FAKE IT Til you BREAK IT

T0343568

USA Today and *Wall Street Journal* bestselling author Meagan Brandy writes New Adult romance novels with a twist. She is a candy-crazed, jukebox junkie who tends to speak in lyrics. Born and raised in California, she is a married mother of three crazy boys who keep her bouncing from one sports field to another, depending on the season, and she wouldn't have it any other way. Starbucks is her best friend and words are her sanity.

FAKE IT *Til you* BREAK IT

MEAGAN BRANDY

ORION

This edition first published in Great Britain in 2023 by Orion Fiction,
an imprint of The Orion Publishing Group Ltd.,
Carmelite House, 50 Victoria Embankment
London EC4Y 0DZ

An Hachette UK Company

Copyright © Meagan Brandy 2022

The moral right of Meagan Brandy to be identified as the author
of this work has been asserted in accordance with the
Copyright, Designs and Patents Act 1988.

All rights reserved. No part of this publication may be reproduced, stored
in a retrieval system or transmitted in any form or by any means, without
the prior permission in writing of the publisher, nor to be otherwise
circulated in any form of binding or cover other than that in which it
is published without a similar condition, including this condition, being
imposed on the subsequent purchaser.

All the characters in this book are fictitious,
and any resemblance to actual persons, living
or dead, is purely coincidental.

A CIP catalogue record for this book
is available from the British Library.

ISBN (Paperback) 978 1 3987 1946 0
ISBN (eBook) 978 1 3987 1947 7

The Orion Publishing Group Ltd
Carmelite House
50 Victoria Embankment
London, EC4Y 0DZ

An Hachette UK company

Typeset by Born Group
Printed and bound in Great Britain by Clays Ltd, Elcograf S.p.A.

www.orionbooks.co.uk

Playlist

'Fuck Love' – XXXTENTACION
'Remember You' – Wiz Khalifa, The Weeknd
'Tell Me You Love Me' – Demi Lovato
'Love Me Like You Mean It' – Kelsea Ballerini
'Bacon' – Nick Jonas, Ty Dolla Sign
'Invisible' – Anna Clendening
'Games' – Demi Lovato
'Starting Over' – Niykee Heaton
'Starving' – Hailee Steinfeld
'Talk' – Khalid
'I Think I'm In Love' – Kat Dahlia
'Porn Star Dancing' – My Darkest Days
'Couple of Kids' – Maggie Lindemann
'Jealous' – Nick Jonas, Tinashe
'Hurts Like Hell' – Madison Beer, Offset
'IDFC' – Blackbear
'Whatever You Say' – Martina McBride
'The Heart Wants What It Wants' – Selena Gomez
'Unsteady' – X Ambassadors
'Nights Like This' – Kehlani, Ty Dolla Sign
'Call Out My Name' – The Weeknd
'Meant To Be' – Bebe Rexha, Florida Georgia Line
'Us' – Carlie Hanson

To the one with many friends who forever feels alone . . .
You're not.

Hold strong.
Someone will come and fill your whole world
as they need you to fill theirs.

Chapter 1
Demi

Chemistry, my least favorite subject, but the class I've looked forward to the most since school started last week, and even more so today.

Finally, we're being assigned our lab partners, and I know exactly who mine will be.

Not counting myself, there are only three others left standing, two being uninterested, academically opposed football players while the third is second in our class, also on the team, but possesses the brains *and* the brawn.

It's an obvious choice.

Mr. Brando looks to his paper, ready to announce another pairing, and I can hardly hold in my grin.

"Nico Sykes."

I step toward Alex only to freeze, my frown cutting to Mr. Brando, *who just read off the wrong name!*

"Wait." I glance from Alex's tense expression to Nico, already on his way to the lab table. I turn toward Mr. B, keeping my voice low. "Are you sure? Shouldn't I be with—"

"I'm going to stop you right there, Ms. Davenport," he cuts me off. "While I asked each of you to list the person you'd prefer as a partner, I gave no guarantees. So, if you are about to make a judgment call on one of your peers, I suggest you don't finish your thought. I'm aware you're a bit of a teacher's pet, however, in my class, you won't make, nor influence my decisions," he states scornfully.

My ears heat in both anger and embarrassment, but my hair

works as a shield to cover it, my expression giving no sign his words meant a damn thing.

Talk about a judgment call.

Asshole.

"Go, Ms. Davenport. Mr. Sykes is seated and ready to go." He dismisses me, turning to the last two standing.

Defeated, I head for the back of the classroom where my 'partner' has chosen to sit — of course the last space up front wasn't the one he wanted.

And ready to go? Please! He hasn't even opened his backpack.

Nico is simply sitting there with his elbows on the tabletop, waiting.

As I approach, he pushes off the cement slab, now lazily leaning against his chair with those eyes, as dark and impassive as always, locked on me.

I stop in front of him. "Guess we're stuck with each other all year."

His gaze narrows. "Guess we are."

When I don't move, he drapes an arm over the back of my seat, tipping his chin.

"Sit down, D. I don't bite without permission."

A heavy sigh leaves me as I walk around, dropping beside him. "Sure you do. Third grade, Ms. Fisher's class, and I've got the scar to prove it." I flip him off with my ring finger, right where his bite mark was left.

"That's called leaving my mark. I was smart at eight."

"Too bad it didn't carry over to eighteen, huh?"

He only stares, not a word spoken, no sign of a functioning train of thought on his flawless face.

I shake my head, pull out my materials, and set them in front of me.

Mr. Brando makes his way to the front of the room to go over how the class will work now that we've been paired up, but I lose track of what he's saying when I notice Alex's attention pointed in my direction.

2

He's focused on Nico, so I peek over to find Nico hasn't a clue. Or at least he pretends not to as his face is buried in his phone. When I look back, Alex's stare slides to mine.

His shoulder lifts in a small shrug, and he nods toward Mr. B as if he doesn't understand the teacher's choice either.

For the last two years, he and I have been partners, and it's worked perfectly. We put in equal time and effort, and the end result is less stress and a perfect grade.

This unpredicted switch, though, means I'll likely have to pull double hours to make up for what, I'm sure, will be a consistently ill-prepared Nico, but hitting the books harder isn't even the worst part of this.

Being paired with Nico puts a twist in my plan.

It's senior year, and I was *finally* going to bite the bullet and go full schoolgirl mode on Alex, make my interest obvious since he's never seemed to catch on. Yes, he typically dates the Round Robin girls, the ones who make their way through all the teams in the school depending on the season and don't care about the commitment side, but still. It could happen.

We're friends, we run in the same crowd for the most part, and usually go to the same parties. We both want to do well in school and sports and have a good time along the way.

We would work well together.

Alex begins to turn to face forward, but suddenly his glare cuts back to my partner.

In the same second, warm air fans across the hollow of my neck and my body responds to the heat, the knot in my stomach tightening even more when Nico's unexpected whisper follows.

"Not that you could be more obvious, but don't waste your time, D." His voice is low and raspy. "He's already chasing tail, Sandra Black."

An instant frown forms, and I force my eyes to Nico.

"Been braggin' about how he's got it locked in at practice all week." He shrugs, focusing back on his phone.

I glance to Alex again.

3

He's observing Nico, a question I can't decipher written across his face, and I don't have much time to try either.

Mr. Brando walks up behind him, slapping a palm on his table to get his attention.

Alex turns around while I sit and trip on Nico's words.

He's not one for gossip, or conversation for that matter, so his bothering to mention it must mean it's true.

Sandra Black.

Five-eleven, gorgeous caramel skin, and my competition for this year's valedictorian, not to mention, the nicest person you'll ever meet, Sandra Black.

Awesome.

I flip open my booklet, about to tell Nico what he can help with when his hand covers mine on top of my paper. My eyes flash to his.

"I got the answers." He doesn't look away as he slides his already completed packet over with his free hand. "You can thank me later."

"Thank you?" I deadpan, attempting to tug myself free of his hold, but he presses harder. "For getting one of your fans to do your work for you?"

He shakes his head, a smirk now playing on his full lips.

"Nah." His grip lessens, his fingertips dragging along my skin with their retreat.

My eyes fall to the contact, a heavy tension tugging at my muscles as I force my gaze back to his, but Nico is no longer looking at me.

His focus has fallen to my chest, and he takes his sweet time bringing it back, leaning the slightest bit closer as he does.

My frown deepens.

"For being the reason lover boy can't stop slantin' back."

With his last word, an angry, almost annoyed, arrogance slips into his gaze, and I realize I'm being mocked.

"I don't need your help getting his attention."

"You sure about that? You're not exactly the forward type."

I glare. "Don't pretend you know me."

4

"Don't forget, I do."

"Did," I correct in a low hiss. "Past tense."

Nico leans forward, his frown sliding between mine with unmistakable tenacity, but his lips remain sealed.

I eye him a moment, slowly moving my focus back to my paper. "Whatever, I don't care what you think of me."

"Lies."

His instant response has my head jerking his way again.

Now it's him who glares. "You care what people think, it's why you're friendly to everyone when they don't deserve it. Like Alex Hammons, for example."

"It's called human decency, you should try it sometime, and I didn't ask your opinion, nor do I care what you think of me or Alex or anyone else for that matter."

"You care he's still lookin' back?" he quips.

He is?

A quiet scoff leaves him, confirming my curiosity isn't hidden well.

"'Course you do." Leaning even closer, a tight scowl in place as he tips his head all cocky like. "Go on, D. Look at him," he dares. "See if what I'm saying is true, you know you want to."

My lips press into a firm line and I'm damn near twitching to know if he's lying or not, but I cover my interest with a glare while commanding my eyes to my paper. It takes all my strength to keep them there.

Nico's low, snide chuckle is proof my struggle isn't lost on him.

I kick him under the table when five minutes later, he rasps, "Your boy's lookin' again."

Asshole.

5

Chapter 2
Demi

"Hey, girl, hey!" my friend Krista announces herself as she drops down at our usual lunch spot, a grassy area in the quad.

"You're quite excited to have been given a seven-page essay in English," my best friend Carley whines, not bothering to open her eyes as she lays there, soaking up the California sun.

"Oh, girl, that's not due for another three weeks." Krista snags a bag of chips from the pile of shit in the middle of us.

"Meaning you'll start it in two weeks and three days," our other friend Macy sasses back, making the four of us laugh.

"Exactly." Krista grins. "But no, I'm peppy because I heard from a bird that you, Miss *Demi*, were paired with hottie McHot Nico Sykes in chem today."

Carley's eyes pop open and she sits up. "Um . . . what?" She gapes. "Why didn't you say anything?"

I ignore her a minute and talk to Krista. "Does this bird happen to be a six-foot-something quarterback you like to call daddy when no one is around to hear it?"

Her jaw drops, and she leans over to shove me backward, laughing at the same time. "Yes, bitch, it does, and I told you that in secret!"

"You told us *all* that." Macy rolls her eyes.

Krista only grins wider. "Yeah, but secret means you don't say it out loud."

I smile and she sticks her tongue out in response.

"K, back on track. Come on, Demi," Macy coaxes.

I shrug, tearing the stem off a strawberry and stuffing it in my mouth. "What do you want me to say, I'm annoyed."

"Annoyed?" Macy purses her lips. "Please, don't lie. Even you can't be immune to the boy and his every single thing."

"Fuck you." I laugh. "What the hell does that mean?"

"It means your vagina must be dead and in need of reviving if not even Nico Sykes gets you going. His fingers alone must be shrimp dick size, and not in a fugly way. If they're that long, imagine the range of the rest of him!"

My jaw drops and then a loud laugh leaves me, earning a satisfied grin from her.

"My vagina is just fine, I assure you, and it has nothing to do with him not being attractive, because duh."

Nico is as perfect as his running game, which is flawless.

He's tall and broad, muscular but not overly so, more full and strong. He has high cheekbones with perfectly thick lips, dark, sandy color hair with darker, always intense eyes. There's this taunting look forever staring back, one he wants spotted but never allows you to decrypt.

He's far from a typical senior, screams experienced and likely has grown women wondering if he's legal enough or not. I'm sure the tattoo etched into the inner part of his right arm is answer enough for them.

He's ESPN billboard material and he knows it.

"So, you admit you think he's hot." Macy nods, proud. "What's the problem?"

"I needed a good partner; one I could trust to do what they say they will." I shrug. "Everyone knows Mr. Brando is the toughest teacher here, always unorthodox, and I can't afford to fail. My mom will wring my damn neck if my grades slip and it'll be back to *medication keeps you focused* before I can even blink."

"Oh please, you're focused on your own. She has to stop putting all of her screw-ups on your shoulders," Krista says.

"She already thinks I'm putting too much time into dance, if I fall behind in this class, who knows what she'll pull."

"Fuck your mom." Carley frowns.

"Someone needs to," Macy mumbles.

The girls laugh, but my head tugs back in disgust causing them to laugh harder.

"Okay, but back up." Carley leans forward. "We know you can't fail, and we know you'd never allow yourself to, but how do you know Nico is a *bad* partner?"

"We've always known him to ditch full days, which means he misses whatever's happening in class, so I have no reason to believe this year will be different, and besides that, have you ever seen him pay attention in a class that isn't PE?" I joke.

"Have you ever had him in a class that wasn't PE?" Carley calls me out on my judgment. "Have you had him in a class at all since junior high?"

I pause to think, and she raises her brows like an asshole.

"Whatever." I shake my head. "Maybe he's not a crappy student, obviously he's eligible to play football, so he must keep at least a baseline grade point average, but still. If he isn't here every day like I am, I'll have no choice but to carry more of our workload. Not only that, he and I don't talk anymore, and on the rare occasion we're forced to, it's small jibes or he goes straight up mannequin on me."

"Maybe he doesn't know what to say?"

I give her a blank look. "He thinks he's a candy bag and all girls have his kind of sweet tooth, and when you don't, you're as worthy as a wallflower."

"I'd take a piece if offered." Macy nods, her lips pursed.

I laugh, shaking my head while Krista pats her knee patronizingly.

"We know, sweetheart, we know," she teases.

"It's not even about Nico, is it?" Carley suspects. "You wanted to be Alex's partner again."

"I've been the last two years, so I kind of expected to be, yeah," I admit. "He wants to be a doctor, like his mom, so I know he's super focused in science where Nico already had his face in his phone all day today. He didn't take a single note

8

while I took three pages. I don't know, I might try talking to the teacher again."

"Screw Alex's pompous ass!" Krista blurts. "He might be good looking, but in a Wahlberg brother kind of way, while Nico is more Mark status, Calvin Klein campaign worthy. *Way* prettier to look at."

I can't help but laugh.

"And he lives right behind you! Think of all the late-night study sessions you could have." Macy's eyes widen in excitement.

"Yeeees!" Krista turns toward her. "She can knock on his door in her tank and tiny sleep shorts, the ones we bought her for her birthday, and be like *I lost my homework, help me.*"

"Help me, I'm poor," they say in unison, laughing.

Carley and I look to each other, chuckling just the same.

"Come on, Demi! You have to use this to your advantage," Macy whines.

"Yeah, take one for the team here," Krista adds.

"You have a boyfriend."

"Exactly!" Her eyes widen mockingly. "Did you not catch the *take one for the team*?"

"Does Trent know you have the hots for his bestie?" Macy teases her.

Krista only flips her off with a grin.

"You guys are crazy, no way. Can you imagine my mom's reaction?" I laugh. "Me and the guy who got kicked out of her precious country club for fucking the owner's daughter in the fountain on the golf course?"

"Don't forget during her daddy's tournament." Macy laughs loudly.

"And that."

"First of all, screw your mom for being so critical, even though I'm pretty sure she'd take him as a win. He's literally all the things on her *Demi must marry* checklist." Krista chuckles.

She has a point there.

"And two, Josie was his girlfriend, so not a big deal other than the whole being caught part, and *three,* a-holes, don't

9

forget Nico is Trent's best friend, Trent is *your* friend. You know him, would he really love and support someone like a brother who was a total douchebag?"

"Total?" I tease, and she throws a chip at me. I smile, shrugging. "I'm not saying he's anything other than the wrong chem partner for me. How he is as a human nowadays, I don't know. He avoids being around me, remember?"

"He doesn't avoid you." Krista rolls her eyes.

"No," Macy says sarcastically. "It just so happens since we started high school, he has something come up every single time Demi comes near, or a shit remark when he has no escape."

I lift my hands as if to say *exactly*. "Literally, today was the most we've talked since eighth grade, and it was maybe five worthless sentences he used to try and get under my skin."

The bell rings in the next second, so we pack up our crap. The girls toss out the garbage while I roll up our blanket and stuff it in the bag.

Ever since freshman year, we've had the same routine for lunch. Whoever is assigned the locker closest to the quad gives theirs up and shares with someone else. We use the other to store snacks and things for lunch as well as the blanket we sit on every day.

It started as a way to have more time since we were spending half our lunch in lines, but we continued because we like having space to quietly talk amongst ourselves. Where we sit is close enough we can call others over if we want, but still have our own friend time.

"Meeting at your house at six to swim?"

"Six-fifteen," I tell her. "I have dance today, but I think I forgot my phone at home, so just come over."

"Cool. Later." Macy and Krista walk off while me and Carley carry everything to the locker to put it away.

"I don't think you should push switching partners," Carley says as she hangs the snack bag on the little hook, stuffing the unused water bottles into the bottom corner.

"Why not?" I hand her the blanket bag so she can toss it on top.

10

She shrugs, slams the locker closed and spins the lock. "You said yourself, you've been Alex's partner the last few years, maybe it's time for a new one."

"But Nico? We're not exactly friends."

"You're not exactly enemies either." She steps backward, winking at me before she disappears.

I lean against the locker a moment, considering her words.

I guess she's right, Nico and I aren't friends, but I can't say we're enemies either. We're simply two people who used to know each other and don't anymore.

Two people that are about to be forced to spend fifty-three minutes a day together for the rest of the year, not counting out of class time we'll likely need.

I'm about to push off the locker when the door at the end of the hall opens, and Nico along with his on-again, off-again girlfriend, Josie, walk through, arguing. Or *she's* arguing while he's ignoring, continuing down the hall, but then his eyes lift, officially catching mine fixated on them and he stops in his tracks.

My gaze slides toward Josie.

She frowns up at him, waving her arms around a moment in an overly dramatic fashion before she realizes he's not paying attention, and her head jolts to where his focus lies.

Solely on me.

An instant and deep scowl takes over, and she flips me off, shoves him lightly — or attempts to, but he doesn't budge — and then storms out the way they came.

The second the door slams with her exit, Nico starts forward again, each step taken seeming smaller and slower than the last.

I stand up straight when only an arm's length of space is left between us, but Nico keeps going, glancing away as he passes without a word, as if he wasn't staring directly at me with each stride taken.

Only when he's out of sight, do I realize I was holding my breath the entire time.

I roll my eyes at myself.

It's about to be a long ass year.

Chapter 3
Demi

Krista, as always, is the last of us four to climb out of the pool. She dries off quickly and ties a towel around her before joining us on the picnic table.

"Okay," she starts. "You're freshly single and in need of some hardcore lovin'. What movie do you jump into to get it?"

"*Fast and the Furious*," Macy shouts, way too eager, making the rest of us laugh.

"Carley?" Krista asks her as she piles her plate full.

"Hmm, how about *The Boy Next Door*." She wiggles in her spot.

"A murderous lunatic is your type?" I tease.

"He brought J.Lo to her knees, literally, okay," she jokes. "That's my man."

"You guys are lame, Christian Grey me, *please*!" Krista shouts.

"As if we're surprised." Carley laughs.

"Demi?" Macy asks, a chicken wing shoved halfway in her mouth.

"*Takers*, all day." I nod.

The three of them pause before they all change their mind and go with my answer, too.

"Talk about a dream team."

"Right?" I agree. "I'd go for Hayden Christianson to TI in a hot second."

The four of us laugh, and then Carley elbows me in the ribs.

I look up and through the screen door to find my mom primping in the mirror.

It's crazy how much I look like her, only the less perfected version, as I'm sure she'd call me.

Long, dirty blonde but not quite brown hair, almond-shaped eyes the same shade of green, a deep, ripe lime-like color. She's always said she blessed me with the heart shape of my lips, though I'm pretty sure hers were created along the way with the help of a needle or two. We're both pushing five-nine, but she stays in four-inch heels to give herself more height.

The difference between us though is she walks around like a California Barbie where I'm more Barbie's best friend.

"You talk to her about my birthday yet?" Krista whispers.

"No." I sigh, wiping the sauce off my fingers before pushing to stand, my towel falling from my middle as I do. "Might as well do it now."

The girls follow behind.

The second we step through the door, my mom openly scrutinizes us in our bathing suits, likely picking us apart in her mind.

"Girls."

"Hey, Ms. Davenport."

"Mom, can I go to Krista's party next weekend?" I ask her.

My mom turns to me. "You want to talk about this now?"

"Since you're here, yeah."

Her features sharpen, but she plays it off, smiling at herself in the mirror before meeting my gaze in the reflection. "So, this is the party that is two nights in a hotel along the beach with its own private bar and DJ? A hotel that has been blocked off for nothing but high school seniors for a spoiled little girl's eighteenth birthday?" She looks over at Krista. "No offense, sweetheart."

"Hey, it's true." Krista laughs.

I hold in my eye roll. "The hotel that's safe and owned by Krista's dad, yes. That's the one."

"Honey, there will be no parents there, and I'll be out of town, so I can't come to your rescue if something happens." She makes sure to shake her head in faux concern.

13

'Course you won't be home, who's shocked?

Not me.

This entire conversation is a pointless one anyway, and all formality.

I ask for something, she plays out the whole scene, makes it seem dangerous, makes herself sound concerned in case my dad asks me about it later, but it's nothing more than a mother-daughter role we play.

A role we both know and understand and don't acknowledge.

"Actually, Ms. D, my parents will be around, they're staying at our property around the corner, but they're coming to dinner one night and they'll be checking in at the hotel here and there. It'll be super chill. Dinner, some dancing, rides on the boardwalk."

I look from Krista to my mom.

"I swear I'll be safe," I add on. "You already know how Krista's dad is, there will be staff security surrounding the hotel, and she just said he'll be around if needed."

My mom nods, in too much of a hurry to get out of here to go full-on *pretend I have reservations* mode. "I suppose that would be okay, so long as you answer when I call and keep in contact all weekend."

She won't call. "I will."

"And please, Demi, safety in the bedroom as well."

Macy sits forward. "So . . . if you don't care if she has wild sex all weekend, what's the point of contemplating her going at all?"

I fight a smile.

My mom, of course, misses the contempt in Macy's question – or chooses to ignore it, she's good at that – and laughs, grabbing her purse off the countertop. "A reminder of safe sex is always worth mentioning. Nobody wants to get pregnant and ruin their lives in high school."

Ouch?

"I have to go." My mom smiles at me. "I'm meeting the Welch sisters for dinner, don't wait up."

14

I turn to my friends who give a rueful smilé.

My mom isn't necessarily a bad mom, but she's basically over mothering. Her and my dad had me their junior year of high school, but still wanted the large, fancy future, so she worked her ass off at low paying jobs while raising a baby, supported us while he went to college – a fact she never failed to throw in his face.

Six years later and four months after he started his law firm, he left her for his business partner.

My mom was bitter at first, even though she drove him away by never being happy with what he gave her, but she quickly decided she enjoyed blowing his alimony and child support checks better than she liked being his wife anyway.

Now that I'm old enough to basically care for myself, can drive, and no longer need her help with schoolwork, she's *living the years she lost* – her words.

I know she loves me, and I love her, my dad too, really, but they're both absent parents more than anything. My dad at least makes an effort where my mom is annoyed when she has to do motherly things, but I mean, I can't complain.

It's what most teenagers would kill for, freedom to do as we wish.

"Oh, and Demi." My mom pulls the door open, her focus falling to my thighs as she says, "I'd say that's enough carbs for you today."

Wow.

I'm a fucking dancer, have been in hip-hop classes since I was five, what the hell does she expect? She should have put me in ballet if she wanted me to be a tighter stick, we work an entirely different set of muscles.

She goes to walk out but freezes mid-step, staring straight ahead.

What is she doing?

After a few seconds, a strong, heavy voice floats around the frame and into the house. "Ms. Davenport . . ."

Nico.

Nico!

My eyes widen, and I whip around to my friends, all who gape at me, Macy holding her hand over Krista's mouth to block her laugh.

Macy whispers with a grin, "Aw shit, he's playing the hot *help me with my homework card* I told you about."

"Shut up!" I hiss back. "You know how she is!"

"She's about to plan your wedding!" Macy wiggles her eyebrows.

"Or your departure to boarding school," Krista adds.

Macy laughs. "Let's bet!"

I shove her, making her fall over the edge of the couch.

"Go over there!" Carley whispers back hastily.

"No!" I gape at her, my eyes pointedly falling to my bikini.

"Here." Macy tosses me her towel. "Go."

I yank it from her hand with a frown, glancing toward the entryway again.

My mom, queen of the fakes and superficial as all hell, pulls out her old pageant smile.

I groan, quickly wrap the towel under my armpits and move closer.

I'm half a foot from the door when the towel is yanked away, and I'm shoved forward.

I stumble toward my mom but catch my footing quickly.

My mom's hand flies to her chest a moment before she composes herself, eyes wide and bright and settled on Nico, saying nothing at all.

I frown at her.

You're really going to stand there silent and stare at him?

I move my scowl to Nico who doesn't acknowledge my mother's ridiculousness, but the corner of his eyes are stiff as hell.

"Hey." He nods.

"What are you doing here?"

My mom gasps, a legit, mortified gasp for once, officially snapping out of her stupor. "Demi!" she scolds, apology in her tone — how dare her daughter not use her manners.

Cue eye roll.

"What?" I say innocently, annoyed that he showed up on the rare occasion that my mom is actually home. "He can't be here, you're leaving."

"Oh." My mom dismisses, flicking her wrist. "Don't be silly. Your friends are always welcome, you know this. Besides, I'm sure I have nothing to worry about."

Her digs are always coated in sugar, served with a bitchy smile, and left up to interpretation – is she saying he's out of my league or I'm far from his?

The way her eyes continue to study him suggests she's undecided, though I'm sure Nico isn't coming to the same conclusion.

It's funny, for someone who pushes me to be the best at everything and make the highest grade, you'd think it was because she wanted a big bright future for me, so I'd never be in the position she was when my dad left her, when really it's all about the bragging rights that come with the scholarly daughter she's after.

I swear she'd marry me to the highest bidder with the prettiest face if she could.

"Nico, wow. It's been some time." She tilts her head slightly, taking him in more and I want to shake her. "You're . . . all grown up."

Oh my fucking god!

My eyes slice to hers.

I can't even look at him.

"It has," he agrees, his stare burning into my cheek.

"Well, it's . . . very good to see you, and *here*, but if I don't run, I'll be late," she announces, her eyes raking over Nico once more, before moving to me.

She gives me a bright smile, reaching out to give my arm a small squeeze that can only be taken as a *good job*.

I bite into my cheek as she squares her shoulders and moves down the driveway to her car, one foot in front of the other like she's on a runway.

I force my expression to remain natural when really her boldness was so embarrassing, I'd rather slam the door in Nico's face than stand here and make eye contact with him after that.

I take a small step back, glancing to the side to find the girls tiptoeing toward the slider, all three being assholes, mock sucking dick or flicking their tongues between their fingers as they disappear from sight altogether.

Jerks.

"Not gonna invite me in?"

Nico's jeering tone has my eyes flying back to him.

His though, they aren't on mine.

They're on my bare legs, and instantly my mom's comment – which I'm pretty sure he heard – takes over my thoughts, and I can't help but wonder what he's thinking.

It's not like I can't hang in a bikini with the best of them. I'm tall with a narrow waist, wide hips, and legs for days. It just so happens I have more muscles in my thighs and calves than most.

Still, there's something nerve-wracking about standing in nothing but a string bikini in front of a guy who has probably seen more naked chicks than Ironman pre Pepper.

Whatever, I've danced in front of hundreds in outfits just as revealing.

Finally, his eyes come to mine and he tips his chin the slightest bit.

"Guys aren't allowed in when my mom's gone."

"Not the vibe I got."

He's obviously trying to piss me off, but I don't say anything.

Nico gauges me a minute before taking a step back. "Right, well, I'd hate to get the duchess in trouble, so let's make this quick, yeah? I—"

"Can you just go?" I cut him off, irritated not only at my mom but at him now, too, for mocking me. "We can talk about whatever it is you need in class tomorrow."

He looks off in the distance, licking his lips before his eyes slowly move back to mine.

"Does that work?"

He gives a slow nod but doesn't move.

After a few seconds of staring, a deep chuckle leaves him. "You have a good night, huh, D?"

He takes a few backward steps before shaking his head and finally walking away.

I close the door, letting out a deep breath. "Well, that sucked," I huff, then remember my asshole friends are outside and head their way.

I don't even get to speak before Krista shouts a loud, "Boo! We were hoping we were about to hear sounds coming from upstairs!"

"You guys are assholes." I pretend I'm walking toward the lounger, but quickly stop and shove Macy, who only had her legs hanging over the edge, into the pool.

She pops up, gaping at me a second before she laughs. "I took that towel quick, huh?"

"You suck." I laugh, dropping beside Carley.

"Oh, please. You should thank me."

"For?" My hands plant on my hips.

"Because, now every time in chem, when he thinks about *being* an ass, he'll instead be *thinking* about *dat ass*."

I frown, but it quickly turns into a laugh when the girls start to crack up.

We lay out as long as the sun allows, and not an hour later, they're piling in Krista's car.

"Demi, is that your phone?" Krista shouts out the window.

I frown, my eyes moving to the hood of my car, where she's pointing.

I walk toward it, noting my glittery PopSocket on the back right away.

What the hell?

Slowly, I pick it up, glancing around, but then it hits.

Nico.

My shoulders fall, and I look to the girls.

"No." Carley gapes. "That's why he came over?"

Damn.

"I must have left it in class, and he picked it up for me." I groan. "I was an asshole."

"It's fine." Krista rolls her eyes. "He's an asshole, too."

A laugh bubbles out of me and she grins.

"Just, thank him tomorrow or something," Carley tells me.

"Or now, whatever works." Macy's brows bounce.

I ignore her and head back inside, locking the door behind me.

I take the stairs two at a time, irritated at myself for being rude when I had no reason other than I was embarrassed by my mom's words and actions.

Fully annoyed with everything, I do my homework, take a shower, and go to bed.

My eyes peel open to find my room pitch black, nothing but the moonlight shining through the window.

I lean over the edge of the bed, snagging my phone off the carpet to check the time.

It's just after midnight when I'd normally be falling asleep.

I drop back, but as soon as I hit the pillow, my body flies forward, my head snapping toward the window.

Is that . . . moaning?

I concentrate, the splash of water against concrete mixing with the proof of someone's pleasure hitting my ears.

Slowly, I pull myself from bed and take the few steps forward until I'm peeking out my blinds.

It takes a second, but the soft laughter pulls my eyes over my fence and right where the noises are coming from – the hot tub connected to the neighbor's pool behind me. *Nico's* pool.

A small gasp leaves me, and I dart away from the window.

He's not . . .

No. My eyes are playing tricks.

I step forward, peeking again, and *holy shit!*

My mouth drops open as I stare at Nico fucking a girl with long dark hair against the side of his hot tub.

He's got his hands braced at the curve of the cement, giving me the perfect view of the muscles working in his back. The girl is bent over in front of him, half her body out of the water, and lying against the cooled cement.

His hand disappears, and I can only imagine it's to grip or smack her ass, but I can't say for sure.

His body moves slowly, methodically almost, like he's taking his time with her, completely unrushed and enjoying, giving her long, slow strokes.

Deep, full strokes?

I take a deep breath, only for my eyes to widen a second later.

Oh my god!

I jump backward again.

Why am I watching him have sex, and better yet why am I imagining the way he's fucking her?

How he'd fuck me?

Wait, what?

No!

I growl, but my hands make no move to close the window, and my feet don't carry me to my bed. No, my eyes close and my ears perk.

The night is dead silent, so even the slightest wallow of water reaches my ears. It's light at first, and then louder, more of a slap against the cement edge.

The moaning starts again. Brash, brazen moaning, both male and female, and I have no self-control. I look again.

He has her on the edge now, her forearms braced against the cement, fingers curled around the edge, head dropped back.

My body grows hot and I swallow. "Good fucking god," I whisper, my hand moving to my throat.

They've moved to the opposite side, the front of his body now facing mine, allowing me to see the cuts of his chest and abs, and the delicious way they tighten with every thrust forward.

I don't realize I've moved closer to the window until my forehead hits the glass and my phone falls from my hand, dropping right onto the edge of my toe.

I yelp and fall against the glass, and then I freeze, my eyes shooting wide.

"Oh no . . ." I whisper to myself, squeezing my eyes closed.

Did they hear me?

Did they see the shake of the open blinds?

I take a deep breath and perk my ears.

When more moaning is caught, I decide it's safe, that they have no idea I went full-on Peeping Tammy.

I open my eyes and I'm instantly rooted in place, heat washing over my body in such a rush I grow lightheaded, my palm flying up to plant on the wall beside me.

They heard me, or more, *he* heard me, saw me. Caught me.

His eyes are lasered on my window. If I didn't know any better, I'd say locked directly on mine, darkness be damned.

Nico has her by the hips now, her ass perched how he wants it as he delivers one *hell* of a show.

A show I couldn't look away from if I tried, a performance I feel deep in my core. One that, admittedly, has need spreading through my body as he works the cum from hers.

A few minutes go by where I can't tell if they're moving at all, and then he suddenly slips back, the bubbles of the hot tub spanning across his torso.

Slowly, his shoulders lift, Nico now standing to his full height, and my hand spans across my chest, my body rising to its tippy toes of its own accord just in case the move allows me to see an inch lower.

Just one more inch to the prize—

My thoughts are interrupted when the girl glides around him, running her fingers across his slick skin as she goes.

In all her naked glory, she steps from the pool like a gleaming goddess, shifting to the side to grab a towel, and that's when I see her face.

Sandra fucking Black.

Chapter 4
Demi

All morning I told myself I'd walk into class today with my head held high.

I'm not embarrassed, and it's no big deal and who knows, maybe I overreacted and he was zoned out. Didn't know I was their willing audience.

I repeat this mantra the entire drive to school, and by the time I'm turning the engine off, I'm feeling good.

Lipstick in hand, I flip down the overhead mirror and take my time applying before stepping out. I shove the door closed, and turn, a gasp leaving me when an unexpected body blocks me in.

Nico.

My hand flies to my chest, attempting to settle my pulse. "You scared the shit out of me," I tell him.

But Nico doesn't speak, instead sliding his feet closer, leaving only inches between us, so I push back against the car.

His stare is unwavering, giving me no insight as to what's on his mind and causing me to grow restless.

I fidget but don't look away as he cocks his head.

"You a fan of porn, D?"

"I—" *Shit.*

Nico plants his hands at the curve of my hood, his arms flexing so damn close to my face my mind transports back to last night, to the tight grip he had on the rock edge of the spa, to the vision of his muscles flexing as he slid—

A raspy chuckle leaves him, and he pushes off.

"You know, I'd have invited you over, VIP seats had I known. Bet Sandra would have been all right with it, she's first-string material and she knows it."

That rouses me, and I shove off the car with a glare. "I thought you said Alex was the one sleeping with Sandra?"

He only licks his lips.

"Weird, right?" I keep going. "Since it was *you* I saw—"

"Watched," he cuts me off, leaning closer. "You *watched* me fuck her."

Oh, screw it!

"You know what, yeah, I did. Until the final bow, in fact," I sass. "If you knew I was watching you guys, why'd you keep going?"

Very slowly, a single, dark eyebrow raises, his tone is even more patronizing than the move. "You'd expect me to stop?"

Right.

As if he *could* have stopped amid that.

They were so lost in each other they didn't even – or couldn't even – realize how loud they were being.

He had Sandra in tunnel vision, a tunnel that leads straight down his shaft.

I mean, he was enjoying her just as much, his groans . . . deep and exhilarated as he chased his release.

The way his—

"Your skin's growing warm, D." Nico pulls me out of my thoughts. "Whatcha thinkin' 'bout?" he whispers, the teasing edge in his heady voice not missed.

The way he studies me with such piercing scrutiny has my toes curling in my shoes to keep focus, and it makes me wonder . . .

How 'lost in her' was he really, if the entire time he was aware of my prying eyes?

"Am I interrupting something?"

My head flies right to find Trent standing near the hood of my car, some sort of drinks in his hands.

Eyes wide in shock, and a stupid grin on his lips, he gawks at his best friend and me.

Nico, though, he doesn't bother to acknowledge Trent's presence.

I roll my tongue over my teeth before glancing back to him.

He keeps his hazardous gaze locked on me the entire time, but if I still knew the boy in front of me, I'd swear humor swims deep within them.

Yeah, he knows what I was thinking.

Nico licks his lips, nods a little, then moves for his buddy. "Catch you in class, D."

Catch me thinking about your perfect form? Please don't!

I groan internally, dropping my head against the car, but quickly remember I need to thank him if not apologize.

"Nico, wait!" I call out.

He freezes mid-step, glancing over his shoulder. Of course, he doesn't bother turning all the way around but nods for Trent to keep walking, so I move toward him.

"Thanks for bringing me my phone last night. You didn't have to do that."

He faces forward. "I don't know what you're talkin' about."

"Right." I roll my eyes at his back, walking as he does. "Well, I'm sorry for being bitchy when you were being helpful."

He scoffs, pushes the door open and shifts to hold it with his back, indicating with a jerk of his chin for me to step through.

My eyes lock with his as I pass him, and he drops his head against the small glass window. "See you in class, D."

Something in my stomach stirs, but I don't say anything, only nod and keep past him.

Trent catches up to me around the corner. "Okay, what did I miss?"

"You don't wanna know."

"That bad?" he jokes.

"Well, your brooding bestie likely hates me more now." I look to him, giving a big innocent smile.

He scoffs, shaking the nasty looking green drink in his hands. "Trust me, he don't hate you."

Right as he says it, Nico comes around the corner, takes one look at us and glares.

I laugh, hitting Trent in the stomach as I walk off. "But he doesn't hate me."

Trent lifts his hands, grinning and moves away to meet his angrily awaiting friend.

I head to first period, making it right as the bell rings, the whole way reminding myself to forget about the scene in the hot tub, knowing for a fact . . . I won't.

From there, the day goes by rather quickly, each class getting deeper into lectures now that the new school year is in full swing, so there was no time to sit and be embarrassed over everything with Nico, who doesn't so much as glance my way when I drop into the chair beside him in chemistry.

Mr. Brando, thankfully, gets right to it, clapping his hands to gain the students' full attention. "I won't say from who, but counting all five of my classes, I have received a total of twenty-one emails from students asking for new partners." He shakes his head, disappointed.

The scoff from Nico couldn't be more obvious – or loud. *Asshole.*

His friends glance our way with light chuckles, but he doesn't acknowledge them. He doesn't acknowledge the glare from his ex, who in a horrible twist of events is the new teacher's aide during our class period, either.

Clearly, he assumes I was one of them when truth be told I didn't even bother, not after the teacher's comment when I first tried.

Mr. Brando folds his arms in front of him. "A little insight for you on me as a teacher? I like to work on more than my required curriculum. The first week is spent going over necessary review, yes, but I also use that time to study each of you as individuals. Everyone, especially those who aren't so sure about the experience you will have with the person you were assigned to, look around the room. Check out each pairing in this class."

26

I do as asked and am surprised by the clear line he drew between each duo. At first glance, it's completely stereotypical – athletes with drama students, shy with exuberant, goth with preppy – but his next words prove this was his exact intent.

"I paired everyone in here with someone as opposite, visually and on paper, as I could find, some may seem subtler than others, but I assure you, there is a reason. I started by looking at who you requested, then went over your schedules from freshman year to now. I know all your extracurriculars, the ones the school knows about anyway, spoke to your past teachers, coaches, and here you are."

I spot Ella Marshal with Samuel Banks in the front corner, and my brows lift in surprise.

Samuel is a rude, cocky basketball player who thinks he's godly and pays no mind to those he considers less than him. And Ella, shit, I don't think she's ever even made eye contact with a guy before.

Right now, Samuel is leaning back in his seat, trying to hide his phone between his legs while Ella is leaning as far away as possible, arms folded in her lap, head slightly down. It's almost cruel to put them together.

But me and Nico? Alex and Evan? What, were we the leftovers? Our pairings don't seem so extreme now.

We run in the same crowd, we're both athletes.

His best friend is dating one of mine, that more than screams 'same circle'.

I glance at Nico, and what do you know, he's already giving me those side-eyes he's practiced in, not bothering to shift his head my way.

Mr. Brando starts talking again, so I face forward.

"There will be many times in life where you are forced to get along with, not just tolerate, someone opposite of you or someone you frankly don't like for whatever reason." He walks to the front of the classroom, scanning over everyone. "I like to think part of my job is to assist you in seeing beyond the hair, the clothes, the crowd, and reach the person

27

underneath. That being said, please place your materials back in your bags."

I frown but do as he asks, glancing around the room to see the same confusion on the other's faces.

"A few days a week, our class time will be spent in different areas of the school. Phones will be left on the tops of the desks, where I can see them"—he knocks his knuckles on Samuel's side of the table and his head snaps up from his screen—"and the fifty-three minutes of class time will be spent simply getting to know each other. I have a prompt for you for the first few days, but you don't have to use it. You can be inventive. Anything you wish to speak about, you may, so long as everyone remains respectful. Today we will be in the quad, neutral ground. So, ladies and gentlemen, phones face down, and make your way out the door, grab a paper from me on your way."

Everyone does as we're asked and we shuffle out and toward the quad.

People start dropping onto picnic tables and grassy areas, some shifting uncomfortably while others have no choice but to follow steps behind their demanding partners.

I glance around, noticing Evan and Alex walk clear to the other side.

"Is here okay?" I ask Nico. We're only steps out the door, but already at the edge of the grass.

Nico doesn't say anything but sits and pats the ground beside him for me to join, like I wasn't already about to.

I get set to read over the paper, but Nico's hand comes down to cover it and I look to him with a frown.

He quirks a dark brow.

"What?"

"Can't ask your own questions, things you might be curious about?"

"Who says I'm curious about anything?"

His jaw tics, and after a few seconds of silence, Nico snatches the paper from my hands, crumpling it in his own.

I gape at him. "What's your problem?"

His gaze narrows. "Let's do this a little different, yeah?"

"Different how?"

"Mr. B said it's about misconception, right?" Nico starts, licking his lips. "So, tell me, D. What do you see when you look at me?"

"I . . ." I start, but quickly trail off.

What do I see?

I look from his hair, shaved at the side, perfect little mess at the top, to his deep cocoa-colored eyes and long lashes. He's wearing a plain t-shirt, nothing fancy, and no sleeves – to show off his arms maybe? And I mean, they're worth the show. Not bulging but clear evidence of the weight training class the team is required to take zero period, and they only tighten, becoming more prominent when he moves them around. He wears perfectly fitted jeans – not skinny but not baggy, and his shoes always match his shirt in some way.

My eyes roam over his form, and I begin to equate his perfection to my own body. I've always been comfortable in my own skin, but more and more my mom likes to comment about how I'm still a 'work in progress'.

"D."

My stare pulls back to Nico, who observes me with unreadable eyes.

"Why do you think he paired us together?" I blurt out.

His frown is quick.

"Look at these other partners, I'd bet they've never spoken to each other. Me and you, though?"

Nico simply watches me, his expression as ungiving as ever, so I glance away.

Way to put yourself on the playboy's level, Demi.

"Look at me." His voice is an easy command.

I do, and disapproval stares back. "Why you comparing yourself?"

"I wasn't," I deny too quickly.

His head drops back. "You're lying."

29

I'm clearly caught, so I give an extremely overdramatic sigh as my affirmation and shake my head.

I swear he swallows a small laugh, though when I quickly search for proof he's human after all, it's gone.

He pauses a moment, then asks, "What do you know about me?"

"You . . . play football, have for years."

He nods. "You dance, hip-hop mostly."

Common knowledge.

I nod, willing myself not to go where I expected him to start.

It doesn't work and the words escape. "You have a thing for sex in water."

He doesn't even blink. "You've never had sex."

My head tugs back at his sudden and so surely stated claim.

I eye him as he does me, and a slow frown takes over.

I'm not stupid, I know what he's doing, and it won't work. He can mock or make fun of me all he wants.

I shake my head. "I'm not gonna confirm or deny what you've heard, so don't bother with this little tactic."

His pointed expression deepens, and the longer he's silent, the more I fidget.

Very slowly, his eyes narrow. "Confirm . . . what, exactly?" He leans closer. "And heard what from *who*?"

I scoff, looking away.

I get it, I opened myself up for this by bringing up his sex life, that's my mistake, but he has to know I'm not a virgin, and I'm sure as hell not going to give him the satisfaction of hearing me say it out loud.

Nico's gaze is laser focused for a long moment before he finally glances off.

He doesn't say another word the rest of class, nor does he the remainder of the week.

When week two rolls around and it's more of the same wasted time, I'm over it and attempt to strike casual conversation, but Nico quickly affirms his attitude.

He falls asleep propped against the tennis court gates, and since I have no material to study, I sit silently, replaying my routine over and over again in my head until we are told we can go collect our things.

Nico is suddenly wide awake and gone as soon as he's excused, but I hang back, cautiously approaching our teacher once the majority of students are gone.

"Ms. Davenport, how can I help you?" The weariness in his tone isn't missed. I can imagine he's getting complaints left and right with the intense sets of pairings he set up.

I take another step toward him, so the stragglers still sliding in to get their phones can't overhear. "I know you asked me not to complain, but I've tried to talk to Nico and he's about as interesting as a cardboard box. He doesn't want to converse, which is fine on a normal day, but I need to know this isn't going to affect my grade because I don't know what to do at this point."

"Is he helpful during labs?" he asks.

"He's getting his work done, but there's no partnering happening at all."

He drops into his chair. "Have you tried getting on his level?"

I scoff. "What level would that be?"

When Mr. Brando frowns, I look away.

"I tell you what," he begins, so I give him my attention. "Since you're the first person to approach not asking me to reconsider, I'll help you out next class," he says vaguely. "The rest will be up to you. Earn the grade, Ms. Davenport, and you might even earn a new friendship, too."

I nod even though I got absolutely nowhere and drag myself to my next class.

Thank god it's hump day because I'm over this shit.

I'm surprised to find my mom's car in the driveway when I get home, and even more so when she's sitting at the little bar top, waiting for me.

Her eyes fall to my sports bra. "You had dance today?"

"Yeah, I was at the studio."

She nods as she sets down her coffee cup and leans back in her seat. "So, Nico Sykes."

Ah. Right.

Guess this is the first chance she's had to grill me.

"He's my new partner for lab."

"Oh?"

"Mom, stop." I wash my hands quickly, drying them on a paper towel. "It's not a big deal."

"I didn't even say anything." She gives an innocent shrug, running her finger over the rim of her cup.

I hold in my eye roll and wait, but it doesn't take her long.

"I asked around, did you know it was him who was caught in a scandalized position with Mr. Clemmons' daughter?"

I pull open the fridge.

Yes. One blue Gatorade left.

I unscrew the top and take a quick drink. "Yes, Josie was, or still is sometimes, his girlfriend."

"Would you say he's a troublemaker?"

"He's a high school senior. It's not like he was arrested."

"Still, public indecency is real."

"And Josie Clemmons didn't even get her black card taken away."

My mom nods, pretending to act casual. "That's a wealthy girl, great family. I bet he seduced her with those . . . those eyes of his."

I fight a laugh, grabbing a croissant from the box on the counter.

Even my dear mother who thinks she's too good for the world can't deny Nico's visual appeal.

"*Those eyes,* Mom? Really?"

Hers narrow, warning me not to say another word, but just as quickly, she smiles. "I was thinking, maybe I should walk around the corner, say hello to the Sykes. Maybe invite them for dinner?"

A scoffed laugh escapes. "You don't cook."

Anger quickly fills her eyes, so I clear my throat and try again.

"Why the sudden interest in being neighborly?"

"He's your partner." She pretends her intent is innocent, when we both know that's never the case when she's involved. "Perhaps you'll be smart, and we'll be seeing more of him."

"What does *that* mean, 'be smart'?"

"Oh, please, Demi. If he had Roger Clemmons' approval to date his daughter, then there must be something promising about the boy. It's worth looking into."

"So, you want to, what, see if he meets your scale of measure?"

Her expression hardens, and she decides to belittle me as she feels I've done to her. "Put the bread away, Demi."

I throw the croissant in the trash, set my Gatorade down with a hard slam, and walk out.

I'm not going to do this with her right now.

She knows Nico's family is wealthy, and now that she's seen his physical appeal, she's interested in learning more so she can come to a shallow decision of whether or not she'll hound me about him constantly or warn me to keep my distance.

My dad mentioned a long time ago Nico and his family inherited a huge estate from one of his mom's late aunts or something that set them up for life and landed them here in Santa Cruz.

It must have been when Nico was a baby or something, because for as long as I can remember, he and I shared a fence.

Now we just happened to share a lab table, too.

There is no way it would ever be more than that.

Chapter 5
Demi

Having Leadership first period is as equally awesome as it sucks.

Now that the voting is over and the class president and what have you has been picked, most of our time will be put into event planning, prep, or tear down, meaning most of our days will be spent outside of the classroom. The weather here is typically on the chillier side, so it's a lot of hoodies and iced coffees all year long.

Thankfully, I had dance this morning and my blood is already pumping and I can manage staying warm while we wait for the sun to eat up all the coastal fog.

"How the hell did we get stuck with the worst job when we did the most work to set this shit up?" Alex laughs as he moves along the fence line, peeling the tape left over from the campaign posters we just got done tearing down.

I grin. "I know, and whoever tied these stupid ribbons made them so tight, I can hardly get the damn scissors beneath the material. I've only made it through the V. At this rate, there'll be a lone T.E left on the fence tomorrow."

Alex sets his trash bag down, pulls off his gloves and throws them inside before walking my way.

"Here." He rubs his hands on his jeans, gently reaching for the scissors. "Why don't we switch for a little bit."

"Are you sure, you basically already did the hard part."

"What kind of guy would I be if I let you struggle when I can do it for you?" He grins, flashing a smile that's almost too perfect.

34

"Okay," I tease. "No need to lay it on thick."

He laughs, moving his attention to the ribbons, so I grab his bag and follow along the fence.

He really did get two times as much done as I did.

Like me, Alex joined the leadership team freshman year, so between now and then, there've been dozens of opportunities for me to make a move on him, but I always chicken out. At the end of the day, it's simple. I can't gauge the guy.

Today is a perfect example. He's been talking nonstop, laughing and smiling and teasing, but it's not anything new. He's always friendly when we work together, flirty to the point of being cheesy sometimes, but I'm pretty sure it's a part of his personality.

He likes attention, loves making girls smile or blush. It can be someone's first day, and his turn as welcoming committee and he acts the same toward them, but it's only ever while he's in class or when we're doing class-related work outside of it.

In any other setting, it's a friendly smile or nod and that's it.

And there lies the problem, his assumed interest only lasts from one bell to the next.

I get to the end of the fence, stepping out from behind the bleachers and pause.

Alone on the field and running full speed from the opposite end I'm standing, Nico flies yard for yard. Every ten or so he spins or does some fancy footwork and slants one way only to go to the next, until he's breezing past me to the end zone, where he slows, only to dart back the way he came.

He stops at the fifty, doing a little roll as if he'd just dove over an invisible defender coming for his legs, and then hops up, jumping from one foot to the other and a light laugh leaves me.

So, he practices his showboating moves.

Why is he even out here? Weight training was zero period, he should be in class by now.

He reaches up, stretching his arms over his head before folding them behind it.

Alex slides into view in the same second, blocking Nico from me completely.

"Hey." His eyes bounce between mine. "All done."

"Yeah, I'm done."

"No." He laughs. "I'm saying *I'm* done."

My mouth drops open with a light laugh. "Shut up."

He nods his head. "Yup."

"Oh my god! How the hell?" I smile, shoving him a little. "I don't believe you."

"Go see for yourself."

"I'm about to," I say, taking a step around him, Alex slides back with me, blocking me again.

"Let's walk behind, do a quick double check on our way back to make sure you're not a slacker," he teases as he moves toward the fence.

"You wish, then you'd have a chance of getting a higher grade than me this year," I shout, but just before I follow behind him, my eyes slide to the field.

Empty.

Huh.

Once Alex and I get done throwing the garbage away, we walk toward the faucet to wash our hands.

"Hey, so I didn't get a chance to clean up my notes from chem, you think I can snag a copy of yours maybe?" he asks.

"Yeah, I have them on me, but I'd need them back by the end of the day, so I can work on some review."

"Cool. I'll make a quick copy and get them back to you in chem?"

I smile. "Yeah, that works."

"Thanks, you're a lifesaver." He grins and walks off ahead of me, even though our destination is the same.

Once again, I'm nothing but an awesome *classmate*.

I'm annoyed as my next few classes go on, and even more so when I end up running a few minutes late for chem thanks to an issue with the computer system in the class before. By the time I get to the room, only the aide is left.

Josie's sharp eyes follow as I set my stuff on the lab table, holding mine as I make my way back to her.

My brows lift expectantly, but she still doesn't tell me where I am supposed to go.

She leans forward, her cleavage pushing against the top she's wearing. "Interesting, you stay and talk to Mr. B yesterday and lo and behold, today's class is on the football field."

"We're on the field?"

Thanks, Mr. Brando.

Josie purses her lips. "How *are* your little 'getting acquainted' sessions going, Demi? He still ignoring you the best he can?"

"Sure is, Josie. Is he still walking away from you in the halls?" I snap back but don't stand there to catch her response.

She told me where I needed to go, and I'm not interested in her drama.

I quicken my steps, easily spotting Nico sitting against the goal post and drop beside him.

"Sorry," I rush out, but when he doesn't so much as acknowledge my arrival, I don't explain further.

We sit there in annoying silence for a few minutes, and in that time, I can't help but notice the way his gaze continues to roam the length of the turf.

He must be running plays in his mind like I was my routine yesterday. Every few seconds his eyes tighten, then snap to another area, like he's playing it all out, visualizing every move, maybe the ones I spotted him practicing earlier.

The utility bin beside the team bench at the edge of the sidelines catches my attention.

Oh, screw it. It's worth a shot.

I push off the grass to stand.

That has Nico's eyes snapping to mine, but I hardly spare him a glance, walking over to snag a football from the container.

I'm tired of this avoidance crap, so . . . I'm getting on his level.

It just so happens I'm wearing my Nike's with a pair of shorts today, so I throw the ball up and try to kick it but of course it bounces off the side of my shoe, landing a sad foot away.

I pick it up, noticing a few of the other groups cutting glances at me, but I ignore them and try again. This time it goes a solid five feet, sideways and wobbly, but still.

I look to Nico.

While his focus is lasered in on me, his expression remains bare.

I pick it up again, tossing it in the air a few times only to throw it a little out, running to try and catch it, but it falls to the grass.

Before I can make another grab for it, Nico's swift hand flies in to snatch it first, and our eyes meet, both of us still bent over.

I straighten first, and he slowly follows, twisting the ball in his hands.

He eyes me a second, but then tips his chin as he positions his fingers against the laces, elbow raised and prepared to launch.

I follow his lead, jogging out a few yards, and he throws a short pass I'm able to catch with ease.

He licks his lips and claps his hands in front of him, his way of telling me to throw it back.

I try kicking it again instead, and he frowns, but the corner of his lips tip up the slightest bit.

"Ah." I point to him teasingly before my hands find my hips. "I knew it."

"Knew what? You can't kick for shit?" He points the ball to the left, so I start jogging that way, and the ball falls right into my hands.

"No." I take several steps back and his forehead creases slightly. "I knew that you couldn't stay padlocked so tight when in your element."

I tip back slightly and throw the ball, it's a horrible throw and spins the wrong way but it makes it close enough to where he can jog up and make the catch.

"What do you know about my element, Pixie?"

"Pixie?" I tilt my head slightly. "I'm less than a head shy of you. *Not* a pixie."

"Maybe I'm not talkin' about your looks."

I swipe a hand out in a *do tell* type of way, but when he doesn't acknowledge me, I answer his question. "Not much, to be honest, but I know it's where you spend every afternoon pretty much all year long, pre-season, regular season, post-season."

We walk toward each other, but Nico quickly spins like he would in a game, a similar move I saw him do earlier, and I laugh, turning with him.

He bobs, slowly swaying back and forth, so I move with him, and when he darts around me, rushing for the end zone, I trail behind.

I'm only two feet from him, so when he stops abruptly, whipping around to face me, my body slams into his.

I yelp slightly on impact and he catches me around the waist, so we don't fall, both of us laughing. I look up to catch him in the act, but slowly his amusement dies, causing mine to follow.

I clear my throat and step back the second he removes his hand.

I glance to the side where Mr. Brando stands at the edge of the bleachers, binder in hand.

He tips his chin, a small smile in place, and then he switches his attention to a few of the other students around, so I turn back to Nico.

Nico who has an icy stare locked in the direction mine just came from.

When he finally brings his eyes back, he does so taking several steps away, and Alex is suddenly standing beside me.

He hands over my notebook. "Thanks again for the help studying," he says.

I laugh, scrunching my nose. "They're only copies, you'll have to put the time in."

A tight laugh leaves him. "Right, yeah."

I offer a small smile and move back to my spot on the turf, Nico sitting once again as well.

"Should we go over some questions, maybe?" I ask Nico, setting my notebook in my lap.

His eyes pointedly fall to the matte black cover only to snap right back to mine.

He goes straight back to silent mode.

And just like that, Nico's done being semi-friendly for the day.

Awesome.

The class ends not too long later, and lunch follows, the pep rally in the gym right after, so I meet Carley at the door, and we file in together.

We're playing a rare Thursday game tonight, but it's still game night, and with our team having had a bye last week, we're all jonesing for some football.

I'm in need of some fun after the taxing week I've had.

Of course, as soon as I think it, the cause of my headache struts in, a large number 24 etched across his chest in big, bold, blue letters.

He's not even the captain, Trent is as quarterback, yet, there Nico is, leading the team down the bench line, and dropping his ass in the space directly in front of me.

Yay freaking me.

Chapter 6
Nico

She couldn't hold in her eye roll if she tried — she'd never try, it's always been her go-to form of sass.

Not my fault she chooses the second row knowing the team sits in the first. It's the same shit every week, been this way all four years.

The difference though, she'd let me ignore her before, never sought out eye contact.

Now? I swear to god the girl takes pleasure in fucking with my head, demanding my attention without a word, causing me to be more measured and sharper with her.

She's testing my patience, and the funniest shit . . . I'm not sure she has a clue.

Like right now, she's pulled her phone out to record her friends who just took the floor to do their little cheer thing, and she's leaning forward slightly to do it, making her naked knees push into my back.

I'm tempted to catch her off guard, mess with her by leaning against them. It's what she gets for not paying attention, but as soon as I think it, she shifts away, knocking Trent in the arm with them instead.

"She's killin' it!" Demi whispers in a laugh.

He chuckles but keeps his focus on his girl.

A scoff leaves me, and he cuts a glance my way, his smirk deepening.

Dick.

Josie tries to get my attention during the routine, but I

purposely avoid her side of the room, and just like that, they're done and running off the floor.

Demi's legs find their way forward again, so fuck it, I push against them, and she tenses.

I drop my head back, so it's damn near planted in her lap and those green eyes widen, her hands lifted and frozen a few inches out.

Her long hair brushes across my cheek so I reach up and move it, and her lips clamp tight.

"You keep kneeing me and I'm gonna do one of two things. One being lifting you up and putting you beside me so you can't anymore, or two, plant your ass in my lap, which will either embarrass or entice you. Your call, Davenport." My eyes move between hers a moment, but the girl is slow to catch on.

Finally, she jumps, swiftly swinging her body away to the point I almost fall over and have to catch myself.

Both Trent and Carley laugh, while Demi simply stares.

"Sorry," she whispers after a second, and then pretends to be focused on Coach, who gives his speech into the microphone.

Slowly, I turn back, hiding my smirk as Trent swallows his laughter.

In the same second, an uglier different shade of blond catches my eye from the opposite end of the bench.

Alex studies me and my muscles lock, but I make sure he's the first to break contact.

Always fucking watching so he can decide what moves he wants to mirror.

Little punk.

I don't speak the rest of the pep rally, and after it I plug in my earbuds and ignore the world until it's time to meet in the locker room to dress for tonight's game.

My peace is short-lived when we start getting into gear and Alex calls me out, like a brave little fucker.

"So, what's up, Nico, you and Josie on or off this week?"

"Here we fuckin' go." Our boy Thompson shakes his head, dropping on the bench beside me to tie his cleats.

"You mean you don't know, Hammons?" I don't bother looking at him but keep tying my game pants. "Thought you rode my jock harder than that."

"Too busy getting mine ridden by the girls you couldn't keep satisfied."

I scoff, pulling my sleeve up and over my bicep. "Tell me, you like what I like, golden boy, or is sticking your dick where I do the only way you can get off?"

I hear him coming and quickly spin, but Trent's already between us before we can touch each other, Thompson on the other side.

A few of our other teammates stand to block the way Coach'll be coming from just in case.

"Watch your mouth, Sykes, or you'll regret it," he forces past clenched teeth.

"You gonna run home, tell daddy?" I spread my arms out. *Try me, motherfucker.*

His nostrils flare with rage as he pushes against Trent's chest, but Trent nudges him back.

Alex nods, backing up and yanking his shoulder pads over his head, glaring at me as he buckles them, so I pick mine up, slipping them on, too.

"You know, I think I'll shift my *energy* for a little while," Alex draws out slowly, looking over his shoulder at me, his spiteful tone causing my neck to stiffen. "Maybe put it into someone new."

My eyes thin and in my peripheral, I spot Trent's head snap toward me.

The air in my throat begins to burn.

"Demi's lookin' good this year," he edges as he tries to read me, to see if I give a fuck about my new little partner. "Think I'll ask her to formal, bet she'd be a lot of fun after."

This motherfucker.

He thinks he can bait me and expects I'll bite? I don't fucking think so.

I take slow steps toward Alex who stands tall.

Trent follows but lets me get close this time.

My expression must be a little wild because the smirk on Hammons' face grows, but slips just as quick when a snide chuckle leaves me.

"You slippin', Hammons?" My lip curls a bit as my glare deepens.

"Nic," Trent warns.

I hold out a hand, not taking my eyes off Alex. I move closer.

"What makes you think I give a fuck about that girl?"

His mask slips completely, his eyes flying between mine in search of truth.

"Why don't you try worrying about catching a fucking ball instead of how to shove yours inside some worthless chick, and maybe you'd get a chance to receive one more."

"Fuck you," he seethes, his anger coming back. "If you weren't sucking the quarterback's dick at night, I'd get the ball way more than you."

Trent tries to bound forward when he's brought into it, but someone grips his shoulder.

"There you go," I mock, his lame ass attempt to offend not fazing me. He's as weak as his words. "Refocus, motherfucker, put more of that *energy* into your own game instead of tryin' to copy mine, bitch, it'll do you some good."

His fist flies, catching me in the cheek, and I laugh, falling back a step only to dart in and punch him just beneath his left eye, but that's as far as it gets before everyone is shouting and pulling us apart.

Not before I spit in his face though.

Piece of shit.

Demi

There's a turnover on downs, and the starting offense takes the field once again.

Wait, where's . . .

"Has Alex even gone in yet?" I squint, spotting him on the sideline, his helmet in his hands.

"I don't think so." Carley offers me a licorice. "Maybe he's injured?"

"Yeah, maybe." He didn't mention it, not that that means anything.

"Dude, Demi." She laughs, leaning back on the bleacher behind her. "Check out your lab boy."

I scoff.

As if anyone could miss him and his neon sleeve and gloves.

If you didn't know by word of mouth, you had no question after any single game Nico is the star player – a starting receiver and the go-to man for Trent.

I swear, even at the away games the announcers love him.

He's metal and the ball is his flying magnet, no matter where Trent puts the pass, everyone knows Nico will be there to catch it.

Too bad his attitude sucks.

The second the ball is snapped my phone rings, my mom's name flashing across the screen.

"Ignore her," Carley says.

"She'll only keep calling."

I answer, not getting a word in before she starts yelling.

"Where are you?"

I frown. "I'm at the game."

Her annoyed exhale isn't missed. "I need to come and get your card, I have a trip out of town with the girls and I need to make sure I have extra, just in case."

I turn away from Carley, lowering my voice. "I have Krista's party this weekend, I need it."

"I'll bring you the cash I have, and Demi, don't mention this to your dad. He'll deduct it from my spending again."

As he should.

"Whatever," I mumble. "Call me when you get here."

"No, come out into the parking lot now, so I don't have to wait around for you later."

"Are you already on your way?"

"Yes, yes," she huffs. "I'm on my way."

The line goes dead.

With a sigh, I stuff my phone back in my pocket and let Carley know I'll be back in a few minutes.

As I should have expected, a few turns into more, and before I know it, the scoreboard sounds, indicating the end of the fourth quarter, and still, my mom isn't here.

I try calling her for the third time, but she doesn't answer, so I text her.

Of course, she responds to *that* instantly.

Mom: sorry, be there in five.

I scoff, shoving it in my pocket.

It's not long before Carley steps out the gate, followed by a crowd of other game goers. "She's *still* not here?" she snaps.

"Says she'll be here in five."

She shakes her head. "Tell her I'll take you home right now to meet her, she's probably still there."

"It's fine." I pass on the offer. "She'll just get stressed out and act like an asshole."

Macy and Krista are out the gate in the next second, their bags slung over their shoulders.

"Hey!" Krista smiles. "You guys ready to go?"

46

We're supposed to be going out for pizza and talking final plans for her birthday, but I'm annoyed now, and my head is pounding. "I'm bailing, I have to wait for my mom. Call me if you need me, though."

"Are you sure?" Macy asks. "We can wait, or you can meet us later?"

"I'll only be a buzz kill, and who knows what kind of mood she'll be in."

"How you gonna get home?" Carley asks.

"She can drop me on her way out. You guys go, I'm fine."

They nod, move in for a hug and then they're gone.

A half hour later, when the parking lot is near empty other than the cars of the senior players, the clean-up crew, and traveling team's bus, my mom sends another text.

Mom: found the cash in your drawer, so I won't be stopping by. Be safe, have fun.

"Ugh." I roll my eyes at my screen, shoving it in my pocket as I kick off the fence.

Love you, too.

"I make you that sick, Little D?"

My head snaps left to find Nico walking out from the other side of the building, his football bag hanging from one hand, protein shake in the other.

"Parents." A tight laugh leaves me, and I glance away with a frown. "They're . . . annoying."

"I heard that," he says, and my stare moves back to his. "Where're your friends?"

"Gone. Where are yours?" I sass back, glancing behind him, but nobody follows.

"Getting chewed out by Coach."

"Yet here you stand."

"I don't make mistakes," he says straight faced, giving a simple shrug.

"Right." I nod and keep past him. "Well, see you tomorrow."
I guess.

47

"There're no cars in the parking lot the way you're walking, Davenport," he calls out after a few seconds.

I spin around as he steps closer to his truck.

"Because I'm doing just that, Sykes. *Walking*."

He tosses his bag in the back, leaning his forearms on the bed. "I'm taking you home."

"Thanks, but I'm okay."

"I didn't ask you."

My head tugs back. "Excuse me?"

He ignores me, walks around his truck and pulls the passenger door open, his eyes cutting back to me. He lifts his chin expectantly.

This guy.

"I said I was fine."

"And I said I wasn't asking," he snaps back, stern-faced. "You're not walking home alone in the fuckin' dark."

"I'll survive."

"You'll get in."

When I don't move but cross my arms, his eyes narrow farther, his words as sharp as his gaze.

"I'm going the same way. I live right fuckin' behind you." He's annoyed. "We don't even have to talk. In fact, I hate talkin' after a game."

"As opposed to what, your usually chatty self?" I joke.

He blinks. "Game's over, your friends are gone. Let's go."

That's right, the game just ended . . .

"You know what," I think out loud. "I'll wait for Trent, have him drive me."

Nico frowns. "Trent got a ride with someone else."

He moves his hand to the rim of the door, eyes on me as a cloud of warning settles over him.

He won't 'allow' me to walk.

With an annoyed growl, I cave.

It's not like I wanted to walk home, I'd have brought my own car had I known the night would end like this. Still, riding with Nico isn't the ideal way home.

He makes me anxious . . . or something.

I walk over, slide into the seat and glare up at him when he blocks me from reaching for the handle to yank it shut. "Happy?"

"Why would this make me happy?"

"Because you win."

He lowers, bringing his face even with mine, and I pull in a lungful of air.

"I always do." His voice is a sultry whisper. "Might wanna get used to that, D."

He slams the door.

Cocky bastard.

I begin buckling as he steps around to climb into the driver's seat.

Right as Nico shifts the truck into drive, the rest of the team spills around the corner, but we're out of the parking lot before they reach the curb.

My phone rings a minute later.

Great. My mom decides to come now?

I don't look but answer as I bring it to my ear.

"Yes," I drag out, aggravated.

"Demi?"

I pull it from my ear, glancing at the screen and my eyes widen.

Oh shit.

"Hey," I say, internally cringing as I clear my throat.

Nico's frown slides my way, but I pretend I don't notice.

"It's Alex."

A light laugh leaves me. "Yeah, I realize that now. Sorry, I thought my mom was bugging me again."

He's quiet a few seconds before he asks, "Are you still at the school?"

I turn away from Nico. "No, I just left."

"Oh."

Oh?

"I didn't see your car," he says.

49

"Yeah, I got a ride home."

"Huh." He pauses. "I was thinking, maybe I could stop by a minute, you know, if you're going home right away . . ."

I squish my lips to the side to fight a smile. "I am. I was supposed to hang at Krista's awhile, but I decided not to."

"Cool." Alex is quiet a moment. "Text me when you're there?"

"I will," I tell him, nodding even though he can't see me, and hang up.

"Who was that?"

Nico fires off, maybe even before the call is ended, and my head snaps toward him.

I scowl. "Thought you didn't like to talk after a game, or you know, *ever* as far as I'm concerned?"

A bored glance is his response.

Now that I'm closer to him, and there's a little light in here from his dash, a small bruise beneath his right eye reveals itself.

That wasn't there in class today . . .

I don't know why, but after an uncomfortable minute of silence and convincing myself not to ask him about his battle wound, I decide to answer his question.

"It was Alex."

"I told you he was talkin' to someone else."

Another instant response . . .

His grip on the steering wheel tightens.

I glance from his hands to his face. "You mean the same person you're *more than talking* to?"

"I'm not."

His eyes, dark and full of something indefinable, meet mine for a short pause before he focuses his frown on the road.

Nico licks his lips but doesn't say another word, and low in my gut, there's a sudden pull.

A minute or two later, he's parking in front of my house, not bothering to look over or acknowledge my thanks as I step out.

He *does* wait until I'm in the door to drive away, though, which was more than I expected.

As soon as I'm locked inside, I quickly send a text to Alex letting him know I'm home.

I find my way to my bed and lie there wondering why Nico decided to share he was no longer sleeping with Sandra and accidentally fall asleep.

Chapter 7
Demi

"Demi," Miranda, my school dance coach, calls. "Get lower on the second count, your booty needs to be an inch from your ankles. You're the most flexible person in here, don't go half ass on me." She claps and moves to the next group.

My friend Ava looks at me sticking her tongue out as she rolls her eyes making me laugh.

Miranda is a stickler for perfection, but it's good. It's what I want, so I like when she calls me out if I'm being lazy. Today, though, I'm so exhausted I almost wish she wouldn't.

Thankfully, it's only a forty-five-minute practice we squeeze in a few days a week before school begins, and it passes quickly.

I rinse in the showers and get ready as fast as I can and then meet Carley and the girls in the parking lot.

Krista hands me an iced coffee the second I approach.

"You're a lifesaver, thank you."

"Yep." Krista spins back to her car, pulling out a stack of lanyards with keycards hanging from the ends, little shot glasses clipped on as well, and waves them around.

"My dad brought these home last night!" she squeals. "I added the shot glasses, obviously, but check it out! We'll have separate rooms, each of ours is adjoining so we can open the middle doors if we want, but Trent is totally sleeping in mine, so that door will *not* be opened often." She gives a Cheshire Cat grin. "Unless someone wants to see what I've taught him—"

"Okay, enough of that." I laugh. "Keep your door locked, *please*."

"And maybe leave your TV on," Macy suggests, making me laugh harder.

Krista glares at her a second but then laughs with us. "Yeah, maybe I should. I'll be drinking so, things could get a little extra, but *anyway*, jerks, we're all set to head out first thing in the morning! I'll hand the cards out there as people start arriving, but ours and a couple others are in a separate baggy with our names on them."

"Sounds good." I nod, I assume she explained all this to the girls last night.

"What time did your mom show?" Carley asks me.

I consider lying, but in case someone saw and mentions it, I admit, "She didn't. Nico actually drove me home."

"Say what?" Macy slides up, ready for some gossip.

"Literally a ride, practically silent."

"It's happening!" she sing-songs, but I walk away, leaving them there laughing.

"Bye, assholes. See you at lunch."

When I woke up this morning, having accidentally fallen asleep the night before, I expected a text from Alex to be waiting for me on my phone, but there wasn't one.

Turned out, while I fell asleep, he changed his mind.

I walk into leadership expecting him to talk to me about last night, but we end up working on different projects, so the chance never comes, and the day quickly rolls on from there.

In chemistry, Mr. Brando passes out a quick, three question pop quiz the second we walk in. It only takes five minutes of class time and then we're off for another 'bonding session', this time in the library.

Nico, of course, moves quicker than me and is around the corner before I'm even fully out of the classroom, which would have been perfect if Alex hung back, but he made it down the hall before me, too.

Now I'm left with no choice but to search for Nico and sit wherever he chose.

I walk through the double doors of the large, brick building, my footsteps slowing when I spot Sandra sitting on the edge of the check-out desk, Alex leaning against it right beside her.

Her eyes lift as I attempt to sneak by, and she smiles brightly. "Hey, Demi. Welcome." She waves.

Alex glances over his shoulder smiling as well, so I give a tight grin back and I hurry past.

Does Alex know she's fucking Nico?

Or wait, *was* fucking Nico if I correctly interpreted his quick and unexplained 'I'm not' last night.

And really? All I get is a smile after he said he was coming over last night?

Whatever.

I shake off the irritation. It was last minute, so not really a big deal, but he should at least say something.

I make my way past the computers, and then the study group areas, and even the darker, more deserted parts of the library I'd expect him to be, but he's nowhere to be found.

When I come back around the opposite side, Alex and Evan are getting seated and I have to walk straight past them.

Alex's head lifts and he falters slightly, but then stands and turns to me.

"Hey." He grins.

My eyes instantly snap to the black rim of his left one and narrow.

"Oh my god, what happened?"

He gives a light chuckle. "Name of the game."

Except you didn't play yesterday.

"Looks like it hurts."

"It didn't." His response is quick and sharp, to the point where I'm almost positive he took it as an insult, but he quickly shakes it off.

"Hey, so sorry about last night," he apologizes, though his tone doesn't quite back up his words.

I don't say anything right away, assuming an explanation will follow, but when he simply stands there, I shake my head.

54

"Oh, you're fine. I fell asleep as soon as I got home, so I'd have missed you anyway, but I better go. I need to find Nico."

Alex laughs lightly, glancing behind him quickly. "How is it being Nico's partner?"

"Pretty uneventful," I say.

"Really?" He eyes me, almost unbelieving.

He expected a different answer?

"So, you guys don't get along, then?" he coaxes.

Is that what I'd call it? I don't think so . . .

"He's not much for talking is all, so it's a little hard sometimes."

Alex nods. "Yeah, that sucks. Well, hey, the reason I called last night was to ask a question about our assignment, but I figured it out so . . ." He nods again.

I blanch a moment and consider reminding him we didn't have an assignment, but I'm not about to make this more awkward than it already is.

"No worry," I tell him, and I can't get away quick enough.

Once I'm back in the middle of the study area, I pause, still not spotting my flyaway partner.

Right when I'm about to give up and take a damn seat, a flash of his unruly hair catches my eye.

Nico holds his fingers to his lips, a deep frown etched across his forehead, and tips his chin, calling me to him.

I glance back at the front desk.

Clearly Sandra is the TA this period and I don't see anyone else around, so I slip into the long, empty hallway he's hiding in.

Nico pushes open a custodial door, and motions for me to go, but when I glare, shaking my head, he grabs my hand and pulls me through with him, letting the door close behind us as he steps ahead.

"Where does this lead?" I whisper, climbing the stairs.

"Roof. Obviously."

I roll my eyes at his back.

Obviously.

He opens the door at the top of the stairwell, grabbing a brick laying just outside, and uses it to help prop it open.

I step out, glancing around as I walk toward the edge, and lean over slightly to look down.

Instantly, large, *strong* hands find my hips, and I'm jerked back.

I inhale sharply, meeting Nico's barren eyes over my shoulder.

Being on the taller side, I'm surprised by how small I still seem against him.

Maybe it's the way he has me barricaded between his wide shoulders that has me feeling delicate.

His dark gaze is displeased, but a concealed sentiment lines his brow. "Don't be dumb," he finally grinds out.

"I wasn't gonna fall."

"Nobody means to fall *when they fall*. It's called an accident."

I stare, my eyes lowering to Nico's bruise.

Wait.

Both Nico and Alex have fresh markings on their faces?

"What happened to your eye?"

He glares down his nose, but his fingers twitch against my hips. "Don't worry about it."

Right. We're not friends, why would he tell me?

"You can let go of me now, pretty sure I'm no longer at risk of plummeting to my death."

In no kind of hurry, he loosens his grip, his hands dropping to his sides as he steps away, nodding for me to follow him to the other side.

We round the air conditioning units to the opposite end of the building where there're crates stacked up. They're raised maybe three feet high, and a solid ten feet from the ledge, a few lawn chairs that look like they might have been nailed down on top of those allowing you to see over the side without being anywhere near it.

It's a perfect view of the entire football field, and right at the fifty.

It's not super close, maybe a hundred yards away, but I'd bet, at night, when the lights are on, it's still a really clear view.

Right now, we can see people running the track during their PE hour.

"This is awesome," I say more to myself than him.

When I go to turn around, a high stool pushed against the brick building at the other end catches my attention.

I take the few steps off the platforms, and walk over, grabbing onto the back of the seat and look out. My forehead puckers immediately, and I swing my gaze to Nico who is standing where I left him, observing me with open, yet somehow still unreadable eyes.

Slowly, he drops into one of the seats. When his chin raises slightly, I break contact and focus forward again. I step toward the ledge, placing my hands on the edge of the brick but I don't lean this time.

I trail every inch of the garden I helped plant my freshman year. The flowers were purposely placed in the shape of a crescent, leaving a large opening of fresh, plush grass in the center and facing the glass wall of the library, giving those inside who chose a window seat, the perfect scenery should they need a minute to breathe.

Me, though, I use it after hours.

Around four or five in the afternoon the sun is positioned against the building just right, allowing for the windows to work as mirrors.

Perfect place for a dancer to work.

It's secluded, uninterrupted. Beautiful.

Leadership chose this side of the school for the garden because there are no classes on this side of the campus, meaning no foot traffic to destroy our hard work.

My eyes fall to the stool and then shift to Nico who is leaning carelessly in his chair, squinting my way.

Does this mean he's watched me practice?

I head his way, settling into the seat across from him.

After a few minutes of neither of us speaking, I ask, "Are you going to Krista's birthday thing this weekend?"

"No."

"Why not?"

"Does it matter?"

With a sigh, I glance across the little set up again and confirm the chairs are in fact nailed to the wood. "Did you bring this stuff up?"

He shakes his head. "Found it freshman year. I guess some teachers used to sneak up here to smoke, but I've been coming up for years and nothing's touched or moved from how I leave it, so I don't think they do anymore." A sudden frown covers his face. "If people hear about this spot, they'll start locking the door."

I regard him a moment before looking off. He wouldn't have brought me up here if he thought I'd rat him out.

"I'm not going to mess up your chill spot, Nico. I have one of my own, and I would be mad if someone ruined it for me."

"The attic left of the theater stage."

My head snaps his way. "How do you know that?"

He doesn't say anything but continues staring with a deliberate emptiness.

"Did Trent tell you?"

That has him blinking hard, and slowly, he leans forward, placing his forearms on his knees as he delivers his question with an icy tone. "And how would Trent know?"

My skin prickles at the sudden shift in him.

It's strange, his expression remains completely blank, but his eyes . . .

Anger?

Frustration?

Maybe.

"You know his mom and mine are friends."

"And that means he knows where you like to go when you get pissed off or annoyed, or just want a fucking break from having to pretend you're perfect all the time?" he spits, his word choice making it seem as if he knows and understands what goes on in my head.

He couldn't possibly.

I ignore the sudden thickness in the air surrounding us.

"I'm far from perfect," I defend myself, affectively changing the subject.

"I know," he says quickly. "That's why I said *trying* to be."

I glare. "I don't—"

"Yeah, you do," he challenges. "You're always at school early, don't leave until late. You have perfect grades and still do extra credit, have had perfect attendance since forever. You say hi to everyone you pass, offer to help more people than you should or even have time for." He tilts his head. "You just smiled and waved at the chick the dude you're hot for wants to fuck, or already has by now."

"You make me sound like some goody-goody, praise chaser. That's not who I am."

"Is everything I just said not true?"

My lips form a tight line and I look away.

I'm not about to tell him I have to do well to appease my mom or that I want to just as much so I can get the hell out of my house and be able to say I did it on my own. Not that he'd care to hear it.

I keep my response simple for his arrogant, hypercritical, ass.

"There's nothing wrong with wanting to do well in school and being nice to other people is the right thing to do. As far as Sandra goes, she's her own person and Alex isn't mine," I snap. "So, yeah. I was nice and I'll continue to be."

"Why?"

My eyes fly to his. "Because."

"You think you'll get that asshole's attention by being *nice*? Tell me, D, how *nice* were you to him last night?" His lip practically curls.

I must give myself away because a dark chuckle leaves Nico.

He shifts, leaning to the right more. "He didn't show."

When I don't say anything, he shakes his head. "Yet you'll still chase him, won't you?"

What is it with this guy?

"It's not like my entire goal is to become Alex Hammons' girlfriend," I bite out.

His face twists. "Isn't it?"

I jerk forward in my seat, pissed off.

"I like him, *sure*. I'd like someone to go with to all the fun senior shit this year, *duh*, but I don't feel the need to have to be a bitch to harmless people to make that happen." My brows jump. "You want to sit here and pretend to know me so well, but if you think for a second, I'm the type who will become what she thinks someone else wants in order to gain, you're wrong. What purpose would it serve to have him if I can't even be me?" I ask, but not for a reply. "If he doesn't like me the way I am, oh fucking well."

Pretty sure he might though, dick!

I don't tell him that.

Nico glares, but yet again, there's an unexpected change in him.

Suddenly, his eyes are less sure, of what, I can't even pretend to understand.

In the next second the timer on my phone goes off, and I shoot from the chair, eager to get the hell out of here. "We need to go back down, there's only ten minutes left, and Mr. Brando might start looking for us."

He doesn't move, his gaze dark and measuring.

Finally, he pushes to his feet, stepping toward me until he's directly in front of me, my entire body wrapped in a shadow of his own.

He stands there, blank faced with a heavy fog of vexation surrounding him, making it hard to breathe.

Nico remains closed-lipped for a solid thirty seconds, and then finally he slips past, his chest brushing mine with carelessness as he does.

Only when the scrape of the brick across the cement finds my ears do I realize I'm frozen where he left me.

A ragged exhale leaves me, and I clear my throat as I step through the frame, leaving him to follow.

I jolt when the door slams behind me, Nico on the opposite side.

I take my time driving home, putting a frozen casserole in the oven for dinner the minute I step inside, and then get busy with my homework.

I've already eaten and am finishing up my weekend assignments when the front door opens and shuts downstairs, my mom's voice easily heard as she argues with someone on the phone.

Why is she home?

It's just after eight when she gets here, but the knock on my door doesn't come for another twenty minutes.

"It's unlocked," I call out, already dreading her entry.

My mom opens the door, glancing around the room before her eyes fall on me sitting in my window seat, surrounded by textbooks and papers.

She walks in, picks up the remote to my TV and turns it off.

"Always studying." She links her hands in front of her.

I swear, she's the hardest woman to please. She wants me to be Miss Socialite *and* the future fucking President while having no clue which she wants more.

If I didn't get all this out of the way now, then I'd be forced to do it at the beach sometime this weekend.

"Hi to you, too," I mock, looking back to my paper.

"Oh, stop. I saw you before school yesterday."

Because that's enough for us both.

She moves closer to my bookshelf, running her finger across it and frowning at the dust. "I was thinking about this party of Krista's."

My brain freezes mid-word and I lift my eyes to her.

She raises her chin. "I'm not so sure it's a good idea you go."

I set my notebook beside me, turning to face her better.

Really? She's doing this without an audience?

"We leave in less than twelve hours and you already said I could."

"Well, I'm rethinking my answer. I'm your mother, I'm allowed."

"But, why?"

"For one, I didn't realize Monday was a furlough day, giving you guys extra time off. Three days is a lot for kids to be running around unsupervised. God knows what will happen there."

You don't even know what goes on here!

"You know Krista's dad is extra cautious, there will be security all over the place, and he'll be right down the street."

"Still." She reaches past me, closing my curtains and cutting off the view I had of the stars. "I have concerns. It's not like you have someone to watch and protect you."

My face scrunches. "Is that not the purpose of security?"

"Don't be cunning. Don't you think it's strange that you're a senior, you hardly date, and you're always home?"

I want to ask her how she would know but decide against it. "No. I don't."

"Well, I do. You have a pretty face, fit body, and great grades," she sums me up with little to no passion. "You need an arm to hold on to."

"Says the person who constantly reminds me I never want to have to depend on anyone and not to make her same mistake and get pregnant in high school."

She blinks. "Birth control is your friend, daughter. It's why you've been on it since sophomore year, and there is a difference between needing someone and having someone. You should never need, but you *should* have what would suit you well." She pretends to be focusing on my trophy case. "I spent some time with Clara tonight."

Clara, being Trent's mom.

Of course.

I shake my head, knowing exactly what she was going to say. "Don't start with this again."

"We don't understand why you and Trent aren't together, is all."

"Because we don't *like* each other."

"Relationships don't always begin that way, Demi."

I gape at her. "I'm pretty sure they do."

"Well, I think it's time you reconsider. Spend some time with him."

I jump to my feet. "He's dating one of my best friends!"

"And your *best friend,* as you call her, is a harlot of a girl who is going nowhere in life and doesn't deserve him. She'll end up forced to join her parents in real estate."

"What's wrong with that?"

"Nothing, if you want to gamble on the market to protect your future."

"Her parents do well."

"And Trent's own an airline. Tell me how that girl is better suited for him than you?"

My mouth drops open, but nothing comes out, so I shake my head instead.

She doesn't know what she's talking about.

Krista is smart and gorgeous; she's kind and respectful to her parents, wants to be a teacher and a mother, and doesn't give a damn about the money her dad has. Does she enjoy spending it? Yes, but what seventeen – eighteen in days – wouldn't when their father is willing to allow them to?

Not to mention, she was a virgin when she slept with Trent – not a *harlot*!

My mom is an asshole and has no room to talk.

She purses her lips. "I will let you go to this party, but I'm going to ask that maybe you and Trent take a little walk or try and get a few minutes alone."

She's a fucking nut.

"You don't have to take it further, but this is your last year of school, and at some point, he's going to leave her because he knows she's not what he needs, and when that happens it needs to be you he thinks of, especially before you two end up at schools on opposite ends of the country."

I move for my door, holding it open so she gets the hint I want her to leave. "I won't, and you should stop saying things like this. All you're going to do is make it awkward when I'm around him because I'll feel guilty the entire time when I have no reason to. We're friends, and if you want us to at least be that, then leave it alone."

A sickening displeasure glares back at me as she walks my way, pausing before she exits. "Friendships should never trump futures."

"Futures are supposed to be earned, mother, not gained by the choice of spouse."

"Don't judge me," she bristles. "Your father was nothing when I met him."

"Yeah, and neither were you."

"If you're not going to help yourself, Demi, I *will* help you."

"Goodnight, Mom, or should I say goodbye, I assume you're leaving again?"

She has the decency to look guilty, but only for a moment before her shoulders square. "I came to drop off my car, I'm riding with the girls to Wine Country. They're waiting out front now."

"Then you better go, and my day was good, thanks for asking." I slam the door in her face and drop my head against it.

"Be smart and let me know when you get there," she says, then her heels carry her back down the stairs and out the front.

I roll my eyes, put all my schoolwork away, and snag my phone. I make my way into the backyard, put on a freestyle playlist, and drop my phone onto a chair.

I take a few minutes to stretch, then when the song switches, I quickly shift to the center of the grass, facing the large windows.

Ne-Yo and Juicy J's *"She Knows"* starts humming in my ears and my body begins to move as it pleases. Without thought or pressure.

Best feeling ever.

I dance through an entire playlist, only pausing when I'm interrupted by a phone call.

I take a quick drink of water, wiping my hands on a towel before picking it up.

"Hey, Dad."

"Hey, sweetheart. Bad time?"

"No, it's fine. I was just practicing." I take another deep breath. "What's up?"

"I got an alert from the bank," he says with a short pause. "There was an overdraft on your account."

I tense.

She did not.

I quickly walk into the house, tearing my wallet from my bag by the door.

"Demi."

I pull back the side pocket and sure enough, my card is gone.

Damn it!

My hand falls and I squeeze my eyes shut. "I'm sorry, Dad. I didn't have a chance to . . . check the balance. I'm going out of town for Krista's birthday tomorrow and . . ." I ramble off a lie, trying to cover when I wasn't prepared.

"You've been spending more than normal," he hedges, but I can't bite.

I have to live with the woman, deal with her more often, which means if I'm lying to someone it unfortunately has to be him.

"I know, there's just been so much happening around here lately. I can drive into the city next weekend, and work it off?" I offer.

My dad's law firm is in downtown San Jose, a solid hour or more in traffic from where I am in Santa Cruz. He commuted back and forth for a long time but ended up buying a place closer a couple years ago.

He's quiet for a moment, and I almost think he's going to call me out on what he must know is a lie. He sees the statements and where the card is being used.

"No, honey," he says quietly, the disappointment, maybe a little guilt, too, easily heard. "You don't have to do that but

65

thank you for offering. Maybe be a little more conscious of your spending is all, you know, if you can."

He totally knows it's her.

I squeeze my eyes shut. "Sorry again, Dad."

"It's all right. Will you check in with me over the weekend while you're gone?"

"I will."

"Love you."

"Love you," I tell him. "Bye."

I hang up and drop my head back, sighing at the ceiling before glaring at my wallet.

She said she came home to drop off her car.

Bullshit.

I can't wait until I'm away at college and she's forced to reevaluate or fall flat on her ass.

Tossing my wallet back in my bag, I grab a blue Gatorade from the fridge, a blanket off the back of the couch, and go outside to lay on the large lounger. I pull the soft fleece over my legs, slip my hoodie on, and allow the music to play quietly beside me while I stare at the stars.

It's well past midnight, my mind having only begun to clear of my own family issues, when the hushed argument of another's floats over the fence.

"I'm not gonna allow this shit from you anymore," Nico hisses.

Cold words from someone else follows. "And how does a punk kid like you plan to stop it?"

Mr. Sykes?

I haven't seen him in years.

"I'm not a fuckin' kid anymore, and I won't stand here and watch you or your new wife destroy her all over again."

Oh shit, the rumors are true. He did leave them and remarry.

"You think you could stop me if you tried?" A loud, clearly intoxicated laugh echoes. "Your mom will never let me go. She begs to see my face. When was the last time your ma's even looked at you?"

66

"You wouldn't know." Nico's voice is a deep rumble that has the hairs on my neck standing. "You keep her so doped up on pills she doesn't even know what day it is half the time."

Shit.

I reach for my earbuds, knowing I've already heard more than I should have.

"Get the fuck—"

Music fills my ears, cutting Nico's words off.

It takes a few songs for my muscles to ease, and I close my eyes, letting the chilled September night's air waft over my face.

Minutes later, my music stops.

I blindly reach for my phone, but when my hand finds an empty space, my eyes pop open.

I jump.

Nico stands tall, his shadow wide and looming, my phone locked tight in his grip.

He glares, jaw clenched, beads of sweat covering his forehead. "You record that?"

My brows jump. "No." I point to my phone and he tears his gaze from mine, forcing them to the screen. "Just music. I plugged in as soon as—"

"As soon as what?" he snaps. "Soon as it got too heavy for your textbook world?"

I prepare to argue, but the longer I look at him, I decide against it.

He's stressed. Tense.

Tired?

My eyes fall to his shirt – torn at the sleeve and stretched at the collar – before moving right back to his.

His face hardens and he cuts his glare to the fence.

"Wanna talk?" I ask when maybe I shouldn't.

He scoffs, shaking his head, still not looking back at me. "I give you one ride home, so you don't have to walk in the fucking dark, and suddenly you assume I want to talk to you."

I eye him and his nostrils flare.

He said after his games he doesn't like talking. Maybe it's the same with all intense situations for him?

"Good, I'm glad you're not up for it." I lift a shoulder and his gaze slowly slides sideways, back to mine as I scoot over on the double lounger, then lay back, gazing up at the sky once again. "You're an asshole, and I don't want to talk to you, either."

He stands there, the heat of his heavy stare burning into the side of my face for a minute or two before a heavy scoff leaves him.

Nico drops beside me.

We lay there in the dark, staring at the stars.

Not talking.

Chapter 8
Nico

Everything was chill, then the DJ had to go and put some fuckin' hip-hop on as if watching her dance to the John Mayer bullshit he was playin' before wasn't bad enough.

This is torture, and I'm only two hours in.

I can't deal with this shit a full weekend.

Demi arches her back, swaying her hips to the music while her friends take turns stepping closer, trying to keep up with her.

They can't.

Swear the girl's hips were meant to roll.

Her long, dark blonde hair is teasing the skin of her slightly exposed stomach, eyes closed and arms in the air. She's lost in her own mind, but only for a few minutes before she opens them again.

For the tenth fucking time, her focus shifts to the asshole whose attention she's after.

Too bad for D, though, lover boy's not looking at her.

No, his eyes are glued on the girls playing beer pong, the ones who jump up and down in excitement, even when they miss. The ones who have yet to put their clothes back on when they've been out of the water for hours and the sun's been gone just as long.

I glance to Demi.

Her shoulders fall half of an inch, defeat sneaking its way out of her, but she quickly wipes it away.

A scoff leaves me, and I shake my head when the small group of girls take several steps left, trying really fuckin' hard to get in Alex's line of sight. She thinks she's being chill about it, but she doesn't know I'm watching.

This shit's embarrassing to witness.

The DJ announces the last song of the night and doing the opposite of what a closer normally would, the dick chooses to hit it harder, and a song more upbeat than the last comes on. Everyone cheers.

A sudden mischievous gleam covers Demi's face, one that has me sitting forward in my seat.

This is bound to be bad.

She drops a little lower, bends a little further and moves spades fucking faster, to the point where her girls have no choice but to step back and sway around, admiring as she does her thing.

When even the DJ's eyes fight for a sight of the blinding blonde in the middle, I push to my feet, and what do you fuckin' know, Demi's head snaps my way in the same second.

She falters slightly, her dance moves slowing a bit, body shifting in my direction, by accident I'd bet.

I head toward her in unhurried steps.

The closer I get, the more uneasy she grows, and by the time I'm directly in front of her, the girl has stopped moving completely.

"Hey," she says hesitantly, her hand coming up to brush the hair from her face. "I didn't know you were here."

I lick my lips, pulling my bottom one between my teeth a moment. "'Course not, D. You've always had blurred vision."

She pulls back slightly but doesn't ask what I mean.

She should.

"You said you weren't coming."

"Changed my mind."

She nods, peeking toward her friends a moment before bringing those eyes back to mine. "So . . . what's up?"

"Testosterone. Your little show was as effective as you hoped."

She bristles, her brows slanting into a frown. "Excuse me?"

70

"That's probably a good idea, or I might have to call your ma, tell her you're not behaving well," I rag her.

Her eyes flash with surprise, hardening only a second later.

I know she's hoping I'll walk away, let her have her fun with her friends, but the night's done, and so is her playtime.

"Who the hell do you think you are?" she hisses, looking around to see who's watching.

Bet money lover boy is now.

The thought has me wanting to walk the fuck away from her.

I don't, but she does.

She jerks from the group, storms across the sand, and throws open the double glass doors, hurrying down the hotel hallway.

Don't matter though, the song was already over, and people are starting to head for their rooms just the same.

I catch her by the elbow right before she passes my door, hers, unbeknownst to her, being the one right beside it, and push her against it, overcrowding her body.

I lock her in, but she beats me to speak.

"When the hell did you talk to my mom?" she questions me angrily.

"You seem as surprised by her little visit as I was."

"What did she say to you?"

"Don't worry about it."

She gapes at me, but it quickly morphs into a frown, one I'm not so sure is meant for me.

"So, Little D, all that for Alex Hammons?"

"I don't know what you're talking about."

"Sure you do."

A laugh bubbles out of her and she crosses her arms. "Why do you even care?"

"I don't, but it was disgustingly obvious," I sneer. "Sad really. You should tone it down a bit, not come off so willing."

Her jaw clenches as she tries to hold back but can't.

"Maybe I am," she says with a fake ass lack of concern.

"Any other girl would realize if a guy doesn't notice her on his own it's a lost cause."

"What do you know about having to fight for someone's attention?" she snaps.

This time it's me that lets out a humorless laugh.

She tries to look away, but I drop my forehead to hers to keep her facing forward, and her eyes darken, in annoyance maybe, but the pink tinting her cheeks has nothing to do with the sunburn she got today.

More and more voices fill the area, so I cut my stare down the hall. My eyes narrow, spotting Alex and Sandra walking this way, to his room, I'd bet.

He laughs at something she said and then looks up, spotting me standing here with Demi in front of me and an instant frown pulls at his brows.

Fuck, man.

He makes an excuse that gets Sandra to pause with him and they talk in place, where he can pretend he's not fixated on us.

I look back to D.

Tension has her face drawn tight as she nibbles at her lower lip.

"You're *seriously* trippin' on him?"

She ignores me but can't hide the dejection eating at her.

The longer I look into her eyes, the more a really dumb thought settles in low in my gut, and once it starts, there's no stopping it.

My mind fucking races, nothing but flashes of the pretty little dancer in front of me spinning round and round and god damn.

No.

No, no . . . bad idea.

Talk about the possibility of full force backfire and now knowing for sure she wants him? It'll be worse. Harder.

Unless . . .

Her green eyes are low and on mine, a hint of gentle concern hidden behind the unease.

What are you worried about, D?

"Nico . . ." She trails off, her gaze roaming across my face, noticing the question written across it.

72

He's seen me with her, in her space. This can be read a lot different than what it is, not much I can do to erase that.

What choice do I have at this point, right?

Right.

Fuck, I shouldn't.

I do it anyway.

I keep my eyes on hers, needing to witness first-hand the look in hers as I slide my hand across her stomach until I reach the loop on her little shorts. I bring her against me.

Her hip almost meets mine she's so tall, five-eight or nine to my six three.

Shock has her eyes widening, but damn, she doesn't fight me in the slightest.

"Acting desperate, *that's* your plan to get what you want?" I question. "You're good with gaining notice that way?"

Her mouth opens but those lips clamp closed just as quick.

"No, no, D," I egg her on with a whisper. "Say it."

"I was dancing, I'm a dancer, there's nothing desperate about it. I was having a good time with my friends."

I fight to keep my mouth shut, but the little cloud in her normally bright green eyes spurs aggravation I can't suppress, and words I shouldn't share fly from me. "He won't want you if you dangle yourself like bait."

That has her frown coming back and she lifts her hands, attempting to push me away, but all it does is make it appear as if she's rubbing on me.

My body is a brick fucking wall against hers.

"How the hell would you know?" she hisses.

"Because he's a punk . . ." *Stop fucking talking,* I curse myself, but it's to no avail, and fuck if I don't say more. "He wants what belongs to someone else. It's all about the chase, winning over another, for an asshole like him."

"Maybe I can be different."

"*Maybe* . . . you can be mine."

Words fail her and she takes in a quick breath through her nose, her brows knitting as she silently studies me.

73

"What?" she croaks after a second.

Slowly, I allow my fingers to slide up her bare side. When my hand twitches against her chilled skin, she pulls her lips between her teeth.

I dip my mouth close to her ear.

"Nico, what are—"

"What the fuck's the point of this thing," I exhale against her, my other hand tugging at the bottom of her wannabe hoodie.

Her swallow isn't missed, and I glare at the softness of her neck as she leans to the side, trying to escape my heated breaths, but all it does is tease me with more creamy, sun brushed skin.

A harsh exhale leaves her. "It's a crop sweater for . . . for over my suit. Nico, what are you doing?"

I shift my feet forward, so one leg is between hers, the other blocking her left hip in. "I told you."

My brain tells me one thing, while also transmitting another.

Shut the fuck up and walk away, but damn, don't she feel good . . .

I keep going.

"Hammons wants what someone else has. You a girl worth his competition's time and attention?"

"Stop acting like everyone wants to be you."

"Stop acting like they don't."

"God! You're so—"

"*Shut up,* D. Your *man* is still watching." She tenses against me, her fingers involuntarily bending, making it seem as if they're fighting to get closer.

"I bet his eyes are trailing my hand," I tell her, allowing my palm to slide lower and this time her little nails do bite into my skin. "Waiting to see how far you'll let me go, right here in the open, for him . . . and everyone else to witness."

I pull back, gliding my tongue along my bottom lip and her eyes follow, slowly raising to mine.

"How far *will* you let me go?"

"I . . ." She blinks, shaking her head lightly as if she's confused but can't focus.

I discreetly reach into my pocket for my keycard. When I pull back, her hands stay glued to my chest, but her head draws away with mine, an unsure expression stamped across her face.

"Turn and look," I instruct her.

As I thought she would, she hesitates a second, but can't help herself in the end.

She shifts her head and mine follows.

Some of our classmates pass, eyeing us curiously, a few girls laugh while a couple guys grin, and others are too buzzed or wrapped up in their own hook-ups to notice, but not Alex.

His feet now shuffle him stupidly slow down the hall, his eyes raking over our position before lifting.

I wait for his stare to move to hers, wait for a hint of the fucking grin I know comes next, the one he gives everyone, and the one I know will have her smiling wide back, all fucking hopeful and shit.

Not happening.

Before she can react, I quickly wrap my arm around her waist, and drop my head into her neck, effectively blocking her from his view. I slip the key in the slot and the door unlocks, so I quickly push her backward into the room.

It clicks shut behind us, my hands falling from her in the same second.

Her palms fly up as she stands there open-mouthed, and finally, she gets her grip and hits me with a little glare.

"What . . ." She shakes her head, eyes flying around my room. "I don't . . . why are you getting naked?" she sizzles.

Ah, there's the anger.

I ignore her, tossing my shirt to the little chair as I kick off my shoes.

"What the hell!" She throws her arms up only to let them drop back to her sides with a slap.

I move toward her and her eyes slice to my bare chest.

She swallows and looks away. "Seriously, Nico, what is this, what was *that*? Better yet, why the *hell* am I in your

75

room – this is your room, right, you didn't just break into someone else's?"

My arm slips past her and she holds her breath, letting it out when I lift the remote in front of her face and step backward until I can lie back on the bed.

"That was me helping you." I can't keep the irritation out of my voice. "Bet lover boy hits you up on the beach tomorrow now."

"Are you joking?!" she shrieks. "He's gonna think we're hooking up!"

"And?"

"And . . ." Her eyes widen, but she has no idea what to say, so she goes with the most obvious response. "He'll think we're dating!"

I level her with a bored look. "That's the last thing he'll think."

Her head pulls back, and like a brat, she crosses her arms. "Because Nico Sykes would never waste his time on a girl like me, right?"

"Wrong." My stare moves to hers. "Because *Nico Sykes* could fuck you either way."

She sneers. "You—"

"Stop talking," I interrupt her, not interested in hearing her crybaby shit over that idiot. "I did you a favor, now you won't have to try so hard. Sit down, play on your phone or watch whatever I put on, something."

"Like I trust you enough to sit on your bed with you."

My eyes jump back to hers and she keeps her glare strong a minute, I'll give her that, but slowly, it wipes away and she looks to the wall.

She trusts me enough, just like she did when we were younger.

We might not have been friendly over the last few years, but I'm not some fuckin' stranger to her.

"Sit."

She scoffs, moving for the door instead.

76

"You leave, he'll think you're a lousy lay and couldn't even help me get it up."

"Or," she snaps back. "He'll think you're a minute man and be dying to show he can hang longer."

A loud laugh leaves me and she rolls her eyes.

"D, he knows better than that, but do what you want. Just don't say I didn't warn you."

"It's not like he's standing out there waiting to see when I leave. I'm sure he's in his room by now, you know, with the same girl you were fucking not long ago."

My muscles tense.

Little does she know that's a perfect fucking example of what I've explained to her. Why I gave her that insight, I don't fucking know. I'll have to fix this and quick.

I manage to lift my shoulders. "Maybe, but I guarantee there're still others out there. Word travels. Want to be the girl known as the tease who loads but can't pull the trigger and cuts before release?"

Her glare gets a little more profound.

She stands there for a solid five minutes, probably playing every fucking situation over and over again in her head, before she growls, tosses down her little bag and flops on the bed beside me.

She twists her body, facing the opposite wall. "My room is somehow right next to yours. I should have left the damn adjoining door unlocked, and I'd be in my own right now."

"Too bad for you."

"I can't stand you," she growls, angrily hitting the pillow to get comfortable.

"Don't care." I toss the remote to the side, lay back and close my eyes. "And unless I'll be waking up with your lips wrapped around my dick, don't fall asleep in here."

She gasps and I smirk.

That'll shut her up.

Chapter 9
Demi

"Demi, wait up!"

I pause mid-step, my head snapping over my shoulder to find Alex jogging toward me, just as Nico said he would.

That alone is almost enough for me to be instantly annoyed.

Almost.

Alex grows closer, so I spin to face him better.

"Hey." He grins, running a hand through his blond hair.

"Hey." I laugh, pushing my sunglasses up on my head.

"Didn't see much of you last night," he says as his hands find his hips.

A slight frown takes over — clearly my efforts were more than lost on him.

I brush it off, allowing a smile to take over. "Me and the girls hung out on the beach before dinner, then the dance floor called my name."

His grin deepens. "You like dancing, huh?"

My mouth opens but nothing comes out.

Is he for real?

He has to know I'm on the dance team at the very least. I mean . . . right?

"So, uh . . ." he begins, pointing to the barstool area of the coffee hut I was headed toward. "I was about to eat, are you grabbing something, too?"

"Just a coffee to bring me back to life. I'm gonna lay out a while, I'm exhausted."

He chuckles, but it's quickly cut off when his eyes fly over my shoulder.

"'Course you are."

My muscles lock with Nico's intruding voice, and I'm stiff as a damn board as he wraps his long arms around my middle, not so gently tugging me against him in a way that can only be his show of dominance. He kisses my cheek and my skin tingles in embarrassment.

I stand frozen, too shocked to do or say a damn thing.

Course, Nico has to go for that extra point.

"If you weren't, that would mean I didn't do my job last night," he mumbles near my ear, his face dipping into my neck and my stomach muscles grow tight. "And we both know that's not true."

What the hell is he doing?

I chance a glance at Alex who eyes me curiously. He pointedly looks from Nico to me and I so badly want to tear myself away right now, but the quizzical glare suddenly taking over Alex has me stuck.

No way Nico was right . . .

"Yo, Alex!"

We both look to the side to find a few of our classmates standing at the top of the small sand hill.

"We're going for breakfast at the cafe," our mutual friend, Frankie, announces, examining me and Nico while speaking to Alex. "You coming? Wait, that you, Sykes?"

The merriment in his tone has me considering elbowing Nico in the gut.

Nico lifts his head, nodding in their direction.

"Mornin', Demi," another guy from school sing-songs.

I offer a flat smile.

"Alex," Frankie prompts again.

Alex swings his gaze back to Nico, then me as he nods. "Yeah. I'm coming." He gives me a smile. "I'll find you later, Demi."

"She'll be busy," Nico tells him.

I have to pinch myself to keep from frowning.

Alex glares as he walks off. "*Nico.*"

"*Dick,*" Nico says.

"Sykes, you guys wanna go?" Frankie yells again.

"No," I say quickly in case he gets a bright idea to agree. "We don't."

The guys laugh.

Nico doesn't move until the group is out of sight.

His arms fall and he strides past me without so much as a glance my way or a single word of explanation.

It takes a second but then I dart forward. "What the hell?!"

"You say that a lot."

"Yeah, well, it's pretty warranted, don't you think?" I snap. "We're hardly even, as in not at all, friends, Nico. You ignore me unless we're in class and no one else is paying attention or around. You're as hot as you are cold and it's ever-changing. Now you're acting all demanding like you have the right."

He gives a half glance over his shoulder, ignoring everything I just said, and then turns back, stepping up to the cashier lady. He orders, coming back to stand right in front of me.

A cross between anger and aggravation is etched across his face, neither of which make any sense.

"It was one thing — still a bad idea — to pull the shit you did last night, but to basically confirm the rumor I'm sure has already started to spread? Dick move."

He shrugs. "Hammons has to think I'm into you, takes more than a night for that to happen."

"Because who could possibly tie you down?" My tone drips with sarcasm.

Nico catches me off guard when he grins. "Exactly."

I'm stuck for a second, the sight so foreign but then I snap out of it.

"Are you insane?!" I shout. "I don't *want* people to think I hooked up with you, let alone that I'm, what, *dating* you?!" My words are laced with a mocking laugh.

80

"Yeah." His expression grows fierce, and he rushes in, closing the gap between us and forcing my spine straight. "And why not?"

My forehead creases. "Why are you pushing this?"

His jaw clenches. "Don't you get it? People saw us last night. Now they'll assume you're a far different girl than they know you to be," he says, almost troubled. "That what you want?"

I squeeze my eyes shut, shaking my head. "Oh my god."

I'm no saint, but there isn't anyone who could claim I'm easy or slutty either. Now they just might. I shouldn't care what others think, it's just name calling, but this is high school, and people can get nasty quick and for less.

My eyes pop open. "This is all your fault!"

"Getting the dumbass you want to notice you is *my fault*?"

"He noticed me before, we're friendly, asshole! This isn't some Pleasantville bullshit, the girl can do the asking and I planned to soon, especially after he wanted to hang out last week."

"Yeah, how bad did he want to, D?" He gets in my face. "Your boy couldn't even show up, bet he didn't respond after you told him you were home, which I'm sure you did the second you got in the door."

He's such a dick.

"I didn't ask for nor do I need your help," I growl.

He scoffs, glaring just the same. "No, you just went video vixen in front of all my friends. What, you thought I was just gonna let that happen?"

I gape at him, lifting my palms at a loss. "I don't . . . *why* do you care?"

"I don't, but you were only allowed on this trip because I'm here. What, I was supposed to let some punk take advantage of you and deal with the heat from your ma? Fuck no."

My face goes slack as I eye him.

That's what my mom told him? After telling me to basically try and steal my friend's boyfriend? What, is Nico her new backup plan?

81

Such a crock of shit.

"You are so clueless it's not even funny."

He lifts his hands as if to say *it is what it is*. "Either way, you're stuck being mine for a while." He dips down. "Get. Over it."

I shake my head doubtfully. "People will never believe this."

The vein in his neck tics against his skin, and he pushes impossibly closer, so close I almost trip in the sand behind me, but with the instincts of an athlete, his arm snakes around my waist as it seems to like to do, keeping me upright.

"Yeah, and why not? You think you're better than me or somethin' because your future's lookin' brighter?" he spits.

My head wrenches back.

Future's brighter? Nico must have dozens of colleges after him at this point in his football career.

Does he not believe in his own abilities?

"That's not what I mean at all," I tell him, my voice quieter than I would have liked. I lick my lips and look away.

"D." His tone is a mild command. "Look at me."

Slowly, I do.

His eyes are sharp and assessing. "Why?"

I hesitate a moment, but when he lowers his chin expectantly, I start. "Fine. Despite how I acted about it when you said it, you're right. Nobody would expect I could keep the . . . *interest* of a guy like you for more than a night."

"Guy like me," he says.

I swear he's trying to be angry, but I'm not finding it when I look at him, and there's nothing but curiosity in his words.

"Yeah. Guy like you. Careless, crass, athletic and overly popular despite your bossy attitude. Let's not forget the fact that we don't speak."

His features smooth some, and he gives me a quick once over. "You act like you're a nerd."

A laugh bubbles out of me. "No, but I'm not some sex kitten either."

His lips smash together and it takes a second, but he releases me, moving to grab his order.

82

When he comes back, it's with a coffee in each hand.

Slowly, he hands the second cup to me.

"Thanks," I say quietly as I accept the drink.

"I think you'd be surprised to learn what's said about you in the locker room, Demi."

With that, he takes off, my eyes trailing his every step.

Once he's far enough, I walk up to the small counter and hand the girl the cup.

She frowns.

"He was . . . I don't know, attempting to be nice, I guess, but I'm lactose intolerant. I can pay for a new one."

The girl blinks. "He ordered both with soy," she says.

My shock must be evident, because the girl smirks, and pushes it toward me. "Seems the boy knows you better than you think." She winks and goes back to her job at hand.

I turn around, finding Nico staring right at me from his place on the pier.

Does he?

Chapter 10
Nico

"Woke up to an interesting string of texts from a freaked-out Josie this morning," Trent tells me of my ex as he drops beside me on the bench.

"Fuck her."

"You have, many times." He laughs. "Pretty sure that's only half the reason for her panic, though."

I offer nothing.

He stays quiet a minute, too, before deciding to go for it. His tone is slightly cautious, as it should be. "Demi, Nic?"

"Don't," I warn right from the gate.

My eyes find her on the beach with no fucking effort. She peels off her hoodie even though there's still a morning chill in the air and doesn't bother laying a towel down before plopping into the sand, leaning back on her hands. She tilts her head so the sun is hitting her how she wants it to.

"We didn't hook up last night," I admit.

"How the hell did she even end up in your room?"

I lick my lips, not giving the answer he's asked for. "I convinced her to make people think we're together."

Trent's silence has me looking his way, and I'm not surprised by the confusion staring back.

"Turns out," I start with a low, humorless laugh. "She's into Hammons."

He watches me closely before a low curse leaves him. "And Alex threw that shit out about asking her to formal."

I nod, sitting back.

"Nic . . . don't do this. This isn't the same as—"

"He already saw me with her, Trent." I cut him off. "It's game on at this point."

Unease lines his forehead, and my best friend can't help himself. He tries once more. "You sure this is a good idea, my man?"

I finish off my coffee and then push to my feet. "Nope."

Not in the slightest.

Demi

"Girlfriend, fucking spill!" Macy's voice hits me, and my eyes open, finding my friends walking up all giggles. Fresh coffees in their hands.

"Spill?" I'm confused at first, but then it hits me.

Shit.

Nico.

Of course they heard!

"It's not what you—" I start to deny it when their eyes lift, big smiles and girly googly eyes take over their faces.

"Speaking of the new boy toy!" Krista laughs. "What up, Nic?"

"'Sup." His deep voice comes from behind me, and suddenly long, muscular legs are caging me in, his wide chest framing me in from behind.

I tense, my stare snapping to Carley's.

Her lips clamp tight, but in a *get it girl* kind of way.

"So . . . this is new," Macy drags out excitedly, none of them moving to sit.

"Tell us how it happened!" Krista's eyes practically sparkle for the juice.

"Krista," I start, ready to distract her one-track mind somehow, but pause when Nico shrugs against me.

"It was only a matter of time," he says with pure confidence.

Only a matter of time?!

Is he serious?

Because the most wanted shithead in the senior class has never *once* done a damn thing to lead anyone to believe we were a possibility. And it goes both ways.

Yeah, okay. As if they'd believe—

"That's why you were drooling over him at the game!" Carley says.

Both mine and Nico's muscles harden.

"I was not."

"I knew it!" Our other friend Ava squeals, and my head snaps her way. "Me and Krista used to bet on when you two would *finally* hook up!"

"Seriously?" I question without thinking and all eyes fly to me.

Shit.

Ugh! I never agreed to this! What the hell am I supposed to do? Lie to my best friends?

"I always thought you had the hots for him but didn't wanna say." Krista grins, all proud like. "I used to plot with Trent, trying to hook you up, you guys are so alike it's unreal, but he'd get mad and tell me not to push it."

Nico's chest flexes against my back and I hold my breath.

Krista smiles wider. "I bet he knew Nico had the hots for you but worried you didn't feel it." She gasps. "We can totally double date now!"

Oh, god. Shoot me.

And did she say we're alike? Ha!

I try to sit up more, to remove my body from pressing against Nico's overheated one, but he only tightens his hold, his lips hitting my ear.

"Stop it," he whispers unexpectedly, and my abdomen constricts. "This'll help us both, go with it. If you keep trying to pull away, I'll whisper something so dirty in your ear it'll have you squirming, and all your friends will witness me turning you on."

What the what?

I try to fight the unexpected pull his nearness seems to have created, but apparently my eyes have a mind of their own, and I can't stop myself from glancing over my shoulder, the move bringing my lips even with his.

87

His eyes are sharp and warning as his tongue sneaks out to flick my lips.

All I can think is thank god for padded bathing suit tops.

My traitorous nipples pebble without permission.

This guy . . .

The breathy "dang" that leaves Macy has my head snapping toward them.

"I just got hot," Macy admits.

I gape at her, but she simply shrugs.

Krista gives her a high five. "Same. I'm going to find my man for a little ocean water rub down."

I can't help but laugh when she runs off to do exactly that, the rest of the girls laying their towels out and piling beside us.

Nico shifts behind me, and then suddenly his shirt is at our sides, the natural heat of his naked skin now pressed firmly against mine, nothing but the tiny strings of my top between us. While tension swims deep in my stomach, my body decides to settle into his.

"See how easy it is, D," Nico murmurs for only me to hear. "No one will question us."

I wish I was as sure as he seems to be, but hey, if he insists on sitting behind me, I might as well use him.

I lift my hips so I can shimmy my shorts down and kick them to the side, allowing my upper body weight to be fully held by his.

"If you don't put those back on—"

"Quiet," I cut him off, not bothering to keep my voice low as he did. "I need your body, not your words."

Carley laughs beside me, slipping her glasses in place.

Nico's chest vibrates with his groan, but after a second he leans back some, so I'm angled just right, the bright California sun beaming down on me.

Not a second after I'm settled in completely, accepting of my makeshift chair, Nico's whispered words find my ear yet again.

"Use my body however you want, D. As far as everyone is concerned, it's yours now." He pauses a minute before continuing, "But remember, if you do, it'll go both ways."

Both ways. Meaning if I use him, he'll use me, but how or in what ways?

Dirty ways?

An involuntary shiver runs through me and his chest shakes with silent laughter.

Asshole.

"Damn, this is gonna be fun."

I'm not sure fun is the right word, but I'll worry about that later. Right now, I'm enjoying the heat of the sun's touch too much, almost as much as his warm body on mine.

I fall asleep.

Chapter 11
Demi

Macy skips into my room and does a little twirl, her neon romper causing her chestnut skin to glow even more, dark curls bouncing all around. "How's it look?" She smiles, posing with her hands on her hips.

I laugh, turning back to my mirror. "Hot. The color looks awesome on you," I tell her as I finish applying the last of my mascara.

"Thank you, thank you. I'll probably freeze once it gets darker, but it's worth it." She chuckles, plopping on the bed. "What are you wearing?"

"I think my white shorts."

Macy bounces over to my bag while I let my hair out of the braids I put them in after my shower earlier. It's not quite dry yet, but the waves are there like I wanted.

"I say this one." She pulls out my plum maxi. It's a stretchy cotton, ankle-length dress.

I shake my head. "I use that as a coverup for over my bathing suit."

She frowns. "Why? It's meant to be a dress."

"Because it stretches around my ass and hips and shows every panty and bra line. At least when it's a bathing suit, it makes sense."

"Well, you haven't worn it here, so it's a dress this time." She tosses it at me. "Wear it."

I roll my eyes, tugging it off my head. "Fine. It's long, so it'll keep me warmer anyway."

"Girl, you could wear your bikini to dinner and I bet that boy'd have you sweating without even touching you."

"Shut up!" I hiss, looking to the adjoining door.

Her eyes widen, her mouth dropping open before a huge, devious grin takes over. "*That's* his room?"

I nod, pull my t-shirt off over my head and slip my dress on, letting my shorts fall to my feet.

I move back to the mirror to put on my earrings.

Loud moaning comes from behind me and I whip around, panicking when Macy lets out another, and then another and another.

"Macy!" I shriek, darting toward her, but she grabs the chair and rolls it between us, darting the opposite way from me. She turns her head, so her mouth is closer to the door and lets out a breathy, "Oh, yes!" and my face flames.

"You little bitch," I squeak.

Footsteps pound behind me, and I look right as Krista and Carley nervously peek around the corner, both of them laughing when all they find is us.

Macy laughs silently, crossing her legs as if trying not to piss herself, and brings her finger to her lips telling them to keep it down.

"I'm gonna kill you!" I force through my teeth.

She laughs harder.

I yank the chair from her and attempt to cover her mouth, but all it does is make her moans sound desperate and muffled by blankets or something.

"Oh my god." I look to Carley and Krista. "A little help, assholes?" I hiss, but they can hardly catch their breaths at this point.

"Why are we even whispering?" Carley giggles.

"Wait for it!" Macy says quietly, tipping her head back for one last sex call. "Don't stop!"

That's it!

I tug my dress up to my hips and jump on her, my hands smashing over her mouth just as she whips open the adjoining door, revealing a half-naked, dripping wet, *frowning*, Nico Sykes.

I freeze, Macy laughs uncontrollably now, and the girls gasp, followed by loud laughter.

His glower flails me, but just as quick, roams the room before settling on my naked legs around her waist. A single, dark brow quirks.

"Something I should know?" he teases.

My glare zooms to Macy.

She smacks my ass, letting my legs drop so I'm standing in front of her now, Nico still in the open doorway.

In a towel.

"She's an idiot," I offer, shoving Macy away with one hand.

"It was experimental, and effective," Macy disagrees, shoving me right back. "If he only wanted to bang it out with you this weekend and ditch you come school, he'd have finished his shower in peace. The glare and balled fists show the truth." She winks at him. "The boy's smart, not willing to share our girl."

Mine and Nico's eyes meet.

Shows how much Macy knows.

Nico doesn't give a damn. He probably just enjoys porn and her noises were, I don't know, appealing or something.

I mean, I watched him have sex for shit's sake, can't fault him for simply listening to what he *thought* was me fucking.

A hard knock followed by a door opening echoes in Nico's room.

"You ready, dickhead?" comes from inside and suddenly Trent is standing in our adjoining doorway.

He freezes, looks between us both and opens his mouth to speak but then something, or someone rather, catches his attention behind me and he glares.

Trent gently moves me to the side, so he can step in my room.

"What the fuck?" he spits.

I spin to see Krista is only in her underwear and bra.

She frowns at his words but then drops her eyes to her body. They pop back up wide and unaware. "Oh, shit!" She reaches for a towel off my floor and holds it in front of her. She grins. "To be fair, I had to run in here so I could see who was fucking!"

"What?!" he shouts.

She laughs loudly, dropping her head back. "Okay, that sounded worse. Come on, baby. I'll explain in my room." She wiggles her brows suggestively, disappearing with the others.

Trent looks at me, his irritation softening some. "Care if I walk through, Dem?"

"Go, just do us all a favor, and maybe close the door to her room?" My nose scrunches.

I swear a hint of embarrassment colors his cheeks, but when his eyes shift back to Nico, it's gone. He clears his throat, crosses through my room and into the next.

I glance at Nico, who now has both arms propped against the door frame staring after his friend with a blank expression.

Slowly, his eyes come back to me.

"Um." I rub my hands against my thighs as my attention falls to his bare chest, and then to the towel barely hanging on to his waist. "You can go back to your shower now."

"I was done."

"Right." I trail a water droplet as it makes its way down his abs, disappearing into the thin, dark trail that leads to his most practiced tool. "Well, you can go dry off now or you know . . . something." I swallow.

When he makes no move to leave, I look up.

His eyes narrow the slightest bit, and he stays put for a few more seconds before finally backing away. Of course, he leaves his door wide open as he moves farther into the room, so I close my side. My hand lingers on the knob a moment before I let it go and get back to what I was doing.

I move into my bathroom to pull off my underwear, smoothing out the edges of the dress so no lines can be detected.

The second I step out, Carley and Macy are walking back in, both dressed and ready to go.

"Is the coast clear?" Macy laughs, dodging the hair tie I flick at her.

"All clear, biatch."

"I think your comment made Trent feel bad cause they went to his room instead," Carley says. "For a quickie, I'm sure."

"Where's his room?"

Carley smirks. "Her dad assigned him to one on the other side of the hotel."

"As if that would stop them." I laugh. "So, do we wait?"

"We should time it," Macy suggests with a grin.

"Or we could go make sure our seats are saved and meet them there?" Carley laughs.

"Like Krista didn't tell them where to put us at the table." Macy rolls her eyes but gives a big fake grin. "Lead the way, oh buzz kill one."

Carley shoves her and together, the three of us head into the hall.

We get a foot past Nico's door when it's whipped open.

I yelp as Nico catches my arm and tugs me inside, the door closing behind us.

He spins me, pushing my back against the wall in one swift move, his large body trapping me there.

"What—"

I cut myself off when he begins to lower his thick lips to mine. At first, my eyes widen in surprise, only to close just as quickly.

A second passes, and then another, and still the pressure of his mouth doesn't land on me.

His breath, warm and cascading across my skin, has me sucking in a lungful of air. My move has our bottom lips brushing each other's but only the slightest bit.

Not a second later, the heat of his body vanishes, causing my eyes to peel open.

While I probably look like a wanton Barbie, plastered to the wall with shock and an unexpected thrill coursing through me, Nico appears completely unaffected, his breathing steady as he steps away from me.

"What was . . . why'd you . . ."

Why'd he what? Try to kiss me?

Why'd he *not* kiss me?

What the hell was I about to ask?

"You're my girlfriend, D," he says with unmistakable aggravation. "I had to know what to expect when I kiss you in public." His eyes slide back to mine as he callously adds, "Needs work."

Dick.

"We didn't agree to kissing."

Did I even agree to anything?

He shrugs. "It goes hand in hand with the title. Couples kiss, should have been obvious."

Right.

Right. Couples also—

No. Not going there.

I eye him as he reaches for the door handle. "You really want to do this, like for reals?"

"We're already doing it."

"But we can still pass it off as a one-night stand at this point."

"I need you for more than a night, D, and I want you all in."

His voice is so strong, so sure, that I almost misinterpret the meaning.

It makes sense, though. Why pretend to date me if he didn't?

He has something to gain here, too.

I'm not entirely convinced this will do anything for me other than piss off Nico's ex and anyone else who might be hoping for a chance with him. Alex already knows me, so it's not like I'm starting at square one.

Maybe I should ask Alex out now and back away from all this?

I let the superficial part of me inspect Nico.

Dark eyes framed by darker lashes. High cheekbones and pouty lips, lips he chooses that exact moment to run his slick tongue across.

A deep, dark smirk hits next.

I mean, what's the rush in backing out?

There's always Monday.

Chapter 12
Nico

"What up?" Trent drops beside me.

"'Sup." I cut him a quick glance, looking back to the girls. They've just finished their appetizers and are now killing time before the meals are here by taking pictures at the end of the pier.

Krista flings her hands all around, and the large group of girls break away, leaving her and her core group standing there. They huddle up for some shots of the four of them.

They take their time, going from big smiles to goofy ass faces and even unflattering poses. That's what I like about their little crew. They don't feel the need to be picture perfect or shoot for sexy all the time, they have a good ass time the way they want to.

Krista whips around right then, shouting across the pier. "Come on, baby," she calls for Trent. "Nic, you too!"

Trent gets up with a grin, downing whatever he was drinking and makes his way to her, but I stay planted in my seat.

Trent growls, lifting Krista off the ground and spinning her around before pausing so the girls can take their picture.

Seconds later, Alex walks by me with our boy Thompson, another player on the team, both headed in their direction.

Krista spots them coming, and smiles. "Yes! Boys come over here, get in on this!"

My eyes fly to Demi, who *of fucking course* has hers on Alex, but the same second, I think it, they shift.

She stares at me with indecision, as if there's something at the tip of her tongue or the edge of her thought.

What to do, Little D?

Alex tries to squeeze beside Demi but Carley shoves him over with a frown, looking this way.

Knew I liked that girl.

"Nico Sykes." She pops a hip out. "Get your never smiling ass over here and take a picture."

I move my gaze back to Demi and she frowns slightly.

Come on, girl, you know what to do. All in, remember?

With a playful roll of those green eyes, meant to hide her nerves, I'm sure, she calls me. "Come on, Nico, don't keep me waiting!"

And there it is, her accepting.

I push to my feet, eyes focused on her as I make my way over. I know the others are watching, not everyone was able to confirm the rumor throughout the day. I'm known to hook up, but I've never attached myself to anyone outside of Josie, so people want to witness us together for themselves, and more than simply disappearing behind a closed door.

They will.

Instead of stepping beside Demi and into the space left open for me, I slip behind her, loosely folding my arms around her shoulders.

Her hands automatically come up to grip my forearms, so I tip my chin a little to whisper, "Now you get it."

She shakes her head, but I'd bet money she's fighting a smile.

Krista snags someone, starts explaining how she wants the picture to be taken, so Demi capitalizes on the free second by tilting her head sideways, peeking at me.

She whispers, "There will be more people around tonight, and everyone here has already been staring."

"And?"

"Last chance to back out." Her eyes narrow, challenging me as if she's assuming I might want to do just that.

Wrong, Pixie.

"There is no 'backing out', Demi. It's done."

Her grip tightens with her stare.

"I told you." I lower my head the slightest bit, so she has to tip hers back even more. "You're mine now."

With a small pinch to her forehead, her tongue comes out to play with her lips and my eyes are forced to follow.

"For now," she gives a sassy whisper.

My smirk is slow, and I look up.

When I do, I find Krista has the camera pointed right at us.

She gives a small wink, then passes it off to one of the security guards.

"All right, everyone, eyes forward!" She jumps in Trent's arms; the guy counts to three and the picture is done.

"The food is coming out now, Ms. Krista!" the staff member shouts from the tables.

"Thank you, Mary! We're coming!" Krista calls back and all the groups make their way over, but I hold Demi back by her waist.

"What are you doing?" she asks.

"Waiting."

She shifts, so I loosen my grip, and she spins in my arms to face me. She surveys me a moment before a small laugh leaves her. "Waiting so you can stand here and stare at me?"

"No. Waiting so everyone sits and notices it's just us left standing."

"Why?"

"Why you ask so many questions?"

Her little nose scrunches. "Don't be a dick."

"Don't ask things you already know the answer to." I shrug. "Why would *couples* stand off to the side or walk away from groups and shit like that?"

She purses her lips, giving a sassy, "Privacy."

"Exactly." I shift her more, so they can't see my face. "Right now, at least half of them are staring right at us, each one thinking something along the lines of how bad you must

98

need me, or how hard I must be for you, if we have to take a few extra minutes to ourselves before we can even consider sitting through a dinner with the rest of them."

She attempts to glance over her shoulder, so I shoot my hand up, catching her chin before she can, my fingers spreading along her jaw and neck in the same move.

Damn, she doesn't even flinch.

I continue. "The girls are wondering what filthy things I'm promising to do to you later when you come to my room, you *are* coming to my room by the way." Her eyes narrow, but it's playful as hell. "The guys are wondering if you're biting into your bottom lip, if your eyes are growing darker, and wishing they knew what that looked like, knowing they'll never get the chance now that you're mine."

"Wow," she teases, purposefully breathy. "You really think you've got this whole *prepped and ready* thing down."

A laugh escapes me before I can squash it, and I tug her a little closer.

She stares a long moment. "So, I'm challenged with convincing everyone your mood swings turn me on?"

"And *I* get to be the possessive boyfriend who doesn't want you outta arm's reach."

"Get to?" She smashes her lips to the side, tryin' real hard not to let her grin slip.

"Get. To. D."

"What makes you think possessive is what I'd like?"

A light chuckle leaves me, and I lick my lips, leaning into her as I slowly slide my arms down. When she doesn't budge, my palms slip a little lower, now resting just below her waist, my pinkies propped on her ass cheeks.

She inhales, waiting.

"Demi," I whisper. "I'll tell you right now, the last thing you want is a pussy ass dude who won't push you. You're too smart, too independent for a doormat of a guy, and too strong to ever be one yourself. You'll take charge . . . but you'll like it more when I do."

Her ass tightens against my hand and instantly my brows snap together.

Hold on . . .

I skim my hand across her waist, gripping her hips and squeezing until she lets out a small yelp. She falls against me, and my mouth plants right at her ear.

"Rule number one, Little D." Her breath fans across my chest. "Don't ever go panty-less again . . . unless there's a *real good* reason for it." I pull back, locking my eyes to hers. "A reason that includes me."

She studies me a minute before her head tips down and a light laugh leaves her. "This is going to be interesting, isn't it?" She looks up again, humor written across her face – hidden heat behind her eyes.

"Fun." I shrug. Letting my arms fall. "It'll be fun."

"Will you always be so . . . extra?"

"Yes. And you'll still want more."

"Uh-huh." She laughs. "We'll see, now let's go eat before it gets cold." She gets a few feet away, and then adds in a mischievous undertone, "And before the wind starts. Wouldn't want my *boyfriend* to get mad when it gives away my lack of underwear."

I dart for her, but she evades, smiling wider.

She skips back to the table, proud of her little teasing, and drops in the middle of Carley and Macy.

I take my seat at the end by Trent, lifting my chin when she looks my way.

She brings her straw to her lips, grinning like a brat.

With a shake of my head, I reach for a fresh beer bottle from the iced beer tub in the center of the table and pop one open.

"Damn, Nic," Trent says under his breath.

I glance his way, my eyes narrowing when he cuts a quick glance toward the girls, only to bring them right back.

"What?"

A scoffing laugh escapes from him and he shakes his head. "Nothing, man."

I drop my arms from the table so my plate can be lowered in front of me, thanking the server as she moves along.

I get it, he's unsure about what I'm doing, but so the fuck am I.

Still doing it.

I grip his shoulder, giving him a little shake. "Let me worry about what needs worrying, Trent."

He lifts his hands as if to say *do your thing*.

I plan to.

Chapter 13
Nico

The boardwalk is pretty fucking crowded, as expected on a three-day weekend, but for the most part, everyone who came for Krista's birthday is sticking together.

Right now, we're all in line for the trolley ride that takes you from one side of the coastline and drops you on the opposite end. Demi ran ahead with the girls and is almost in the front, while I'm stuck several spaces back with a few guys from the team.

Of course, I'm not the only one with eyes on her.

Alex snakes his way through our crowd, slithering right in line beside her.

She's talking with her friend Ava when he inserts himself in their conversation.

Her head snaps his way, and instantly she throws her head back, laughing at whatever lame ass joke he's spit.

"Now *they* look right together."

I don't bother to turn when Josie's voice finds me. "Who invited you?"

"Does it matter?"

I scoff, moving forward as the next group of people are let on.

"So, is it true then?" she asks. "Did the princess see the toad?"

"Get the fuck out of here, Josie."

"Oh, so much tension. It must not be what it seems," she guesses.

I turn my glare on her. "What the fuck do you want? Why you standing here right now? We're not together anymore. You couldn't keep your legs closed, remember?"

Josie's gaze falls a minute but comes up stronger. "Don't judge me. You didn't even care."

My head pulls back. "What the fuck did you expect, me to grovel? Fucking please, Josie. You know better than that." I lower my voice. "You didn't come at me when you found out I slept with Sandra, but now that you heard about me and D, here you are. Worried you'll never get another chance to slide down my dick like you've been able to in the past? Tell me, Josie, if you didn't give a damn about the girls I've fucked since you, why you trippin' on little Demi Davenport?"

That pisses her off. "She's not just *some girl*, is she Nic?" she forces past clenched teeth.

"You're right, she's *my* girl, something you'll never be again."

That has her dark eyes hardening. "Look whose side she's by right now."

Despite myself, I do, finding her and Alex now next in line to ride.

Irritation tightens my muscles, something not missed by Josie, and a dark chuckle leaves her.

Demi chooses this moment to cut her smile this way, spotting me standing a few rows back. Her brows knit the slightest bit, the tip of her lips straightening.

Josie leans closer to my ear, and Demi's eyes cut her way. "Seems none of us can resist a perfect white boy—"

My glare slices to Josie and she stops short, swallowing hard on her words.

"Forget about her, Nic," Josie backpedals, a desperate flare taking over as she takes a step in. "She'll never want you like you—"

"Hey." Demi's peppy voice surprises us both, even more so when she slips in front of me, leaving Josie at her back as if she didn't see her standing here at all.

She did.

Her big green eyes stare into mine, unsure of what she can or can't do right now, but even though she doubts her place, her voice is strong. "It's our turn."

"Excuse you," Josie spits, stepping to the side slightly.

Demi's hand plants against my chest as she turns toward Josie. She smiles sweetly at her. "Hey, Josie."

Josie glares, opens her mouth to speak, but Demi grips my hand and tugs.

"Come on," she says, throwing one long ass leg after the other over the chain that closes off the line and I'm right behind her.

I don't look back at my ex once.

The ride attendant pretends she's annoyed for us holding up the cart an extra few seconds, but a small smile tips her lips as we pass.

Demi slides inside, not letting go of my hand, so I drop right beside her.

I glance over, eyeing Alex who stands at the head of the line, only for a split second before the cart jolts forward, and he's out of sight.

The second we're moving, Demi lets go, scooting over several inches.

We're both quiet the first few minutes, but it's me who breaks the silence.

"What happened, lover boy didn't want to ride?"

My flat tone has her head snapping toward mine.

"He did."

"And?"

She eyes me mockingly. "And then I remembered everyone thinks I'm dating someone, so I did what I would if I really was."

"Ditch the asshole trying to get at what he knows to be mine?" I throw out.

"Make sure the ex knows where she stands," she counters, holding my gaze. "Behind me."

Damn if heat doesn't spread through my groin.

It's been a minute since anyone's felt greedy for me. Fake reasoning or not.

"Rule number two." She scowls.

I sit back, nodding my chin.

104

Let's hear it.

"Don't make a fool of me by sleeping with your ex while people think we're dating or whatever."

"Just my ex?"

She frowns but doesn't ask for more. She should.

"Demi, I won't be fucking anyone."

"That's not my business, but if you do, at least avoid people we know or go to school with. I'll do the same."

A scoffing laugh leaves me, and I shift on the seat. "You'll do the same?" I crack. "Meaning you'll fuck if you feel the need, but not someone we know and not your boyfriend?"

"Fake boyfriend."

"Same fucking thing."

"Not at all."

"You're a virgin."

She gapes, slowly shaking her head. "I'm not a virgin, Nico."

My muscles curl, my eyes locked on hers. "Don't play with me."

"I'm not." She gauges me. "I thought you knew this and were just teasing me when you said it before."

"Who?"

Her eyes widen, panic flashing across her face. "No way."

"Who, Demi? When?"

"Look." She turns toward me.

I don't let her speak. "A boyfriend would know these things."

"Not necessarily," she argues. "Girls lie about this stuff all the time."

"Are you for real right now?"

"I'm not telling you," she snaps. "So, you can stop with all your angry eyes and this deep chest voice thing you've got going."

I throw myself back in the seat, looking away from her, glaring out the window.

"You should have ridden with Alex. Might have been able to cut this thing quicker."

"I'm sorry, am I cramping your style so soon?" she cracks. "Don't forget you're the one that said we needed more time. If you wanted to get it on with your ex, who you must have invited because Krista and Josie don't even like each other, then you should have said something."

My eyes slice to her. "If you think I'm gonna back out of this so easy, and for pussy I've had plenty of, you've got a rude awakening coming. I said I was all in. I am."

"So, this is some sort of 'Nico Tantrum Time'?" Her brows lift jeeringly. "Can I expect this type of shit every time things don't go your way?"

My eyes narrow but she doesn't back down right away.

She stares, attempting to read me, but after a moment she looks off, randomly saying, "She was jealous."

"Let her be."

Demi hesitates before asking, "Do you *want* her to be?"

"Why do you care?"

"Well, *asshole*, if you do, you might as well use me."

I glare. "Use you how?"

"I bet she's planning to come back to the hotel for dancing tonight. Obviously, I'm all over that. So, if you want to go . . ."

"If I *want* to go?"

"Yeah." She shrugs.

"If you're going, I'm going," I tell her matter-of-factly. "Possessive, keep you in arm's length, boyfriend, remember?" I lean in. "And so there's no confusion in that pretty head of yours, I don't give a shit what Josie wants, does, thinks, or sees. Fuck her. I will *never* touch her again, but I'm not interested in purposely trying to piss her off either. She gets mad seeing us together? Oh fuckin' well." I confirm, "This isn't about making *anyone* jealous."

She considers my words a moment. "It's not?"

I shake my head.

"What is it then?" Her tone is doubtful. "What are you hoping to gain?"

So fucking much I could say right now, none of which I

106

should. Instead, I go with a solid amount of truth. "I want everyone to believe it."

"Believe what?"

"That you want me."

She shifts in her seat, looking at her hands. "I guess that would be the first step in faking being together." She glances my way, but only with her eyes. "Making people believe we're into each other."

"It won't be hard."

That has her lips smashing to the side to hide her grin. "Is that right?"

I nod. "*Everyone* will see how attracted you are to me."

Her eyes narrow, but just as quick a loud laugh leaves her, and I hold in my smirk.

"Did we just make up?" she teases.

"That what you call a fight?"

She chuckles, looking away. "You know, I'm not afraid to admit I think you're more than okay looking," she clowns. "So, I guess all we really have to work on is getting them to believe *you* are into *me*."

"They already do."

Her mouth drops open slightly, and she smiles. "Nico Sykes, so sure of himself and his unspeakable plan, even though, to everyone around, you and I *together* will have come completely out of left field."

I ignore her statement. "I'm gonna need you to use football references from now on."

"Should we use code when we want the other one to do something, go all Peyton Manning and shout 'Omaha' when we need to cut and run?"

"Cut and run?"

She nods with a grin. "It'll happen, you watch, and are you not impressed I know who Peyton Manning is?"

"Everyone knows who Peyton Manning is."

"Thanks to his horrendous acting in those insurance commercials, right?"

I laugh and she gapes at me, blinking hard.

"Multiple laughs in a day from the silent killer?" she mocks.

I shake my head, and lean closer to glance out the window, then wrap my arm around her outer thigh and pull her to me.

Wide eyes slice to mine.

"We're coming up to the curve," I tell her. "All the carts ahead of us will be able to look back as we round it, and then everyone will be waiting there as we climb off, too." My gaze holds hers. "My girl wouldn't be sitting so far away from me."

"Oh, no?" She cocks a brow, playfully. "And would she . . . simply sit right here beside you?"

My head tugs back.

She chuckles. "Did I surprise you?" She smiles, and I lick my lips. "I'm not shy, in case you thought different, I'm also not the *in your face* type, so of course you wouldn't have noticed."

It's not a dig at me, she's only speaking what she knows.

What she thinks she knows.

"If you're not shy, why haven't you asked Hammons out already?"

That has her pausing. It takes a second but then her eyes come back to mine.

"I don't know, maybe because while we're friends he's never shown interest past that. I'm sure he'd be down to hook-up or something, but I've never gotten the feeling he would want to date past that and I don't know, I don't want to waste the chance if there is one by going the fling route."

"So, you don't want to be rejected?"

"Would you?" Her tone is sharp.

"I've been rejected."

She scoffs, her eyes flicking upward.

"I have."

"By who?"

"You."

Her head snaps my way, a small frown pulling at her forehead. "What?"

"Yup."

108

"You lie." She crosses her arms, but her tone is unsure.

"Nope."

"When?"

"I invited you to wake me up with my dick in your mouth and guess what?" I lean in and her brows jump. "I woke up in an empty bed."

It takes her a second, but she busts up laughing, hitting my chest with her little hand and I can't help but grin.

We're at the bend now, so before she can pull back, I grip her wrist to hold it there.

Out her window, I spot our friends in the carts ahead, all of them looking around at the others, so I scoot closer and her laughter slowly dies.

"People are watching now."

Demi

Something about the way he whispers has me swallowing.

"Demi!" Krista's shout hits my ears.

I jolt, tugging free from Nico's grasp and spin around to wave.

She throws her hands up, letting out a loud scream that follows each cart after hers.

Nico scoots up behind me and I lean over slightly so he can fit his head next to mine.

Trent throws his arms out to his buddy and Nico's low chuckle wafts across my neck and I convince myself the sensation it creates is a natural response to the warmth against my skin.

"Is that Carley and Thompson?" he asks.

I look in time to see them finish their kiss. Both of them start laughing when they realize they got caught.

"Sluuuut!" Krista yells with a laugh, and then her and Trent's cart disappears from sight, each other's right after it.

With a laugh I turn back, my breath catching as I do.

Nico is *right there,* right against me, his hand sliding into my hair, mouth moving in only to skim across my cheek.

My arm shoots up, gripping his wrist as a heavy knot forms in the pit of my stomach.

"Almost, D," he murmurs, the vibration of his word raising the hair on my neck. "Keep still."

My features pull, my grip tightening with his.

What the hell is wrong with me?

The whistling sounds have him pulling back, a smirk on his face as he releases me and turns for the door that the ride attendant is about to open.

He climbs out and I sit there frozen, only moving when he pops his head back in, his hand extended for me to grab.

I do, and he pulls me from the cart, yanking my body to his the second my feet touch the ground.

He drops a chaste kiss to my cheek, slides a hand around my waist and ushers us forward, our friends waiting just a few steps away.

While my girls give me wiggly eyebrows for a whole two seconds, nobody else dwells or makes a big deal.

It's as if seeing the two of us like this is normal, accepted, and we're just another couple having fun on the boardwalk, laughing and smiling and ready for the next ride.

I don't hate it.

As a group, we get in line for the rollercoaster, everyone chatting amongst themselves as we wait. After a few minutes, I take a second to look at Nico.

His backward hat is covering the messy top of his hair, showing nothing but his perfect fade.

He jokes with Trent and Thompson about something, laughing as he pushes off their shoulders. His fist comes up to his mouth when he smiles as if he doesn't quite want to share it with the others, but from my angle, his white teeth shine.

I've never really known him to laugh much, though, I assume it's something he does often with his friends.

I hope he does; he looks good doing it.

Thompson swats Nico's arm, and Nico's stare slices over — the entire group catching me staring.

His laughter slows, but the corner of his mouth stays raised.

He winks, and I pull my lips in, biting down to keep from grinning back.

Such a crowd pleaser.

"Bet he winks like that *right* before he goes down."

My eyes widen and I'm positive I look like a deer caught in headlights.

Nico's questioning frown is instant, and his eyes fly to Macy.

I whip around, hissing, "Shut up!"

She smirks, turning her attention back to him. "Mm. Yeah, and that little stubble he's got going right now, the light scratch it would put off against your inner thigh." She nods to herself. "Oh my god, you'd be aching before his mouth even landed."

"Macy, for fuck's sake," I force past clenched teeth. "*Sh*!"

"How often do you shave, Nico?" she shouts, leaning an elbow on me.

This bitch.

I drop my face in my hands, peeking at him through my fingers when he's quiet longer than five seconds.

"Usually every other morning." He reluctantly moves his eyes to her. "Why?"

"So, she needs to catch you late night." Macy nods, crossing her arms over her chest.

Nico's gaze slides back to mine.

"Ignore her."

"Oh, no." He saunters over, licking his lips, looking all sorts of cocky. "I gotta hear it now."

His friends are right behind him, everyone in line turning to see what we're all doing, huddling up like this.

Well, this is awesome. Nothing to do but indulge her ass.

I spin around, facing her. "Macy?"

She shrugs, grabbing a piece of Trent's popcorn and tossing it in her mouth. "Just wondering if you use the stubble as a tool. You know, slide it across the inner thigh, maybe the stomach first on your way." Her eyes fall to his jaw and I gape at her. "We dig that shit."

"True dat." Krista comes out of nowhere, raising her hand in agreement.

Everyone starts laughing and I shake my head, right there with them.

The line moves forward, so the group shifts, going back to their spots and restarting their previous conversations.

Nico slips in behind me, his chest at my back. "How 'bout you, Pixie, that something *you* like?"

A light laugh bubbles from me, but I keep facing forward.

112

He interprets it correctly, my way of saying *nice try, boy*, and I'm about to tell him not to worry his pretty little head over it, like he did me, when he reminds me of the roles we are playing.

"I know you disagreed already, but as your man." He pauses. "I should know these things, yeah? 'Case your girls ever try to pop quiz me." His arms make their way around me and he squeezes. "Need to ace that test, D."

He has a point, sort of, even though he might simply be teasing, but nothing says I can't tease back.

"You know," I lead with a grin he can't see. "A *real* boyfriend has to work hard and *learn* these things about his girl."

The second it leaves me, I regret it, internally cursing myself. *Why* did I say it?

I know he's about to joke, throw out an offer, something, so I give him what he wants before he can. "Yeah, I do."

"So, you've been eaten out before?"

Heat spreads in my abdomen at his instant question.

"I have," I admit, quietly.

Only a couple times, and for a few short minutes. It was sloppy, but the warmth of a mouth on me was enough to get me going. Unfortunately, not enough to *keep* me going either time.

He doesn't need to know that part.

Macy was right, though. Us girls have talked about this before, and while the person who went down on me was smooth faced, it doesn't take a lot to imagine what it would be like with someone who has occasional stubble.

A prickly face is like a rough palm, I'd think, tantalizing all on its own. Raising your pulse with nothing but a slow slide across your body, forcing the arch of your back, even when you're still standing.

Yeah, I can get down with a rough textured hand.

Suddenly Nico's fingertips are grazing across my shoulder blades, his palms joining as they slide down the length of my arms in a feathering manner, the barest of touches against my skin that I feel down to my toes.

113

"Like this?" he rasps.

My body shivers in response, and his heated chuckle only makes it worse.

"Good to know." His arms fall.

It takes me a second, but I glance at him over my shoulder. He's as straight faced as ever, but those eyes . . .

The hint of arrogance is expected, but I wasn't prepared for the rest.

Eager.

Greedy.

Wanting?

Confusion draws my brows in, something else entirely burning low in my core.

He doesn't look away until Trent bumps into him from behind.

With a rapid blink and a hint of a frown, he turns away.

I face forward right then and not a minute later the ride attendant opens the chain, ushering me and Nico through.

He steps ahead of me, choosing the front of the rollercoaster.

He pauses before climbing in, shifting around to look at me.

He nods his head, indicating for me to step past him into the small steel cart. "You first, *girlfriend*."

Tell me why my stomach clenches.

Chapter 14
Nico

Demi, Krista, and the other two run into the haunted maze with a bunch of other girls while us guys stay out front, both Trent and myself walking toward the exit the moment they disappear.

Twisting the lid off my water bottle, I take a drink and offer one to Trent, but when I glance over, finding him eyeing me curiously, it's obvious he's got something to say.

"What?"

He hesitates. "I know you don't want to hear this, but I don't think what you're doing is a good idea."

"Yeah, why's that?"

"Demi's not like the girls you've dated, Nic. She stays out of drama, cares about school, thinks about her future."

"You think I don't know all that?"

"How would you, you've steered clear of her for years. All of a sudden you're forced to be her partner in class, and you've changed your mind?"

I glare long enough for him to look away, not speaking until he forces himself to face me.

"You're acting like you don't know the ins and outs of why, man. You're my best friend, or you're supposed to be, but right now I'm gettin' the vibe you're against me here."

"I'm not," he says. "But I don't want to see this end up in ruins either."

"It's been a fuckin' day, bro. Less than twenty-four hours if you wanna be technical."

"That's my point." Trent frowns. "Less than a day, and all the girls believe it, you're touching her, and she's letting you?" his eyes widen. "And I don't know if you just played it right or what, but it looked like you kissed her."

"And if I did? What's the issue, Trent?"

He shakes his head. "I'm just saying it's kinda soon for you two to be acting this comfortable with each other."

"Maybe we are."

His head pulls back. "Are what?"

"Comfortable with each other." I toss my water bottle in the garbage. "Like you said." The girls' light screams have me stepping closer to the exit, knowing they're coming out soon, but I keep my body facing his. "She's chill. I'm chill." I give a small shrug. "Faking it ain't all that hard, my man."

The girls rush out in the next second, each one in small fits of laughter, and our attention shifts to them.

Macy smiles but then lets out a small growl as she shoves Demi into me. "Spank her, Nico, she deserves it."

Demi's hand plants on my chest and she looks up, green eyes full of laughter. "Sorry. She's being a hater because I pushed her through the clown part ahead of us."

A low chuckle leaves me, but all I can focus on is the *spank her* part.

Demi clears her throat, smiles and turns to her friends.

"I'm hungry," she announces. "Can we go get some food now?"

"We just ate a few hours ago!" Macy points out.

"Shellfish," Demi argues, looking at her like she's crazy. "I'm a normal human. I need hardcore carbs to fill me up."

"But the swing line is low!" Krista pouts and tries to reason. "There'll be snacks out for us when we get back."

Demi's shoulders fall, her head snapping my way when my arm lands across her.

"I'll take her to get some food while you ride the swings, and we'll meet you on the next ride."

Krista crosses her arms, narrowing her eyes on me. "And no delaying for a quickie in the boardwalk showers?"

Demi laughs goodheartedly, reaching out to pat Krista's arm. "No, honey. That's only you and your man who can enjoy the filthy, sandy, shower floors."

My head slices to Trent who rubs the back of his neck, giving a small shrug.

I laugh, looking to Krista. "Where you goin' next?"

"Snacks, drinks, and a DJ will be set up in the conference room at the hotel at nine, so let's do the skylight ride last, then we can head back and party?"

"Sounds good." Demi nods, looking to me for confirmation.

I agree, and the two of us break away from the rest of the group.

We get a few feet away when she nudges me in my ribs with her elbow.

"You can take your arm off me now," she teases.

"Nah." I tug her closer. "Others could be watching."

She chuckles. "Ah. Right."

I steer her toward the food court, but she turns me the opposite way, headed straight for Dessert Row.

"I thought you were hungry?"

"I am. For some deep-fried Oreos."

I laugh and she looks up at me, smirking.

"What?"

"Before this weekend I didn't even know *Nico Sykes* knew how to laugh." Her feet stop moving so I'm forced to stop with her. "Now here you are, smiling, laughing." She tilts her head to the side, a coy grin on her lips. "And to top it off, you've only had one or two temper tantrums today."

I glare. "I don't have temper fucking tantrums."

"Mood swings, tantrums, random moments of dickishness. Call it what you like," she mocks. "But careful, *fake boyfriend*, or I might start to think you're having a halfway decent time."

"You clownin' on me?"

She chuckles as she pulls away, so I let my arm fall, shifting to face her as we step into the line.

"Maybe I am, D."

She squints. "Am what?"

"Not miserable."

She eyes me a second before a small laugh leaves her and she steps up to the order window. As quick as she pays, Demi's being handed a paper bowl full of deep-fried Oreos covered in powdered sugar.

"I'll eat as we walk so Krista doesn't strangle me for being gone so long." She lifts one of her pieces up, biting into it with a soft moan. "So good."

We look at each other, and she chuckles.

I'm sure she can see the need in my eyes, while hers only hold a playfulness I enjoy as she covers that sexy mouth of hers that's still full.

I'd like to fill it up with something else . . .

"Sorry." She fights a smile, wiping her mouth, before going in for another bite.

"Moan like that again and—"

The ringing of my phone cuts me off, and I drag it from my pocket to find my dad's name flashing.

My feet stop moving, tension wrapping around my shoulders as I glare at the screen.

He never calls.

"You can answer that if you need to," Demi says and I look to her. "I can walk ahead."

No.

I hit ignore, shoving it in my pocket and fall in place beside her, the two of us heading where we know the others will be.

My dad calls three more times between the walk there and the end of the ride.

We're back with the group and entering the hotel lobby when it rings again.

"Damn, who's blowing you up?" Trent whispers. "Is it Josie?"

I scoff and glance around to make sure nobody is in earshot. "It's my dad."

"Whoa." His eyes widen. "Why you think he's calling?"

I frown. "I don't know. Could be about my mom, I'm about to try and call her right now. If not that, then it's about the fight with the fuckhead in the locker room."

"He's been watching you guys all day, you know," he says, referring to Alex.

"Good. Let him think he can take her; it'll be that much sweeter when she decides she don't want him."

"And if he goes in now while she still does, or if she keeps on wanting him, then what?"

I shove my phone back in my pocket, my eyes sliding across the room where Demi is. "Then I find a reason to force her to stay."

"Blackmail?"

I look to my friend. "If I have to."

Trent shakes his head with a sigh. "You need to be careful, Nic. For real."

"I told you to let me worry about this."

"I'm tryin', my man," he says, eyeing me a moment before changing the subject. "You goin' to your room first or straight over to the party area?"

I look to Demi who laughs, letting go of Carley's legs so she can slide off, ending the piggyback ride she was giving her.

"D," I call.

She says something to the girls and heads our way, her long hair laying half over her shoulder. She bumps into Trent, smiling at him briefly when he chuckles.

I frown, pulling her attention back to me. "You goin' to your room first?"

"Hell yeah. I can't dance in this thing." She pats her hips.

"Restrictive attire on the front liner?" Trent teases her.

"I know, right?" She smiles. "Blame Macy. She made me wear it."

"She make you leave the underwear behind too?" I bite out.

Trent's eyes go wide, as do hers, and while he clears his throat and walks away, Demi prickles.

She waits until he's far enough away before she steps toward me. "What the hell was that?"

"Nothing." I tip my head back. "Shouldn't have let him in on that."

My phone starts ringing again, and her eyes fall to my pocket a moment before coming back.

"So why did you then?"

"Don't ask stupid questions."

Her head tugs back and she opens her mouth to speak but pauses, bringing herself even closer instead. "I've never been able to figure you out," she whispers.

I push against her chest. "You sayin' you've tried, Little D?"

She tilts her chin, observing me with a feisty fire. "I might have answered that if nice Nico was standing in front of me. It's one thing — still shitty — to be an ass when it's just the two of us, but in front of others?" She clicks her tongue. "Better work on your attitude if keeping this charade up is important to you."

My eyes slim. "That the key, playin' nice?"

She shakes her head, placing her lips a breath away from mine.

"Don't play," she whispers. "*Be*. You've got it in you."

"Yeah." I place my hands on her hips lazily. "And how would you know, Pixie?"

She slides free of my grip.

"Your mask slipped today," she tells me. "You're not what you pretend to be."

"And what do I pretend to be?"

"Cold and cavalier." She eyes me as she steps back. "That's not you, it's your go-to defense."

"Defense from what?"

A small smile plays at her thick lips and her features pull in thought. "I'm not sure yet, but it seems I'll have time to find out, yeah?"

A heaviness settles over me as I look at her, and I'm not sure what to make of it.

"Wanna know something I decided today?"

I lift my chin.

Tell me.

"I've decided . . . you're not a *total* asshole."

An unexpected chuckle leaves me, and as a result, a pleased smile spreads across her face.

Demi laughs, spins on her heels and catches up with her friends. The three of them take off down the hall, but not before she jerks to a stop, so she can shout over her shoulder. "Find me on the dance floor, Neek!"

Neek, huh.

My muscles lock when the thought is echoed by the last fucking voice I want to hear.

"*Neek*, huh."

I glare after her, taking my time to whirl around and face the little bitch behind me.

I step into his space and he doesn't back away.

"I see you decided to get her ready for me after all." His lip curls.

"Touch her while she's mine and I'll break your fucking fingers. Then you really won't be catching shit, but hey, at least you'll have a solid excuse to run home with."

Alex shoves me, and I let him, stumbling back a few steps.

I smirk, tip my chin and point at his bitch ass. "Catch you later, Hammons. I'll save a seat for you at breakfast, huh?"

"We'll see about that." His eyes harden.

My phone rings again, and a sinister smirk covers his face.

"Better get that, Sykes. Might be trouble at home."

My jaw clenches, and I reach out, gripping him by the collar and tugging him in. "Watch yourself, Alex. If you haven't noticed, I'm done with your bullshit. *Done.* You're not untouchable, even though you think you are, so go ahead, play your fucking game, I'll be here playing it better." I shove off him, and he stumbles, hitting his back against the wall. "Tell your pops I said hi, motherfucker."

I take a few backward steps before turning and heading for my room.

121

Fuck him.

I've just got the door closed and am tugging off my shirt when my phone rings again, but I ignore it and dial my mom instead.

As I figured, she sleeps through the call.

I toss it on the dresser where it'll stay the rest of the night and run my hands down my face.

This is what he wants, me to stress the entire fucking weekend, to ruin any chill time I might have. All I wanted was a damn day to forget, but I guess that was too much to ask.

Demi said I come off cold and careless.

I'm not.

I don't speak because my thoughts are constantly racing, my fucked-up reality sitting at the forefront of my mind at all times.

I work my ass off at sports to try and get picked up by a college team, even though I likely can't accept any offer that may come in.

If I go, who stays here to watch after my mom?

I can't leave her alone, my dad is already slowly killing her, and she refuses to see it, refuses to let him go even though he has a new home and wife and preferred son, a better version of me, as he loves to say.

I drop back on my mattress, staring up at the cracked ceiling.

Demi and her friend's loud laughter floats beneath the adjoining door of our rooms and despite my shitty fucking mood, the corner of my lip tips up.

I don't know what the fuck I'm doing, but that doesn't mean I'm going to stop.

I close my eyes, take a deep breath and let it out.

Fuck it.

I'm taking a few more hours, shoving everything to the back of my mind, and dealing with the damage of it all later.

Chapter 15
Demi

Krista fans her face, nodding toward the tables, so we all step off the dance floor for a quick break so they can catch their breath.

She steers us where the guys are huddled near the open bar.

Krista drops onto Trent's lap, the others grabbing an open seat around him while I hop up, sitting on the edge of the table.

"Damn, Dem. You've got Krista breathing all hard," Trent jokes.

"You try keeping up with her ass out there and look at Carley," Krista says. "She's sweating more than I am."

"I'm a sweater, asshole, and you know I can outrun you," Carley throws back.

"True, but still." Krista laughs, downing half a water bottle before sipping on Trent's drink.

"Dude, Nico is the fastest on the team, too." Macy gasps, glancing his way. "You guys could prolly go all night if you tried."

My mouth drops open, but then Nico is suddenly in front of me, pushing my knees open so he can slide between them. I stare, unmoving and a little buzzed, as his fingers come up to lift my chin.

"Stamina is key," he says, all deep and gravelly like. "Ain't it, baby?"

My muscles tighten unexpectedly, and I have to remind myself to nod.

It's delayed and beyond obvious.

The chuckles from around the table have my hand coming up to push his away, and a breathy laugh escapes me.

"Let's go back out there, but with the boys. My dad told them to pull the plug at one." Krista hops up.

The rest of the group stands, and they all rush off, but Nico continues to block me in, his attention on their retreating bodies before it moves back to me.

"*Not a sex kitten,* she said," he says with a heavy rasp. "Gotta tell you, if hip-hop is your jam, club shit is your spirit. Not sure how I missed that."

I blink innocently. "So much to learn."

"Trust me, D, I know plenty."

"What, you spy on me from that window of yours, Neek?"

His smirk is instant and my jaw drops, a laugh bubbling from me.

"Oh my god, you do, you perv." I hit his chest playfully.

"Not my fault you get half naked and have sex with the air in my line of sight."

I laugh loudly, dropping my head back. "Sex with the air. Nice."

His gaze falls to my neck, slowly and seductively lowering from there.

Suddenly, with his head still pointed downward, his eyes pop up to meet mine through thick, dark, lashes.

It's too much.

I clear my throat. "Do you dance?"

He gives a slow nod.

"Show me."

"Nah."

I frown. "Why not?"

A smug expression slides over his face. "'Cause my girl would dance for me, not ask me to dance with her."

I roll my eyes as I jump down, but his body is a barrier and unbudging, so all it does is smash my hips against his.

He cuts a quick glance to my lips.

"You couldn't handle it if I did," I tell him.

124

He brings his mouth close. "I could handle all of you, Pixie. Believe that."

I squish my lips to the side, pushing him away slightly to get some air between us, and this time he allows it.

"Good thing fake boyfriends don't have to prove things to their fake girlfriends," I whisper. "Now, are you ready to get schooled?"

"You think so, huh?"

"I know so, Neek. Like the field is your home, an open space is mine."

Nico licks his lips. "Okay, pro. Let's go."

He walks backward toward the dance floor, reaching for my hand.

I slide mine into his, and he tugs me to him, his hold quickly shifting to my waist. "Time for my girl to show me what she's made of."

"Make sure to keep up." I turn in his hold, my back now to his chest.

"Quit talking, D." He gives a small squeeze. "Move."

I chuckle, doing just that.

My hands stay in front of me and I swing my hips back and forth, slightly swaying in and out with each movement. When Nico keeps up, his grip firm, I add a little more of a bend, arching my back.

The song changes and the extremely played out but highly effective for this moment, "Low" by Flo Rida comes on. I know instantly it's Krista's doing, it's her go-to hype song.

A grin splits across my lips, and I wink at Nico over my shoulder.

I lock my feet in place on the ground and shake my ass lightly against him, and his hands slip farther around to my front before slowly sliding up my ribs, down my stomach, then his fingers slide into the loops of my shorts, but I break free. I step out half a foot and drop down only to pop back up and do it again, swaying my hips on the way up the second time.

When his chest suddenly slams into my back, I laugh, dropping my head back, but my laughter trails off as I'm caught in his eyes.

Low and dark and on me.

His hand begins trailing along my arm, until he reaches my fingertips where he links our fingers together and slowly wraps our intertwined hands behind his head.

I take his cue, and lock my palms across his neck, grinding against him as his hand makes its way back to my hips, eyes still holding mine hostage.

When he pumps his hips, causing me to jolt slightly forward, I laugh.

I spin in his arms, bringing us face to face, but we keep moving.

He licks his lips, his top teeth tucking his bottom one in for a second.

I smirk, running my hands up his shoulders and holding them at the base of his hair.

I glance around finding several eyes on us.

"People are watching."

"They see."

I look to him. "See what?"

"Chemistry."

I lean in and he stops moving.

I whisper, "Mr. Brando would be proud."

Nico starts busting up laughing, his hands sliding higher, and pulling my chest against him.

"You should kiss me now, D. They're waiting for it."

I push up to my tippy toes, bringing my mouth to his, and his fingers spread out against my back.

"Not a chance."

Nico grins, his arms falling from around me as he nods toward the mini bar ran by Krista's housekeeper.

We step off the dance floor, and grab a quick drink, then wait for the others to join us. Once they have something for themselves, the six of us walk out the side exit and into the cool night air.

Krista's dad had long stakes placed along the hotel, bright lights wrapped around them to allow us a lit up place to hang out at night, so we kick off our shoes and drop to the sand in the middle of them.

"To the final drink of the weekend." Krista smiles, lifting her cup in cheers.

Thompson comes out next with a handful of waters he passes around before joining us.

"Thanks, man." Nico takes two, handing me one.

"Did you see Josie showed up at the boardwalk today?" Krista asks Nico, her eyes cutting to mine quickly.

"Uninvited, I'm bettin'?" he asks her.

I'm pretty sure his response is for my benefit, considering I pretty much accused him of inviting her earlier.

"I sure as hell didn't ask her to come." Krista laughs.

"We all know why she came. Her sister is here and told her Nico and Demi hooked up." All eyes fly to Macy as she says this. "What, it's true. I'm surprised she didn't come tonight."

"She did," Trent tells us as he looks from me to Nico. "I wasn't about to let her piss Krista off by fucking with you guys. She had no business coming around the party. The boardwalk . . ." He shrugs. "Can't control that."

"What'd you say to her?" Krista asks.

"Told her to get lost or be embarrassed when security escorted her out."

Krista grins, looking my way, but I glance at Nico, expecting a small frown or something similar, but he's talking with Thompson, not even paying attention to – or caring – at all.

"Demi, you and Nic were lighting the floor on fire in there! Super hot, but I expected that." Krista giggles, leaning against Trent who shakes his head as he wraps his arms around her.

"He surprised me, that's for sure," I admit with a grin.

"Bet he'll keep surprising you." Macy rolls her hips, digging her ass into the sand.

The others laugh and we break into separate conversations amongst the group.

A few minutes later, Nico's voice fills my ear.

"I need to go."

"K," I whisper back.

"Get up, Demi."

I pull back, shifting to look at him.

A weighty command stares back, and he doesn't bother holding it in. "You're coming with me."

I fight a grin. "Am I, now?"

His eyes slim in warning. "How will it look if I go to bed without my girl on a parentless trip?"

Like a lie.

I nod, and the two of us stand, but before we can say anything, the girls start teasing.

"Oh shit, there they go."

"Bedroom heat coming our way."

"Keep the moaning down, would you?"

"Yeah, I don't wanna hear you and Nico on one side and Krista and Trent on the other."

"Would you guys shut up." I scowl, taking Nico by the hand and getting the hell out of there.

They laugh harder, yell louder, and then everyone around is whistling as we step back in the hotel.

I shake my head, grinning as I look to Nico. "So, are we gonna hang out?"

"Guarantee your idea of hanging out is nothing like mine."

"I'm not the prude you think I am, Nico." When he gives me a bit of a dirty, enquiring look I add, "But I also have no intention of *entertaining* you either."

The corner of his mouth lifts slightly, but it's quickly washed away, a full-fledged glare taking its place.

I face forward, slowing when I spot Alex posted against the wall, only a few doors down from our rooms.

I peek at Nico again, but his expression no longer matches the tension rolling off him. He appears relaxed, poised really, but considering the way his hold on me tightens, I'd say he's anything but.

We reach Nico's door, and he slips his hand in his pocket for his keycard but I tug on him.

His jaw flexes, assuming I'm pulling myself free, but when I produce my keycard, he relaxes a little.

I open my door, and Nico keeps his eyes locked with mine as he enters, pausing right beside me. He leans down, skimming his lips across my cheek before disappearing into my room.

As I turn, my stare locks with Alex's.

He pushes off the frame, and winks, but there's something hidden behind his grin I can't quite place, a vibe I've never gotten from him that has me looking away before he spots my frown.

I close the door, turning to Nico, wondering for the first time tonight if this is a mistake and more than that, why it doesn't feel like one.

Nico leans against the small TV stand with a black layered look.

"I figured you left your adjoining door unlocked. This way, when you're ready, you can go in your room and no one will know we aren't together," I explain.

He stretches to his full height and opens the door revealing his is still wide-open as I suspected.

But not for long.

With an air of sudden coolness surrounding him, he steps into his room and closes the door behind him.

I stand there, stuck a moment, but the clink of a latch has me moving toward mine.

Well, okay then.

I gently close it, but something keeps me from turning the lock, instead moving to the one connecting me to Carley's room. I secure it, telling myself it's not to help drive home the ruse I didn't agree to at first but seem to have fallen in perfect line with.

I grab snacks from my mini cooler and lie down to watch *Takers* for the dozenth time.

*

The light tap of a knuckle against wood has me pressing pause on the TV. Seconds later it sounds again, so I crawl from the bed, and over to the door blocking me from my fake boyfriend and pull it open.

Nico is leaning there, a shoulder against the frame on his side, his head also propped on the white wood.

He pins me with a fixed stare, but there's no anger or irritation in it as his expression might lead one to believe.

They're heavy, weighted.

Overwhelmed?

"I didn't hear a click," he rasps, exhaustion coating his already deep voice.

"I didn't lock it," I admit.

"Why not?"

Yeah, why not?

I cross my arms over my chest, giving a small shrug, and Nico's gaze lowers, boldly raking over my body and pausing at the apex of my bare legs.

The longer I gauge him, the more obvious it is that while here he stands, in nothing but his sleep shorts, his mind is far from present.

"Everything okay?" I ask.

The corner of his lip tips up, but there's no joy on his face.

Those eyes come back to mine and hold. "I don't wanna talk, D."

I frown, and his focus shifts to the wall.

He doesn't want to talk . . .

Of course. I keep forgetting.

"Well, I'm tired," I say and he starts to turn his body away. "So good thing, huh?"

His gaze cuts to mine, and slowly I move aside, welcoming him into my room.

Nico steps through, waiting until I climb back into the bed to walk to the other side, where he lowers himself on top of the comforter beside me.

His phone rings from his room the moment we're both seated

and his head falls against the headboard with a soft thud. He lifts it, gently knocking it once more.

It's on the tip of my tongue to ask, but when I meet Nico's eyes and the closed off expression within them, I face forward and press play.

If sitting in silence, with me, is what he needs, I can give that to him.

We spend the next several hours *not talking*.

Chapter 16
Demi

I jolt in bed when persistent loud banging reverberates throughout the room.

The first thing I notice is the space beside me is empty, my TV is still on, and the doors connecting mine and Nico's rooms are still wide open.

"I know you hear us, slut face!" is yelled, laughter following.

I pull myself up, unlocking the door blocking me off from my friends.

Carley, Krista, and Macy pour in, running right for my bed and plopping on top. Macy jumps off just as quickly as she lands though when she realizes Nico's door is open. She races right for it.

"No, wait," I hiss when she runs right inside without warning. "Macy!"

A few seconds later she's walking back in with a small pout. "Boo, he's already gone. How could you let us miss the walk of fame?"

I have to force myself not to frown.

Gone as in he left?

"Yeah, Demi. Rude." Krista laughs, digging into my cooler and pulling out a bag of grapes. "So how was it? Did he take his time or was it hot and quick?"

I open my mouth to tell her to shut the hell up when Trent walks in with sleepy eyes and a glare.

"Busted!" Macy laughs and Krista smacks her, climbing to her knees and holding her hands out to her boyfriend.

I quickly grab some shorts and slip them on. "Thanks for knocking."

"Shit, sorry," Trent apologizes but doesn't walk out.

"What time did Nico leave?" Carley asks and all eyes turn to me.

"I—"

The knock on the room door saves me so I run to open it, my eyes widening when I find Alex on the other side.

"Morning." He grins.

"Uh, hi, I mean good morning." I smooth my hair down, running my fingers under my eyes.

"I wanted to see if you . . ." He trails off, frowning at something over my shoulder.

I look to find Trent standing there, and he only moves closer. I frown and step away, turning to face Alex again.

"Did I interrupt something I shouldn't have?" he asks slowly, his insinuation loud and clear.

"What?! No!" I shout, pushing the door open farther which forces Trent back.

Alex glances past me to spot the girls inside.

"Ah. Now it makes sense." He chuckles. "I thought we could walk down to breakfast together."

"Oh . . ." I subconsciously look to Nico's door.

He left without a word; does this mean our fun is over?

We made everyone think we were partying together all weekend; Alex is standing at my door at eight in the morning.

Is that not the endzone?

Either way, it's a harmless walk that my friends will be on, too.

"Um, I just woke up." I motion to myself. "Obviously, but . . ." I look to the girls. "How long until you're ready to go eat?"

"I'm only changing, and ponytailing it," Krista says, and the other two nod.

I turn back to Alex. "Ten minutes?"

He smiles. "I'll wait by the lobby."

"Awesome."

I shut the door behind me and all four of them stare with wide eyes.

"What?"

"What'd he want?" It's Trent who asks.

"To see when we're going to breakfast, why?"

He shrugs, then turns and walks out while the girls giggle lightly.

"Damn, Demi. Pulling two in one weekend?" Krista grins.

"It's breakfast."

"And last night's dessert was Nico. Or was it you who was dessert?" Macy teases.

"Cute." I flip her off. "Can we get dressed now?"

They hop up and within a solid twenty all of us are headed to our last breakfast before we go home and back to school tomorrow.

Alex sits by me but spends most of his time talking to the people around us until we're about done and people begin taking pictures.

He turns to me with a smile. "So, are you heading back with Krista?"

"Yeah, the four of us drove in together."

"Well, if you want, you can ride with me. I drove myself." He grins.

"You sure you can handle me for a whole two hours?"

"I can manage."

I smile, looking to my drink as I pick it up, something about a 'yes' tasting sour on my tongue. "I'll talk to the girls about it. This is kind of our trip, so I don't want to upset anyone."

"Didn't you ditch them last night to spend it with Sykes?"

My muscles lock and my eyes fly to his.

Well, that was bold and delivered a little gruffly.

"I didn't ditch them, I . . ."

I sort of ditched them, but little does he know the girls would have carried me and dropped me inside with Nico if I tried to turn him down to hang with them, they're awesome like that.

I don't say this to Alex.

He gives a tight grin. "I wasn't trying to give you a hard time."

"No, you're fine. I guess, in a way, you can say I did." Not really.

"So, you hung out with Nico last night?" he probes.

I take a deep breath, looking away a moment.

What is he doing?

He saw us go into my room, so why question me at all?

And why am I hesitating on answering?

The sole purpose was for him to think I was with Nico, right? *Right.*

Still, all I give him is a side smile and small shrug.

Alex eyes me, his lip tipping up. "Ah, come on. Let me know if I have a shot here."

My eyes shoot wide and he chuckles, but then someone at the end shouts his name, gaining his attention the rest of the time.

Once everyone is done, we all exit together, us girls hanging back to wait for Krista as she and her parents thank the restaurant staff for having us.

I walk a few feet out to look over the water, and Trent approaches with his hands in his pockets.

"Nico, huh?"

I cut my eyes his way, but I don't say anything.

"Weren't you just telling me he hated you?"

"Weren't *you* just telling me he didn't?"

"Yeah." A low chuckle leaves him. "I've been telling you that for a long time, Dem."

We're both quiet a moment before he sighs, and I know what he's thinking, but neither of us says it out loud.

This is — maybe *was*— only temporary, so no need to consider long term issues.

Instead of speaking his mind, Trent asks, "Are you really riding back with Alex?"

I nod, smashing my lips together. "I might."

"You know, him and Nico have . . . problems."

"They play the same positions, so it makes sense they compete with each other."

Trent scoffs, shaking his head and looks away as if there's more to it.

"What?"

"Nothing," he says. "I thought you and Nico were having fun this weekend is all."

I frown.

Never thought I'd agree to such a statement, but I did have fun. "He's not as heartless as I've known him to be."

"Why are you leaving with Alex, then?"

I shake my head. "It's just a ride home, Trent."

"Right." He nods, turning when Krista's voice floats from the doors. "I think you should ride with Krista and the girls."

"If this is about having your friend's back, I can promise you Nico wouldn't care about me going with Alex."

Trent catches my eyes, a serious look in his I don't see much, and his words are just as pointed. "I can promise you he would."

With that, he walks off, picking up Krista when she reaches him and spinning her around.

Trent has no idea how wrong he is.

This was Nico's plan, not mine. He'd be fine with it, I'm sure.

Alex laughs a few feet out and my eyes pull his way.

He happens to look over at the same time and lifts his hand in a small wave.

Yeah, I'm riding with him.

We make our way to the beach and walk around a bit before heading back to our rooms to pack up.

Twenty minutes later, I'm ready to go, but Alex isn't at my door yet, so I decide to slip into Nico's room and peek around since he's gone.

The bed is unmade, but other than that, there's no sign of anyone having stayed in here at all. I walk toward the bathroom sink, running my hand across the cool marble, and drop down on the edge.

I pull my phone out, deciding to scroll through Instagram until Alex gets here.

My notifications are insane, dozens of tags and mentions from friends who spent the weekend with us.

I start scrolling, reacting to each post, but my finger freezes when a picture shared by Nico pops up, or should I say pictures?

It's almost like a moving image, a small collage of four images. They're from yesterday on the dock before dinner.

It's me and him, a few of our friends on the other side of us, Macy right beside me looking up with a grin, but we're the focus and . . . holy shit.

You'd think we planned out the pose and each one after, but I had no clue a camera was pointed my way.

In the first shot, Nico has his arms draped around my shoulders while I'm gripping his forearms. His mouth is slightly open, his lips at my ear. This must have been taken when I blinked, because my eyes are closed and that's the only explanation for it.

In the second picture, I've turned my head, our faces are only an inch or two apart and we're looking into each other's eyes. The third, I'm licking my lips and his gaze is lasered in on my mouth, and the fourth, his eyes are locked dead with the camera while mine are glued on him.

We look . . .

Like way more than a weekend fling.

The tagline reads, 'Bay this weekend', and he hash tagged it *bay with my bae*.

His bae?

I look to the timestamp, and something stirs in the pit of my stomach.

Less than an hour ago.

After he left.

I go to his profile, hovering for a moment before I decide to send him a message.

Me: saw the pictures.

I pause to think before adding to it.

Me: thanks for an entertaining weekend.

I wait about a minute, staring at the chat to see if it'll show if he's read it or not, but then I stuff my phone in my pocket and move back to my room right as Carley shouts from hers.

"Demi, you still have sodas in your cooler?"

"Yeah!" I tell her. "I have Gatorade, a few waters, and candy left, too."

I pull my door open, propping it with the little desk chair right as Alex walks up.

"Ready?"

I smile. "Yeah, I—"

My phone beeps, cutting me off, so I pull it from my pocket.

It's a text from a number I don't have saved, and a screenshot of the message I sent to Nico, *thanks for an entertaining weekend* highlighted.

Another text comes through.

Unknown: funny, D.

"Should I grab your bags?" Alex offers.

"I, um . . ." I trail off, slowly lowering my phone to my side, but it beeps again.

Unknown: we're not done.

I pull my lips in.

"Demi."

My head pops up. "I'm . . . I need to ride with the girls after all. I have all the snacks so . . ."

Alex frowns at my horrible excuse, and a forced grin follows. "Yeah, cool. See you at school."

I nod, smiling after him as he turns and walks away.

Once he's out of sight, I frown.

What did I just do?

My phone dings.

Unknown: good girl.

I can't help it, a laugh bubbles out of me, but then I pause.

How did he . . .

138

Trent steps into the long hallway, coming out of Krista's room a few doors down and heads right for me, her bags flung over his shoulder and another hanging from his hands.

He tries to fight a smile.

Wow.

"Really, Trent?" I raise a brow as he walks by.

He laughs, glancing over his shoulder with a shrug. "Gotta share those snacks, Dem."

I laugh back, shaking my head.

Yeah, that was *pretty lame.*

Of course, Trent had to go and call Nico.

My phone beeps again, but this time when I look down, it's a notification on Instagram.

Nico posted another picture, tagging me in it this time, even though I'm not in the image.

It's him in a hoodie, half his face covered with his arm, nothing but those dark eyes, and thick lashes showing. It looks as if he's lying in bed, but I can't be sure. The caption though . . . no mistaking his meaning as it reads *get that ass home @ DemiTheeDancer. Your man is waiting for you.*

I roll my eyes, stuffing my phone in my pocket.

My man, huh?

I guess we are playing our roles a little longer.

Chapter 17
Demi

"Okay, girls!" Miranda claps her hands. "I hope you enjoyed your three-day weekend, because we're pulling doubles the rest of this week. We already know we won't be performing for the school until Senior Night, but what I haven't shared yet, is the principal has asked the dance team to lead the varsity players onto the field at the game."

"Cheer always leads the team," one of the girls points out.

Miranda shakes her head with a grin. "Not this year. This year *we* are the show."

Holy shit.

The dance team is geared more toward hip-hop in style, which is why when they recruited me freshman year, I agreed, but to take over Senior Night that's not only full of students, but parents and faculty? Kind of crazy being our dances are on the risqué side, a lot of booty popping is involved.

"There's like forty of them and only seventeen of us," another says.

"Only the seniors will be escorted, but we'll still be a little short which is why I've asked the JV dance team to help out, but only during the escorting. They won't be performing our full routine with us," she announces. "I'm still working on costumes for the performance, but I'm thinking we'll incorporate the team to help make it fresh in some way."

"How so?" I ask.

"Well, we can add eye black for fun, and knee-high socks. We can ask Coach Parks if we can borrow the boys' away jerseys since this is a home game or another option is lettermen jackets. The entire team was awarded one free last year when they won state, so every player should have one that can be worn."

"It might be hard to dance in."

"Yes," she agrees, then smirks. "But it would be a great show starter, and a piece you can easily toss when the chorus hits."

"Yes!" someone shouts. "A transition piece into our costume reveal!"

"Do we get to pick who we escort?" Ava asks with excitement, making us laugh.

"Hell no, you think I want to deal with the fallout of that when these boys aren't what you imagined in your heads?" she teases, making us laugh. She's only twenty-one, so she's always super cool when it comes to boyfriends and things. "This is about our team performing well. Hear me?"

"Yes, Coach," is said in unison.

"Okay." She rolls her wrist. "Three laps around and then fall in."

After our quick warm-up, we run through our routine twice and then there's a hard knock on the gym door.

Miranda smirks, skipping backward toward the door. "Did I mention they'd be here today?"

My eyes widen and I glance around the room.

Most of us are in tiny booty shorts and tanks or a sports bra. Since this is only practice and not an actual class, we can get away with that.

The boys, though, they have zero period weight training, so they're on the clock right now. Still, when she opens the door and shakes the coach's hand, half the guys are shirtless, the rest sleeveless.

Thompson and Trent walk in first, Alex and a few others behind them, followed by more of their teammates.

Trent nods in hello, so I wave, my eyes shifting along the line and catching Alex's. He grins, then looks around at the girls.

Where's Nico?

This makes three days now he hasn't shown up to school.

"Okay," Miranda starts. "Boys, solid straight line across the wall, shortest to tallest. I'm gonna place some girls in front of you and check height so I can get a good idea of what will and won't work for entrances. I know you normally just walk out with the girls while your stats are read over the speaker, but this year we're involving you a little more for fun."

She has us do the same once they're placed in order.

I'm shuffled around a few times, and in the end, placed in front of Thompson who is at least six-five and has been since freshman year.

He throws his arms over my shoulder. "Wassup, Demi?"

"Not much. Did you guys know we were pairing?" I glance at Trent who is a few bodies away.

He shakes his head no as Thompson says it.

"We've got a couple bodies not here, Miranda, just so you know," Coach Park tells her. "I can send you their height if you wanna preplan in just a bit."

"That would be helpful, thanks," she says, moving girls around at the beginning of the line. I'm moved one more time, now placed in front of Carlos, the defensive end.

Miranda steps back, nodding slowly. "I think this—"

She's cut off when the gym door slams shut and all eyes fly in that direction.

Nico walks in wearing joggers and a hoodie pulled over his head.

He pauses by his coach a moment, saying something no one else can hear. The coach slaps him on the shoulder, pushing him our way.

"Miranda," Nico mumbles as he walks by, not looking at her.

"I need to pair you, Nico," she says sternly.

He ignores her, stopping in front of me, and his eyes narrow before shifting to Carlos.

There's a light shuffle, and then Nico slips in, his chest pushing against my back in the next second.

I inhale, slightly annoyed he thinks he can walk in here and take control, especially after no word for three days.

142

My eyes move back to Miranda.

She won't allow him to mess up the flow or visual of the performance, even if he does think he's privileged.

Nico pushes even closer. "I'm paired."

I tense, waiting for her to set him straight as she would us, but Miranda only frowns, staring a moment longer before she snaps out of it and places one of the JV girls with Carlos. "Let me grab my phone so I can go over this later to be sure, but it's looking good."

When she comes back, she starts taking pictures, moving a few people over with each shot until she's happy with what she sees.

"Okay boys, when I say one, place your hands on your partner's upper ribs here." She indicates to a few inches below our breasts, continuing to show them what she means as she says, "On two, slide them down to the hips, on three, hold, and on four, she will jump as you lift. On five, her feet should be on the ground, your hands at your sides. Girls, by six, I want you laid out.

"This is just a quick, off the top try and not necessarily what we'll be doing for the routine. I want to see how clean it looks height-wise." She repeats the counts and moves once more, then pulls her phone back out, clipping it to the tripod. "Go ahead and grab on now."

Heavy, strong hands plant on my ribs, and I straighten my spine, getting ready. When I do, his hands slide up, now brushing against the edge of my sports bra.

I glare straight ahead. If he still wants to keep this fakeness up, he needs to understand that it doesn't come before or between dance, and that what my coach says goes. Yes, this is only my school team and not my competition team, but still. I'm on the front line for a reason and his power trip isn't getting in the way of the gold stamp that this puts on my college applications.

"Demi," Miranda barks and my head jerks her way. "Sass, not anger."

I clear my throat, quickly putting my game face on.

I don't miss Nico's chuckle.

Considering Miranda left him with me, I guess she agrees with our pairing.

Miranda pushes play on the recording. "We're already at one, but I'll repeat it for the sake of the steps."

She continues to count, and in what seems like slow motion, Nico slides his hands down my ribs, fingers spreading out at my hips. Mine come up to cover his as I jump a foot into the air. The second my feet hit the floor, I nudge him off as he forgets to let go.

In the next second, all of us girls are dropping into a left split, and the guys start freaking out, completely losing their cool with whoops and *oh damns* making us laugh.

We push to our feet as a laughing Miranda turns to the grinning coach. "Maybe I should have explained what they were about to do."

He laughs lightly, then heads for the door. "Give them five minutes to change at the end, but they're all yours for now. Can't give them to you this week but starting next you can have them for twenty minutes, twice a week and in the morning only. Boys, this means I get twenty extra after school, so plan for it."

"Yes, Coach," is shouted by the guys.

He nods and walks out.

Miranda's tense gaze comes back to me. "Demi," she calls on me as I'm the front liner. "Keep steps one through three and give us the last seven."

I nod and take a few steps forward. I lift my arms, assuming Nico will understand to place his hands back on me, but when no movement follows, I glance over my shoulder to find Nico glaring at my bloomers.

I snap my fingers, and a few others chuckle as that glare cuts up to mine.

He looks around, realizing everyone is watching the two of us, then he steps out. "What?"

I roll my eyes. "Do what you just did, but leave your hands loose on my hips, so I can move them while adding steps."

He doesn't hesitate, scooting in so close his sweats are rubbing against my ass.

I ignore the thickness of him brushing against me and start counting.

Nico's hands go from my ribs to my waist and hold.

"Five." I spin to face him, gripping his hoodie mid stomach. "Six." I drop down, my legs butterflied, face at his crotch. "Seven." I'm back in his face, chest to chest. "Eight." I push off of him, and just like I knew he would, he creeps back in with a frown. I smile. "Nine." His brows knit. I grip his hand and spin out, both of us now facing forward, our elbows bent, hands up. "Ten."

She said we're escorting them, so I take a few slow, dramatic steps forward and he moves with me before I drop his hand and turn to the others.

A few girls whistle and clap while Miranda stands there processing.

After a moment she nods. "That's perfect. Messy, needs serious precision, and practice, but a perfect entrance. They come in hot, get knocked down a peg, but fire back with a dominant flare. Complete story to tell before a big game."

Nico's eyes slide to mine, and I almost detect a flash of satisfaction coming from his, but he blinks, and it's gone.

We only have time to run through it once with everyone and it's a shit show, but Miranda advises us to try and get together to practice this week if we can swing it.

The boys are dismissed while us girls hang back to go over our schedule for the week, and then we're let go.

I use the time I have left to take a quick shower and dress in my normal clothes, but I'm too exhausted to mess with my hair, so I tie it back in a slick ponytail, throwing some mousse in to give the illusion of natural body.

As usual, I'm one of the last to leave, rushing out the door, only to slam into Nico on my exit.

"What . . ." I trail off as he uses his body to drive mine back a few steps, trapping me in the small divide that leads into the locker room.

"What are you doing?"

His eyes narrow. "I gotta ask to hide away with my girl?"

I frown and he holds a finger to his mouth, telling me to keep quiet.

Right then, a girl on my team comes out of the locker room door, squealing when she sees us.

"Sorry." She laughs as she disappears.

Nico waits for the door to close completely then looks back to me. "I had to leave the beach. Today's the first day I could make it back."

From where I want to ask but don't.

I nod instead. "I gathered when I woke up and you were, you know, *gone*, and when I didn't see you in class all week. You and Trent thought you were really cute, by the way."

That makes him mad.

"I never said I was done," he says sharply. "You shouldn't have been planning to go with Alex in the first fuckin' place."

A laugh bubbles out of me. "What was I supposed to think? You took off, I assumed that meant mission accomplished."

"Whose mission, because there's two of us, *remember*?"

My shoulders fall instantly.

Well shit.

"I didn't even—"

"Think past your boy? Yeah, I know." He steps back, his eyes flicking over my form with a void expression. "See you in class, D."

He leaves me standing there, but not before Miranda steps in to watch him angrily walk away.

Awesome.

She waits for an explanation, but I offer nothing more than a flat smile and walk out.

I'm officially an asshole.

I never should have entertained Alex like I did without

having spoken to Nico first. This pretend relationship was a mutual agreement. It wasn't fair for me to act how I did.

If I knew what he was after, I could work that angle more, turn it on when it needs to be, stay low key when it's pointless and others aren't around. I could play a better part all around.

I'm mopey all day, and it doesn't help I'm constantly asked about Nico and me, more so than I've been all week now that he's actually here.

I disappoint each person, giving a smile or laugh because I don't really know what to say.

It was one thing at the beach where it was more or less all the same people we hang with every weekend or at lunch sometimes, but here on campus where there're hundreds more, it's sort of intimidating.

Nico has always been the guy people stare at when he enters a room, but he's also pretty standoffish. He doesn't make a scene or show off, doesn't like or need to be heard. You really only catch him interacting when it's his core group of friends or teammates.

I mean, when he's on the field, you'd think he was constantly being showy, but it's simply him giving nothing but his best. It's a raw, natural talent he possesses, and it shows.

Other than that, he sits back and relaxes, and yet, people still gravitate toward him as if he's the life of the party.

He's definitely capable of being the life of the party after dark if the rumors from the girls here are true.

"Demi Davenport."

I'm pulled from my thoughts by a familiar voice.

I lift my eyes, meeting Josie's in the bathroom mirror.

Great.

"Hey, Josie." I turn off the water, moving for a paper towel before facing her.

"You have fun over the weekend?" she asks as she steps up to the sink I vacated.

And here we go.

"I did. You?"

147

"Bunches."

Right.

I'm not doing this.

I toss my garbage in the bin and turn to leave when she speaks again.

"I care about Nico."

Slowly, I look over my shoulder, spotting the sincerity in her eyes. It's the only reason I don't walk out.

"You guys were together a long time." I nod. "I'm sure he cares about you, too."

She scoffs a dejected laugh, and I swear sadness clouds her expression. "You'd be wrong," she says, pausing as her gaze scours over me before lifting to mine. "He's brave. I never thought I'd see the day, you two together."

"Well, you have, so get over it." I push on the door, but she halts me once again.

"You need to be careful with him."

That irritates me and I turn around fully. "And you need to mind your own business."

"Like I said," she snaps. "I care about him, so I'm standing here telling you to be careful with him. He has issues, Demi."

"He's my boyfriend to worry about, Josie, not yours."

"Just watch yourself with him."

"Not that he would, but I'd never allow anyone to walk all over me. I'm not some naïve little girl."

She nods, one side of her mouth lifting as she throws her paper towel away without looking, stepping in front of me in the same move. "Funny, you automatically assumed I was talking about *him* hurting *you*." Her tone is terse and as bitter as I'd expect from an ex of his, but it's the concern laced through her gaze that confuses me. "Maybe you are as naïve as you're pretending *not* to be. Have a shitty day, Davenport."

She pushes out the door, leaving me to trail after her.

Trent and Krista are in the hall as we exit, and Josie flips them off as she passes while I take a deep breath and stop beside them.

"What was that about?" Krista asks. "Did she hit you up about Nico in there?"

I look to Trent. "Why'd they break up?"

His eyes widen, and he hastily shakes his head. "No fucking way."

"You obviously know, just tell me."

"You're his girl, right?" His tone is laced with something I can't quite put my finger on. "Ask him."

"Come on, babe," Krista whines, gripping his arm. "Please."

"Nope." He pulls free, kisses her quickly then starts down the hall. "Meet you after math."

Krista and I fall in line together, walking to our next class. "Are you gonna ask Nic?"

"I think so." Maybe.

I sort of have to. He and I need to sit down and talk this out, get on the same playing field or we'll screw it up and people will question us.

"Oh, did you hear?" Krista turns to me. "Alex asked Ava to formal."

I stop in my tracks and Krista slows, turning toward me.

"Does that bother you?" she asks with worry.

"No," I say, maybe too quickly.

She gives a slow chuckle, and the two of us start walking again. "Are you sure because it's okay if it does. You and Nico are still new, and you've had a thing for Alex for years."

"I'm a little surprised is all. I didn't know they talked." It's the truth, but even more honestly would be admitting it doesn't necessarily bother me. He dates all the time, so it's not like I had a chance and lost it.

Right?

"You know how it is when dances roll around." Krista chuckles. "Tons of people who have never dated start hanging out. Most of the time it doesn't go past the after-party."

I grin. "True."

"Okay, see you at lunch later." She walks into her next class a few doors down from mine.

I smooth my shirt down and pull my hair from where it's gotten stuck under the strap of my backpack and walk into chemistry.

Alex looks away the second I enter, and I have to force myself not to frown. He's ignored me all week.

I turn down a ride and he wants to act like a child about it and avoid me?

Ugh.

Nico is looking at his phone as I walk toward our table.

I don't know what I expected from him, so I drop into my seat and continue to face forward, but not five seconds pass before he's hooking his foot in the bottom of my stool and pulling it to him.

He shifts so his knees are spread wide, one in front of mine, the other behind me. His left arm comes around to drape across the back of my seat while he leaves his right laid out on the tabletop in front of me.

Nico leans in, so close I consider pulling back, but I can sense other eyes on us, so I stay planted where I am.

He gauges me. "How hard is it for you not to fidget right now?"

"Not hard."

He leans in farther and I inhale.

His lips are less than an inch from mine when he asks, "How 'bout now?"

"You're going to get me in trouble."

"Maybe you need to get in some trouble, Pixie," he taunts, his voice liquid smoke.

I narrow my eyes.

So, he thinks he can play his little sex games and not get it back?

Sorry, Neek.

I lift my chin, my eyes purposely moving to his lips and back. He glares.

I lick mine, letting warm air flow from my mouth, knowing it's carrying to his.

"I thought I was a *good girl*, Neek?"

His jaw flexes slightly, the dark of his eyes amplifying the slightest bit.

Nico, not one to back down, scoots his body closer. "Prove it, D. Lay them thick lips on mine. Right here, right now."

I fold and a heavy chuckle leaves him, but he doesn't scoot away. He stays put until the teacher comes in and announces where we're to 'get to know' our partners today.

The theatre.

Nico jumps up, grabs my hand and tugs me out the door.

I can't help but notice the shock on Mr. Brando's face as we fly by him.

When we enter, Nico looks at me.

"We're not going to my spot," I tell him.

"Why not? I took you to mine."

"I didn't ask you to, but we do need privacy. We have shit to talk about."

"No."

My mouth drops open. "No?"

He nods. "I'll come over later, we can talk then."

"To my house?"

He steps closer. "That a problem?"

I guess not. "What time were you thinking?"

"Practice isn't over until five."

"I have a studio class today, so I'm across town until six."

"Fine. Seven?"

"Okay, but what about right now?"

He looks around, spotting Evan and Alex on the stairs to the stage, and then looks back to me. "Come on."

Hesitantly, I follow.

I squeal lightly when he suddenly lifts me by the hips and sets me on the edge so my legs are dangling over the side. Nico hops up beside me.

"Why did you and Josie break up?" The question flies from my mouth before I can stop it.

Nico's glare swings to mine. "Why?"

151

"Shouldn't I know that?"

"No." His answer is instant.

"But you tried to convince me you needed to know about my bedroom preferences and experiences," I whisper, mockingly.

"That's different."

"How?"

"Because I have to know how to please you, Demi. It's all a part of being your man. You don't need to know why my ex couldn't do the same for me."

I look away, willing the heat creeping up my neck to go away. I glance back at Nico to find him frowning.

"Why you asking?" he questions.

"I don't know how I'm supposed to act when it comes to her, she knows you more than anyone I'm guessing, so it's a lot," I admit. "Being yourself is working just fine for you, I don't want to be the one to screw this up without even realizing it."

Nico doesn't say anything at first, but then hops down.

He nudges my knees open so he can step between them causing my inner thighs to rest against his ribs due to the added height of the stage.

A seriousness slides over his face and he holds my attention.

"You're supposed to act like you want me. *That* is your job."

After a moment I nod, reiterating what he said to me before, "Make people believe this."

He shakes his head, reaching up to tuck a loose piece of my hair behind my ear.

"No?"

"No," he confirms. "Not people." He leans in skimming his nose across my cheek, his lips pausing at my ear. "Me. Make *me* believe it, D."

Goosebumps spread across my arms, and his eyes fall as he notices, ever so slowly rising back to mine.

I'd be lying if I said they were caused solely from nerves.

Make him believe it, he said.

Why does it sound so enticing to try?

The challenge in it maybe, or the doubt I assume he has, that everyone will have soon when all they get from us is some middle school hand holding bullshit.

No way does Nico think I could possibly act so well that even he would believe we were an us. That's where his challenge lies.

Or at least that's what I tell myself when I drag my ass to the edge of the stage, my center pressing into his ribs, lips aligned with his, and wait.

There's zero hesitation from Nico.

His hand shoots to the back of my neck, and an instant, low groan leaves him as he applies a heavy pressure to my mouth, one I feel between my legs.

My thigh muscles clench against him and his tongue attempts to pry my mouth open, but I tug away.

Holy shit my heart is beating like crazy, I'm pretty sure it's visible through my shirt.

Nico frowns as he licks his lips, tasting mine on his skin and his hand lowers, now cupping my outer thighs.

There, we did it.

We kissed for our classmates to see.

For Alex to see.

For show.

Right?

Chapter 18
Demi

Snack bag in hand, I drop beside Macy on the blanket. "Where are the girls?"

"They went to the vending machines to get us drinks really quick. Here." She hands me a sub sandwich. "Trent's mom dropped off a bunch of sandwiches for us."

"Awesome." I set it in my lap, pulling some pretzels from our bag while Macy chooses Hot Fries.

"Turkey and avocado, hold the cheese, Dem," Trent shouts from where he and the boys are, a picnic table a few feet over.

I laugh, lifting it up in thanks.

Nico's eyes tighten but when I tilt my head, not looking away, his lips twitch and he turns his attention back to his friends.

"You guys are so cute." Macy smiles.

Krista and Carley walk up right then, lowering to the blanket.

"For you, my dear." Carley sets a blue Gatorade in front of me.

"Thank you."

Krista passes Macy a soda. "So." She peeks toward the guys quickly. "I told you I'd find out, and I did."

"Find out what?" Carley asks, filling her sandwich with potato chips.

"I found out why Nico and Josie broke up." Her eyes cut to mine.

My muscles tense, but I try to hide it. "Tell me."

Krista is a bit of a gossip mill, mainly just for us, but if she got the details, she made sure to confirm them first.

Her hesitation has me on edge.

"Out with it, Krista." Macy rolls her eyes, tugging her mini jean jacket off.

Krista nods, leaning closer. "So, you know how Nico and Josie had that fight at Trent's bonfire over the summer?" She doesn't wait for a response but keeps talking. "*Apparently,* Nic found out Josie had fucked someone else."

"But they'd broke up for the ten-thousandth time the week before that, right?" Carley asks.

My eyes slide to hers.

"Yeah, who cares." Macy shrugs. "He can't get mad after the fact."

He can if he still has feelings for her and that's what all this is really about.

Krista shakes her head. "The fight was because he found out the entire reason she broke it off with him when she did, was to try and hide that she fucked someone else earlier that morning."

My mouth drops open. "Wait, so she cheated, then broke up with him right after, all so later she could claim it wasn't cheating?"

"Exactly, she was hoping to play it off like she hoed-out after the split if he ever found out, when really she cheated, then broke up with him hours later." Krista takes a quick bite of her sub. "I guess she showed up to the bonfire in the hopes of getting back with Nic, tried to use her planned excuse, but I guess he told her he knew what she did before she even broke it off with him. He was waiting for her to admit it."

"And then he told her to fuck off," Macy adds, remembering the tail end of the fight a large group of us happened to walk up on.

"Wow." Carley chuckles. "Girl needs to have some class and stay away."

"She needs to stay away period," Macy snaps, then smiles all dreamy-like. "He's Demi's now."

I give a tight chuckle, quickly covering it by taking a drink.

Krista eyes me and I slowly screw the lid back on the bottle.

"What?" I draw out.

"I sort of . . . sugar-coated part of the story . . ." Krista says slowly, pulling her lips back to show her teeth.

"Just tell me."

"I don't think it matters."

"Krista."

"It was Alex," she rushes out.

My face falls. "Wait . . . what?"

Alex?

Macy and Carley both gape at Krista then look to me.

"Alex." I lower my chin. "Josie slept with Alex while she was with Nico?"

Krista chews on her bottom lip as she nods, then quickly shrugs it off. "It doesn't mean anything, Demi. I just thought, you know . . ." She trails off.

"Thought it was a strange coincidence?" Carley asks suspiciously.

Krista nods, her eyes moving between the three of us before once again landing on me.

"Okay, well, who cares." It's Macy who says this. "Demi is the one who has, or maybe had, I don't know, a thing for Alex. So, for any of this to matter, it would have needed to be the other way around. It's not like Alex was into Demi and so Nico . . ."

"Pretended to be into me?" I give them the truth covered in a lie, my chest growing tight for reasons I'm not ready to admit.

Is that what this is? A way to get to Alex for screwing the only girl Nico cared enough about to keep around?

"Oh, no." Krista sits up straight. "There is no way, no how, that's the case. It is *so* obvious he's hot for you. I wasn't trying to insinuate anything, swear, but I mean, I had to tell you. I can't help but think if he knew you had the hots for Alex before him, it might make him nervous or angry or something, thinking it could happen again."

"Yeah." I give my best fake chuckle. "Good thing he doesn't know about that."

Awesome, Demi. Keep offering unnecessary lies.

The rest of lunch I'm useless and lost in thought, but what Krista said was true.

My gaze travels to Nico who's talking with Thompson.

What purpose would it serve for Nico to want to *fake date* me when his ex cheated with the guy he's supposed to help me get?

The simple answer is it wouldn't.

That doesn't stop me from coming up with a million other reasons why, none of them making any sense to me.

After a moment, Nico's eyes slide my way, and as if sensing the tension building in my gut, his expression tightens, and he nods his chin in question.

I give a half smile in answer, and after a moment he nods, looking back to his friends.

It shouldn't comfort me that my fake boyfriend knows how to read me.

Yet, for some reason . . . it does.

"Can I ask you something?"

Trent looks up from the blender, nodding his chin as if to say go ahead before focusing back on the margaritas he was asked to help make.

Every time Thompson has a party, he puts Trent behind his parents' bar to mix drinks.

"Did Josie really sleep with Alex?"

Trent's glare flies to the kitchen table where Krista sits, and he curses, finally looking back to me.

"Does it matter if she did?" he deflects.

"Trent, come on." I cross my arms, leaning them on the countertop.

It's Monday night, so three days since Krista filled me in on Alex and Josie and I need extra confirmation, so I can stop thinking about it which is pretty much how I spent my weekend.

Trent turns off the machine, quickly pouring a cup and handing it to me. He grips the edge of the marble. "Yeah, she did."

157

"Did she break Nico's heart?"

Trent scoffs a small laugh. "No, Dem. Not even a little bit."

When I frown, he sighs, cuts a quick glance toward the living room where Nico sits, then leans closer. "Nic liked Josie, a lot. They dated for a long time, but it wasn't so much love as it was comfortable, a way to escape. Someone to hang with." He lifts his shoulder, adding. "Sex on hand."

I roll my eyes and he lifts his palms.

"So . . . he wasn't hurt by it, like at all?"

He studies me, inquisition in his eyes.

"Are you falling for him?" His tone's suspiciously full of surprise.

My muscles grow tight. "We're . . . dating, Trent."

He's quick to shake it off. "No, yeah. I didn't mean anything by it. I'm sorry."

I eye him and after a bit, Trent licks his lips, looking at Nico a long moment.

He hangs his head, a deep exhale leaving him as his attention slides back to me. "It hurt him, Dem, yeah, but not in the way you're thinking. It's more complicated than you realize, it was a low ass blow from Josie. Don't ask me anything else, all right? Please."

"Why not?"

"Because it's not my place, and when you look at me like this, all genuine and with honest curiosity and concern, it's real fucking hard to deny you." His eyes widen. "*Always has been.*"

A light laugh leaves me, and I drop my stare to my cup. "You know, I always thought you were a bit of a blabbermouth, like your girlfriend."

He laughs goodheartedly.

"But now I know you're not."

He winks, then walks away, a tray of Styrofoam cups full of margaritas to be handed out in his hands.

My focus shifts toward the living room where Nico sits on the couch across from Carley, but something keeps me locked in my chair a few moments longer.

158

Nico

I didn't get to see Demi at school today because she was gone on a field trip for some leadership bull. I texted her twice but when all I got was one-word answers, I turned my phone off and did my best to forget the fact she was on a two-hour bus ride, where she should have had plenty of time to talk. The same bus dickhead Hammons was on.

Now, though, I'm annoyed as fuck, doesn't help she stayed locked in her room all weekend. I know because her light stayed on around the clock.

We're chillin' at Thompson's and Demi's been nothing but quiet all fucking night. At least, where I'm concerned.

She seems to be in there chatting with everyone else just fuckin' fine.

"What are you pissy about?"

Carley calls me out, and my eyes snap to hers.

"What are you talkin' about?"

"The *I might murder you in your sleep* look on your face." She folds her feet in the chair.

With a frown, I unscrew the cap to my Mountain Dew. "Nah, I'm just chillin'."

"Liar."

The bottle pauses at my lips, my eyes moving to hers. Slowly, I take a drink and then shift toward her. "What makes you say that?"

"You're making faces at her like you're angry, but your jerky movements are a clear sign of frustration. Something about her both stresses you out and intrigues you." Carley narrows her eyes. "I like you and I think you're good for her, but I can tell you're hiding something."

"Oh, yeah?" I give her a bored look. "What am I hiding, Carley?"

"I don't know, but I do know Demi. Not everything around her is as black and white as it may seem . . ." She trails off.

"What are you tryin' to say?"

"The gist of it? Don't make her life outside of home suck, too."

What the fuck does that mean?

Carley stares a moment, only looking away when Demi walks up, dropping beside me.

Without a word and leaving several inches between us.

What the fuck?

She was playful, confident – sexy as fuck – a few days ago, we didn't get to hang this weekend, sure, but suddenly today, after a couple hours with that prick, she's taken a page from my playbook and gone silent?

Fuck this.

I set my drink on the glass coffee table with a hard thud and shoot to my feet.

"I'm out," I announce, my eyes falling to hers. "You ready or you gonna get a ride from someone else?"

She frowns.

Yes, we've only been here for a little over an hour.

No, I don't give a shit.

"I planned to ride with you."

So, get up. Leave with me.

She stares a moment and right when I'm positive she's saying bye to me, she turns to Carley.

Carley smiles at her. "Text me when you leave for school in the morning if you want me to grab you a coffee."

Demi nods as she stands.

She could easily walk past me and out the front door. She doesn't.

She grabs my hand, gingerly lacing her fingers into mine, but there's something in the way they hold on that has my skin tingling. Her tired eyes meet mine.

Fuck me, my chest muscles pull, and I discreetly clench my teeth.

Movement behind us lets me know Carley has walked out, and I can't stop my feet from shifting closer.

I lift my right hand, using my pinky to brush her hair from her face, allowing it to fall through my fingers at the curve of her breast.

Her chest expands, the edge of her shirt feathering across my knuckle.

"What's on your mind?" she whispers.

I don't know how or when I moved, but suddenly she's sitting on the edge of the couch looking up at me with low, heady eyes.

My hands drop, sliding up her sides and her chin lifts to keep our eyes connected.

"You mad at me, D?"

She shakes her head.

"You sit by Alex on the bus today?" I ask, unable to cover the aggravation in my voice.

She shakes her head again.

"Did you want to?"

She licks her lips. "That why you've been giving me angry eyes all night?"

"Yes."

My instant response has her chuckling but just as quickly, a question crosses her face.

I'll bet she's asking herself what it means, why I'd be angry, or say I was, for her getting closer to who she's supposed to be getting closer to with this little deal of ours.

"What if . . ." she whispers.

"What, Pixie?" I lean in, my grip tightening, and she sucks in a deep breath. "What if . . . *what*?"

Her lips part the slightest bit, so I take them.

I drop my mouth to hers, my dick twitches in my jeans when hers opens even more and my tongue is awarded with the full taste of hers, but it's quickly deflated when laughter and mocking noises echo around us.

She tugs back, a small frown on her face as she looks at me before it's wiped away and a forced chuckle escapes her.

Some of my teammates walk by, clapping me on the back like dicks, but it's Alex who my eyes zone in on and the stupid fuckin' smirk on his face.

I look back to Demi who focuses on her fingernails until a few of the guys say hi to her as they pass.

Demi gives them tight waves, then slowly slips past me and out the door.

I wait for them to disappear around the corner, then drop my head back. A sigh leaves me and I walk outside to meet her.

I never got my answer.

What if what?

Chapter 19

Nico

I juke left only to slant right for a quick, short pass, and then Coach blows the whistle.

"Good, good. All right, blue squad off, white on," he calls, lifting his hands for me to pass him the ball.

Other than the O-line, the rest of the team steps off the field so second string can get a couple reps in.

I grab a water bottle, squirting some in my mouth before passing it to Trent.

He watches as his backup QB steps into the pocket. With a little pressure put on him, he releases too early, throwing an interception on his first drive.

Trent scoffs, looking my way as he hands the water back. "Better hope I don't get injured. This fool can't throw for shit. He's been playing scared ever since he got sacked against Joho a few weeks ago."

"That's 'cause he's a bitch."

Trent grins, his eyes moving to the bleachers and mine follow. "Speaking of bitches."

Josie sits there with her friends like she has the last several years just bullshitting until the last bus leaves.

"Demi asked me why we broke up."

Trent frowns. "When?"

"Couple days ago."

"Fuck," he curses, a deep sigh leaving him as he moves to face me.

I lift my foot to the bench to tie my cleat. "What?"

"She knows."

My head snaps his way. "What do you mean?"

"Demi. She knows why you and Josie split."

"You tell her?"

He licks his lips, looking off.

"Trent."

"Nah, man. I didn't tell her," he says. "But I confirmed it when she asked."

"What the fuck, man?!"

"Not confirming would have been just as much confirmation at that point. She asked me point blank. What was I supposed to say?"

"No. You say no, asshole, or better, tell her to talk to me, and I'll tell her no."

"I tried that. She asked me a while ago, and I told her to ask you. What's it matter anyway? It's not like she wouldn't eventually find out, right?"

"I wasn't ready for her to know yet." I frown. "This is why she's been quieter than normal."

Trent eyes me. "Why didn't you want her to know?"

"Why you playin' dumb?" I ask him.

"I'm not, but don't you think you're running with this a little too hard? I heard you kissed her in class this week, and I saw you kiss her Monday night."

"And you care why?" I glare. "I was on her. And? She fucking let me. Baited me the same if you really wanna fuckin' know. She's been single a long ass time, Trent. She likes this."

"Likes pretending?"

I study him. "Likes the playfulness, the attention, the lack of pressure. I'm telling you, you think she's this schoolgirl who likes studying but lightly parties with her friends. She is, but she's not. She's bored."

"You hardly know her, Nico."

"You think you do?" I turn toward him. "'Cause your ma and hers are friends? That don't mean shit."

He looks ready to say something but thinks better of it and looks away. "No, you're right. I don't."

I sigh, putting my helmet back on and strapping it up. "Look, shit's twisted right now, so I'm not trying to complicate it even more. And I know the girl better than you think."

"I'm just saying be careful, she's had a thing for Alex for a long time. What do you think happens when she finds out the truth, the *entire* truth?"

Coach Park's whistle rings through our conversation, so I squirt some water on my mouthpiece, quickly looking back to Trent.

"I don't know, but don't help her out anymore, huh?"

I jog back on the field and get into position. I'm not mad at his ass for this because he's right. If he didn't answer her straightforward question, that would be an answer in itself. I'm pissed off he has my mind spinning now.

What would I do if she found out now, before I'm ready for her to?

Damn fuckin' good question.

One that's on repeat the rest of practice, leaving my chest feeling heavy and my mind muddled when I finally step off the field.

I hang back after everyone's gone, taking a long shower to try and clear my head before getting in my truck and driving home to a house I hate walking into.

It's pitch black as always, the curtains drawn as tight as they've been for months now, lights off, so I have to use my phone to navigate my way into the kitchen for some water.

There's a bottle of pills laying spilled over next to the stovetop, an overboiled pot of noodles sitting beside it, raw meat dropped in a pan but never turned on like she got halfway through before the meds kicked in and she abandoned the idea of cooking dinner, something she used to love to do before my dad took her soul with him when he traded up.

With a sigh, I clean up the mess and put the pills back in the container. I go to put the lid on, but resentment flares in my chest as the little red pills mock me, the life I used to have and the life I have now.

Pills that caused me to have to rush home from the beach because my mom decided to take a few too many after a late-night visit from my asshole dad.

I know he found out I was away with friends, which is what led him here that night. I haven't decided yet if this was out of spite, all to ruin the one weekend away I tried to allow myself or if he was simply taking advantage of my absence.

He's a sick piece of shit with no regard for the woman he once loved and married and had a son with. If she dies, he inherits all her fortune because while they're divorced, he's still in her will and I can't convince her to change it.

Fuck it.

I tip my hand, letting the poison spill into the sink, running the water to wash them into the disposal, but I don't turn it on and risk waking her.

I'll pay for this later, one way or another, but I'll deal with it as it comes.

As quietly as possible, I open the slider door, grabbing the bag to take it out so it doesn't stink up the whole house by morning.

I make it halfway to the can when Demi's voice breaks through the silence of the evening, and I pause in place.

"Are you joking?" Demi laughs, scornfully.

"I don't know what you're so upset about," her ma fires back.

"It's the seventh of the month, Mom."

"I'm aware, thank you."

"How have you already spent all your alimony?" Demi questions. "This makes six months now you've asked me to give you money. Dad's driving into town next weekend to visit. He's going to ask me where it all went. We always go over my finances when he's here. I had a savings started he was helping me build. Now I don't. How am I supposed to explain this? He already called me when you overdrew my card last time, you know, when you took it without even telling me?"

"You'll say not a word, Demi. Tell him you're a typical teenager who loves to shop and go out to fancy lunches and things. Tell him you want to live the life he promised us when you were five."

"You mean the life *you* live, the life he promised *you* that he worked his ass off to give you while you sat back constantly telling him it wasn't enough?!" Demi shouts, but I'd almost say anger is absent from her tone. "I don't want to live like you. I don't *need* to."

"You have no idea what life is. You're going to be hit with a rude awakening one day and see it all through my eyes." There's a long pause before her mom continues. "It's no wonder you lost the boy to that floozy friend of yours."

Whoa, what?

"Don't start."

"Then wake up before it's too late, and she ends up pregnant or something stupid!"

"I don't understand what you're playing at, Mom. You give me your little speech that comes after *every* outing with Clara, before you go, and then you approach Nico about me, for what? To make sure I have a back-up plan you can't stick your nose up at?" Sarcasm drips from her words, but more so than that, she sounds tired. Fed up with . . . life, maybe. Like me.

"I have every right to worry about the wellbeing of my daughter. If I have to intervene in areas, I will. I spoke to Krista's father before the party, we had a long conversation and he shared he sees a lot of the young man," her mother says in a plummy voice. "I wasn't aware he and Trent were such great friends."

"What?"

"It wasn't a big deal, I kindly asked him if he could ensure the boy's room was beside yours, is all."

Good looking out, lady.

"Of course you did," Demi says monotone. "What did you say to Nico, Mom? That your daughter is weak and needy because she wishes her mom would be around more?"

"You act as if you don't enjoy the freedom you have."

"What did you say to him?"

"All I asked was for him to make sure you were safe since you went alone. I have to say, he was rather eager."

"You're ridiculous."

"It was only a little fun I thought I'd try out, some healthy competition to see if we could evoke jealousy."

"You . . . *what?!*"

"Honey, we have to get the ball rolling."

"It's never going to happen. Like ever. You're insane and you don't listen to anything I say!"

My head tugs back.

What the fuck are they talking about?

"You know what," Demi adds after a long second, defeat driving her words. "I don't know why I asked, I should be thanking you."

"That's what I keep trying to tell you." The smug smile in her mother's tone is easily caught.

She didn't pick up on her daughter's hurt *at all*.

Does she even know her?

"No, I mean I should thank you for talking to Nico."

Silence stretches a moment, so I move closer to the fence until I can see through.

There's a tight crease at the edge of her mom's eyes. "What do you mean by that?"

"Me and Nico, we had fun at Krista's party and we've been having fun since."

Her mom lifts her head, squares her shoulders. "That . . . is great then. He's a fine boy, promising athlete."

Demi shakes her head and the two stare at each other before her mom speaks again.

"Right, well, I'll be—"

"Back in a few days even though this is the first I've seen you since you got home last night?" Demi finishes for her, an unexpected helplessness woven in her words. "Yeah, Mom, I know the drill."

She stares at Demi a moment before giving a small nod. "There're groceries in the fridge you can make something

168

with. I'll be grabbing your card from your wallet on my way out."

Her mom disappears into the house, while Demi drops her head back to look at the sky.

With a defeated sigh, she sets her phone on the lounger and walks to the edge of the pool. She steps out, penciling straight into the water with every piece of clothing still on.

I wait for her to pop up, almost to the point where I'm ready to scale the fucking fence and dive in to get her when finally a mess of blonde emerges. A deep gasp follows, but she doesn't climb out.

She lays back, floating there with her eyes closed, a tense expression covering her forehead, water wafting over her mouth as she uses only her nose to breathe.

Quietly, I open the connecting gate, finding her lock was never put back on, and walk through.

Her eyes pop open immediately, a deep frown taking over her face when she spots me looking down at her as I tug off my shoes.

She allows her body to drop, now swimming in place, only her head sticking out of the water, her eyes following my hands as I pull my shirt over my head before meeting mine.

Only when my belt clinks against my thigh, does her gaze fall to my jeans. I kick them off, quickly toss my socks, and then drop to the edge of the pool, slowly allowing my body to slip into the water.

I don't have to move.

Demi swims to me, dipping her mouth beneath the water so only her makeup streaked eyes are showing, the deep blue of the water reflecting in her stare, making the green seem impossibly darker.

Our legs kick against each other's slightly, and simultaneously, we both edge closer to the shallow end, swimming sideways so we're facing one another as we move.

Once I'm able to reach the bottom, I stretch out, grip her by the hoodie and tug her toward me.

Demi already knows what to do – what I want – and her long legs find their way around my waist, bringing her body close.

Her breathing speeds up, now coming in short, quick puffs, her eyes moving between mine several times before she finally allows them to fall to my lips.

"Neek . . ." Her voice is a breathy whisper, and her fingers slide across my neck, skimming up and across my fade. "I don't wanna talk."

I hold in my groan, but my dick twitches against her.

Her eyes fly to mine, fingers spanning out, covering the base of my skull.

Slowly, *torturously* fucking slowly, she brings me closer. My groin tightens when the heat of her mouth brushes mine.

Her eyes close.

"Oh, shit, sorry."

Demi jerks back with less than a second to spare, her head snapping toward the interrupting voice.

Trent stands there, right inside her house with a fuddled expression.

I glare, but then Krista's head pops up around him, a wide smile spreading across her face.

"Hey, girl, hey!" She laughs mischievously. "Should we join you or are you about to get out?"

We were about to fuckin' kiss.

Demi snaps out of it, her limbs fly from mine and she falls back into the water, dunking under to swim to the stairs so she can climb out.

"Damn, girl!" Krista teases. "In your clothes?"

Demi laughs, pulling her soaked hoodie over her head and letting it fall to the ground before wrapping a towel around her.

My dick is as good as limp now, so I'm right behind her, and she passes me a towel.

"What are you guys doing here?" she asks them. "And how'd you get in, did my mom leave the front open?"

"Yeah, it was open. Didn't mean to creep, thought you might want to go eat or something?"

170

I grab my shit off the cement, finding Demi staring at me once I turn back around.

"Want to?" she asks me.

I study her a moment, half expecting her to shy away but she doesn't so much as fidget, so I agree. "Be right back. I need some dry boxers."

She rubs her lips together, nodding.

A gravelly chuckle leaves me, and I tip my chin at Trent before stepping into my yard.

It's only when I get into my room to change that what her mom was saying dawns on me.

Ms. Davenport's first choice for her daughter is my best fucking friend.

A golden boy, both visually and literally – 4.0, scholarship offers, a solid household, and a successful family business to take over when he's done.

Much like the other asshole she thinks she wants.

On paper, I can agree Trent or fuckhead Alex are perfect.

I pull my clothes on and head back to Demi's house.

When I walk in, she's waiting for me, an easiness in her eyes that's new to me.

What her mom fails to realize is being perfect and being perfect for Demi are two *very* different things.

Would she be happy with a carbon copy of herself?

I'm thinkin' not.

Chapter 20
Demi

I can't stop staring at his mouth.

"You literally haven't stopped staring at his mouth," Krista whispers the second the boys walk off.

I laugh, pulling my feet onto the booth seat, and wrapping my hands around my knees.

Way to read my thoughts.

"Be honest. You two haven't fucked yet, have you?" She sets her phone on the table.

I cut a quick glance at Trent and Nico as they order our pizza and drinks. "Why do you say that?"

"Because you're both screaming blue balls."

My mouth drops open and she laughs.

"I'm kidding, but it's cute. You guys are like ready to pounce, but both holding back."

Not holding back enough.

I can't believe I almost kissed him. I straight up climbed him, made the first move and everything, with *no* audience, and he didn't fight me on it!

I'd almost say he wanted it.

Wanted me, for a second anyway.

It was more than that, though.

I know he heard me and my mom, just like I heard him and his dad. That's the problem with connecting yards, your drama is shared with everyone around you, but Nico didn't step through that gate to judge me.

He came over knowing I needed a break from my own mind,

172

something I'm beginning to realize he's all too familiar with thanks to the heavy he deals with in his own home.

That move alone speaks volumes for the boy I used to know and the man he's becoming.

My eyes seek him out, and as if sensing it, Nico glances over his shoulder, his stare locking onto mine.

I was unfair to judge you.

A slow frown begins to form on his face, but Trent grabs his attention and it's washed away. A few seconds later the two start back for our table.

"I say you take him home and find a way to keep him there." Krista pulls me from my thoughts with her whisper, falling against the booth as the boys return.

I shake my head, fighting a smile as Nico drops beside me, and faces forward.

"Sorry I couldn't find my card," I say to Trent, not missing how Nico's head snaps my way. We both know that's a lie, but he doesn't call me out. "Give me the receipt and I'll give you my portion at school or something."

Trent scoffs and Krista rolls her eyes.

"Oh, please." She sips on her straw. "We invited you guys. Like we didn't plan to pay."

"I don't care, I don't want your boyfriend paying for my meals."

"Yeah, well, Nico didn't let me cover it anyway, so if you owe someone, it's *your* boyfriend," Trent says, dropping his arm around the back of the booth so Krista can scoot into him.

"Oooh," Krista teases. "I can give you some ideas for how to work off that debt."

With a light laugh, I look to Nico and slip my tongue between my teeth.

His lips press together in a one-sided grin as his hand lands on my thigh for a playful squeeze.

We rock this role play thing.

The rest of the dinner is spent talking about all the fun and embarrassing things that happened over the weekend.

An hour or two passes and then we're driving home.

My eyes keep sliding Nico's way on the drive and finally he turns his head my way raising a brow like an ass.

I laugh, glancing away right as we pull in front of my house.

Krista hops out to give me a quick hug, whispering in my ear, "Details tomorrow. All of them."

"Shut up and go," I whisper back, making her giggle.

"Nic, take care of my girl, would you?"

"I'll take care of my girl, don't worry." He grabs my hand leading me toward my own house. "'Night, Krista."

I unlock the door as he waves bye, and then it's just me and Nico.

I lead him into the kitchen, pulling out two sodas and holding one up in offering.

He nods, so I move toward the cabinets to take out some glasses.

"Where's your ma?" he asks.

"Gone." I pop back to the fridge, filling the cups with ice. "Where's yours?"

"Sleeping."

"Your dad?" My eyes slide his way.

He shakes his head, not willing to speak on it, not that I expected him to, but it was worth a shot.

I open the can, applying a little too much pressure and the top pops up, the tip jamming into my thumb and leaving a small cut.

"Shit," I hiss, pulling my thumb in and shaking my hand.

"What happened?" Nico walks closer.

I turn on the sink, running it underneath the cold water. "The cap got me, but it looks like a clean little cut."

"Let me see it."

"I'm fine."

"Now, Demi." He doesn't wait for me to show him but grips my wrist and drags my hand to his face. "Yeah, it's not deep, a Band-Aid should do it."

I fight a smirk. "I told you it was fine, but since you insist on helping, get me one from the cabinet above the microwave?"

He walks over, pulling it open.

"The plastic container to the right, grab that," I tell him.

He does and starts digging through it, finding the perfect size for my finger. "You got some Neosporin or something?"

I pull my thumb from the water and pat a paper towel against it. "I don't know. In the drawer maybe? If not, I have another first aid kit in my car."

Nico pulls the drawer open and starts digging around, but suddenly stops.

I shift on my feet when he stands there, unmoving a long moment before slowly looking over his shoulder at me, his body following after a moment.

My eyes tighten, roaming his face before a flash of orange catches my attention and my stare flies to his hand and the small pill bottle held in it.

I dart forward, attempting to snag it from him, but his hand wraps behind him and he stands to his full height, a blank expression masking his thoughts.

"These yours?" he asks, even though I know he read the name printed across the label.

"I don't take them."

"Don't lie," he throws back, the small tablets knocking against the container as he shakes the bottle behind his back. "They're half gone."

"I didn't say I never took them, I said I don't, as in not lately."

Nico doesn't look away, and the longer we stand here the more guilt gnaws at me, the need to explain winning over.

"My mom . . . she doesn't accept mediocre." I shrug. "That was how she made sure she never got it."

"Do *you* feel like you need them, to focus or any other reason?"

"Did they help? Yes. Do I need them? No."

"Then don't take them. You're not a child who doesn't understand what helps you and what doesn't. Don't let anyone control what you put in your body." He brings the pill bottle around, grabs my hand and sets it inside. He leans against the counter. "Throw them away."

My head tugs back and then it hits me.

Pills.

The night he argued with his dad in the yard, he accused him of getting his mom addicted to pills.

Is that why she's asleep now?

Is she always asleep?

There's an angry sense of helplessness slipping over him, one he can't control or can't hide. One that has me removing the lid off the container and dumping them into the sink. I wash them down with the soda I cut myself on and grab another, pop the top and pour.

I turn to Nico, passing him a cup. "I haven't taken them since finals last year," I offer quietly. "It was never about addiction. It was appeasing my mother, which I guess is sort of what I was addicted to."

For what seems like a lifetime, he stares, but finally takes a small drink. His shoulders lower with his glass.

There's a shift in the air, and suddenly the tension in the room is an entirely different kind.

I replay him and I in the water in my mind, and I've got a feeling he's doing the same as his eyes darken before me, the tip of his tongue coming out to tease his bottom lip the slightest bit.

I focus on my drink, his nearness so overwhelming that I lead us into a larger space, my living room.

Tell me why I'm nervous?

"Because your body is leading your mind."

My head snaps to Nico and he chuckles.

"Yeah, you said that out loud."

I laugh anxiously. "I'm sorry I'm a mess. It's been a *day*. I'm so sore from double practices, then this unintentional sharing session we've just had, and the whole my mom's bleeding me dry thing . . ." I trail off, looking at him. "Thanks for not saying anything at dinner."

His eyes narrow in query. "Your friends don't know?"

"That my mom spends more than most people earn in a month in a week?" A dejected laugh escapes. "No, they don't know. They know she's all about her outings but . . ." I shrug.

My friends don't necessarily love my mom, but they don't hate her either, and I'd like to keep it that way. Knowing she takes from me would piss them off and once you lose respect for someone it's really hard to get it back.

I shouldn't care to preserve their feelings toward her, but I do it anyway.

Nico looks around, taking in the picturesque living area that clearly goes unlived-in. "How often is she gone?"

"There's, what, typically thirty days in the month? So, twenty-two, twenty-five."

He frowns. "You're alone more than not."

I turn, focusing on the bland images along the wall. "I don't mind."

"Yeah, you do."

That has me glancing over my shoulder. "What makes you say that?"

"You spend most of your time outside," he says, flicking the ugly tassels dangling from the edge of a couch pillow. "Bet it's because you hate being in here by yourself."

Like you, you mean?

Is he by himself as much as me?

I shrug, trailing the length of the fireplace before I spin and give a roundabout answer. "I'm used to it."

"That's shitty."

"Maybe." I nod, moving us back into safer ground. "But I told you I didn't want to talk about it, remember?"

His chuckle is full of innuendo as he cocks his head, leaning on the edge of an armchair. "Yeah, Little D. I remember."

Okay, not safer ground!

I quickly turn, flipping on the TV as an excuse to look away.

Why do I like him here?

I shouldn't.

Should I?

The light shuffle of Nico's feet should have been expected, he won't accept my holding back. The hairs on the base of my neck stand as my was-steady hand begins to wobble against the remote.

Am I seriously this pent up?

Nico's fingers wrap around mine and he gently takes it from me.

He makes no other move, his breath purposefully cascading over the exposed skin on my shoulders, so I attempt to settle myself and spin to face him.

It must be what he wanted, my attention fully and completely on him — my fake boyfriend I almost real kissed.

He wastes no time, instantly stepping in until the heels of my feet meet the entertainment center.

His hair falls into his eyes, blocking the smallest bit of his face from me.

For some reason, I'm not at all okay with that.

I pull my lips between my teeth, reaching up to brush it away, but my touch is too hesitant for his liking, so he helps apply some pressure, keeping his fingers on mine as he leads them to his neck, dragging them around to trail over his throat where he releases me, allowing my hand to fall to my side.

"You're my girl, right?" he rasps.

"That's what we agreed to . . ."

His glare is quick and he pauses. "The answer is yes, Demi, and since the answer is yes, that means when you touch me, you mean it."

My pulse beats heavy in my throat and I think I nod.

"Know what else it means?" He shuffles closer, one dark brow jacking up. "You can touch me anytime you want, however you want, and I won't stop you."

I free my lips from between my teeth and his eyes darken.

"Because of our arrangement?"

Nico's soft chuckle fans across my mouth and he steps back, tossing the remote to the couch. "No, D. I won't stop you because I'm not a fool . . . or a saint." He shrugs unapologetically.

"Does this mean it's the same for you? You can touch me whenever you want . . . how you want?" My chin lowers, but my eyes stay on his.

He licks his full lips. "You tell me."

What's it mean if the answer feels a lot like a 'yes'?

This is bad, right? I'm not prepared for Nico's hands to have free rein of my body.

Who am I kidding . . . there is no preparing for a guy like him.

Fake feelings or not.

The hint of his grin further proves he's in my head more than he should be. "'Night, D. Keep these doors locked."

"Yes, Dad."

His smirk is slow, and I laugh, pushing him away.

I'm more than happy to end the night on a lighter note.

He starts across the yard, and a question pops in my head.

One I shouldn't ask but can't handle not knowing the answer to.

"Hey, Neek!"

His feet pause in the grass and he glances over his shoulder, nodding his chin.

"Will you make me want it first?" I ask, not spelling out what 'it' could mean.

Knowing him, there's a long list of answers to be named.

Nico's brows jump, but a knowing look quickly replaces his surprise, and in true Nico fashion, he calls me out on my obvious physical response to all that is him.

The corner of his mouth tips up, half his face blanketed by darkness. "As opposed to you, what, D, *not* wanting it?"

And then he's gone.

But the heat in my abdomen isn't.

Nico

I've been lying in bed for over an hour, and sleep is the furthest thing from my mind.

Straight up, I'm in fucking trouble.

I'm not sure what I expected when I flipped the fuck out and threw this idea of faking *us* on her.

Once it was out, there was no taking it back, and the second Hammons saw us together, going easy wasn't an option.

The part had to be played and played well.

I knew people would believe it, that it wouldn't take much effort, but what I didn't anticipate was how easily she'd accept me as hers.

Accept the lie.

I was being real when I told Trent I think she likes this. I told him she was bored, but now I'm realizing it's more than that.

The girl's not only bored, but lonely as hell and that's fucked up.

She's a gorgeous, smart, talented – *single* – girl, with good friends and a lively personality.

People don't get it, how someone with popularity and looks and a gifted ability, loved by many and envied by more can stand before hundreds and feel completely fucking invisible.

I get it.

I was able to read her today with unmistakable, relatable precision.

The starved look in her eyes, the need in her touch, the plea from her body.

She wanted to feel something and decided quickly, I was it.

Had Trent and Krista not interrupted, I'd have let her take what she wanted, giving twice as much in return.

I've imagined what her body would feel like against mine more than I care to admit, how soft her thick, dancer's thighs would be, how quick her heated breaths would come. How quick *she* would come.

I groan, and before I realize it, I'm gripping my dick in my hand, squeezing in an attempt to alleviate the ache.

I scoot up to my headboard, my head falling against it as I begin to stroke myself, the quiet pants from her mouth replaying in my ears. I slide my hand from base to tip, groaning lightly, remembering the greedy way she pulled me to her, and the strength of her legs locked around my body, begging for me to come closer.

An unexpected shock wave rushes down my spine causing my knee to jolt, and I pump faster.

A small flash has my head snapping toward my window in time to catch Demi having just turned off her patio light.

I jump up, moving closer to the glass to see her better.

It's dark as fuck, nothing but the gleam of her white bikini helping me trail her as she lowers herself into her hot tub. The small underwater light kicks on with the jets, and the water starts splashing across her breasts in gentle waves.

With one hand still on my dick, I squeeze, a deep frown marring my forehead as I decide if I should stop.

It's one thing to imagine, it's another to watch her as I work myself.

But then Little D's head turns and tilts the slightest bit, now aimed right at the second floor of my house. At what she knows to be my bedroom.

Adrenaline flares and I place my hand on the frame, leaning over slightly as her head shifts back and forth the littlest bit.

Lookin' for me, baby?

Demi rests against the wall seat and pulls her bottom lip between her teeth. I can't be sure, but I'd swear her legs spread wider beneath the bubbles, the creaminess of her skin no longer centered in the water.

My pulse jumps, my dick, still hard as a rock right there with it when her little hands disappear under the froths.

Her head tilts, exposing her neck some, and fuck me, she keeps her eyes locked this way.

She can't see me; I know this for a fact. My house is pitch fucking black and the moon doesn't shine against the backside of my place as it does hers.

But damn, if it doesn't stop her from trying, or maybe, if she's as much like me as I'm learning, her imagination is doing just fucking fine.

For now.

My features pull, and it's done.

If I had any chance of stopping before, I don't now.

My grip tightens, my dick swelling even more, flexing in my palm.

She must like a slow start as she's calm and relaxed, her forearm hardly moving so I follow her lead in secret, with slow and measured movements, squeezing every few strokes to add some extra pressure.

Demi shifts, both her feet coming up to plant on the concrete seat near her sides. Her legs are so damn long the new position has her knees completely out of the water, giving me a tiny glimpse of how fun her flexibility could be.

When her other hand moves to grip her own neck, I fall forward, my arm now holding me up as I jerk harder, faster.

My hips jolt forward, a deep groan leaving me as heat spreads through my veins.

Her head falls all the way back and her lips part, her chest rising above the steam as she gasps into the air.

I imagine the sounds escaping as her hand trails lower, slipping under the tiny white scrap of material covering her breasts. She massages herself, her core lifting in the water as she fights for her release.

Come on, baby.

Demi's legs stiffen, shooting down into the water as her chin falls to her chest, and I swear I can feel her fuckin' trembling from here.

My toes curl into the carpet and squeeze, my free hand flying down to catch the cum she unknowingly pulls from me, my shoulder knocking into the window.

A shockwave shoots through me and my muscles clench tight before everything in me relaxes.

I drop my head against the glass.

I just got off with Demi Davenport, but she hasn't the slightest fucking clue.

And me? I have not an ounce of fucking guilt for it.

None.

Chapter 21
Nico

She's been straight smiles and happy sighs all day.

Not that she's ever overly bitchy, but her 'good mornings' and 'hey, how's it going' are on overkill.

"Okay, so I'll take care of the definitions if you want to find what pages the diagrams are on? It'll help save time when we have to reference back." Demi tilts her head, looking over her notes.

When I don't respond, her eyes swing to mine.

I know I look curious as fuck, which is confirmed when she frowns. "What's wrong?"

I got off with you last night and you have no idea and now you're peppy as fuck and I can't help but wonder—

"Earth to Nico?" She laughs.

Another obvious sign she's not her typical self this morning. Normally, she'd roll her eyes at me.

Girl's smiling.

"When's the last time you had sex?"

Her eyes shoot wide, quickly darting around the classroom before coming back to me. Her voice is low and squeaky when she asks, "What?"

I drop my pencil on the tabletop, twisting in my seat to face her better. "You say you're not a virgin." I lean in, speaking lower, "So, when was the last time you fucked?"

She studies me a moment, her green eyes slowly moving between mine. "Why?"

When I don't let up, she inhales deeply, offering a hesitant, "Awhile."

"How long is *awhile* to you, D?"

"How long is it to you?" she challenges, her attempt to delay.

"I haven't had sex since the last time you watched it happen, and it feels like a fucking year's passed. *Especially* now."

A hint of confusion lines her brows before she realizes what I'm saying — *she* is making it harder.

Literally, though.

She fights a grin, looking away, but I quickly pull her eyes back to mine.

We're in class, people are all around, so every touch counts.

"You haven't given me much," I whisper, running my fingertip down her jawline. "Tell me."

She licks her lips, her focus deepening before a light chuckle leaves her. "You're really good at this," she murmurs.

Now it's me who laughs and I let my hand fall. "I'm just sayin', I think I deserve it."

"Oh, boo hoo," she teases, shaking her head, but then she must think for a long moment because she gives in. "Sophomore year and don't make fun. Not everyone is the same and needs it the way other people do."

I heard nothing after sophomore year.

Two years ago.

She hasn't fucked in two years.

"When did you lose your virginity?"

She tilts her head, giving me a bratty glare that says it all.

That was her first time.

"One person?"

She nods.

"Multiple times?"

"Oh my god, Nico. Stop." She looks around.

There are eyes moving around the room, but nobody is sidled up beside us listening. Mr. Brando isn't even in here; he left Josie in charge and walked out.

I tug her chair closer, laughing when she scowls as it scrapes loudly across the floor and more people glance our way.

She smacks my arms, but I grab her hand, and she rolls her eyes yanking it back.

We get back to working on our assignment, a few quiet minutes passing, and then she clears her throat, admitting in a whisper, "Twice."

We turn toward each other, and a light blush creeps up her neck.

I know what she *assumes* I'm thinking, how she's inexperienced, possibly incapable of pleasing a guy, or at the very least would have a lot to learn.

She's wrong, so wrong.

She's an empty playbook.

"It's gonna hurt when you fuck again."

The head of her pencil finds its way between her teeth. "What makes you say that?"

"Two times, two years ago, and likely with another first timer who doubtfully made you come, and probably didn't thoroughly stretch you out, too afraid to hurt you. You're basically a virgin."

I expect her to blush harder, pull away and shut this down. She doesn't.

She leans in, tilting her head up to mine, her long, dark blonde hair falling over her shoulders, and smirks.

My eyes narrow.

"Oh, Nico," she sing-songs, eyes gleaming. "You think you're so sly, don't you?"

"What are you talkin' about, Pixie?"

"This sudden conversation, the real reason behind it. The extra, *obviously noticeable*, pep in my step today." She doesn't let me speak, but straightens her back, and slides off her seat. She comes to stand behind me, drapes her arms around my shoulders and places her lush lips covered in a shiny gloss today at my ear. "You think I'm not as human as you are? You asked when I last had sex. Let me ask you, when was the last time you *came?*" she whispers. "Could it have been maybe last night . . . like me?"

When my chest rumbles, her husky laugh fans across my cheek.

She decides to kill me even more with her next purred words.

"Yes, Nico. I was pent up. Yes, fake boyfriend, I had a sudden need to take care of myself last night for the first time in months. And yes, *baby*, it was all. Your. Fault." She embellishes every word. "Now, your jeans are getting a little tight, so stay in that seat of yours . . . or show the class what little, born again virgin me does to big, bold, *overworked* you."

She pats me on the shoulder and walks to the front of the room. She doesn't ask Josie's permission, but snags the bathroom pass from the wall and disappears out the door.

Fuck me if my starved stare doesn't track her ass every step until she's gone, but as my eyes slide back, it's Alex's they catch.

He keeps his face neutral while I can't, and an instant glower takes over. Slowly, he pushes to stand.

The little bitch grabs the male pass and off he fucking goes.

In my peripheral, I catch Josie's head snapping my way as I shoot to my feet, but as quick as I'm standing, the bitter and cold reality freezes me in place.

The asshole chasing her tail is the one she claims to want riding it.

She might want him on a normal day, but no matter the reason, last night she wanted me.

The thought knocks my ass back to the cheap wooden stool, but the next is the only thing keeping it planted.

I can work with that.

Demi

Holy shit! I just admitted to masturbating to the thought of my fake boyfriend to my fake boyfriend.

I drop my head against the bathroom mirror, shaking it a moment as a light laugh escapes.

I wash my hands and then give myself a minute to stand there and think, but it takes no kind of convincing.

Plain and simple?

I like Nico.

I'm *attracted* to Nico, and who the hell wouldn't be?

He's tall with strong shoulders and muscular arms, a small tattoo under his forearm adding a little mystery, not that it's needed. His dark, dangerous eyes are enough to pull anyone in, and with sexy, perfectly messy hair to match, full lips and bright smile, he's more than easy on the eyes and enticing to the body.

Only, he's so much more than what you get at first glance.

I'm slowly starting to learn who he really is, and Nico Sykes is beyond what I knew him to be.

A few weeks ago, he was nothing but the guy to the left who loved to stare, glare, and then glanced away. The seemingly too cool for school guy who disappeared whenever I was near. Or at least, that's how it felt.

Now, though, I know better than to assume who's behind the mask he gives so many of us.

Nico is witty and daring. He's athletic and determined, and the most surprising to me, as judgmental as it might make me seem, compassionate.

He's supposed to be a stranger to me, yet he showed up as if he knew I hated the feeling I was left with every time my mother walks out the door, leaving me behind like I'm no longer important enough for her to care for.

Every day I discover something new about the guy, none of which I don't like. That's the scariest part.

Yes, he's moody, but I can handle it, and honestly, I think he enjoys when I challenge his snappy attitude. Sometimes he shuts down completely and without warning, but so far, he's always come out of his funk. It's sort of part of his appeal, not knowing what you're going to get, but being okay with it either way.

He's exciting and unpredictable and temporarily mine.

What the hell am I supposed to do with all this?

And how the hell did things shift so quickly?

Nico didn't agree to the idea of more, he agreed to pretend.

This is a problem because I no longer want to fake date Nico.

I sort of want to keep him.

Would he ever be open to the idea of keeping me?

As if the universe couldn't allow me to wonder a little longer, I exit the bathroom to find Alex standing right outside, waiting.

I stutter step, offering a tight smile, and go to walk on by, but he reaches out to stop me.

"Hey, running off so fast?" He chuckles.

I give an anxious smile. "Sorry."

It shouldn't feel wrong simply standing here talking to the guy, yet it does in every way.

I'm so screwed.

"What's the rush?" He grins.

"I've been gone a few minutes too long." I give a light laugh.

"I think your ninety-eight percent in the class can afford you a few extra for bathroom breaks."

"Ninety-nine, but who's counting," I joke.

"Right." He chuckles.

"I better go." I edge away.

"Yeah, yeah. For sure."

I give a small wave and head back, but he catches up to me before I round the corner.

"Demi, hang on a minute."

I hesitate but then turn around. "What's up?"

"I forgot to ask. I need a little help with the routine for homecoming."

I straighten at the mention of my team. "Oh, right. You can ask—"

"You're the main girl, right?" he cuts me off.

"I'm center, front line, basically, but we're still a team."

"You think you could help me out? After I get out of practice maybe?"

"Oh." Shit.

Well, if this isn't a clear ass sign, I've officially switched teams.

"Sorry, but that's not really a good idea," I tell him, not missing the way his eyes tighten. "But hey, we haven't started practicing with you guys yet. I'm sure you'll be fine after this week."

"Well, your coach, who is really young by the way." He feels the need to add for some reason. "She mentioned we should practice now."

"If you really want to, Alex, I'm sure Katy would be happy to help you," I mention his partner.

"Yeah, but I don't have her number." He reaches out to grab my hand. "Help me out?"

I stare at him a minute and the gorgeous green of his eyes I used to daydream about only weeks ago. Suddenly they look more like seaweed than shiny emeralds.

I gently pull my hand from his.

His eyes harden the slightest bit.

"Sorry, I can't, but I'll text Katy and ask her to find you."

I leave him standing in the hall with a staggered expression.

I walk around the corner, skidding to a stop when Nico is leaning there, his hands in his pockets, head tilted down, glare focused on the linoleum beneath his feet.

Slowly, and only with his eyes, he glances up, gauging me.

My stomach warms, and I feel the tension surrounding him, but the longer he stares, the more his features smooth. Still, he doesn't give me much.

Sliding his shoulder against the wall, he moves closer until I'm only a foot's space away. His hand slips into my hair, his focus now on my lips.

I keep my arms locked at my sides, my toes curling in my flats, fingers digging into my skirt as he leans in.

Waiting.

But he doesn't kiss me.

As soon as the disappointment stirs in my gut, the warmth of his lips press down against the throbbing pulse of my neck, creating a deeper kind of heat, and my eyes close.

He has to feel it, right?

The way it kicked up the second his hands landed on me, only to grow faster and faster with every breath I took.

My control begins to break, and I'm about to yank him to me, when his mouth finally lands on mine.

I open for him and he shifts closer, his hand digging into my hair with a gentle tug.

My arms wrap around his neck, tugging him in and his chest vibrates against mine causing my nipples to harden behind my bra.

"Damn, D," he rasps, his mouth pressing back to mine a second later.

He shifts, nudging my back into the small cut out of the wall when the squeak of footsteps across freshly polished floors passes.

Nico's mouth falls from mine in the same second, his breathing out of control.

He eyes me a moment, then cuts a quick stare over his shoulder, at the back of Alex's retreating body.

The reason for the show.

The warmth of Nico's body disappears, but he grips my hand and pulls me back to class, leaving a small piece of me in that empty hallway without even realizing it.

I don't talk much the rest of the period, a question spinning in my mind the entire time.

What happens when this show's over?

Chapter 22
Demi

Miranda takes a drink from her water bottle, setting it on the floor before she claps to get our attention. "Okay, that was halfway decent, but I do need to make some changes. A few of the pairings just . . . aren't working," she announces, her eyes instantly meeting mine. "Demi, partner with Mr. Rodriguez."

I look to Trent who is focused on Nico.

"Gina, you're dismissed," she tells the JV girl she had dancing with Trent. "I'll let you know what I need from you later."

Nico's chest presses against my back in defiance, and I glance at him over my shoulder.

But wait . . .

I look to Miranda. "I'll be teaching Nico and Trent then?"

"I'll make sure Nico is taken care of." I don't like the way she smiles as she says it. "And I'll assign him a new partner after I make a decision."

"I can teach him what he needs to know."

Several heads swivel our direction at my instant and accidentally argumentative tone.

Miranda's eyes narrow. "Fall in line, Demi. Ten seconds to start."

I pick up my towel and water, ready to walk off, but Nico jerks me back with a scowl.

"What are you doing?" he snaps.

"What she told me to."

He glares, his eyes focused over my shoulder and narrowing. "Tell her no," he says almost too low to be heard.

192

"She's the coach in this room, Nico. Would you tell yours no on the field?"

"Now, Mr. Sykes," Miranda says with a hint of a threat.

His jaw tics, a harsh breath escaping through his nose.

He's pissed, and he doesn't bother hiding it as he glances at me, only to jerk right past me. Slowly, he makes his way toward her.

Trent ends up at my side, so I set my items back down and we work in the spot I started.

He scratches the back of his neck, glancing around. "Sorry."

"Not your fault," I tell him, spinning around and getting into position, my back to his front.

"We'll run through it once more as a group," Miranda shouts. "Then work independently with your partner to make sure they're doing as expected, perfect what you can, ladies. We only get them for twenty minutes at a time."

Just as she says, we go one more round, cutting after the sliding walk — we don't show them a single step from our actual routine that will follow.

Trent is a quick learner so we're basically chatting as we repeat the steps in slow counts to keep going like we're busy. It's not as if the boys have a whole lot to do other than hold on and follow our movements. They aren't dancing with us, it's just a presentation welcoming them onto the field, and then it's our routine.

As much as I try not to, I repeatedly glance toward the end of the gym, where Miranda and Nico practice independently.

I can't look away as she starts from step one again, foolish frustration flaring when Miranda drops in front of him.

His eyes following her form as she slowly lifts has me looking away.

"Your coach is a trip."

A laugh leaves me and my eyes widen mockingly. "Yeah. I like to joke she's a stripper at night and sometimes lets it show in here for fun."

"She probably is." He laughs. "No way she can afford to live how she does on a coach's salary."

"Trust me, she's making money." I look to him. "She dances for Jay Productions."

"The record label?"

I nod. "Yep, she's their top dancer. Featured in over a dozen videos this year alone."

"Damn." He nods, impressed.

I squint their way, finding Miranda smiling and pushing on Nico's chest. "Yep."

"Are you jealous?"

My head snaps toward him. "What's with the tone of surprise lately, Trent?"

"Shit," flies from him, but he recovers quickly, his expression smoothing out. "I meant seeing another chick on your man like that. Does that make you jealous?"

I look back to the two, tracking Miranda's hands as she reaches behind her to grip Nico's, and places them a little too high on her middle.

I swallow and turn back to Trent.

"No," I lie. "Chemistry, sexuality, it's all a part of what we do as dancers. People have to believe what they're seeing. It's our job to make sure they do."

If he doesn't believe me, he doesn't say so, instead going with, "Not sure I could handle it if Krista was doing this instead of cheer."

"Yeah," I frown. "I imagine it can be a lot."

Like right now, for example.

"Demi . . ." Trent trails off, gaining my attention.

"What?"

He eyes me a moment, before shaking his head. "Nah, nothing. Let's keep going."

So, we do.

The rest of the day I'm stuck with a headache I can't get rid of and end up going straight home to sleep it off, not waking up until my alarm rings for school the next morning.

*

The second I walk into dance class; I'm tempted to walk right back out.

Miranda and Nico are the only two in the gym, both tucked in the back corner, only half the lights turned on for some stupid reason and providing them with too much privacy for my liking.

I stand there, frozen, watching as she drops in front of him, then rolls her way back up his body. When she spins, walking out with his hand in hers, the last move that involves the boys, I begin to step the rest of the way through the doors, but the music continues to play, and Miranda keeps fucking dancing.

She twists her knees left, her elbows locked and shifted right, then as she jumps up, her stance widening as she tugs her jacket open, revealing her sports bra beneath it – the move I choreographed to go with the lettermen's jackets we'll be wearing at the beginning of our performance.

I look to Nico, who while his eyes are pointed in her direction, wears a deep frown.

Slowly, his feet move toward her, and just as slowly she walks into him. Her hands slide across his chest, as his move down her ribs, gripping her hips so he can tug her forward.

That's not part of their entrance.

"Damn," is whispered in my ear, and my head jerks over my shoulder to find Alex. He's watching them. "Guess you weren't the only one asked for a private lesson."

I look back to the two.

"Shit, I'm sorry, Demi. I wasn't—"

"It's fine," I whisper.

Why am I whispering?

Why not go right in, make my presence known?

"Wanna go somewhere?" Alex offers, his hand finding my lower back. "I doubt you really want to stand here and watch this."

I don't answer, but lift my bag in the air, letting it go when it's well over my head to ensure it hits with a loud, echoed thud across the near empty gym.

Miranda, I would think, would fly away from the student whom she has her filthy hands all over. She doesn't.

Nico either.

He locks in place, a hard glare taking over as his hands slowly fall to his sides.

But his eyes, they aren't on me.

They're on the guy beside me, or more, the hand still fixed on my back.

"Hey." Miranda laughs, dropping her palm to Nico's chest, officially forcing my attention back to her. She looks to the clock quickly. "Early as always."

"As always."

Her eyes pull, but then she shifts her focus to Alex. "You should have told me it was Demi you've been meeting early. I totally would have asked the janitor to open up for you guys. Seems you found a private place to practice, though. Awesome."

I grow stiff. "What—"

Alex's sudden closeness has me stopping short. I frown, having not even realized he and I walked farther inside.

"Yeah, we're good. Just finished up actually," he lies, tipping his chin as if asking me to go with it.

Is he crazy?

The tension in the air is so thick, it takes me a second to react.

I take a step out, away from Alex and look to Nico, who knows I turned Alex down when he asked for help.

I'm the one missing something here, not him.

I look to Miranda. "You can get your hand off him now."

Shock flashes across her without her control, but she covers it with a glare just as quick.

As if he hadn't noticed before this moment she was touching him, Nico's eyes slice to the contact and he shoves her off. He studies her a moment, then his head snaps toward Alex, and something passes between them.

Nico steps toward him, but I slide in the middle, positioning myself directly in front of Nico, and nothing but rage glares back as he looks at me.

His features are hard, the cuts of his jaw more profound as he clenches it, the cords of his neck raised and tight.

He might be mad, but so am I, and I glare right back.

Show her, Neek.

I tip my chin the slightest bit.

Nico's forehead pulls, but then it dawns on him, and his hand slips into my hair at the base of my skull, his lips lowering to mine.

It's a short, quick skim, but it's effective enough.

For now.

I reach up, sliding my fingers across his, my eyes moving over his shoulder to a pissed off Miranda.

"I'm going to run to the restroom. Should I . . . I don't know, maybe wake the place up on my way out or are you wanting the class to practice in this shadowed, burlesque type lighting you've got going on?"

It comes out with more of a bite and I'm glad for that.

Her eyes narrow, but she finally snaps out of it, and realizing she should have some tact, or at least be more careful in the school gym with a student when technically she's a teacher, she offers a tight smile.

"You can turn them on." She starts backward, her narrowed gaze sliding to Nico. "Help me grab—"

"Just," I cut her off, tugging Nico with me. "*Don't.*"

I don't wait for her response, if she gives one, but pull Nico out the door with me all to drop his hand and storm into the bathroom a door down.

I'm so fucking annoyed and pissed, and an array of other things I don't even want to think about right now.

My dance coach? Is he that careless?

This is someone I have to work with for the entire school year. It's not like we announced to her that we were dating – fake dating – but based off how he came right to me the first day, the interest was at least laid out in front of her and the rest of my team. To make matters worse, Alex, who acted like an ass just now and *does* know us to be together, saw the same thing I did.

It's embarrassing.

It's so much more than embarrassing.

Taking a deep breath, I step in front of the mirror, staring directly into my own eyes.

What the hell are you doing, Demi?

A mocking chuckle escapes and I shake my head.

It would be so easy to stand here and play the comparison game, but I'm not going to do that. I'm happy with who I am, with my body and skill set. Miranda and her scandalous tactic this morning has nothing to do with the anxiety building in my chest right now.

This is all about Nico, who steps through the door behind me.

Nico shifts closer, his body now aligned with the mirror as he stands only a few paces back, and a single step to the left, eyes on mine, a heavy hostility surrounding him.

"Demi." The bridled anger in his voice has my own returning.

"Are you in need of a hall pass, Nico?" I snap.

Shock flashes across his face, but fury quickly takes its place. "Are you fucking kidding me?"

"Answer the question."

He scoffs, looking away quickly only to come right back. "She told me to come here early, said we had to start going over the rest of this shit. I had no fuckin' clue it would only be us. You really think I'd be here if I did?"

I stare, forcing the possibilities flaring in my gut at bay.

He shakes his head and charges for the door, but pauses with it half open, his eyes finding mine in the mirror once more. "Is this your game, how you wanna play it so you can go fuck Alex and call it a draw? Or maybe you two just slipped outta his backseat before you walked in the gym, with his fuckin' hands on you!" he lashes out as he tosses the door open and exits.

I whip around to chase him out and the few feet down he's gotten, hastily forcing my words past clenched teeth. "I am not you, and I'm sure as hell not *Josie*."

His muscles lock tight and he freezes in place.

After a long moment, his chin tips over his shoulder, only half his face visible to me, but it's enough for me to know that was the wrong thing to say, also noticing he doesn't exactly look shocked I know about what she did to him.

I cross my arms. "Alex is a fucking liar. I don't know why he tried to make it sound like I helped him, and I don't know why he's here early, but it wasn't to meet me. I turned him down, Nico. You heard it with your own ears."

Something shifts and he keeps me locked in his gaze until he disappears into a classroom door a few feet ahead.

My heart beats out of control as I follow.

I only make it a foot through and then he has me pinned.

His voice is low, not a hint of cruelty laced within his tone, though the words he chooses seem to be. "You realize I need no hall pass to fuck whoever I want, right?" His nose brushes mine briefly. "But, tell me something, would my sticking my dick in someone else not bother you none? 'Cause all that, D, everything you just said to me in there, it tasted a lot like jealousy, so I'm thinking it would."

When I don't speak, he lifts his head, looking me in my eyes.

I am jealous. Completely.

"Why did she have attitude toward you the first day of practice?" I demand.

"Because I fucked her this summer," he admits instantly.

My shoulders fall and I try to look away, but he doesn't allow it, shifting to stay in my line of sight.

"I haven't touched her since, and I have no fuckin' plans to. She was good with it when it ended, I don't know why she's acting like a fool right now."

I'm not sure if this is supposed to make me feel better or not, but it doesn't.

He didn't exactly do anything wrong, so I'm not mad at him, but I am mad at the entire situation.

As if reading the thought the second it crossed my mind, Nico cocks his head to the side, whispering, "Tell me you're not as dumb as you are blind?"

"I don't know what that means."

He nods, allowing his hands to fall before he steps back. "Then I guess the answer is yes, D."

With that, he walks out and I'm left wondering what wrong turn I took to get here, falling for the guy who only promised me a lie.

I'm a zombie the rest of the day, and thankfully we're watching a film in chem so talking isn't necessary.

I skip my after school dance practice for the first time in all my four years, because fuck Miranda, and head straight home.

I'm showered and lying on my bed within minutes, left with nothing but my thoughts to further ruin the day.

The light knock on my door a couple hours later has me pushing up on my elbow.

My mom opens the door and walks in, her lips pursed in an unpleasant smile.

At this point, I'm already emotionally spent. I'm prepared for her words, whatever they might be, another trip announcement probably, but when her mouth smooths out, concern lining her forehead as much as the Botox allows, my bottom lip begins to tremble.

"Demi . . ." she whispers, a softness I haven't heard from her in . . . I don't even remember when, but she hasn't seen me like this . . . ever.

She steps closer.

And I break.

I cry for no real reason other than fear of what hasn't even happened yet.

Surprising me even further, my mom doesn't say what she came in here for, but instead sits on the edge of my bed.

She doesn't speak, doesn't touch me like a normal mother would feel comfortable enough to, but she doesn't get up either.

She's there when I fall asleep but gone when I wake.

It was enough.

I push to my feet and move toward the closet to grab some clothes.

I take my time getting ready, having no intention of getting to school early today. My mind is overworked and an anxious mess.

How I allowed myself to get to this point, I don't know, but if I'm sure of one thing, it's that I should give myself some room to breathe.

I need to distance myself from Nico because . . .

When he says it's time to break, I just might.

He and I, we're nothing.

Fake as the smile I'll wear today.

Apparently, I even lie to myself now.

Once I'm ready to go, I grab my phone and my backpack and make my way downstairs, and sitting there, beside a slightly melted iced coffee is a note.

Prep for finals begins today.

But the words aren't where my focus lies, it's on the little pill that sits on top of the paper.

I take the stupid thing.

Chapter 23
Demi

I left my phone at home and went to all my classes without a word to anyone in between, but then when it was time for chemistry, my nerves were through the roof. So, instead of going to class, I walked up to the office and cashed in on my performance card for the first time since freshman year. I used the class pass, went into the open study hall room and worked on reviewing in there.

I'm pretty sure the office staff caught on to my off day, though, when I suddenly had a stomachache during my lunch period, one that was miraculously better when the following class began.

Thankfully, my last one of the day is teacher's aide, so I'm already allowed to leave five minutes prior to the bell every day, but I decide to slip out a few early. All so I can jump in my car and take off before anyone spots me.

I know the girls, and they'll sense something is off the second they lay eyes on me and I can't exactly explain what's going on without giving up mine and Nico's secret and I'm not ready for that.

So, to kill time and make sure they can't seek me out, I drive to the coffee shop across town and study until my eyes begin to burn.

It's almost six-thirty when I look at my watch, and I know the girls have called me at least a half dozen times by now with it being game night.

Other than the few away games the girls' squad didn't travel to over the years, there hasn't been a single game I've missed.

Carley and I are always around to cheer them on. Now, if you add in my *boyfriend* being on the team, I'm expected even more to be loud and proud and present.

I won't be today. At least, not where they can see.

Not when I know Miranda will be there trying to get attention.

She said she needed to get a better idea of space for proper placement since the gym is more wide than narrow like the field and apparently being there with her handy little GoPro for cheer's half-time performance will help with that.

I let out a heavy exhale.

The last thing I need right now is to be angry with an instructor of mine. Of course she's hot for Nico.

He's an eighteen-year-old high school senior with the body of an NFL star and the allure of Hollywood's finest.

Still, I want to tell her to fuck off and find a new center who can do what I can. I have my normal dance studio and team, and if I didn't need this on my college applications, I might not even go back.

Shaking off the annoyance, I park on the backside of the school so I can walk the long way around the building and slip into the library.

I take the stairs Nico led me up when he shared his spot with me, not bothering to move toward the edge of the rooftop this time but drop into the chair Nico sat in the day we were up here together.

I drop my Gatorade and survey the sky as the sun begins to set while I wait for the game to start.

Sure enough, right when the wind blows in, and the summer night's air hits, I can only faintly hear Mr. Freeman's voice float across the field as he announces the game.

Thankfully, I have perfect vision, so when I move closer, I can make out each jersey.

Not that number 24 allows himself to be missed.

After the National Anthem ends, the team captains take the field for the coin toss, and then it's game time – Spartans set to receive.

I stay there, on the edge of the roof, my eyes trailing Nico's every move. Before I realize it, it's halftime, and the team gathers at the far right of their endzone.

The cheer squads walk out, meeting in the middle, before they run over to the opposite side to watch as the visiting team performs before switching back for their turn.

I smile when they give a small booty pop and point to the crowd, fighting the urge to clap when it's over even though there's no one around to hear me if I did.

My joy is short lived, frustration taking its place as Miranda keeps her stupid camera pointed forward and walks for the guys.

They're just beginning to stand and snap their helmets back in place as she approaches.

Of course, she makes her way around the group, pausing when she's only feet from Nico.

And just like that, I'm over the game.

I take the stairs two at a time, making my way to the studio room.

The lights are all off, but the door is open, so I go right in, taking a few minutes to set up the sound system. Right when I get it ready to hit play, a voice catches me from behind, and I jump.

The janitor stands there with a frown. "Ms. Davenport?"

I smile meekly. "Sorry, Jan. I was hoping to get in some extra work if that's okay?"

She nods, lifting a shoulder as she glances around. "Well, I haven't hit this room yet, and I've got at least fifteen more to go, so I don't see why not. Just be sure to leave it how you found it?"

"Thanks." I smile, turning back to the stereo when she walks away.

I kick my shoes off, toss my sweater beside them and press play.

I face the mirror, wait for the bass to hit, and then I let go.

Nico

I drop my shoulder, running right through the defender who comes in for the tackle.

Too high, asshole, gotta go for the legs.

The safety dropped back, so it's only him and I left, or so I thought.

I'm blindsided by some prick who slipped passed his block and I slam to the turf with a groan.

I jump up, leaving the ball where I landed and push off the guy who attempts to pat me on the back.

That's when I notice the flag that was thrown, and we're hit with a penalty.

Thirty-yard carry, fucking busted.

I jog to the huddle and spit out my mouthpiece. "What the hell happened?"

"Personal foul." Trent turns to Thompson. "I don't give a shit about your beef with that guy out there, let it go. You just cost us Nic's yards, and another fucking fifteen." His glare quickly flies to me. "You, chill the fuck out, too. Don't go gettin' another fuckin' flag."

"Fuck you, roll out."

He scowls but calls off the next play and we're back in formation.

I'm wide open, but Trent throws the ball to Alex.

The bitch catches it, taking it down to the twenty-yard line.

He jumps up, knocking shoulders with Thompson, smirking as he passes by me.

His eyes cut to the stands on his way back, and fuck if mine don't do the same.

Carley sits there, and as if she knows I'm looking at her, she lifts her hand.

Still no Demi.

But as my eyes move down the bleachers, they freeze.

My dad sits there, clapping his fucking hands, while simultaneously shaking his head.

"Nic!"

My head snaps forward and I hustle back to the huddle.

Everyone breaks, but I stick back when Trent does.

"What the fuck's wrong with you?"

"You've got a big fuckin' mouth, that's what," I spit and he glares. "Give me the ball."

"No," he snaps. "Line up."

"Trent—"

"You're hot headed, clearly pissed about something." The coach shouts for us to hurry up in the background. "I'm not risking a fucking pick because you wanna showboat."

"My dad's here."

Trent's eyes cut to mine and he curses.

"Get to the fucking ball and stop being a prick," he growls, and we rush into position before a delay of game is called.

I go out for the pass, jumping up and over the safety who hung deep.

I catch the ball, my feet touching the ground right before I'm tackled, but the pass was successful and that's a touchdown for the Spartans.

And because there's something twisted about me I can't control, I look at the poor excuse of a man in the bleachers, telling myself all I want to do is prove him wrong in life while refusing to believe any part of me still wishes to please him.

My frustration is only fueled more by my dad's lack of response, even though it was fully expected.

He sits there in his slacks and button-down, arms folded over his chest.

Piece of shit.

"What's the matter, Nico? Daddy not impressed?" Alex taunts.

I lose it.

I shove the punk, yanking his helmet off in the process before the ref blows his whistle in warning.

Before I can be ejected and risk having to sit out the next two games, Coach pulls me, sending me straight to the fucking locker room.

Once inside, I slam my helmet against the wall several times before dropping to the bench. I run my hands over my face, then fall back and close my eyes.

Fuck. This. Day.

I tug my shit off, not bothering to shower before putting my gym clothes on.

I try Demi for the millionth fuckin' time and when she doesn't answer, I toss my phone across the room.

Where the fuck is she? She agreed to be with me and being at my games comes along with that.

This is bullshit.

With a deep breath, I move for the door, picking up my phone along the way, and glare at the shattered screen.

The last thing I want to do is go home to a dark house, and everyone I hang with is still on the fucking field, so I head for the rooftop. Straight to the fucking edge.

The game is about over, and we're gonna win, but I can't find it in me to care.

Why isn't Demi here?

And what the fuck is she trippin' on anyway?

I told her I didn't do a damn thing, but what if I did?

I could have easily fucked Miranda again. Shit, the first day I walked in the gym I saw the want on her face, noticed her watching Demi and me more than she was the others, but I thought she was being a professional, perfecting her shit.

I should have walked my ass out yesterday morning when ten minutes passed, and I was still the only one there.

Stupid fuckin' me, I thought I could get ahead, already know the moves before Demi had the chance to show them to me. She'd be impressed.

I groan, dropping my chin to my chest.

"Suck it the fuck up, Nico. You sound like a bitch." I shake my head at myself, turning to lean my elbows and back against the bricks.

A shine of blue catches my eyes and I freeze.

Slowly, I make my way over to pick it up.

A blue Gatorade.

Still cold.

She's here.

Chapter 24
Demi

I over exaggerate every move, locking my hips fully with each pop, flipping my hair and using my hands to add more sensuality.

I spin around, my chin lifted as I sassily walk toward the mirror and grip the barre attached to it, slowly swaying from right to left.

My eyes close, giving my body full control as I freestyle through the rest of the track.

With a tight hold on the glazed wood, I slowly butterfly to the floor, bouncing lightly on my tippy toes, and then make a slow and provocative rise.

My hands lift into my hair only to trail right back down the length of my neck.

The air in the room shifts in the next moment and my skin prickles as my eyes fly open, instantly connecting with a pair of dark, wild ones.

I gasp, falling against the glass slightly, but I don't look away.

Nico stands in the open doorway, lips pressed in a firm line as he makes slow and deliberate strides inside, each one causing my pulse to pound harder.

It only gets worse when he pauses an arm's length away.

He stands there unmoving, not so much as a blink, but his gaze grows ten shades darker and I know what he wants.

Unhurriedly, I begin moving again, hesitant at first, but when his tongue touches his lips, his focus falling to my ass, I give more.

He snaps instantly.

With a quickness I couldn't prepare for if I tried, he rushes forward, his chest now pushing into my back as his eyes remain glued to mine in the mirror.

His gentle yet firm tug to my arm has me spinning to face him, my hair sticking to my lip gloss when I do.

I lick my lips, blowing it off lightly, and he follows the movement.

Suddenly his eyes pop up to mine.

So eager.

The vein in his neck tics angrily against his skin and I can't help myself, I move in, running my lips across it.

It hits harder.

What are you doing, Neek?

His hands are quick to find my ass, and without warning and zero effort, he dips, lifting me with ease.

My grip flies to his shoulders to help steady myself, but in the same second, my back is pushed to the mirror, my ass now perched on the small barre as his palms trail around, up my stomach until he's cupping the underside of my breast.

He steps closer, tugging me to the edge so he's pressed against me, nothing but both our workout shorts between us.

My eyes cling to his, a rapid, throbbing, unbearable ache taking over my body.

And I can't help myself, not when his hard-on is resting on me with a subtleness that should be forbidden.

I grind into him.

A tiny bit at first, almost enough to be considered a shift of my body, but then his forehead tightens.

A sign of slipping control?

I do it again, harder, longer, with a deeper sway, and a small whimper escapes from my own actions.

Nico's response is a reckless growl.

His lips crash into mine with a hard and heavy need, and all I can think is fucking *finally*.

I moan instantly, and when he pushes his dick against me, shifting his hips the smallest bit, I gasp into his mouth.

As if expecting it, Nico is ready, his tongue delving inside my mouth, his hand coming up to force me impossibly close and leaving no room for air to breathe, nothing but him to fill my lungs.

My legs lift, sliding across his thighs, before wrapping across his back and locking.

He groans, ripping his mouth from mine as he gives a strong squeeze to my thighs. "I've been dying to feel these around me again."

He nips my lips and my head falls back, gently knocking into the mirror.

Nico slides his mouth down my throat, and my eyes squeeze tighter. I grind harder into him, my hands sliding along his biceps.

When he bites at my neck, my toes curl, and my eyes pop open.

My entire body grows stiff in an instant, a shrill coldness filling me to the core.

No.

Alex stands there, phone at his side, bag over his shoulder. With a subtle shake of his head, he keeps walking past, and I wish I could disappear just the same.

I am such a fucking fool.

It takes Nico a second to realize I've locked up on him, his head lifting as he does.

I refuse to meet his treacherous gaze, not when I know my unrestrained desire is written across my face while all he was doing was driving a point home.

I drop my legs from around him, and he doesn't relent right away, but finally releases me, allowing me to fall back to my feet.

I try my hardest not to touch a single inch of him as I squeeze away, quickly moving for the sound system to turn it off.

My shaky hand misses the button twice, and I take a deep breath, steadying myself a moment before trying again.

God, I'm an idiot!

"Demi." His voice strained as he attempts to catch his breath. I don't reply, hastily slipping into my track pants.

"Should I be apologizing right now?" he edges. "'Cause I don't fuckin' want to."

"No." My response comes out quick and raspier than I had expected, so I clear my throat and try again. "No, it's fine. Everything is fine."

I slip my shoes on, then tug my sweater over my head, pulling my hair out.

It takes all my will, but I manage a forced blank stare and turn to him.

Nico's face is drawn up tight, his chest rising and falling in quick spurts as he studies my every move.

"You did what I asked." My shrug is rigid.

Why the hell did I ask him to make me want it first?

Nico's head jerks back.

"I wouldn't worry about having to do that again."

"*Having* to do that again," he drawls slowly.

"He, uh." I look away. "Caught the entire show, so I'd say we're good for a while."

"What the *fuck* are you talkin' about?" Nico shouts.

"Look, I'm going to Carley's tonight, we're going out of town in the morning to visit her grandparents," I lie, moving for the door. "So, I'll just . . . see you Monday."

Or never, that would be awesome.

I go to walk away, but he calls me out.

"You're lying," he accuses flatly.

I tense, turning around. "Excuse me?"

"Carley, like the rest of us, has been trying to call you all day. When she couldn't get ahold of you, she asked me to let you know she was leaving right after the game, going with Krista and Trent to go get his brother from the airport."

Shit.

He tips his head back slightly. "Why you lying, D? Got plans you don't wanna share?" He glares.

Oh, fuck him.

212

"I was trying to be nice," I shout, taking him off guard, but only the subtle lift of his brows would tell you so. "But, fine, since it seems we're going all out, how about because I don't *want* to see you tonight, or for the rest of the shitty fucking weekend for that matter."

"Why the fuck not?" He takes a step toward me, and this time unexpected turmoil stares back. "What the hell just happened here, D?"

My anger is kicking higher the longer I stand here, and the hinted hurt in his eyes only confuses and pisses me off more. "I'm not really yours, Nico, so stop acting entitled to things you aren't. If I don't want to tell you something, I don't have to, so go ahead, feel free to lie to me all you want, too, because I don't really give a shit."

He eyes me a moment, licking his lips as he nods. "Right. Fake it 'til you make it, huh, D?"

"Learned from the master, huh, Neek?" I mock him. Moisture fights its way into my eyes, so I end the conversation with, "Awesome acting."

That felt pretty fucking real to me.

I walk out, afraid I left a part of me behind and unsure of how the hell to get it back.

I thought he kissed me for us.

I thought wrong.

Nico

What. The. Fuck.

Awesome acting?

What the hell just happened?

I kissed her, a real fuckin' kiss, like I'd been waiting to do for a long ass time. Shit, I've been fighting against myself since the second she agreed to this stupid ass lie, since I let my hands touch her that night in the hotel hallway.

There've been several times when we were alone, so there was no hiding what it would be like, when I was sure she wanted it, wanted me, but I waited. Until I couldn't anymore.

I knew she'd like it; knew she'd respond to my every move with one of her own.

I fuckin' knew we'd fit.

She pushed back harder than I did. Sought out what she needed more than I allowed myself to. Then boom, a bucket of fucking ice dropped, and she flipped her switch, walked out like nothing happened.

She's not mine, she said.

Ain't that some bullshit?

I have no fucking clue what she's truly been thinking the last few weeks. All I know is what's going on in my damn head, and it's not easy to admit when I can't positively say she's not on the same page. Still . . .

When I think of her, I want more.

When I touch her, I hate to stop.

When I look at her, I see *mine*.

I need her to feel the same.

A half hour passes before my phone rings and I finally find

myself walking out of the studio and toward the parking lot.

I answer Trent's call.

"Your truck's still here. Where you at?" he asks, right as I step through the double doors.

"I'm coming," I tell him, hanging up.

His eyes travel over all the exit points of the school until they land on me, and he leans back against my hood.

"What up, man?" he asks when I make it to him. "Where'd you go?"

I scoff, shaking my head and nodding at the cab. I hit the unlock button, and he follows my lead, climbing in the passenger seat while I slide into the driver's.

"Thought you were going to get your brother?" I ask him, leaning back.

He shrugs, looking away.

I turn toward him. "She called them, didn't she?"

He hesitates a moment before looking my way. "She didn't have to. Dem walked out when we were getting in the car. Girls got one look at her and off they went."

I nod, then put the truck in drive. "Lock up, we'll go get him."

"You sure?" He eyes me. "I can go by myself, call you later?"

"Yeah, bro. I could use the drive. He'll have to sit bitch, but . . ." I trail, and we both laugh lightly.

He pushes the button on his keys and off we go.

"So, what's going on, Nic? Why was she cryin'?" he asks once we're on the highway.

She was cryin'?

"Fuck if I know." My grip tightens on the wheel. "She flipped out. She . . ." I cut a quick glance his way, and he tilts his head expectantly.

Fuck it.

I break down all the bullshit that happened with Miranda, the switch of partners, and how her and Alex showed up together that next morning, catching us in a fucked up looking position.

"Damn," he draws out, looking away. "So, you really didn't touch her this time, Miranda?"

215

My glare snaps to his a moment before I focus on the road. "Are you for real?"

"What? Don't act surprised. I'm the one person aware this shit between you and Dem is fake, remember? I had to ask." He lifts his hands. "Keep going."

I flip him off and he chuckles.

"Every time we've kissed it's been when others are around, played off as all part of the deal, you know? But man, I know that's bullshit."

"What do you mean?"

"I mean what I've been telling you – I can fucking read her, bro. She's wanted me to kiss her, touch her, something, several times, and not so people would see. It hasn't been easy, but I held myself back every fuckin' time when it was the last thing I wanted to do."

He thinks on that a second before he says, "You kissed her when you were alone."

"I fucking kissed her, and I wasn't subtle or gentle, and she turned to putty in my arms, Trent. She was into it. Fully. Fuckin' completely." *I know it.*

I fuckin' felt it.

"I'm not really seeing the problem here, Nic."

"My point exactly. She just froze, and that was it. She talked some shit and took off."

"Maybe she freaked out. Too much too quick? This was supposed to be fake. Maybe she's not looking for more?"

You don't have to be looking to find the best fucking thing for you.

Sometimes all you have to do is open your eyes and realize it found you first.

I glare out the front window.

"You got a thing for her?" I ask him point blank.

"What?! No!"

His answer is instant and I breathe a sigh of relief.

"I love Krista. I'm *happy* with Krista and plan to follow her ass around like a little bitch after graduation." He laughs lightly. "I like Demi, and I care about her, but no . . ." He trails off, and I cut a glance his way.

"What?"

A heavy tension lines his eyes, and he curses under his breath. "I gotta tell you something."

"Tell me what?" I ask, merging over and turning down the road that leads to the airport.

He shakes his head, blowing out a long breath. "Look, this—"

Trent's phone beeps.

With a sigh, he pulls it from his pocket, frowning at the screen.

"Goddamn this girl." He shakes his head.

"That was Krista?"

"Yeah."

"What did she say?"

He lifts the phone for me to glance at the screen.

A picture of the inside of a liquor store bag full of junk food and a bottle of Hennessey, he scrolls up to show the other one that came with it.

It's of the girls walking, a near empty bottle at Krista's lips.

"They're walking?"

In the fuckin' dark?

He types away. "She don't listen."

I chuckle, turning into the terminal that leads to the pickup line. "They never do."

Trent laughs, looking out the window.

"We gotta talk, Nic," he says.

I shake my head, not up for this. "Not right now, your brother's coming out in a minute."

He turns to me, an overwrought expression on his face. He nods. "Yeah, all right, man, but later, yeah?"

"Yeah," I agree, when I have no desire to hear him tell me for the tenth time this is a bad idea.

We're so fuckin' far past that.

Chapter 25
Demi

I lean over, sticking my tongue out and touching it to Macy's while Krista takes a picture, laughing.

Carley plops down beside us, but slides off the bench, falling to her ass on the grass and the two of us drop with her.

"Hey, don't leave me out!" Krista whines and throws herself onto the pile.

We giggle, letting our empty snack containers tumble to our sides, and lay there silently.

After our first few shots, we decided to walk along the green strip that leads to the golf course. Halfway through, though, the Hennessey kicked in and the snacks ran low, so we sat down, drank some more and here we are — a mile from the golf course one way, and a mile from Macy's house the other.

I sigh. "Why do guys suck?"

"Because it's the only way they know how to work the clit from the outside."

The three of us bust up laughing while Macy smiles, proud of herself.

"I'm so drunk," Krista hiccups. "And hungry. Are you guys hungry?"

"Starved." I blink several times, following the lights of a plane flying overhead.

"What did Nico do, Demi?"

Made me believe in us.

"He kissed me."

Carley and Macy push up on their elbows while Krista's head snaps my way.

"I'm confused." Carley tries to frown.

I groan, closing my eyes. "So am I! My boyfriend is supposed to kiss me, right?"

"I think she's trashed," Macy says.

"She's definitely trashed." Krista yawns. "And I'm definitely dying from starvation."

"Let's finish the walk to the country club. We can charge some shit to my mom's account," Carley says.

We all agree, but nobody moves, and a few minutes later we're chuckling for no reason, but mine dies when a familiar face is suddenly glaring down at me.

"I think I'm having a nightmare," I whisper.

The girls chuckle, then open their eyes.

Macy screams before she rolls over laughing at herself and Carley groans, throwing an arm over her face.

Nico looks left so my eyes follow, finding Trent glowering at Krista the same, but she only smiles up at him.

When she lifts her arms like a child, his grin breaks free and he sighs, bending to pick her up off the grass. She wraps her arms around his neck, then looks at us. "I solved our food dilemma. No more apocalypse."

I push onto my elbows, but my head starts pounding and I fall back slightly, blinking hard.

Nico grips my arms, stupid flat expression on his handsome asshole face. "You good?"

My eyes search his, and the ache in my chest comes back harder than earlier. I tug free and have Carley help instead. It's not the best idea, but it works.

Nico stays bent on one knee, glare pointed my way, while I attempt to help Macy stand. Neither of us are steady on our feet and we stumble, but Nico's reflexes are sharp, and he's able to grab ahold of us both before we fall.

Macy looks up at him, letting out a whimsical sigh. "You should share, Demi."

219

"Sharing would imply he's actually mine," I murmur, and Nico's glare cuts to me.

My eyes widen and I cut a quick glance to Macy who, luckily, is already headed for Trent's truck.

I shrug away from Nico, following my friends.

"My truck is behind his." His words are a firm warning, one I choose to ignore.

"Might wanna move it before he hits you then," I say over my shoulder, dragging my ass in with the girls while Trent drops Krista in the front and shuts the door to talk to Nico.

"You mad at me, Demi?" Krista asks as she attempts to put on her seatbelt.

"Yes." I drop my head back. "But if you feed me, I'll forgive you."

She yawns. "Deal."

Trent hops in a moment later, announcing we're following Nico to his house to drop off his truck before we find somewhere to eat, and within minutes, my friends are climbing into the third row, my *fake boyfriend* who I thought *real kissed me* has weaseled his way to my side.

He wraps an arm around me, and I attempt to slide away, but freeze when his lips brush my ear.

"We haven't ended this." His words are a harsh whisper. "You said you aren't mine, I heard you loud and fuckin' clear, but to them you are, so act like it or I'll make sure everyone knows what we're really doing."

I jerk my head toward him, glaring at those deceitful lips. "And what are we *really doing*, Nico?" I hiss, my gaze snapping to his. "Because I'm not even sure anymore."

"What does that mean?" he hisses right back, frustration burning deep in his tone.

But his eyes . . .

A powerless pain.

I don't understand you, Neek.

"Where should we go?" Trent's voice breaks through our hushed conversation.

I clear my throat, facing forward.

"Oh, let's go to the place we used to eat at every Friday night before they kicked us out!" Krista shouts.

"No way! They'll recognize us," Carley says.

"Yeah right. We were flat chested, brace-faced kids. Besides, no way it's the same workers there!" Krista adds.

Trent meets my eyes in the rearview mirror. "Dem? You good with that?"

I pop a shoulder. "Go for it. This day sucks as it is, can't possibly get worse."

Nico shakes his head, tears his arm from around me and lets it fall to his lap. He scowls out his window the entire twenty-minute drive to Downtown Daisy, the small diner in town and the only place open around the clock.

We're seated almost instantly, choosing the open picnic area on the back lit patio instead of in the main room.

Krista laughs, knocking her shoulder into mine as she drops beside me. "I told you!" She grins. "And we haven't been here since sophomore year!"

"Think of all the pancakes we've missed. Sad face." Macy pouts playfully.

"Ohhh shit." Carley drags out each word, her wide eyes glued to the screen of her phone.

Macy scoots over to get a glimpse, a smile spreading across her face, and Krista snags it from her hand next.

The boys drop across from us, eyeing them suspiciously.

"What is it?" Trent asks.

Krista's smirk bounces from him to Nico and then lands on me. "Please tell me this isn't why you're mad at the boy, looks like he did *good*."

"What are you talking about?" My eyes fall to the phone when she tucks it to her chest. "Wait, is that *my* phone?"

She nods, wiggling her brows as she turns the screen toward me.

She presses play right as I snag it from her.

Soft music sounds, but the screen is dark, and then slowly the image comes into focus.

221

The camera zooms out, and there we are, me and Nico in the school studio.

The lens focuses on the two of us right as I lock my feet around him, our bodies moving against each other's, my hands latched tight on his arms while his are gripping my thighs. A moan follows, my moan.

Trent's "what the fuck?" has my eyes snapping up.

I fumble with the phone, quickly turning off the sound and lowering it to my side.

"What is that?" Nico drags every word out slowly.

A slow sweat breaks across the nape of my neck at his heated tone, and I shake my head.

Krista snatches it back, wobbly on her feet as she jumps off the seat, Macy just as unsteady, joining her.

"You guys!" I shout.

Krista leaves the volume down but grins at the screen. Macy just as excited beside her and I swear my face burns bright red.

I chance a glance at Nico, who is still glaring right at me.

Did we really kiss that *long?*

"Wait . . ." Macy says, taking the phone from Krista. "Alex sent this to you?" She looks up, lowering it to her side. "I don't get it . . ."

"Demi," Nico calls sharply. "What the fuck is that?"

My muscles lock, and I jolt when the table bounces with Nico's quick shoot up.

He has the phone in his tight grip before I even move.

He's shaking, trying to open it but the password is back on and he doesn't know the code like the girls do.

He stalks toward me, holding it out in front of my face so facial recognition opens it for him, and I just stand there and let him.

His lip curls, disgust and fury burning across his face.

He holds my gaze a moment longer before stepping back and forcing himself to glance to the screen. He presses play.

Everyone is quiet, looking on as he views the video of us, me so lost in his touch I had no clue it was all for show, or that we were being recorded.

I'm mortified, my stomach is in knots and I want to run away.

Slowly, Nico lowers the phone, confusion blanketing his features. "I don't . . ." He trails off.

"Oh my god!" Carley's eyes cut to mine a moment, before returning to him. "You heard the moan on the video, heard Alex is the one who sent it, and then what? Gave yourself two seconds to jump to the conclusion it was of her and him fucking around?"

My eyes fly to Nico's, a tight pinch in my brow.

He ignores her and everyone around us.

His breaths are coming quicker now, and he edges toward me. "You . . . all that shit after, it was because of that?" he rasps, almost so low I miss it.

I don't.

I can't admit to it, right?

What right do I have to get mad over him doing what I agreed he could, making me want his touch, making others believe in the lie?

Making me believe?

He keeps coming for me, and I can't move.

Carley snatches the phone from his hand and he lets her, not once turning away.

Nico's palms land on the sides of my face, eyes moving between mine. "You saw him standing at the door," he says for only me to hear.

It's not a question, but I nod anyway.

"You thought that was for him."

My gut tightens, my face wrenching up at his words.

He dips the few inches needed to make us at eye level. "Listen to me, right fuckin' now. He is the last motherfucker on this planet I would ever . . . *ever* want to see you like that."

My hands come up to cover his. "Don't lie to lie," I whisper.

His eyes glance to the side, remembering we have an audience who has no idea what's really going on between us.

What is going on between us?

Nico walks me a few feet away.

He slides his hands into my hair, tipping my head so he can whisper to me.

"I was fucked up all day after what happened with Miranda." He steps closer, letting out a long breath. "I got kicked out of my game tonight."

"You did?"

He nods. "Couldn't keep my cool knowing we were fucked up." His eyes stare into mine. "I don't wanna be fucked up, D," he admits.

Me either.

"I went to the roof to breathe a minute," he tells me. "To think. I found your drink, and knew you came even though you were mad, so I went to find you."

My chest inflates with a deep inhale, waiting for more.

"You were dancin', killin' me with that body I can't stop thinking about, and I fuckin' snapped. I had to feel you, kiss you. So I did, and the *only* thing on my mind when you were against me was how to get closer. There was no show. No plot." His lips press down at the hollow of my ear, and my eyes squeeze shut. "Me and you," he rasps. "That's what that was. If he showed up, if *anyone* showed up, I had no clue. I kissed you because I had to, Pixie. Wanted to. Plain and fuckin' simple."

My muscles tense a moment before a light zing runs down my spine.

I pull back.

His eyes are open and honest and laser focused on mine. "I don't want your lies. I want your all."

An airiness takes over my chest, a light pull at something deep within me the longer I stare. I drop my hands from him and a frown creeps over him.

I take a step back, heat spreading up my body as I whisper, "Prove it."

Confusion etches across his face before that slow, sexy smirk, takes over and all that's left is determination.

Nico grips my hand, ready to yank me away when suddenly the video is playing again, louder this time.

My moan echoes around us.

"Oh my god." I cover my face.

Nico whips around. "What the hell, man?"

My eyes pop open as Nico tugs my phone from Trent's grasp, and the girls, all three huddled around him pull back with drunken giggles.

All three tease by doing awful, drunken slutty dance moves, then drop onto the bench seat.

"You guys are assholes." I laugh lightly, stepping toward the bench, but Nico pulls my arms, so I turn back.

He eyes me skeptically, his arms gingerly sliding around my waist as he pulls me into him. "We good?"

Can we be more than good?

Can we be real?

I confirmed I was upset because I thought he only kissed me so someone else would see, for the sake of the stupid deal we made that states he's not really mine nor am I his.

How long before he reads into that for what it is?

How long before he realizes I want to be an *us*?

"Don't, D," he whispers, and my eyes fly back to his. "Don't think."

Don't think.

Don't think . . .

Fuck it.

"I don't want him anymore." The words fly from me before I can stop them.

Fully and completely, every muscle in his body locks and my stomach begins to stir.

Holy shit, I said it. It's out.

"What?" His tone is harsh, but I know it's not coming from anger.

"Alex," I admit quietly. "I don't want him. I can't even remember why I ever did."

His grip on me tightens, a heavy sense of possession radiating from him to me, warming my body from the inside out. "Don't play, baby."

225

"Tell me I am," I rasp.

When his brows dip, I continue.

"Your baby." My eyes hit his. "For reals, not for fakes. For keeps, not for now."

The heavy thump of his heart beats against my hand, and I flatten my palm there, not wanting to miss the way it's climbing.

"Pixie." He leans in, brushing his lips over mine. "You are. You've been," he stresses. "Even when you had no fuckin' clue . . . you were my baby."

He kisses me, and the overbearing weight on my shoulders lifts.

His.

That's what I am.

He pulls back the slightest bit, whispering into my ear. "And in case there's room for question, let me clear it up for you. You're mine, D, and I'm yours. That's as real as it gets."

Finally.

Chapter 26
Demi

Since Friday night, Nico hasn't stopped touching me when he's near, and he makes sure he constantly is. It's like when he teased before about *getting to be* the possessive boyfriend and keeping me within reach, that's exactly what he's doing.

He'll go from holding my hand to moving my hair, touching my waist or arms, anything.

Today, we're at Caper Cliffs, rock jumping and barbecuing, so it's been snapping the strap of my bikini top or running his palms across my arms, but this afternoon's touches are lingering, slow and far more deliberate.

It could be because we're basically naked in nothing but swimsuits, so the heat of his body radiates to mine even more than normal or maybe I'm imagining the lasting effect of his fingertips because I want them to drag a little lower and stay there for a while.

"Girl," Macy whispers in my ear. "You need to stop, take a dip in the water, something."

My frown finds her.

She rolls her eyes. "Your lady boner is showing so hard right now, and don't look, but the little bit of padding your suit top has isn't hiding the rocks poking out behind them."

I can't help it and a loud laugh leaves me, gaining the attention of the others climbing on the rocks to the side of us.

Carley shakes her head, shouting, "What crazy shit is she whispering to you over there, Demi?!"

I give a playful shrug, and the others smile. "Ah, nothing that isn't true."

Macy and I laugh, and like I knew he would, Nico jumps down off the rocks and stalks my way. Shirtless, trunks hanging nice and low over those magical hipbones.

Hipbones I have a sudden urge to trace with my fingertips.

It really is too damn bad our friends didn't take the hint when we tried to sneak ahead of everyone to higher ground for some privacy, but no. Suddenly they were all eager to start jumping and came with.

The only person who stayed down at the bottom is Trent so he could get the barbecue going.

"Do I go or do you need me to stay and be the fire extinguisher?" she whispers.

I laugh, pushing to my feet and dust off my ass.

Nico slides up, raising an expectant brow at Macy who winks and takes the spot I vacated.

His attention shifts to me, and he moves in, planting his hands on my bare ribs.

Always touching.

"What'd I miss?" he asks.

"Oh, you know, Macy being Macy, and advising I jump into the water before I . . . jump on you."

His frown is instant. "That's some shitty advice."

I laugh, dropping my head back, and his chest rumbles with a low growl.

"You keep giving me your neck like that, I'm gonna take it."

I lean in. "Maybe I want you to."

He has the tip of my ponytail in his hands in seconds, tugging, forcing my head back as far as he wants it.

"Oh, hell no!" Krista shouts. "If I can't get Trent to run off with me, you don't get none either."

I turn to smile, but my eyes shoot wide.

She and Carley are rushing for us.

My hands fly from Nico just in time for them to block me in. "Back off."

"Jump or you're going in." Carley's hands find her hips.

I look at Nico who smirks, lifting his chin.

I gape at him. "Really? No help? I'll remember this."

He steps forward. "See you in the water, D."

Nico jumps off the rock ledge, penciling into the deep pool of water below.

I look over, and slowly he emerges, shaking his head to clear his hair from his face.

He smiles up at me, swimming in place as he moves over a little. "All clear down here, girls."

I gasp and he laughs, lifting his hands quickly, beckoning me to him.

I look back to the girls. "You're assholes."

"And you're the driest one here, I've jumped twice already! If I have to have ratty ass hair, so do you." Krista pops her hip, smiling.

I groan, turn and glance out over the flat rocks that circle around the deep water below and jump.

Their hollers have me flipping them off over my head as I hit, quickly coming up to the top and taking a breath.

"It's freezing!" I yell with a laugh.

Nico chuckles and I swim toward where he's sitting on a moss-covered flat plain, half his torso out of the water, and dripping wet.

His hair is a mess on his head, so once I'm where I can put my knees on a rock, I squeeze between his legs and reach up to smooth it out.

One little curl keeps falling in his face, so I hold it back.

My chest is even with his face in this position, so he drops his chin on my breastbone and stares up at me.

"You've got goosebumps." His eyes fall to my arms, hands coming up to wrap around them, sliding up and down and creating twice as many as before. "That got anything to do with the water?" he rasps.

I can't answer him, though.

I'm stuck.

I stare at his mouth, only inches from my breasts, taking in nothing but the sensation of having so much of his skin on mine.

I could reach up and untie my top, and without direction he'd know what to do.

My nipples harden and his focus moves directly to the proof.

His grip tightens, his fingertips biting into me like I want his teeth to.

"D . . ." He licks his lips, reluctantly dragging his gaze back to mine.

Suddenly I'm tugged back, splashing into the water again.

I come up laughing and shove Carley away.

Krista is next to jump, popping up and swimming to the left of us to climb out the one shallow spot at the Cape.

We love this place and come here at least once a week during the summer.

Parking is down at the bottom with built-in barbecues and picnic tables, small games and things all around. It's not very large, only around ten carloads can fit in the area, so when we come, we leave before the sun even rises.

It's beautiful and quiet, green and clean, nothing but the sounds of people having a good time or the mini waterfalls that filter through the rocks and the small stream it all leads to.

"Yo!" Trent comes around the corner, tongs in one hand, towel for his girl in the other. He tosses it at her and she drapes it over her shoulder. "Foods ready."

"Yes!" Krista smiles with a shout, wringing her hair. "And now that Demi can pretend her vagina is wet from the water, let's be quick about eating so we can go kick these people's ass playing volleyball!"

"Oh my god!" I slap the water, but she only grins wider.

"Did they even invite us to play?" Macy climbs out.

"No, but they have six and we have six. They'll let us." Krista starts to walk away, but jerks to a stop and adds, "Carley, don't climb out until Demi does or Nico will never let her go."

I laugh, looking to Nico who finally drags himself to his feet, as if he planned to do just that.

"That's it, I'm gonna fuck with Trent's ass now," Nico mumbles as he passes Krista.

"Good, do it. He's all tense today, loosen him up for me, please." She looks to us, fighting a laugh, and then follows after him.

We spend the rest of the afternoon playing volleyball with the random people who set up beside us, and dip in the water to cool off here and there.

It takes longer to clean up than it did to set up and by the time we manage to head home, it's starting to get dark out, and everyone is hungry again, so we stop at a small taqueria for dinner.

They sit us around a large table, and my phone rings the second I get seated, my mom's name flashing across the screen.

I hesitate a moment, then Nico taps my shoulder, nodding to the screen.

With a sigh, I answer and walk a few steps away for some privacy.

"Hey, Mom."

"Hey, sweetie."

Sweetie? I frown. "What's up?"

"I was calling to see if you were home, I'm about twenty minutes out. I thought I could bring home dinner."

It's already after eight-thirty, later than I would normally eat, so I don't tell her I've just sat down to. "I'm not home right now, I'm with the girls and we already ate, but thanks."

"Oh, well, in that case maybe I'll stop for a salad at the club." The ding of her car door being opened lets me know she was betting on my answer and is already stepping out. "So . . . your dad called today."

Ah! That's what the 'sweetie' was for.

"Why'd he call you? I just texted him this morning."

"You did?" she asks, seemingly surprised.

It's as if she convinces herself he and I speak as little as *her* and I do.

"So, what did he say?" I get us back on track.

"Oh, he mentioned coming into town next week, he wants to have dinner." She pauses and I wait, knowing more is coming.

231

"You'll let me know if he mentions the specifics to you, I know he had to cancel his last trip last minute?"

So you can make sure to plan and be home to save face, sure, Mom.

"Yeah, Mom. I will."

"Great. I'll see you later, Demi." The line goes dead.

I take a minute to breathe, get out of the funk every conversation with her seems to put me in, before I turn back to my friends.

They're all laughing and cheering as Trent flicks a paper through Nico's fingers that he holds up as if they're goal posts.

Macy preparing to block Trent's next shot, switches seats, taking the open spot beside my man.

A smile takes over my lips as I look at Nico, who happens to glance my way at the same exact time.

Holy shit.

My man.

That's *my* man.

I stuff my phone back in my pocket and head right for him.

His eyes cling to me, and his body seems to relax into his chair. He licks his lips, his legs spreading wider.

I drop onto his lap, slide my hand into his hair, and kiss him.

Because he's mine and I can.

Chapter 27
Demi

"I've got the Kahlua!" Krista lifts the bottle in the air as she pushes open the door to Trent's truck.

"I got the Kahlua." Macy frowns, pulling open her backpack to show us the A&W Root Beer bottles inside. "I already disguised them and everything."

"Krista, you were supposed to get the coffee."

"I thought you were getting the coffee." She puts her hand on her hip.

Trent rolls his eyes and walks over to Nico who is sitting on my patio chair.

"I'm snacks, Carley's blankets, Macy's alcohol, and you were supposed to be coffee."

"Ohhh . . . that's why my alert went off at lunch! I thought I forgot to turn it off from this morning," Krista says.

"You remind yourself to get coffee in the morning?" Carley teases.

"No, biatch, but if I'm not out the door when it goes off, that means I don't have time to stop." She laughs, then looks to Trent. "It's fine, we'll go get the coffee?"

"I can't," he tells her. "I have to grab my brother on the way and drop him at my dad's office."

"I'll get it." Nico pushes to his feet, moving toward me.

I love how his shoulders sway the slightest bit with each step, and how he's always got a little lift or tip of his chin, giving him an *I'm coming for you* look, making me want him to do exactly that.

He plants his feet directly in front of me, grabs the snacks from my hands and lifts them over my head to set the bag into the little container in the back of my car. "What are you thinkin' about, D?" he smirks as he asks. "A night under the stars with your man?" he jokes.

I pretend to gag and he laughs, bumping my body into the car with his.

"Please, never be the cheesy poet."

"I thought it was cute!" Macy shouts as she walks off.

I hold in my grin while Nico's deepens.

"You like me better when I'm bein' a dick."

"I like you better when you sit there and look pretty," I joke.

He pushes closer. "You think I'm pretty, Pixie?"

A laugh bubbles out of me, and I wrap my hands around his neck, leaning into him, and satisfaction burns deep in his eyes.

"I think you're a fine specimen, Nico Sykes, but if you don't get your ass to the coffeehouse and to the school in time to have our bags checked, I might change my mind and—"

He captures my mouth with an unexpected kiss, but I'm ready for him, and need no time to think. I've been waiting to feel his lips again.

Nico's lips are soft, but his kiss is hard, a strong pressure from his mouth to mine that doesn't last near as long as it should. His tongue ghosts the edge of my lips, not invading, and quick.

Too quick.

He tugs away and my body tries to go with him.

A raspy, *sexy*, chuckle escapes him, and he whispers in my ear. "Watch it, D," he teases and my core heats. "I might pull you into the house."

"I might let you," I whisper.

His laugh is louder this time as he tugs free and heads for his truck while I'm stuck, practically panting, as I stare after him.

"You need help, Dem?"

Trent pulls me from my mind. "Huh, no I'm good. We're good."

He studies me a moment before glancing around — the girls are digging through bags in the trunk, and Nico's already in his vehicle turning the engine over.

"Dem." He gets my attention once again. "Are things getting serious between you and Nic?"

I frown, an instant stir in my stomach putting me on edge. "Why are you asking me this?"

Tension lines his forehead and he takes a small step forward. "You know why, Demi."

"Wha—"

"Ride with me, Trent," Nico shouts from the driver's seat of his truck, cutting off our conversation.

He's got his window rolled down, eyes sliding from me to his buddy.

"My brother, remember?" Trent reminds him, slipping his hands in his pockets.

Macy overhears and walks over, holding her hand out with a grin, so I pass over my car keys.

I cut a quick glance at Trent who rubs at the back of his neck, looking off, and then skip around Nico's truck. I tap the hood as I go, his eyes following me until I'm sliding in the passenger seat.

"Rude." I take my time buckling the seatbelt, my stare slowly making its way to his. "Ask your boy before your girl?" I tease.

Nico leans over, and I meet him halfway with a smirk.

"My girl." He damn near hums, just to hear himself say it I'm guessing. "They watchin' us?"

I look past his head to find everyone is climbing into their designated vehicles. "Nope."

Suddenly, my neck is in his hands and his mouth is on mine.

It's even shorter and quicker than the other, not even giving me an extra second to meet his eyes before he's gone, yet somehow, this kiss manages to leave me wanting more than the last.

More than this short ride alone with him.

More of it all.

I've been looking forward to Senior Sunrise for weeks, now I wouldn't mind skipping it completely. I don't tell Nico that though, and five minutes later he's disappearing inside the coffee shop while I wait in the truck.

It's not until he exits, both hands full, that I realize what he did back at my house.

It was simple, subtle, and small, and even though we admitted this is more than pretend, he still did exactly what I asked of him last Friday night.

He proved it.

Nico

As soon as I get the table set up, Trent pushes the ice chest beneath it and the trucks parked alongside ours follow our set up, laying their shit a few feet out from the tailgates.

It's Senior Sunrise, so all the seniors come back to school at eight in the evening, set up and play games, eat and bullshit all through the night, the entire class – or everyone who makes it out – watching the sunrise together.

The school allows those with a truck and the grades a first come first serve ticket to park along the outer edge of the fencing, so there are about thirty of us making a large U around the open field while the others parked in the parking lot and brought random shit and filled up the middle.

They've got everything from tables and chairs to blow up mattresses and even a real one, and another group is inflating full blown rafts to chill in.

"Is that a fucking futon, bro?" Trent laughs.

I glance over my shoulder, finding four guys carrying it across the grass. I chuckle, shaking my head. "People are for real about this shit. I heard a couple years ago the basketball team took the entire center, made a fat ass circle with dozens of trampolines."

"Yeah, I saw that. I was helping set up games out here that year when they were bringing them in." He laughs.

"That's right, you were on leadership with Demi that year."

He nods, looking to Krista. "I'm uh, I'm gonna go help her get the rest of the shit. Be back."

He takes off right as Demi steps up.

She bumps her hip into me, setting out the paper coffee cups and making a full coffee station with straws and spoons and shit.

"Where do you want the snacks?"

"Oh!" She turns back to her little tub and pulls out two small buckets, setting them at the other end. "Here, I'll pour them in there."

She reaches out, but I tug them away, swinging the bags behind me.

A small smile plays across those thick lips of hers and she leans in. "I can do it."

"I know you can, but so can I." My eyes shift between hers. "You should kiss me now."

A laugh bubbles out of her as she scrunches her nose. "Oh, yeah? Why is that?"

"Because I want you to, that's reason enough."

Demi pushes up, bringing our mouths even. "I'd say it is." She chuckles, pats my chest and pecks my cheek before hurrying away.

"That's not what I had in mind!" I shout after her.

"Oh, I don't doubt it," she calls from the other side of my truck.

Krista and Trent walk back with two trays full of enchiladas his mom made us for tonight, setting them on our table with the rest of the shit right as Carley and Macy walk back, Demi right behind them.

"Are we just eating and snacking as we want?" Macy asks, peeking into one of the enchilada trays.

"Yeah, no reason to make it complicated." Demi nods, hopping into the bed of my truck.

"Cool, I'm going to go play water pong," she says.

"Water pong?"

"They couldn't exactly bring beer."

"Demi, did you seriously bring your homework?" Carley whines.

I glance at Demi, who brought beanbags for us to sit on.

She laughs, pulling a blanket over her legs. "What? I have to get it done, and we have ten hours out here. Why not?"

"Ugh, I'm going with Macy. Come find us in a little bit or we'll be back."

"I don't have much, I'll be done quick. Swear!"

They tease her a little more as they walk off, but she simply smiles, her focus moving back to the notebook in her lap.

I grab my backpack from the floorboard of my truck, hopping in the back with her.

When I drop beside her, pulling my own shit out, she swings a grin my way, offering me a piece of licorice.

I lean forward, capturing it with my teeth and she laughs, biting from the same part I did.

We sit and work in silence, but only manage to keep focused for a little over a half hour before we give up.

Demi stuffs her papers in her bag, and drops her head against the window, looking at the sky. "Think you'll be able to stay awake all night?"

"I can think of a few ways to make sure I do." I slide my eyes toward her.

She laughs, shaking her head. "I bet you can."

"Want me to name 'em?"

She smiles, but doesn't say anything, her attention falling to my mouth when I pull my bottom lip between my teeth.

Man, she's gorgeous.

Wild green eyes locked on me, shiny, dark blonde hair she left laying long across her shoulders, and plump ass, pretty polished lips.

She shifts on her beanbag.

It's not hard to tell she's got something on her mind.

"Talk to me, D."

Her tongue slips out, unease written across her forehead, but she doesn't allow her concern to keep her from speaking. "What if I told you I needed this?"

"I'd tell you to be more specific," I reply instantly. "I don't like vague and I don't like assumptions. If you mean it, say it. If not, don't."

She chuckles, reaching up to push my hair from my forehead.

"You're kind of an asshole," she says, her voice lowering with her next words. "But I kind of like it."

"Liar."

Her mouth drops open.

"You more than like it." I smirk. "I should be an asshole more often."

Her lips twitch, and she moves her blanket, covering my lap with it as she scoots closer. She shakes her head. "You're good how you are."

My hand slides over her jeans on her left outer thigh. "How am I, D?"

"Unexpected." She thinks a long moment. "Do you think something built on a lie could ever . . ." She trails off.

My stomach muscles tighten as she tucks her lips between her teeth.

Keep talkin', baby.

She hesitates, so I try to ease it from her.

"Ever what?" Reaching up, I slide my hand into her hair. "Ever . . . *last?*"

I swear she blushes and something pulls in my chest, but then we're interrupted by a few of our classmates, and her focus shifts.

"Stop fingering my friend so she can come play with us," Macy calls as she jumps up on the tire well of my truck.

Demi can't hold it in, and a loud laugh leaves her.

"Go away, we're busy."

D cuts a quick smile my way.

"Please!" her friend Ava begs. "We need a couple more people."

Demi playfully rolls her eyes, stands and jumps to the grass, while my ass stays planted. "Let's go, Neek. We're needed over there."

You're needed right fuckin' here.

I must be frowning because she chuckles, offering a flirty smile as she follows her friends, leaving me where I sit.

Half-cocked and blue balled like a motherfucker.

Chapter 28
Nico

In no hurry, I climb from the truck.

I finish off a full bottle of water, throw back a pack of peanuts and text my mom to check in on her as I head for Demi.

Some of my teammates are parked next to each other, so I stop and chat, making sure the girls are still where they're supposed to be every few minutes.

A few minutes too long . . .

Sandra Black slides up.

"Hey." She smiles, leaning in.

I go to give her a one-armed hug, but her shoe knocks into mine and she stumbles closer.

She giggles, her vodka breath fanning across my face as she looks up.

"Damn." My head tugs back. "Gettin' fucked up, or what?"

"It's Senior Night." She smiles, shrugging against me. "Why not?"

"Might wanna pop a piece of gum in your mouth. Campus security is scattered all around."

"Or . . ." she whispers, her hands come up to pull my head down. "We could hide out in your truck, or my car. You up for it?"

I grip her wrists, freeing myself from her grasp. "Back up, girl. That's not happening."

"Oh, come on." She pouts, running her hands through the ends of her long, dark hair. "We can even try for a quickie, even though we both know we need longer than that."

I go to step past her, but she's quick to wrap her fingers around my arms and peers up at me through her lashes.

She opens her mouth, but when a small shriek follows, my eyes narrow only to widen in the same second.

Demi tugs her back, stepping in front of me. "I always thought you were sweet. A little loose, but sweet."

Sandra's jaw drops and people begin looking this way.

"I realize now you're just another girl who thinks she can have whatever she wants because you're pretty and say please, but that's not going to work here. You can screw whatever guy you want, Sandra, with the exclusion of mine."

Sandra blushes, her bloodshot eyes filling with moisture. She peeks around before stepping toward Demi.

Macy and Carley move closer, but when Sandra only reaches out to grab D's hand, they pause.

"I didn't realize—"

"Yeah, you did." Demi gently pulls herself free. "If acting shitty embarrasses you into lying, then don't be shitty. It's *really* not hard."

Demi locks her fingers into mine and leads me to my truck.

There's commotion behind us, but she doesn't spare another glance, instantly releasing me when we're back to our area, and busies herself pouring a cup of coffee.

She's jerky with her movements, so when she drops the stack of lids for the third time, I snatch them before she can, pull one off and hand it to her.

She cuts me a quick look before walking over to Trent's front seat where she pulls out one of the root beer bottles full of Kahlua and pours some into the cup.

She takes a small sip, attaches the lid, and takes another.

She's frustrated, pissy as hell, and it's got everything to do with what just happened.

My groin heats, and I can't hold it in. "Thought you said she wasn't hurting you and you were gonna be nice?"

Her head snaps my way, nothing but sass to be seen. "When did I say that?"

"When she was gettin' at Alex in the library."

She glares. "Alex wasn't mine. She could do with him as she pleased, *you are*." She looks back to her cup, blowing into the little opening. "She doesn't get to touch you."

Fuck me, there it is.

The claim, the absolute sense of possession, the fire in her gut she lets ride, no longer having a reason to hide it.

Demi tries to spin away, but I catch her, swiftly take her drink and set it down, and then sneak her between our trucks, pinning her in with my hips.

Her eyes grow heavy and she lets her shoulders fall.

"For the record." I run my hands up her ribs. "I'd already told her no and was walking away."

She's pissed but not at me.

Demi reaches up over her head, gripping the roll bar inside my open window. She holds on, lifting her legs off the ground and wrapping them around me, her arms slipping over my neck once her body is hooked just right.

She pulls her mouth to mine, nipping at my lips with hers.

"Would you tell me no, Neek?" She pauses a second. "If I asked you to put me on my back in your truck, right now . . . would you deny me, too?"

I groan, pushing into her and her harsh exhale lights a fire under my skin, sending a shiver down my body.

Her eyes darken before me, a heavy need taking over.

Damn.

"Here, where all these people would see? Yes. Anywhere else?" I skim my lips over hers and she leans in, fighting for more. "*Never.*"

"Then move your feet," she whispers, gripping me tighter.

My chest rumbles against hers, and a slow smirk spreads across her face.

"You better be careful, D."

"And you better start walking, Neek. Take me to this . . . *anywhere else*. Somewhere where you won't tell me no," she says coyly, closing her lips over mine.

Her hands slide across my shoulders and down my chest as much as our closeness will allow.

I'm hard already, aching, and the want in her eyes only makes it worse.

I squeeze her ass cheeks and her lips part.

She's not asking, but commanding I take her somewhere, play with this body.

I run my hands across the back of her thighs, hesitating, but knowing damn well I won't deny her even if I should for my own fucking sanity.

A little of her would never be enough.

A taste would only leave me starved.

I'm what she wants, and what my baby wants, she gets.

I drop her to her feet and damn near drag her ass across the field, through the campus and into the only open door I can find.

She laughs at my eager steps as we rush down the silent, dark halls until we're walking into the open theater, and sneaking up the stairs that lead to her safe place – the attic above it.

I give her no time to think, I'm on her in an instant.

She shudders in my arms, a small gasp leaving her as my mouth lands on hers, the anticipation alone lighting her up.

Her mouth is mine to take, and she gives everything she has, her arms quickly wrapping around my neck, tightening and tugging me impossibly close.

I kiss her and I don't stop.

She doesn't either.

Demi clings to me, whimpering in protest when I pull back to glance around the area as I walk her backward toward the wall, but she has other ideas.

She leads me to the opposite corner where there's a small blanket she must have laid out up here at some point.

She tugs my hand, her eyes low and aroused as she draws me to the floor with her. She lays herself across the soft fleece beneath us, her legs falling open, so I settle between them.

I let my eyes soak in the sight, Demi Davenport under me, turned the fuck on and deprived as hell, but she's impatient and refuses to wait any longer.

She pushes to her elbows to bring her mouth back to mine, her tongue demanding entrance I'd never refuse.

My hands roam her sides, and I take a deep breath as I slide under her shirt, gliding across her skin.

"So damn soft," I murmur.

She moans, whispering against my lips, "Touch me, Neek."

I groan, dropping my head into her neck.

I don't need a second invitation, and I don't hesitate, but slip past her bra to find a perfect handful of silky skin.

Her nipple is already hard as a rock, so when I trace the pad of my thumb across the sensitive bud, she cries out, right into my fuckin' ear, the sexy ass, desperate rasp shooting straight to my dick and making me throb.

I push against her reflexively and she reacts instantly, her hips rolling, begging for more.

She grips my hand, squeezing, then drags it down her stomach, pushing the tips of my fingers into the waist of her pants, and then leaves me there to work.

I flick open the button of her jeans, and adjust my position, so I can slide my hand inside without having to take them off and she lifts her hips. I tease over her underwear and her legs drop even wider.

I pull back, my eyes on her dazed ones as I inch the edge of her panties to the side, feeling the smallest piece of what I guarantee is the softest spot on her.

I run the tips of my fingers up and down, slowly moving the rest of the stretchy material to the side, until I'm ghosting right over her clit.

She gives a slow blink. "What are you waiting for?" she whispers with a dare.

My touch falls on her, pressing harder the lower my fingers slip, and a small smirk finds her lips, her eyes closing at the same time.

I drop my mouth to hers, but she doesn't kiss me.

Demi pulls my lip between her teeth, biting lightly, an airy "yes" escaping as she releases me.

Her hands find their way under my shirt, and her fingertips dig into my skin as she explores my body for the first time.

"Take it off," she pants.

Right as she says it, laughter echoes beneath us and we freeze.

More and more voices float up, and I look at Demi.

Her head lifts and falls back to the wooden floor. "Fuck. They're putting in new chairs. The crew must work through the night to avoid class time."

She lets out a deep sigh, her head tilting to the side.

My smirk is slow. "You poutin', baby?"

Her eyes fly to mine, darkening by the second, and damn if she doesn't nod.

I suppress a groan, pushing on her clit even harder than before as I drop my lips to her ear. "Can you be quiet?"

"I don't know," she answers with a moan, a little too loud. "But don't stop."

Her pussy clenches and she pushes her hips into my hand, rolling with me.

"Put your mouth on my skin," I tell her. "Bite if you have to."

She nods, and then her tongue trails across my neck, her mouth covering the spot a second later.

A jolt runs deep in my body, and her small smile is felt.

I pinch her clit, swirling quicker and quicker until her body starts to quake, her mouth pressing harder and harder into me as she fights to hold it in.

I want to hear her let go.

"Can you open your legs a little wider for me?" I whisper, dragging my teeth across her earlobe.

"I'm a dancer, Neek," she breathes, locking onto my biceps with a death grip. "You have *no idea* what I can do with my legs."

"Fuck," I groan, pushing my hard-on against her outer hip, and she starts shaking even more.

I pull back so I can watch as she blinks in and out of her orgasm.

Her lips are spread, a deep tension lining her brow as she twitches.

It takes several minutes for her breathing to slow; she drags those hazy green eyes to mine.

I expect her to retreat into herself a bit, maybe pull back a little or feel unsure.

She doesn't.

She slides her hands up my neck until she's got a good, solid grip on my face, and pulls my lips to hers.

Demi fights her laughter as we push against the wall then quickly dart out the door before the staff inside spots us. As soon as we're through the double doors and back into the cool night air, she lets it go, dropping her head back as she laughs loudly.

And god damn it, I have to hold her again. I grab her by the ribs and lift.

Instantly, those long ass legs wrap me up and she smiles, slowly lowering her lips to mine.

"We should go back in there," I tell her.

She smiles wide, shaking her head. "You should come over tomorrow night," she requests, her arms loose around my neck. "Stay with me."

There's a tender, nervous air surrounding her, one that has me reaching up to brush my knuckle across her cheek and her lips twitch.

"That what you want?"

Her hand runs through the top of my hair sliding down and pausing over my left pec. "Yeah, Neek. I want you."

She kisses me, a little slower than she has before, and when she tugs free, shimmies down with a giggle, and trails ahead . . . I know.

For the first time since we started this, I'm undeniably sure when Demi Davenport walks away, leaving a piece of herself behind for me to have. To keep.

I'm keeping her.

At this point, I wouldn't let her go if she tried to walk away, so I'm glad she agrees.

I jog forward, but she hears me coming and breaks out into a run herself, darting toward the field where the others are, only to come to a full and sudden stop when she realizes campus security is now guarding the gate we slipped through.

I fight to hide my laugh while she doesn't even breathe, nervous we've been caught, but I wrap my arms around her, and she starts moving again.

They do give us the evil eye, but they don't say shit. They know what people sneak around to do, and since we weren't caught, there's no point in hounding us.

She doesn't relax until we're at my truck, where she bursts into laughter, leaning her head back on my shoulder to look at me.

I can't fuckin' help myself and take her lips again.

She's more than with it, keeps her mouth locked on mine as she spins in my arms and deepens the contact.

Macy, the cockblocker she is, whistles and Demi tears away, hiding her face in my chest a second, and then finally looks to her friends.

"Where the fuck did you guys go?" Macy teases with a smile.

"Yeah, and why didn't you tell us?" Krista whines. "We couldn't slip past the gates for shit."

I laugh, looking to Trent who frowns at Demi. He senses my eyes on him and cuts a glance my way.

I nod my chin, but he shakes his head subtly, his way of saying we'll talk later.

He's got to be picking up on what I've been trying to explain to him.

Demi isn't with me to get to Alex, not anymore.

She fell, just like I wanted her to.

Demi

"So." Carley bumps my hip, sticking her hands under the sink water I've just pulled mine from. "You guys snuck off."

I grin. "We did?"

"Did you have sex in the school, you dirty ho?"

"Sex . . . no." We look at each other and both start laughing.

She studies me, a small smile on her lips. "You really like him."

I nod and mock myself. "Weird, right?"

Carley shakes her head, wrapping an arm around my shoulder. "What if I said no, that it's not weird at all?"

I glance her way. "You've been team Nico since the beginning. Why?"

She shrugs, walking out first, so I follow.

"I always wondered if he had a thing for you when he first stopped talking to you. It was the typical 'pretend you don't want what you can't have' attitude he always gave."

"Yeah, I never picked up on that." I grin, my eyes finding him on the field right away. "But I'm happy with where things are going."

"I'm glad, Demi, you deserve some happy."

"My life isn't sad, Carley."

"No." She looks at me. "But it was lonely, and not a lonely having us over to hang several times a week could fix. You need this."

I smile, my eyes locked on Nico's as he moves toward me and I him.

I more than need this.

I want this.

Nico plants his feet in front of me, and Carley keeps moving.

He runs a knuckle down my throat, his lips twitching after I do. "So easy to excite," he draws out, anticipation laced through his dirty whisper. "Are you wet, D?"

My breath lodges in my throat, and I grip his arm.

"Yeah, baby, you are, aren't you?" He presses a kiss to my erratic pulse behind my ear, and it jolts even higher. "It's only three in the morning, how you gonna make it through the sunrise, through the day, and into the night, hmm?"

"Don't tease me, Neek, or I might tease back," I caution, my fingertips slipping into the edge of his joggers. "But I won't be so subtle."

"Prove it. Grab me, D."

A heavy throbbing pulses between my legs, and thinking he won when my move isn't instant, he chuckles and pulls back, only to freeze when I'm suddenly cupping what I can fit of him in my palm over his boxers. I give a gentle squeeze, tugging the slightest bit.

He twitches in my grip, his fingers wrapping around my arms in a tight hold as he presses into my hand, only to yank away completely.

He glares, but it's in warning, not anger. "Next time you touch my dick, be ready for it to be inside you, nice and slow. Got it?"

I inhale, nodding.

He starts to smirk, but groans instead when I ask, "Promise?"

Chapter 29
Nico

"Nic. I need to talk to you."

I shake my head, stuffing my phone in my pocket. "Don't, my man. I don't want to hear it."

"You need to."

With a sigh, I turn to him. "I get it, you don't like how this happened, but we're good. Things have changed." I don't say it out loud, Thompson is by us, and nobody else needs to know we started off as a lie.

"I *know* things have changed, that's why you need to hear me out."

I shake my head and turn around, ready to walk and find the girls.

"Sophomore year, two times."

Tension wraps around my shoulder blades, locking me in place as I replay Trent's rushed words.

It takes several seconds, but slowly, I look behind me, my body shifting until I'm fully facing my best friend.

"What?"

Thompson falls a few feet back, rubbing at the nape of his neck, and my eyes dart back to Trent.

He hangs his head, taking in a deep breath before he stands tall to meet my glare. "I've been trying to tell you."

My pulse hums in my ears, my steps like heavy lead as I force a foot forward. "You think this shit's funny?"

"Trust me, Nic. I know it's fucked up."

I shake my head, denying what he's saying. "What are you tryin' to do? Why you fuckin' with me?"

He holds my gaze, my best fucking friend. The only person who knows the truth about *everything* in my life. My dad, my mom, Alex. *Demi.*

Demi.

I lunge at his ass.

Demi

"Get over to the truck, now, but don't run or security will follow you."

I look over my shoulder, my smile fading when I recognize the seriousness of Thompson's face.

He glares. "Take your friends with you."

I glance to Carley nodding my chin and walk as calmly as I can toward our area, the girls a few feet behind.

It's dark, but I manage to see between the trucks as I grow closer, and I gasp.

Nico and Trent are fighting, their bodies slamming into the bumper of Trent's truck and rolling off onto the small patch of grass in front of it.

Or more, Nico is fighting while Trent more or less allows him to toss him around.

"Oh my god! Nico, stop!" Krista hisses, her wide eyes flying to mine as she rushes forward. "Demi, what the hell?!" She glances back.

Oh my god . . . shit.

This isn't happening, not tonight.

Not after we finally got to spend some alone time together as a real couple, away from all the fake.

Away from everyone.

Thompson is suddenly grabbing Krista by the sweater and tugging her back. "Nu-huh. You're not gettin' hurt, girl."

"Then stop them!" She starts to cry.

Thompson glances past her, wincing when Nico lifts Trent from the ground, punching him square in the jaw, not the slightest attempt to block it.

Thompson looks to Krista. "He's got it comin' and he knows it. Leave them. I'll step in if it gets nasty."

Nico nails him in the gut and Trent groans, stumbling around and slamming into the side mirror a foot from where Thompson stands.

Krista screams again, gaining Trent's attention.

Concern lines his eyes and he lifts his hands to Nico, stepping toward the fence to put some space between them.

"That's enough. You're scaring the girls—"

"Don't," Nico seethes, shoving at him again, his shoulder hitting the metal wiring. "Talk about her like she's yours to worry about and I'll break your fucking hand, quarterback."

"Nico, what's your problem?!" Krista fights to get past Thompson again, but he holds her still.

"Say it. Right now, to my fucking face, Trent." Nico creeps closer to him.

Trent's eyes fly my way before going back to Nico's, pleading. "Come on, man."

"You were man enough to do it, not man enough to say it out loud?"

Trent only shakes his head, leaning against the fence, blood dripping from his lip.

"Don't act like you aren't proud, asshole. Say it!" Nico's jaw flexes repeatedly, but I can't see his face. "Now, Trent."

Trent's eyes are solemn, regret slipping over him. "All right," Trent relents. "Dem and—"

"Enough of the nickname! It's one letter, motherfucker!"

Trent sighs, at a loss.

There is no calming Nico or hoping he calms himself.

All Trent can do is lay it out and all I can do is hope we don't end as quickly as we began.

Trent does as he's asked. "Demi and I slept together, but it was a long time ago."

"Fuck, man." Nico's hands fly from him, sliding over his head and folding behind his neck.

He blows a harsh breath into the air, and my lungs feel the loss.

"How was I supposed to tell you? You've—"

"Wanted her since *before* you had her and told you all about it?" he shouts. "Yeah, I fuckin' have."

Whoa, what?!

"It was two years ago, and yes, I should have told you when it happened, but you stopped talking to her after everything with your dad, and the threat from—"

"Watch it," Nico warns.

Trent's body sags, and he tries to reason with him. "I didn't know she was still inside you, man, and I didn't realize where the two of you were headed. I thought you dancing with Miranda would have—"

He cuts off, his eyes darting to Krista and then back to me.

"No." Nico shakes his head, running his hands through his hair. "Are you for real, man?"

"Nic," he says quietly, walking toward him. "It's not—"

"Not what?" Nico shouts, punching into the crossed metal of the fence on the side of Trent's head. "Not what I think? Then why *would* my best fuckin' friend purposely go behind my back and try to fuck what I had going by inserting drama between us? And this on top of the bullshit you just stood here and fuckin' told me? Let's hear it, asshole. How the *fuck* is it I'm supposed to take *this*?"

"Trent . . ." Krista starts forward, and this time Thompson moves to the side. "What's he talking about?"

Trent's face grows taut. "I asked Demi's dance coach to switch us, make Nico her partner and me Demi's for the practice part. I knew she'd agree or might have already planned to do it herself." Trent glances from Krista to Nico. "I was only trying to speed up the inevitable."

"Inevitable?" Nico laughs, but there isn't a hint of humor in it. "That's my girl—"

"She wasn't!" Trent explodes. "That's the thing you kept forgetting, Nic!"

Krista gasps as my body stiffens.

What the hell?

The fall of Nico's shoulders is instant and everyone is quiet a long moment.

"That what this is about?" Nico pushes. "I asked you, point blank. *You* said no, was that a lie? You want *my* girl? Or am I supposed to say you want her *again*?" he spits harshly.

"I can't do this," Krista cries and runs off, Macy and Carley following behind her.

"Krista!"

"Krista don't leave! It's not how it sounds!" Trent shouts urgently. "Fuck!"

Nico scoffs, slapping a coffee cup off the edge of the truck, and glares at the sky.

Krista running off is where Trent draws his line.

He scowls, taking a small step toward Nico who stands just as tall. "I don't want to fight with you, man, I love you and I'm fucking sorry. I wish I could take it back, but I can't. I know I deserve everything you've got to throw at me right now, trust me, I get that, but the shit you're saying is way off base, and I can't stand here and take it because it's fucking with *my* relationship. My *real* relationship," he broaches.

My mouth drops open.

He knew *this was fake?*

"I can't allow that, so I'm going after my girl." Trent takes a few slow steps away before breaking out in a full run.

Thompson clamps a hand on my shoulder and walks off next and soon it's just me and Nico.

Nico drops his forearms on the hood of his truck and hangs his head between them. "Go away, Demi. I can't look at you right now."

"That's not fair."

"I don't care. *Go.*"

"Just like that? You don't want to talk about this, ask questions? Explain how he knows this was fake?"

Nico scoffs, then lifts his head. His face is blank, eyes hardly open. "Don't even. And what kind of questions, D? 'Cause I'm not interested in the positions you fucked my best friend in, or how long it lasted, or where it took place." He blinks carelessly. "You were right, a fake boyfriend doesn't need to know a damn thing. You do you, D." He pushes off the hood, and steps toward me, but only so he can glide by. "I think I'll find Sandra. Take that hall pass you offered before."

"No, you won't." A heavy pressure weighs in my chest, and I spin to face him. "You won't because you know you'll lose me if you do."

His lip curls. "What makes you think I care?"

"Neek . . . stop," I whisper. "We're past this — no more tug of war. I want you and you know it. So just . . . stop."

His face is a picture of rage, but there's anguish in his eyes. "You fucked Trent."

"A long time ago."

"And you never felt the need to tell me this?"

"I didn't think about it!" flies from me, and a wave of nausea rolls in behind it. "When we talked about my not being a virgin, I thought you were mocking me, using it as a way to talk crap or something. I figured he had told you after it happened. I had no clue he kept it to himself until later."

"And still, not a fuckin' word about it, huh?"

Damn it!

Anxiety builds in my gut.

I have nothing but the truth and it's a pathetic one.

"I didn't think about it," I say quietly. "I get it's messed up, and I'm sorry, but I . . . didn't think about it."

He shakes his head. "I don't know what I'm supposed to do with that."

"Don't push me away over something that happened before we did. How was I supposed to know we'd be standing here two years later?"

"You were supposed to come clean when you finally woke up and realized I wanted you." His anger dissipates as he pushes against me, his fingers lifting to brush across my cheek. "You were supposed to be mine and only mine."

"I am."

257

"But he had you first."

"So have me last."

His lips hit my ear. "I'm walking away, Demi. Let me."

Sensing there's no other choice at the moment, I do.

Chapter 30
Demi

After Nico took off walking, I grabbed my blankets from the back of his truck and moved to my car in the parking lot. I texted Carley who told me Krista got home safe and none of them were coming back unless I needed them to, but I wanted to be alone, so I told them we'd chat later.

Right after, I called Krista and talked to her a few minutes to make sure her and I were okay, but Trent was pounding on her door the entire time, so I let her go to deal with him.

That was two hours ago.

Now I'm lying here trying to rest, but sleep won't come, so it's about to be a long ass day.

While seniors are allowed to skip the first half of their schedule after Senior Night events, senior athletes aren't. We participate at our own risk, so after a night of zero sleep and high-strung emotions, in this gym for practice is the last fucking place I want to be.

It's the last place I expected Nico to be, too.

I should have stayed home last night.

"Demi," Miranda snaps. "Stop being lazy with your dip. Roll your hips all the way and tug them into your partner."

I clench my teeth but nod and get back into step one, waiting for the music to end so she can replay.

"Are you going to talk about anything that happened last night or are you going to ignore me, too?" Trent asks quietly.

"I haven't had a chance to talk to Krista or Nico, so why the hell would I want to talk to you?"

"Me and Krista are fine, Dem. You told her years ago, and I explained where my head was at last night. It sounded bad the way Nico said it, but it wasn't like that at all."

I shake my head, going through the moves lazily to keep attention off us. "And you and Nico, are you good? 'Cause guess what?" I spin, pinning him with a glare. "We aren't. I shouldn't even be dancing with you right now! Why the hell did you have to tell him like you did? We could have talked to him alone, explained—"

"It wouldn't have mattered, Demi. You don't know everything, there was no breaking it to him easy. He would have reacted the same no matter what."

"But it didn't have to be then or at a school function with everyone around. I should have thought to tell Nico everything weeks ago." I get back into position, facing forward. "Look what your way led to for you and Krista."

"I told her everything."

"You tell her I don't really have a boyfriend?"

His hands tense, then fall from me as he steps around to face me with a scowl. "No. I didn't, so I still feel like shit, like I'm lying to her."

I shrug. "Might as well have told her. We're done with the role play."

"Demi." Concern thickens his tone. "Don't walk away from him when he gets mad and acts like a dick."

"I didn't walk away," I hiss. "He did."

"Fuck." Trent's eyes fall to the floor.

"Demi." Miranda sing-songs, "Waiting on you. Again."

My head snaps around and I glower.

Her hands find her hips. "You know what. Switch with Hammons, he needs the help anyway. You two can pair back up for the performance."

"I'm not switching," I refuse. "There's no point."

"You are, because I said so," she bites out.

Alex steps up, moving right behind me when Trent bumps past him and moves toward the girl he's now forced to work with.

Alex grins. "Hey."

I offer a flat smile, quickly cutting my eyes to Nico.

He stands frozen, glaring this way with a scowling Miranda beside him.

She says something to him, but he isn't listening, and after a moment, I have her attention too.

Slowly, a nasty smirk forms on her bitchy little face.

She steps toward the rolling speaker to press pause and drags it to the center of the room.

"Everyone, gather in the center and sit," she instructs, quickly adding, "Demi, stay standing if you would."

I force a blank stare but I do as she instructs, stepping forward a few feet and slightly to the left.

"Why don't you ditch the sweater." She lowers to her knees.

Slowly, I untie the hoodie from around my waist and toss it toward her, leaving me in my stretchy workout shorts and sports bra.

"Everyone, Demi is going to perform the full routine, on her own, for you so you can have a good idea of what we'll be doing Friday night."

I run my tongue over my teeth, squaring my shoulders in preparation.

I don't know what she's thinking, I have no reservations about performing for people. I'd dance in front of the President if he asked me to and not bat a damn lash.

I know what I'm capable of.

She presses play and I do exactly as she asks, not missing a damn beat.

She doesn't look so smug when the music stops and everyone cheers.

"Again," she snaps as she sits back, and I move into position once more, my muscles locking when she calls out, "Alex. Run through the first part with her."

Is she joking?

Alex steps up with no hesitation whatsoever, planting his chest to my back, but I jerk away, unease twisting in my gut.

I whip around, glaring at her. "I'm not doing this."

"Excuse me?" Miranda barks.

"I *said* I'm not doing this."

She crosses her arms, gauging me.

I look at Nico, but he's blocked from my view when Alex slides over, reaches out and grips my hips roughly. "Come on, just do what she asked."

I don't even have time to peel his filthy hands off me when Alex is suddenly tackled to the ground, causing me to fall as well.

Everyone shouts, scooting back.

"Nico!" Miranda screams. "Enough!"

Her shrill cries do nothing to derail him.

Nico jolts to his feet, towering over Alex, and serving him with a swift kick to the side.

Alex grunts, rolling over as Trent hurdles forward, driving Nico back to stop this from getting any worse.

"Get the fuck off me!" Nico throws his hands up, knocking Trent's away with disgust.

Raw grief is written across Trent's face, so clear I know Nico sees it, too, but he refuses to acknowledge it, and jumps in his face, clearly ready to shout something else, but suddenly he looks at me.

I swallow past the sudden ache in my throat.

His nostrils flare, his chin lowering, and I'd swear he's shaking.

My body lurches forward, ready to stand and step toward him, but he quickly shifts, bumping his shoulder into Trent's with a fixed force.

Nico kicks a chair, sending it flying across the gym floor, and throws open the door with a hard shove on his exit.

I push to my feet, ignoring all the wide eyes focused on me, and follow.

"Demi!" Miranda shouts. "You're not excused."

I jerk to a stop, my shoes squeaking on the flooring as I whip around. "Fuck off, Miranda."

262

The girls gasp, some giggle and cover their mouths, but I don't stay back to hear anything else. I run out the door.

Nico is nowhere in sight, so I dash to the parking lot, catching his door right before he slams it shut.

His head snaps my way, his glare quickly turning into shock only to switch right back.

"Get out," I snap.

He scoffs, sitting back in his seat. "Nah, I'm good. You finally got the hands on you you've been waiting for, why don't you run back in there, D? Wouldn't want to keep your boy waiting."

Anger ripples down my spine and I step closer.

"Are you *fucking* kidding me right now?!" I shriek.

Nico's eyes narrow.

"That's how you want to play?" When he doesn't respond, I step closer, forcing words past clenched teeth. "My *boy* is right in front of me, but if he can't see that, after everything that's been said, this week, *last night*, then my standing here right now is as pointless as ever."

I step back, my frustration taking the form of moisture and threatening to spill from my eyes with my next blink.

His gaze doesn't leave mine, following with every foot away, I grow, and hope flares in my chest when he suddenly jerks, dragging himself to the edge of his seat as if he was about to step out, but not a half second later those eyes fall to the ground, and when they pop back up, they're blank. Cold and void of life.

He doesn't climb from his truck, but slams the door, blocking himself off from me instead.

Left with nothing else to do, I walk off, hooking right to take the long way around when I spot Trent headed for Nico, who has yet to drive away.

Thankfully, all my things are in my locker, so I take a quick shower and prepare for class.

Stupid leadership means I can't get away from my thoughts, but instead I'm forced to the same place it all imploded last night.

263

I have to sweep in with the rest of my classmates and clean up what's left of the mess now that all the vehicles and personal items have been moved or picked up. The only way we get to keep going with these types of traditions is if we leave shit how we find it.

There are about fifteen of us in total, so we're all on the field cleaning the left-over garbage and taking down all the banners and balloons we had hung up yesterday morning. I don't know who came back and cleaned up all our shit, because it wasn't me, but there's no sign of spilled enchiladas and our table and everything else is gone.

I hunker down and work as quickly and silently as possible, and before I know it, I'm sweating.

"Dang, Demi." My friend Ava laughs. "You got this entire half by yourself."

I laugh, wiping my hand across my brow. "Yeah, I've got a lot on my mind. I want to stay busy . . . and for this day to end."

She hesitates before asking, "Wanna talk about it?"

There it is.

My arms fall, the garbage bag in my hand spilling over the edge, and instant tears roll down my cheeks.

Because no, I *don't* want to talk about it.

I want to sit and *not talk*.

With Nico.

"Demi?"

A heaviness in my chest has my heart pounding harder.

"Yeah." My voice comes out scratchy, so I try to clear my throat, but when I swallow it stings.

I lose my breath.

I pull my gloves off, tossing them into the bag and look at Ava. "Do we have more water?" I rasp.

Ava's forehead tightens and she nods, jogging off.

I twist with her, following behind with slower steps. Sweat beads across my neck and I lift my hair, fanning myself.

My eyesight grows fuzzy, so I stop walking, blinking a few times.

My teacher walks up right as I start to stumble, and he gently lowers with me as I fall to the ground.

Ava uncaps the water bottle, handing it to me, and I take a few small sips, fighting for a deep breath.

"Did you get any sleep last night?" Mr. Course asks.

"About as much as any of us."

He nods. "You eat?"

I pause to think and then shake my head.

"Okay, let's stand you up, and get you to the nurse. I'll run to class and grab you something from our stash."

Mr. Course calls for campus security on his walkie talkie and a few minutes later, the little golf cart is speeding across the field.

They help me onto the back and off we go.

Trent is in the hall when we cruise by and he rushes toward us.

"Dem? What happened?"

"Nothing," I say, looking away from him, happy security keeps going.

Against my protest, the nurse calls my mother, and shocker, she's home, and even more surprising, shows up at the school only minutes later.

"Demi?" she asks expectantly.

"I'm fine. No sleep and no food apparently does this to you."

Her eyes thin and she steps closer, opening her mouth to bitch, I'm sure, but then the nurse walks in again.

My mother turns to her. "We're stepping outside."

"Of course, Ms. Davenport." She smiles at me. "Feel better, Demi."

My mother speaks the second we're planted in her car, away from prying ears, but still in the school parking lot. "I didn't know you had an event last night."

"You don't know much, Mother. You're never home." I look out the window.

She ignores my response. "How did you expect to get through your classes after staying up all night?"

I tense, realizing where this is going. I look at her.

When she hesitates, I roll my eyes and lay my palm open between us.

She drops the pill, already in her hand, in mine, nodding to a fresh, unopened bottle of water that happens to be sitting in her cupholder.

After a bit of a stare off she guesses, "Is this about that boy? Did something happen?"

"Nothing happened. Everything is fine." I take a deep breath, reach for the door handle, and push it open.

"What are you doing?"

I swallow, looking back to her. "I ate in the office, I'm feeling better, so I'll see you when I get home."

"Demi." She frowns. "The pill."

I turn to her, setting the pill on her dash and level her with a hard glare. "Hand me another one of these and I'll finish the year living with Dad."

I slam the door shut and head back inside.

I don't go to class.

Chapter 31
Nico

"Thought that last one was perfect," Trent says as we step inside the locker room after practice.

He's right, he threw a bomber, a hell of a pass.

I slowed my game and let the fuckin' thing drop.

I shouldn't have come back for practice today.

Opening my locker, I ignore him, set my helmet inside, and start unclipping my shoulder pads, bending to shimmy them off.

Hands grip the edge of my gear, and I jerk away, tugging them over my head completely.

I glare, moving to work on the belt of my practice pants.

"This how it's gonna be, man?" Trent throws his locker open, dropping his helmet inside. "Not gonna talk to me, don't want my help, purposely drop passes?"

When I don't respond, he dares, "Maybe I'll have to throw to Hammons more—"

When my head snaps his way, he closes his mouth, looking away as he unclips his own shit.

"I shouldn't have said that," he mumbles a moment later.

I grab my bag, leaving my pants open, shirt off, and cleats on. I slam my locker closed before getting in his face.

"You shouldn't have fucked Demi either," I hiss, shoving his ass into the metal as I pass him.

The second I step into the fresh air; my shoulders fall and I head for my truck.

I throw my shit in the back and drop against the seat.

I fuckin' hate fighting with Trent. It's rare we argue, and when we do, it's over stupid shit we can laugh about later, but this is different.

I know it's not fair for me to be pissed about something from years ago when I've spent the last few dating Josie or hooking up with other people, but I am anyway.

The thing is, if he'd have told me this then, I might not have her now.

Do I have her now?

I pushed her away, but she tried not to let me. She tried to keep me there, and I walked off regardless.

Just like I did with Trent years ago.

After my dad left my mom, I dropped all my friends and stopped conversing with adults I knew.

My mom was miserable, and I was partially to blame for it, so I told myself I was supposed to be unhappy and alone, too, but Trent refused to go.

He fought me, literally a time or two, when I'd try my hardest to get him to back off, but no matter how shitty I was, he never would.

He knew I was bleeding on the inside and he was too good of a friend to walk away, and he has been ever since.

His sleeping with Demi doesn't change that, but it fuckin' sucks and I can't stand thinking about it.

I can't help but believe it'll always be right there when I look at him or her, or them together, the image of him *with* her.

A thought hits, and I call someone I'd never expect to.

She answers on the first ring.

"Nic?"

"Hey, Krista. You still at practice?"

"No, I just walked in my house, hang on." There's a light shuffle, and the sound of a door closing before she asks, "Are you okay?"

I scoff, and her soft laughter floats through the line.

"Yeah, I had a rough night, too," she admits. "I feel better now though, always do after I talk to Trent. I take it you haven't yet?"

"Nah, not yet."

"Demi?" she asks.

I scoff a light laugh. "Does gettin' my shit handed to me count?"

"When it's coming from Demi, I say yes," she jokes. "She doesn't lose her cool all that often . . . only when something means enough for her to. Or someone."

"Yeah, I hear you." I lick my lips, my eyes closing. "Is it weird?" I rush out before I change my mind.

She knows exactly what I'm asking. "Not anymore, but it was. Sometimes it was pretty bad, if I'm honest, and I'd get super insecure. She had already given him what I wasn't ready to, so I felt pressure, but as soon as Trent realized it, he went out of his way to change it."

"Does it make you jealous, when they talk, or do you get mad or curious when they're alone?"

She's quiet a long moment before she says, "I don't, but is that what worries you the most? The possibility that she could want him again?" She pauses. "Because if it is, Nic, I think you might want to take a second to consider how she must feel about the girls you've been with. That was her first time and two years ago. Who was the last person you were with and how long ago was that?"

Fuck man, she's right.

She saw me with Sandra, knows I left Josie because I was cheated on, and I told her about Miranda, then she was forced to watch me dancing with her.

"Nic?"

I clear my throat. "Yeah."

"I didn't say any of that to take away from what's happened. Trent should have told you a long time ago, and if not that, then Demi should have before you two started dating. It wasn't fair how they went about it, and I'm sorry you found out how you did."

I nod, sighing into the line.

"Now, tell me the truth, how much of an asshole were you?"

I laugh and she follows.

"Talk to them, Nic. If you're hurting, they are, too. That sucks for everyone."

"Thanks, Krista."

I hang up, take a deep breath and drive home.

I head straight for the shower when I get inside, but my mom's soft hums have me poking my head back out and walking to her room.

Concern pulls at my gut when I find her on the floor, surrounded by papers, a loopy smile on her face.

I drop beside her. "Ma?"

"Nikoli," she rasps, her palm coming up to slide down my cheek. "You're home."

"What is all this, Ma?"

Her hand falls, and she looks to the mess. "He's promised to take care of us."

I pull back, slowly pushing to my feet. "What'd you do, Ma?"

"Your father. He came with papers from lawyers, had everything ready for me, wasn't that nice of him?"

"No."

Tears fill her eyes and she smiles weakly. "He's letting us come live with him. Isn't that great? We'll be a family again."

"Please, no." I run my hands down my face and get back on my mom's level. "Tell me you didn't give him the house? Tell me you didn't sign *anything* without me here?"

She tilts her head. "You know he only comes to see me when you're gone."

"Fuck!" I start pacing the room. "He screwed you, I know it."

"No, no . . . he loves me, Nico. He'll take care of us."

I shake my head. "Like he's been taking care of us, Ma? He steals from you, and keeps you so doped up you don't even realize it."

She looks to the wedding ring she refuses to take off. "He's good to me, makes sure I have the medicine I need."

"You aren't sick!" I yell. "Not in the way he's made you believe." I drop beside her, grabbing her hands gently. "Ma, you lost your husband, and it broke you. You're sad, depressed,

270

and that's okay. I get it, I swear. I tried to find someone to help you, remember? But you only wanted him, and he used that to control you."

"You're wrong. He cares. He pays our bills."

"With your money," I stress gently. "And now you probably just gave him control of everything."

"It'll all be okay, son," she whispers, her eyes growing tired, whatever fucking cocktail he cooked up for her when he was here obviously kicking in. "He promised me."

I glare at her, having so much more to say, but unable to let the words out.

She's fucked up, he's in her head, and she doesn't want to know the truth.

What's she gonna do when I'm gone next year?

I wasn't sure how I'd leave before, but I really can't get out of here if she has no place to go.

That's got to be why he's doing this.

Her head tilts up a little, and she smiles at me.

I swallow my sigh, moving forward to scoop her in my arms, and gently place her on the bed.

She pats my cheek, her eyes already closed. "My sweet, sweet boy, I love you so much."

My chest grows tight.

I want to shake her, hug her, her to hug me back, instead I look down at her from the bedside.

"Love you, Ma," I whisper, but she doesn't hear me.

She's already knocked out.

I turn off her light and bypass the shower, stumbling my way down the stairs, and out the back door.

Before I realize what I'm doing or where I'm going, I'm already shoving open the gate connecting Demi's yard to mine.

I spot her instantly through the large window, little and perfect and not quite mine.

She's in her kitchen, pulling something down from the cupboard when her head snaps my way, her eyes locking on mine through the glass.

She takes me in, still half dressed in my gear, and worry clouds her eyes.

I need you, baby.

She rushes for the sliding door, pushing it open right as I reach it.

"Neek—"

I cut her off by slamming my mouth into hers.

Her lips tighten a moment, but she gives in the very next, letting me take what I want from her.

What I need from her.

Every little bit she'll allow and more.

Her arms wrap around me as I scoop her up and walk us backward toward the stairs, kicking my cleats off as I step.

I drop her on top of the small table near the foot of the stairs so I can kiss her better, dive deeper into her mouth, and then she tears away, dropping her head back as she gasps for air.

I let my lips fall down her jawline and to her neck, where I suck gently.

Her little hands slide up my back, her fingers spanning out against me, pulling me in.

She's so welcoming, so ready to give—and she doesn't even question us despite everything—that it's overwhelming and my head falls to her shoulder.

I grip her hips, squeezing slightly.

Her hands loosen, one making a lazy path up and down my back, while the other slides past my cheek, and across my fade. She lightly brushes her fingers in repetitive, soothing movements.

I lift my head, locking eyes with her perfect green ones.

Words aren't needed, she can see as I can, the hurt we caused each other. The unnecessary pain we didn't have to deliver and can and will move past.

She's mine and I'm hers and that's what matters here.

I'm standing here with fucked emotions and a weighted mind.

I need her and no kind of fight would be changing that fact.

Demi knows and slowly raises her hands over her head.

I lick my lips, tug her to the edge and meet the skin of her waist with my fingertips.

I don't take my eyes off her as I trail them up purposely, torturously, slow.

Her deep breaths quickly switch to short pants, her face giving the illusion of pain, when it's need coursing through her every vein and all I've done is run my knuckles along her ribs.

When I get to her bra line, I lean forward, and her lips part. I lift her shirt so it's blocking her face, stealing her sight as I blow warm air across her breastbone, smirking when goose-bumps rise in response.

She loses some patience, and helps the thin cotton over her head, tossing it to the side.

Her palms land on my chest, and she drags them down, then back over my pecs before leaning in. Thick, warm lips press against my skin, and my hand shoots up to close around the back of her neck.

Her eyes pop up, the emerald within them hardly visible she's so stirred up, and she slips her fingertips into the band of my boxers.

Her eyes fall, tracking her own movement as she pushes my practice pants to my thighs, then brings her feet up to help them the rest of the way down until they've fallen to my ankles. I kick them somewhere behind me.

Her greedy hands quickly slide across the front of my boxers, cupping my dick with a light squeeze causing me to flex in her grasp.

I groan, slide my palms around her ass, and lift her again, her legs quickly latching on.

I spin us, carefully climbing the stairs with her in my arms while she lets go to unlatch her bra and tosses it aside.

A raspy giggle leaves her when I stop dead, hitting her back against the wall with an urgency I've never felt as I quickly bring my hands up to feel her better.

I bring my mouth to her skin, wrapping my lips over her nipple and tugging until it pops free.

My eyes snap to hers. "Mine."

"Yours," she moans, grinding against me and I apply pressure with my hips.

She slips her hands between us, pushing my boxers down and I pull back, forcing her to watch me as she does it.

That has her slowing her movements, but still, she keeps going.

I let her legs fall, but she keeps her back plastered to the wall, not dropping her eyes as we push my boxers down together.

My dick springs free between us, the head brushing where her jeans end at her waistline, getting the tiniest taste of the feel of her skin, and my thighs clench.

"I've thought of this," she admits with a breathy whisper, her untried senses on full fire. "Imagined it."

"Me too, baby. More than I'll admit." I move in again, but she has other ideas.

She nudges me away gently, and takes backward steps down the hall, unbuttoning her jeans as she goes.

She's eager, it's easy to see, but she pulls at her restraint, and when her eyes fall from mine, it's in a slow savoring appraisal. One I'm guessing she's in favor of if the way her steps falter when her eyes meet my hard and ready cock for the first time tells me anything.

Her chest inflates as she halts altogether, hips swiveling as she works those tight ass jeans all the way down, now standing in nothing but a deep blue thong.

Her hand comes up to grip the doorframe closest to her, and with her head angled toward me, her body twists, giving me a full, straight on, side view of all ass.

"Fuck, D," I groan, and I rush toward her.

She laughs and quickly disappears behind the door.

I fucking follow.

She's leaning against the wall just inside, a smile on her face, her tongue sitting between her teeth, waiting for me.

I lick my lips, slowly walking toward her, and damn if a deep flush doesn't creep up and across her skin with my advance.

We're in her room now, so it's getting more real by the second.

I'm about to have her, take her.

Fuckin' claim her.

I slide my palms down her chest, feathering my fingers across her hard nipples only to slide them back up and cup her breasts fully. I massage them gently, before dropping my lips to Demi's.

She inhales deeply, her mouth perfectly in sync with mine. "You got a shower in here?"

She nods.

"Take one with me."

There's no hesitation from her as she links my hand with hers, pulling me along and into the closed door at the left side of her room.

She lets go, spinning to turn it on and reaching out to feel the water.

I step against her, her bare ass lined up perfectly with my dick.

She gasps when I slide it against her, my arm raises and I trail my fingers along her raised one until I can intertwine our fingers again.

I bring both our hands down, wrapping them around her middle and she pushes into me, her head falling back to my shoulder.

My free hand comes around, gripping the side of her face and turning it to mine.

I kiss her, deep and full, and she melts into me, spinning in my arms and pressing her near naked body into mine.

My hands skim across her panty line and she pulls her lips free.

Her heart beats wildly against me, those hazy, utterly aroused, eyes locking with mine. "Take them off, Neek."

"Not yet," I rasp. "I need to feel how bad you want me first."

Her gaze darkens and she squirms, but her center pushes in closer, ready for me.

I slide my fingers inside the material and trail them down until the center meets my skin. Instantly they freeze there, the proof of how ready and wanting she is right there for me to touch.

She's soaked.

"Bad," she moans, delivering the answer I've just discovered.

"So fuckin' bad, right baby?" I hook my fingers in the sides and step back, my eyes on her as I drop to my knees, slowly sliding her underwear down her legs.

Her head tilts forward slightly, so she's looking at me down the bridge of her nose, waiting to see what I want to do next.

So many things, baby.

I reach over, tapping the edge of the shower.

She knows what I want.

She lifts her leg, placing her foot flat against it and I scoot in.

Her scent hits me first and I groan, squeezing her thigh as my hand glides up and across to her ass cheek. I lean in, blowing slow, warm breaths across her center and her hands fly to my head.

"I didn't shave today, baby." I lick my lips, and hers fall open. "You wanted to feel my stubble on your inner thigh, yeah?"

Her eyes blacken and she nods.

I glide my chin along the apex of her thighs, and her muscles tense, even more when I allow it to lightly brush her clit as I pull back.

"You want my mouth on you, D?" I rasp, squeezing her ass cheek.

"I want all of you," she whispers.

I'm struck immobile.

I stare up at her, Demi Davenport, stripped bare, stimulated, her eyes open and on me. For me.

Wanting me.

I slip my hand farther into her ass crack and tug her to me, my mouth clamping around her throbbing clit instantly.

I groan at the taste of her, my chest rumbling and her heavy moan fills the room. Her grip on me tightens.

I roll my tongue as I suck her into my mouth and her legs start to spasm, her whimpers growing longer, deeper, and when her legs try to close on my head, I pull away, shooting to my feet and smashing my lips into hers.

She tries to protest, but when I slip my finger inside her, she dives her tongue into my mouth, fighting for the orgasm I just denied her, but I pull away again.

This time a low, angry groan leaves her, and I smirk.

I climb into the shower, lifting her in with me and spin her to the wall, closing us inside.

She tries to sneak her hand between us, but I catch it, pinning it back with my own.

"I need to get clean for you, baby. I just got outta practice."

"I don't care."

I fight a grin, grinding into her, my eyes flying across her face as she moans. "I do."

She pouts but then raises a brow as she reaches to the side blindly grabbing a bottle of soap. She squirts some in her hands and lets the bottle fall to the floor.

She trails her hands over my shoulders, gently nudging me back as she washes my body. She hurries through my top half, but when she reaches my abdomen, she slows, teasing along my skin until she's gliding across my dick.

Her eyes shoot up to mine as she wraps her soapy hand around it. She starts pumping me, her other hand sliding behind my balls and gently massaging.

I drop my forehead to hers, pushing into her hand more.

Her teeth sink into her bottom lip as I grow stiffer in her grasp, and she pumps quicker, her hold tighter as my muscles clench.

I tear away from her, letting the water run over me for a quick second then I rush her.

She laughs when I practically toss her in the air to get her body as high as I need her. Her legs latching around me, her ankles locked tight at my back and I spin us under the spray while keeping our heads out of it.

Her features soften and she pulls her body in, pressing her chest tight against mine. She eyes me, then drops her lips to mine, kissing me with deep, erotic strokes of her tongue. She shifts her lower half, aligning the head of my dick with her entrance.

She releases my lips, opening her eyes to look at me as she pushes her ass into my hands, and the tip is suddenly wrapped in her wet, warm flesh.

"You on birth control?"

Her grip tightens and she nods. "We're good."

Fuck, yes.

"It might hurt more like this," I tell her, sliding my lips across hers. "You're wide open for me, baby."

She pushes more and at first I keep my grip, when her pupils expand, I let up, let her body slide down my shaft until her pussy has swallowed me whole.

She gulps, tugging me close, her pussy clenching around me as I grow even harder inside her.

I pull her ass in, lightly pumping my hips in and out of her and she nods.

I moan, catching her lips with mine again and her hands start roaming, trailing across every inch of me she can reach.

I push inside, grinding against her.

"Oh, fuck," I gasp, my eyes closing.

The feel of her is unreal, silky and tight. Fucking burning.

"Neek?"

"Hmm?" I kiss her neck, her throat, pulling and pushing back in as her nails dig into my back.

She pants. "I want you in my bed."

I groan, shove in deeper only to pull out and set her on her feet.

I quickly shut off the shower and step out. I reach for the stack of towels, but then Demi is in front of me, kissing me again and then she hops up, so I let them fall and instead carry her straight to her bed.

I set her down, but she doesn't let me go, so I crawl with her as she scoots up to her pillows and lies back.

Her legs hook my thighs, pulling me close and I'm back inside her in seconds.

A shudder runs through me and she squeezes my dick within her walls.

I hold still, and our eyes meet. "Tell me what you want, so I can give it to you." I make a slow circle and she squirms, fighting for more, but I grip her hips, holding them still. "You want me to fuck you good, baby? Make you come?"

I quickly dip to scrape my teeth along her nipple and a ripple of excitement shoots through her. "Oh god."

I flex inside her and her eyes widen with need. "How bad do you need to come, D?"

I pull back, until only my tip is left inside her, and then slowly drive back in.

She whimpers, her nails finding my ass, a sexy little warning glare filling her eyes. "I'm pretty sure I can come just feeling you like this, but if you want to earn it, you better move, 'cause I'm ready. Ready for you. For this." She licks her lips, a heavy need blanketing her features as she rasps, "Give me all of you, Neek. Now."

A shiver runs along my spine and I don't hesitate.

I pump in and out, faster and faster and her knees draw back, her head diving into the pillow.

I lean down, kissing across her collarbone and she starts to shake. I pull one of her legs in, holding it against my ribs and tilt my hips, giving her a deeper, fuller angle and her back flies off the bed, a loud, airy and unrestrained moan filling her room.

"God, damn, baby."

With long, slow blinks, her eyes hit mine before they close completely, her hips pushing into mine before her entire body twitches and she grips me, attempting to keep me still so she can ride it out, but I grind harder, push deeper and then my toes curl and I come with her, both of us shaking and sweating and holding on tight.

After a few minutes, her feet slide across the mattress, her body growing limp.

I climb off and go to stand but she shakes her head, so I drop down again.

Her hand comes up to brush my hair from my face and she smiles, the first sign of any shyness I've seen tonight.

"Don't go getting nervous on me now," I rasp, reaching out to run my knuckle over the edge of her breast, sliding it back and forth across her nipple, grinning as it plumps up.

"I'm not nervous."

Our eyes meet. "No?"

She shakes her head, scooting closer, and leaning over so I have to fall on my back to stare up at her.

Her wet hair falls onto my chest, so I wrap it in my hand, laying it behind her.

"What are you then, Pixie?"

The crimson on her cheeks spreads a little more. "Okay maybe a little nervous," she admits, and both of us chuckle.

Her hands trail along my abs and she tilts her head. "Why do you call me Pixie?"

"Because that's what you've always been to me, and you were right, it's got nothing to do with your height, baby, but what I see. How I felt when I'd look at you, which was often."

I bring my hand up, my stare following as I glide the pads of my fingers across her collarbone.

"My little Pixie," I whisper, my lip twitching when she shudders. "An elusive, unattainable creature. Can hardly see it. Can't possibly catch it." My eyes snap to hers. "Could never keep it."

Her forehead wrinkles, her eyes flying between mine as my hand falls to my side.

She twists, now lying on her side, facing me, and pulls her blanket over us both. Demi slips her hand in mine, folding it between us. "That's how you felt about me before, but what about now . . . after everything, and now that you know what you didn't before?"

"Now I'm keeping you even if you try to leave."

She laughs lightly, her eyes roaming mine before shame fills them. "I'm so sorry, I should have told you. I should have thought to."

It stings, but the reality is I'd never walk away from her, and she doesn't deserve to have guilt over something she did years ago, having no idea it would tear me apart then. I run my knuckle across her jaw. "I think you would have, if we started differently."

She's hesitant as she asks, "What you said to Trent, about wanting me before he had me. Why did you say that?"

"Because it's true. I've wanted you for *years*, Demi. Years."

"I never knew."

"I know, but you do now."

She smiles, looking away. "My mom brought me a pill today." It takes a moment, but she glances back. "I was stressed, exhausted and couldn't focus after everything. She knew I was off."

Unease stirs in my gut as I wait for her to say more.

"For the first time, I gave it back," she whispers. "I told her if she tried to give them to me again, I'd move in with my dad."

Warmth and affliction spread through my gut for so many reasons, one because Demi was strong enough to stand up to her mom, and the other because my mom can't seem to stand up for herself.

She leans over, pressing her lips to mine in a slow, promising kiss. "Stay, Nico."

"That doesn't sound like a question."

"That's because it's not." She tucks into me, a smile ghosting her lips. "Now, close your eyes before I change my mind," she teases with a yawn, sinking farther into her mattress.

I don't say a word.

I close my fuckin' eyes.

Chapter 32
Demi

Warm breath fans across the back of my neck and my eyes slowly open. My alarm clock reads five in the morning, we have school in a little over an hour.

I twist in my sheets, looking to Nico who is sound asleep, lying flat on his back, one hand under his pillow, the other resting low on his stomach.

I gently turn all the way, lifting the covers slightly to get a better look at him.

His tan skin glows against my ivory sheets, and even when at ease as he is right now, his muscles are sculpted and curved to my kind of perfection.

I look to his face and I fight the urge to lean over and meet his lips.

His commanding, control seeking, perfect lips.

I replay moments from last night in my head and my core warms.

He was so in tune with what I liked, knew exactly how to set my body off and I tried to give him just as much back.

When I had sex before, I felt clueless and unsure, self-conscious.

Last night, all I felt was Nico.

His want and his need, his desire to please and the greed in his movements. Every time his hands touched me it was purposeful. Every kiss was more heated than the last and every moan he earned of mine only seemed to make him work harder for the next one.

Last night was completely intoxicating.

Nico is intoxicating.

I quietly climb from the bed, snag my robe from the hook near my door, and move to use the restroom in the hall so I don't wake him.

The last thing I expected yesterday was everything I had hoped for — Nico to show up and erase the memory that threatened to ruin us.

He did, and then some.

I know nothing is forgotten, but to have him here, knowing we can move past this is more than enough.

After washing my hands, I splash some water on my face, gently patting it dry with a hand towel and sliding it across my neck.

My robe falls open slightly and I spot a small hickey just over my breast.

I lean closer to the mirror, tracing it with my fingers and then look into my own eyes.

No guilt. No shame.

I step back, push the door open, and my eyes fall to my discarded jeans, then slide down the hall where Nico's boxers lie.

A small smile tugs at my lips and I follow the trail, laughing at his football pants on the stairs, and my shirt by the entrance rug, his cleats a few feet from there.

I pull the corner of my bottom lip between my teeth and reach into the fridge for a bottle of water.

I unscrew the lid, taking a drink as I close the door.

I scream and jump back, gasping in the next second as the cold-water spills onto my chest.

My hand flies to my robe and I pull it closed tighter.

"Mom." My wide eyes snap from her to me and back. "What the hell!"

My mother narrows her eyes, tilting her head slightly. "What the hell?" she repeats.

"I only mean thanks for creeping up on me, you scared me."

"Maybe if you weren't so lost in thought, you'd have noticed I was standing in the living room as you passed by." She blinks.

She was?

"You were?"

She crosses her arms. "Is this what you do when I'm gone? Shack up with the neighbor boy?"

"You know his name."

"Demi."

I put the lid on my water, setting it down I then turn around, leaning against the countertop. I lift my hand. "It's not like you'd know if I was telling the truth or not, but no," I say and the corner of her eyes pinch the slightest bit. "Last night was our . . . was his first time staying over."

Her gaze tightens, but her lips smooth out, so I can tell she appreciates the honesty.

"Protection?" she asks.

I nod even though, no, we didn't pause for that like we should have. I am on birth control, but we should have gone for double protection.

My mom looks away a moment, pretending to pick lint from her blazer before looking back to me.

"I like him."

"I'd hope so," she comes back instantly, judgment burning in her stare, but concern is also evident.

My shoulders fall and I step toward her.

"Mom . . ." I pause. "I'm serious," I whisper. "I like him."

It takes her a few seconds, but her features smooth and she glances away. "Is he . . . are the two of you . . ."

"Dating?" I help her out.

She gives a stiff nod, so I nod back.

"You know, Trent is—"

"Mom." I stop her, moving closer. "Trent is Nico's best friend, my friend's boyfriend, and even if he wasn't either of those things, he would still only be a friend to me. I don't and I won't want him. That's never going to change."

"Friends . . ." she tests the word, her lips pinching.

I shrug. "That's all."

After a moment, my mom surprises me when she clears her throat and nods, a fitted smile on her face.

She reaches out, gently touching my cheek, a bit of dejection plaited in her words, "Don't be late for school, Demi."

She steps back, grabs her purse and her keys, and walks out the garage door, locking it behind her.

It's odd, for a mother to do nothing else, but mine has no clue what to do, and leaving is easier for her than facing the fact that she's oblivious to how to parent a teenage girl. I can't fault her for it, but sometimes I almost wish she'd try.

I take a deep breath, my eyes stuck on the way she exited before I pick up my water and head back for my room, but as soon as I step around the corner, I find Nico standing there, leaning against the wall, his boxers on and a throw blanket draped over his shoulders.

"Hi." I grin.

"Hi."

"How long you been standing here?"

"Since you stepped foot in the kitchen." He eyes me, a gentleness I haven't seen in his before. "Thought you were sneaking out of your own house on me."

A small laugh escapes.

"She left?"

I nod.

His eyes blaze. "Come here."

I do.

He lifts his arm, running his hand along my neck before leaning in to kiss me lightly, the blanket falling to our feet as he grabs my hand.

He pulls back, nodding his head so I follow him up the stairs and into my in-house studio room.

There's a few small stools in the corner, a sound system in the other and that's it.

He walks over to the stereo, glancing back at me as he turns it on. "What's in here?"

I shrug, not remembering since I prefer to practice outside. I lean against the frame, eating up every inch of his body standing in nothing but boxers for only me to see and enjoy.

After a moment, The Weeknd's "Earned It" comes through the speakers and he moves to one of the stools, dropping onto it as his head falls against the wall.

"You said I couldn't handle it," he rasps, a slow smirk forming on his lips. "Prove it."

"Prove what?"

He lifts his chin, calling me to him and I don't hesitate.

I stop right between his legs.

Nico scrapes his teeth over his bottom lip, his hands coming up and sliding under my robe at my shoulder. He slips his hands around and down my arms, taking the soft, fleece material with him, his hands staying on my skin until I'm left standing how he wants me.

Completely bare for only him.

"Dance for me, baby," he whispers, his fist gliding across his hard-on.

My eyes are forced to follow.

I give him what he wants, and Nico gives even more in return.

Chapter 33
Demi

"Why'd you want to meet here?" I ask my dad, taking a quick drink of my water.

"I thought it would be nice to have a meal with my daughter."

"Mom always orders in food when you come." I smirk.

He lets out a low laugh. "Yeah, she does do that, doesn't she?"

"You didn't tell her you were here, did you?"

"Would we be sitting here so peacefully if I had?"

I scoff. "No, we would not."

He gives a small smile, tilting his head. "I hear you have yourself a boyfriend? Any threats I should be making?"

I laugh, covering my face with my hands. "Oh my god, Dad, no."

We don't talk about my relationships, ever, but maybe that's because I've never been much of a dater.

"Do I know him?" he asks.

"Mom told you about him, but didn't tell you who it was?"

"Who is it?"

I stretch my lips over my teeth in a nervous smile. "Nico."

His instant frown makes me laugh.

"Little Nico, who lives right behind you, way too damn close, and used to stare at you through the fence every second he could, *Nico*?"

I'm pretty sure I blush. "He's not little anymore."

My dad throws his head back with a laugh, but when he looks back, there's a softness in his eyes. "No, I guess he wouldn't be. Neither are you, baby girl."

He lets out a deep sigh and I know he brought me here for a reason that makes him feel uncomfortable.

I lay my forearms on the table, giving him a soft smile. "What's up, Dad?"

"Your mom called me the other night, she said she was worried about you." The corners of his eyes pinch. "Considering all the spending lately, and how you don't text me in the evening as often as before made me wonder if she had a right to be. I can never really tell with your mother, so I wanted a chance to chat with you away from her, just in case."

A knot forms in my throat even though I knew this was coming, but still, I delay. "Why didn't Leah come?"

"We have an issue at the firm, and one of us had to stay in town just in case."

"I'll have to drive over soon to see her, it's been a while."

He nods, tilting his head to the side. "Is everything okay, sweetheart?"

"Actually, Dad, yeah." A light laugh leaves me. "More so than any other time I've claimed so."

"Do I have the boy to thank for that?"

I smile, shrugging.

He chuckles. "All right, I won't pry . . . yet." He winks. "So why do you think your mom freaked out and called?"

I lick my lips, looking to my hands a moment. "I . . ."

"Come on, Demi."

Our eyes meet again.

"She's been giving me pills again, here and there, so not like before, but I don't need them, so I told her so." I hesitate. "I also might have threatened to move in with you if she tried to push me."

My dad laughs loudly this time, thanking the waitress for his drink as she sets it down. "That will definitely do the trick."

"Yeah, she's . . . something else."

"And the extra spending, your savings . . ." He eases into the big issue, an expression that says he knows the truth, but expects I won't share it.

I won't.

I don't want to deal with my mom when her world crashes around her.

My eyes fall to the table, my knee bouncing beneath it. "I'm sorry, I . . ." I look to him. "I'll try to do better."

He gives a sad smile, not outing my lie, but nodding as he finishes off his drink and sets down the empty glass.

He leans forward. "I was thinking, what do you think about having the firm set you up with a new, separate account that will be inaccessible and unconnected? I can take a percentage from what you currently get and put it into the new one. An out of sight, out of mind type of account. I can have them play with some numbers, see what needs to be moved to get you where you want to be by the end of the year and then you can adjust. What do you say?"

Yeah, he knows exactly who is spending the money.

"That would be awesome, Dad." I nod, trying to keep the moisture from my eyes. I hate to lie to him, but to completely throw my mom under the bus isn't easy.

He understands, so he doesn't ever really push. I'm pretty sure it's because he has guilt for being so absent, but I don't hold it against him as much as I do my mom. He has a company to run in another town and he still manages to call or text me a few times a week where I live with my mother and speak to her less. He tries where she no longer seems interested.

We spend the rest of dinner talking about school and the work he's currently doing, safe topics that don't cause too much thought.

Within an hour, I'm saying goodnight to my dad, climbing back in my car and heading home.

I text Nico, but get no response, so after a shower, I decide to call it a night and head for bed earlier than normal.

The next day, when I still don't hear from Nico and he doesn't show up at school, I figure it's another one of his random miss days he used to have more often, but when the final bell rings and it's time for his practice to begin and he's still not here, I grow concerned.

I try calling, but it goes to voicemail after a single ring and I force myself not to dwell on it, going about my normal routine instead.

On Tuesday, when it happens again, I decide I'm as angry as I am concerned. I consider talking to Trent, to see if he heard from him, but I have no idea if he and Nico have talked yet and I don't want to step on anyone's toes, so I throw out the thought as soon as it comes.

As soon as the bell rings, I head home, and walk around to his front door. His truck isn't in the driveway, but it could be in the garage, so I knock.

I'm about to walk back home when the silvery voice of a woman floats from the other side.

His mom. Shit.

I take two backward steps, turn to leave, and bump right into Nico.

I stumble, and the bags in his hands fly to the ground as he swiftly jerks forward to catch me.

He's slow to let go, heavy creases paved across his forehead, his under-eye heavy from a clear lack of sleep.

Concern pulls at my brows, and I step back, smoothing my hands over my shorts. "Hey."

"One second," comes from inside, and his glare intensifies, snaps to the door and back to me.

"What are you doing here?" he asks quickly, a sense of urgency and something I can't quite place in his tone.

Not necessarily anger but a deep frustration I'm not sure is for me.

"You've been gone."

He sighs, brushes his hand across my jaw swiftly as he bends to pick up the medication bottles that slipped from the bags, so I get down to help him.

"You didn't answer, so I figured I'd come by and make sure everything was okay." My eyes lift to find his narrowed on me.

I know what he's doing, and it saddens me he still feels so guarded.

Not only had I overheard a bit when he argued with his dad before, but Nico himself shared his mom's troubles with me already.

He can stand here and search all he wants; he'll find no judgment from me.

The door clicks and his glower snaps over my head.

Slowly, I look over my shoulder to find his mom, thinner than I remember, but still just as beautiful, standing there in a nightgown.

Her eyes, as dark and captivating as her son's, fall to mine, and then shift to the pill bottles in my hands. She gives a faint smile.

I push to my feet, bringing my hands together. "Ms. Sykes. Hi."

She tucks her long hair behind her ear. "My husband must have sent you," she guesses and my smile grows stiffer by the second.

Does she not recognize me?

And did she say *husband*?

"You brought my medicine," she says. "Thank you."

Her eyes slide to her son then, and I force mine to follow. Nico glares at the ground.

"I told you he'd keep taking care of us, Nikoli."

Our eyes meet a moment, but he quickly glances away.

He gently tugs the bottles from my hands and stands. "Guess you were right, Ma," he says tenderly, stepping inside and closing the door.

He leaves me there without a word.

It takes me a moment to turn to leave, but as I take a few steps down the path I spot another small pill bottle that rolled into the dirt. I pick it up, turning around to knock on the door once more to give it to them, but the prescribing doctor's name catches my attention and I freeze.

Dr. Avery Hammons.

Hammons. As in . . .

Alex's mom?

I set the bottle close to the door, and walk back home, my mind spinning more and more with each stride.

When I step inside my door, I don't get a foot farther before my mom is in my face, a smile far too wide for my liking.

"What?" I ask hesitantly.

"I just got off of a very promising phone call."

I slowly close the door behind me. "What phone call?"

Her smile spreads impossibly wider.

This can't be good.

Chapter 34
Nico

Never once has my father *ever* reached out to me with the intention of asking me to come to his new house for a visit, the house he bought with the money he seduced my mother into giving him, money left to her from her family.

The shitty part is he doesn't even need it. His new wife is worth even more, but he's a greedy prick, and nothing is ever enough for Nikole Sykes.

The fact that he pulled some shit on my mom and still called me to come here is fucking with my head and bad.

I've been driving up and down his neighborhood for a half hour now, my leg bouncing against the seat, fingers tapping against the steering wheel, I'm so stressed the fuck out, and I hate myself for it.

I hate how he still has a way of getting under my skin when I do my best to pretend his existence and all that goes with it means nothing.

He's nothing.

There's no doubt in my mind he's aware I found my mom under the mountain of paperwork he left her with. He knows I know what he's trying to do, even if I'm still missing pieces. Not that he cares, but still.

Invite me here for a fight in front of his wife who probably has no fucking clue he's still screwing his ex when it's convenient for him?

To say I'm on edge is an under-fucking-statement.

At first, I flat-out refused, but when he used my mom as a threat against me, I had no choice but to cave to the asshole.

Who knows what he'll pull on her next time I'm out of the house. I've already fallen even more days behind in school because of him and his latest stunt, I can't afford to miss any more. He knew I'd take the time to try and figure out what exactly he accomplished by getting those documents signed.

I spent hours going over the paperwork he left, but it was all out of order and seemed pages were missing to the point where I couldn't make any sense of it. I'm not a damn lawyer and most legal terms are lost on me, so it was more wasted time than not.

It didn't help that whatever it was he gave my mom had her vomiting and sluggish into the next day. I'm the only one she has who cares about her, so of course I was at her side through it. I had to feed her more meds when she started shaking and getting even sicker once they began to wear off, so the two days that followed the first were spent watching my mom sleep and wishing she'd wake with a clearer mind than the one she'd laid down with.

He's getting more reckless with her and I have no clue how to end it. Denying his request wouldn't help any, that much is clear.

So here I am, parked outside of his place, glaring at the long walkway that leads to the front door, a giant ass welcome wreath hanging from the center of it.

I pull my phone out to check the time, but before I realize what I'm doing, I'm dialing Demi.

My muscles constrict even more when she doesn't answer.

I haven't talked to her since she came to my house, and it feels like too long already. She showed up, worried because I had disappeared. I should have taken the time to call her when I was out, but when shit at home gets so fucked up, I get lost.

I fuckin' hate it.

There's no way she didn't see the prescribing doctor's name on the pill bottles, and I need to prepare to talk to her about that.

I toss my phone to the side and look up again.

Fuck it.

I climb from my truck, taking my steps two at a fucking time. *The quicker I get in, the quicker I can get the hell out.*

This isn't my house and I know I'll never truly be welcome here, but I walk in without knocking anyway.

Respecting this place is the last thing on my mind, so I don't bother with closing the door, allowing it to slam shut behind me as I walk through the entryway, following the voices floating from around the corner.

"That must be my other son now."

Other son.

Please. I have no brother.

Man, fuck this.

I lick my lips, stand straight and mask my fucking face before moving into view.

The little bitch is the first one I spot, and his eyes meet mine, a sick, satisfied gleam staring back as he sits beside my dad as if it's where he belongs.

Maybe it is. On the inside they're one and the same. Both as fucked up and manipulative as the other.

"Nico," my father says, pushing off his place against the wall.

I step farther into the room giving him nothing but a blank stare.

"Don't be rude, son." He's gotten good at acting, his smile comes off generous, but his eyes are as vicious as always. He sweeps his hand out and says, "We have guests."

Right as he says it, a little hand with pink polished nails folds over the edge of the high-backed chair facing away from me.

Inch by inch, long, dark blonde hair from scalp to tip appears, a frame I'd recognize anywhere that has no place in this living room.

My feet grow numb yet heavy, my body swaying in place as my lungs squeeze in my chest, blocking my airway.

Time fucking slows, my veins running cold when slowly, her head turns, those green eyes needing no directing, but landing right on mine.

I've never witnessed such an array of emotions flash across a person's face and so quickly.

Anger, disappointment, discomfort.

Sadness.

Confusion.

Concern.

Fear?

What are you afraid of, baby?

I want to step toward her, but I'm rooted in place, fucking frozen.

"I didn't know you had a brother," she says, her tone cool and collected when she's anything but.

My eyes move between hers, a sharp ache puncturing between my ribs, a pain so strong I have to look away, my glare settling on the asshole she's referring to. "I don't."

Alex smirks, and I force myself to glance back to Demi.

Her face contorts, but she doesn't say a word, and in the next second, her mom is standing beside her.

My eyes cut to my dad. "What is this?"

"I called Ms. Davenport and asked her family to join mine for dinner."

In my peripheral, I see Demi's head jerk toward her mom.

My dad continues, "We were just discussing formal next week, and the possibility of Alex being Demi's date."

Anger pulls at my every muscle, and my eyes fly to her.

She slowly shakes her head, looking from my dad to me. "That's not—"

She cuts off when her mom grips her by the arm.

Demi pulls her foot back the half a step forward she had started to take.

"Oh, honey, don't be silly." Her mother tugs her closer, an undertone to her words that can only be interpreted as a warning.

My pulse spikes, but I force myself to stay put, keep fucking calm because the last thing I'm about to do is give anyone in this room the satisfaction of witnessing my anxiety.

Demi, though, she surprises me when she tugs free from her mom and steps away. Despite how pissed off and confused she is right now, my baby attempts to clear the air. "I'm not sure what my mom told you, Mr. Sykes, but I think there's been some confusion."

"Are you not dating my son?" He cocks his head to the side mockingly.

"Yes. Your *son*, not your stepson." She cuts a quick glance my way, uncertainty in her eyes but confidence in her words. "I'm with Nico."

My dad isn't deterred. "Is *Nikoli* taking you to the dance, Demi?" he asks her.

She hesitates, her eyes snapping toward mine.

Is that not an obvious answer?

She keeps her focus on me as he adds, "Has he so much as mentioned it, let alone asked you himself?"

Doubt creeps over her and my throat begins to itch.

I glance across the room, from my dad's silent, porcelain wife to Demi's carbon copy mother. From Alex to my dad, my eyes settling on Demi last.

"Nico and I are going together." Her answer is straightforward, but it kills me to hear it.

She had to be careful with her words, not let on that, no, I haven't mentioned it, and no we haven't spoken of it at all.

I know what she's thinking.

Am I really going to stand here and not say a word? Not confirm I'm hers and she's mine, allow Alex to think she's free game when she's anything but.

Why the fuck am I playing statue?

Why haven't I grabbed her and dragged her from this toxic place already?

Maybe I want to test her when I have no right to, maybe the pressure of being in my dad's house with his new wife and chosen son is too much, or perhaps it's that her mother so quickly disregarded my being what her daughter wants when she realized Alex fucking Hammons, my unclaimed, bitch of a stepbrother wanted her, too.

Whatever the reason, I say nothing at all, forcing an emotionless expression when all I really want to do is fall at her feet and erase the hurt in her eyes.

Alex, though, he opens his mouth.

"You know, I was surprised when I found out you two were hanging out." Alex smirks and pushes to stand.

The fucker dares walk closer to her with me standing right here.

He's baiting her and damn if she doesn't fall for it, unable to hold back in asking, "Why is that?"

"It's just, everyone knows Nico to be a bit of a hothead, so it was interesting he didn't tear into me when I told him, and most of the guys on the team, I was planning on asking you out."

Demi's eyes fly to mine and narrow before she slowly moves them back to Alex. "That is interesting. When was this . . . exactly?"

My stomach muscles tighten and I grow light-headed.

Fuck.

This is not how I wanted this to happen.

"After our Thursday night game," Alex tells her, sliding his hands in his pocket like the prick, preppy boy he is. "You know, the night Nico gave you a ride home, and I called to ask if I could come by?"

Instead of focusing on what he wants her to, she asks, "How did you know Nico gave me a ride?"

His pretty boy smile slips, but only for a second before he realizes and puts it right back in place. He lifts his hands. "You caught me. I saw you get in his truck, got worried I'd miss my shot and called you."

I fucking knew it.

That's the one and only reason he called her that night. To take her attention from where it could have possibly been, on me.

"Wait . . . the Thursday game . . ." Demi trails off, shaking her head.

Tension wraps around my body, making it harder to breathe. Alex has no problem clearing it up for her.

"Yeah, the week before Krista's birthday weekend, *before* you and Nico got together?" He chuckles, but the malice within it is easy to find. "I should've gone that night, and maybe asked you then, huh?"

Demi's eyes fall to the hardwood, and she rubs her lips together anxiously, before lifting her stare to mine. "Yeah . . . maybe."

Anger builds in the pit of my stomach, my eyes twitching and unable to meet hers while desperately wanting to.

I fucked up.

"Competition between siblings, it's quite healthy," my dad says loudly. "I bet had you known of Alex's intentions in advance, Demi, you would have made a wiser choice, am I correct?"

I keep my head straight, but cut my eyes to her, my pulse beating like crazy while my skin starts to crawl. I need to get out of here before I'm gutted, fucking torn apart from the inside out, for all these assholes to see.

Demi's smile is tight, and I prepare myself for the sickening gleam that will fill my father's eyes when the son he's chosen is chosen or agreed upon by her, be it in anger or in truth.

It doesn't matter, it'll sting the same.

She opens her mouth, my chest tightening more and more by the second, but then she clamps it shut.

Demi shakes her head, anger clouded by fresh tears, transforming my favorite shade of green into a murky mess it slays me to see.

She moves her focus to my dad, pity leaking into every word spoken. "I'm not even sure how to respond to such a foul question, Mr. Sykes." She's quiet but resilient. "Your obvious and ill-placed insult of your own son makes me sick, and I'm positive the answer isn't one you want to hear anyway."

Her mother gasps while my heart threatens to tear from my chest.

Demi turns to Alex next. "I'm not going to formal or anywhere else with you. The fact that you so easily disregarded how you already have a date to formal who, I'm sure, is excited to go, speaks to how shitty of a person you are."

"Demi!" her mom shrieks.

Demi rolls her eyes and looks to her mom. "And, seriously, Mom. Will you ever stop?"

"Demi!" she hisses.

Demi isn't discouraged. "Quit trying to use me to set yourself up. Be happy for me and what I want or back the hell off," she snaps.

Demi spins, pins me with a heavy glower that warns me not to follow and storms out.

I'm stuck until the door slams with her exit, and then I fucking chase her.

I catch her rushing down the driveway.

"Demi," I call, but she hustles even more. "Baby, wait!"

Suddenly she halts, a little growl leaving her as she spins and stalks toward me. Eyes heated and ready to fight. "I cannot *believe* you pulled this shit!" She shoves me, but I don't budge. "You *knew* he was planning to ask me out before you suggested we pretend to be together!"

"Yeah. I did," I say unapologetically, and fear gets the best of me. "What, you mad? Now you know he wanted you all on his own, you ready to say fuck it and run to him?"

"Did it look like that's what I was ready for?!" she shouts, throwing her arms out. "I was the only one speaking for us in there, or should I say the us I thought we were."

"What the fuck does *that* mean? All the shit that was said between us goes out the fuckin' window now that all you originally wanted got dropped in your lap?!"

"Don't." A quick breath hisses past her mouth.

I know my words aren't fair, but this is what I've feared, her walking away from me.

"Don't you dare try to turn this on me. You played me this entire time."

My head tugs back, shock sending a zing down my spine. "*What*? No! *Fuck* no!"

"Yeah, Nico, you did." She nods. "Maybe something changed along the way, or maybe everything you've said and we've done was a part of the lie, but from the first fucking day, this was about using me to get to him. Admit it."

What the fuck?!

Chapter 35
Demi

I'm shaking I'm so. . . . I don't even know what, but everything hurts worse when Nico shouts his denial.

"That is *not* what this was." He glares, daring to show a hint of anger he has no right to give. "Not even fucking close."

A humorous laugh leaves me, and I cup my face with my hands, shielding myself a moment before pinning him with a hard look when I'm feeling anything but tough right now.

"Your dad, Josie, Sandra . . ." I trail off as a thought hits, my mouth falling open as his grows tighter. "Oh my god."

"Demi. Don't."

"Miranda. He fucked her, too, didn't he? That's why you two stopped hooking up over the summer, isn't it?"

He licks his lips, looking off.

I scoff, but it comes out as more of a cry. "Of course. *Of course*! You would have fucked her again, wouldn't you? If only she didn't let Alex stick his dick in her after you, right? It wasn't about me or us or anything else you led me to believe."

"You're wrong," he argues weakly, but can hardly meet my eyes.

"Ugh. This must have been so fun for an asshole like you." I shake my head. "What, did you look at me and say poor, pathetic, boyfriendless Demi, bet she's naïve enough to fall for my bullshit?" His features grow stiffer. "You said you had something to gain from this, now I know what it truly was — convince me to pretend to date you to weasel your way in, and then make it feel so natural, so *easy*, that I forget the lines

302

between us and believe the lie. All this so you could finally say you screwed him like he has you, and fuck the collateral damage along the way, right?" My brows lift. "Literally, in our case."

Nico's spine shoots straight, his jaw clenching. "You don't even know what you're saying. How fucking backward you have it."

"Whatever." I sniff, looking away, suddenly hit with a wave of exhaustion. "You didn't have to take it this far." I shake my head. "You could have walked away before we got here. Unless this was your plan, fake it 'til you break it."

"Nothing is fucking broken!"

"I am!" I scream, my voice cracking and making a bigger joke out of me.

Suddenly, Nico is in my face, gripping mine and holding it up to his, and a strong sense of desperation flows from him to me.

"You should have told me," I whisper, my hands coming up to clasp around his wrists. "You didn't have to break me to win."

"Don't you get it?" he hisses, but the bitterness in his tone does nothing to hide the anxiety in his eyes.

It only confuses me more.

"Why I stayed away from you all this time when you know now how long I've wanted you? Why I went about it the fucked-up way I did?" He stresses his question. "I had to trick you into seeing me, Demi, when all I saw was you."

"All you had to do was show me who you were, Nico. No games, no pretext. I'd have fallen either way." I'm certain of this.

"You're not getting it . . ." He trails off. "It never would have worked."

"You don't know that."

"Yes, I do. I can't *have* what I want, Demi. He takes *everything*."

"Am I nothing then?" My question is instant, but my voice faint.

His face contorts, his eyes flying between mine. Nico's words leave him on a strangled breath. "What are you talkin' about, baby?"

I swallow, slowly pulling away from his hold and his hands fall to his side as I walk backward into the street.

"You said Alex takes everything from you, but he didn't take me, Nico," I whisper, a defeated shrug leaving me. "You just stood there, quiet, ready to give me right to him, *like nothing.*"

I turn and walk away.

There's no doubt in my mind he's standing there, following my every step taken, but I don't dare look.

Once I'm around the corner and out of sight, I allow my shoulders to fall and text Krista to see if she's home since she's the closest house to this one, and she texts back instantly, letting me know the girls are over, so I head straight there.

Never in a million years did I think my day would end like this.

When my mom told me Ms. Hammons called and asked us over for dinner, I was shocked and confused.

I had no clue what to expect or why the sudden invitation was extended since I had no knowledge of Alex's mom and mine ever conversing outside of social events. I tried to refuse out of respect for Nico, I knew he wouldn't like it, but she was persistent and wouldn't take no for an answer.

I planned to tell him at school since he wasn't answering calls, but then he no-showed again, and there was no way I was going to text him something like that.

The last thing I expected was to walk into Alex Hammons' house and find my boyfriend's dad standing there with a fake smile and condescending demeanor.

I would have turned and walked right out if I wasn't so shocked. I don't remember speaking a word until Nico's voice rang through my ears, simultaneously soothing and irritating everything inside me.

It takes me a solid hour to get to Krista's on foot, and I don't even get a chance to knock before Carley is whipping the door open and tugging me inside.

Her eyes travel over me with sheer concern.

304

Krista and Macy come around the corner right then, both rushing over.

"What happened?" Macy tilts her head.

Krista grips my hand and pulls me toward the couch to sit, and the other two drop onto the coffee table in front of me.

My makeup must be all over my face at this point.

I went from being angry to downright sad and back again at least twenty times on the walk here.

I fall against the cushions. Closing my eyes.

"It was all fake," I admit to them for the first time.

"What was fake?" Carley asks.

"Demi wait—" Krista starts, but I interrupt.

"Me and Nico." Tears form behind my eyelids, so I don't open my eyes right away, hoping they'll disappear.

But when a familiar throat clears, they fly open, but I don't bother sitting up.

The tears spill over, running down my cheeks as I look to him.

"Awesome," I whisper.

"I was trying to tell you," Krista says quietly.

Trent looks down and I manage an eye roll, but when I blink, it only makes more tears fall and I look to my lap.

There is no doubt in my mind Trent knew about Alex and never said a word.

Not that I'd expect him to give up his best friend, but I knew it was fake. He knew I knew it was fake. I just needed the heads up not to get too close.

I should have known this on my own.

He's Nico Sykes, the star receiver, insatiable playboy, and mine?

Yeah, okay, Demi.

"She needs us right now." Krista gets up and directs him toward the front door. "I'll call you later," she tells him before shutting it behind him and moving back beside me.

"You two are okay?" I ask her.

She gives a small smile, nodding. "Yeah, we are, but this is about you. Are you okay?"

"I'm fine." I kick off my wedges, pulling my feet onto the cushion.

"Tell us what's going on." Carley leans forward.

I lick my lips and get right to it. "Nico and I, we weren't really dating . . . it was all for show."

"Whoa, hold on." Macy lifts her hands. "What do you mean? Like you pretended to be together?"

"Exactly."

"Why would you do that?" She shakes her head.

"Macy," Krista hisses.

"What?" she snaps back. "I'm just trying to understand."

"Well—"

"Krista, it's fine," I say, looking to Carley and then Macy. "Nico realized I had a thing for Alex, told me Alex was only interested in girls who were taken, and then suggested he and I pretend we were dating."

Their eyes shoot wide.

"He said he had something to gain from it, too, but I didn't really care what it was, so I went along with it." I clear my throat. "Little did I know then, it was about so much more." I look across to the girls.

"What was it about?" Carley asks.

"Alex."

Confusion covers all three of their faces.

"The night of the Thursday game, in the locker room, I guess the team was talking about formal, who they wanted to ask, who they already asked."

"No . . ." Carley trails off.

I nod. "Alex told the team he was going to ask me."

"That's the day before they both came to school with black eyes, right?" Carley remembers.

"I forgot about that . . ." I trail off.

What does that mean?

Does it even matter?

"Wait, that was also before Krista's party." Macy frowns. "He knew Alex wanted to ask you out before you two started pretending?"

306

"Yep, he played me." I look to Krista. "You were right to question him when you told us Josie cheated on him with Alex. Nico knew all about my being interested in Alex."

"Jesus," she whispers, pity in her eyes.

I nod. "And remember how I said Nico told me Alex was talking to Sandra? Well, I never said anything to you guys, but Nico and Sandra were hooking up the first few weeks of school, so when Alex was after Sandra, she was already sleeping with Nico."

"So, Alex fucked Josie while her and Nic were still together, then Alex goes and fucks Sandra while she and Nico are hooking up?"

"And not only them two." I frown. "Same thing happened with Miranda."

"What?!"

"Holy shit!"

"I knew she was fucking students!"

They all fire off at the same time.

"It gets worse."

They sit, wide-eyed and wait for more.

I hesitate, holding myself back a moment from spilling the secret nobody else seems to know, but I've lied and hidden things from my friends enough lately, and they have no reason to tell anyone what I'm about to share.

"Alex is Nico's stepbrother."

The three of them gape at me, at a loss for words.

"Turns out Nico's dad is married to Alex's mom."

Krista frowns, sitting back. "How the hell could I not have known this?"

"I don't think anyone does."

"Trent?" She lifts a brow.

"It's not his secret to share. Mine either but . . ." I shrug.

"Who told you?" Carley leans forward.

I scoff, shaking my head. "It was an interesting night." I sigh. "My mom told me *Dr.* Hammons called to set up a dinner when really it was Nico's dad who called her. Imagine walking into that home, knowing all you do now about our relationship, to find Mr. Sykes standing there, Nico walking through the door only minutes later."

"Holy shit," Carley whispers.

I look away. "Everything made sense all at once. Nico found a way he could get even with Alex, and he used me to make it happen."

"What an asshole," Macy mutters.

I nod, wiping under my eyes, looking at the black now covering my fingertips. "When Nico first suggested this stupid fake relationship, I thought it was nuts, but something had me saying screw it. It was the weekend, and I could change my mind when the week rolled around if I wanted, you know?" A sad laugh leaves me and I sniffle.

"But you never changed your mind," Carley says quietly. "You fell for him instead."

"I fell for the lie." I look to the girls. "Being with him was so easy, fun and I don't know, exciting. The more time we spent together, the more I thought he might have been thinking the same thing, but now I know it was all his plan."

Krista reaches out, touching my hand. "I'm so sorry, Demi."

I glance at Macy, who has a troubled look on her face.

She eyes me. "Did Nico admit this?"

"No, but he did stand there in front of everyone, in front of *my mom*, and say absolutely nothing."

"You slept with him, didn't you?" All eyes fly to Macy only to cut toward me.

I nod, and all three of my best friends climb on the couch beside me.

We sit there in silence a few minutes before Krista says, "I know it doesn't help, but it didn't look fake, Demi."

It didn't feel fake either.

Chapter 36
Nico

The clink of the gate has my hands falling from my face as I lean back against the cool wicker. I already know who it is, so I don't bother looking, my eyes sliding over the pool instead, trailing the light ripples the vacuum creates across the top as Trent drops in the chair opposite of me.

After a few minutes of nothing from me, he stands, lifting his seat with him and sets it directly in my line of sight.

He stares at me.

I stare right fuckin' back.

He nods, pushes to his feet once more and grabs the football off the grass. Tossing it in the air, he steps back and waits.

He knows I haven't touched a ball once this week. Shit's fucked up and fucked up good when this happens.

He's seen it before, when my dad first left my mom, and a few times in between.

I drag my ass from my seat, walking backward to the opposite side of the yard.

He tosses me the ball and a sense of ease floats over me when the hard rubber hits my fingertips, but it quickly fades.

We toss it back and forth a few times before Trent breaks the silence.

"You okay, man?"

"Does word really travel that fast or do you have a habit of checking up on her?"

His eyes narrow, but quickly smooth out. "She showed up

at Krista's a couple hours ago. I left so she could talk to her friends, but it was pretty obvious shit got spilled."

"You happy about that?" I throw the ball a little harder.

He catches it with a glare. "Happy about my best friend losing the girl he's always wanted and finally got? Nah man, can't say I fuckin' am." He takes an extra second to bullet it back.

I drop my hands, allowing the ball to bounce off my chest. "How the fuck could you keep that shit from me? Two fuckin' years, bro. You had two years to tell me you guys slept together and never did."

Trent's head falls before he meets my eyes again. "I fucked up. I've got no excuse. You told me freshman year you and her would never happen, and you started dating Josie on and off. I was the fool who believed you let Demi go just because you said you did. I get I should have stayed away from her regardless. You have no idea how shitty I've been feeling since I realized you still had feelings for her. Dirt," he spits hatefully to himself. "I feel like straight-up dirt, man."

"Not enough to open your mouth, though, yeah? Not until you had to?"

"I was straight-up terrified to tell you, didn't wanna lose my best friend over something that didn't mean what I knew you'd think it did. Nic, I swear on my life, man. I would never do something knowing it would fuck with our friendship. You're like a brother to me. I would never risk that knowingly."

I shake my head, and we both move back to the chairs.

It takes me a minute, but I look to him. "Why even fuck her? If it didn't mean shit, Trent, why?"

"You really want to talk about this?"

I glare.

He sighs, sits back, and answers fuckin' honestly.

"We thought it would be fun. Most of you guys had already lost your virginity at that point. She had no interest in anyone and didn't see it happening anytime soon, and I . . . was a guy." He shrugs. "I wanted to learn what to do so I'd be ready when it happened with someone else. We were pushed together so much by our moms that we trusted each other, so we drank a little to calm our nerves and then . . . yeah. It was really that fucking insignificant, man. Shirts were left on and all."

"And you thought that's what she deserved? Something purely fuckin' meaningless?"

Trent looks away, wincing slightly. "It's shitty, but uh, I didn't even consider it, not once until the night I took Krista's virginity. I wish I could say I regretted it before then because of you, but I didn't until I realized what it meant to sleep with someone you love for the first time. I gave that memory to Krista and took it away from Dem."

I sit there a minute, unsure of what to say to him.

"I'm sorry, Nic. I knew you crushed on her back then, and that should have been enough for me to tell her no. I'm sorry I didn't tell you after it happened, but honest to fucking god I didn't think you'd care or . . . fuck." He drops forward, placing his elbows on his knees. "I guess I didn't think at all. The minute I realized, though, I should have been honest. I know it only makes it seem worse, but at that point, it felt like we were in too deep." He sighs. "I was afraid, plain and simple."

"It's never too late to be honest, but there is being honest too late."

He nods, looking to his clasped hands.

I glare at his form a minute, then I lick my lips and say, "Luckily I've made some fucked up choices, told some big lies and lost a lot along the way."

Trent's head pops up and I lean forward.

"I'm not looking to lose my best friend, and sure as fuck not right now when I've got a lot of fuckin' nothin'."

I reach out with my fist and he pushes his knuckles into mine.

He knows I'm feeling cross, and that this will take time. We've got a fuckin' field to walk, but I'm more than willing to spare the tread on my cleats to get us back. He's family in every way that counts.

"I'm sorry, Nic," he says, his eyes earnest.

311

"I know, man." I nod, a deep sigh leaving me as I kick the ball at my feet across the concrete and into the pool. "So, you were at Krista's?" I move the conversation, my eyes sliding to his while my head remains forward. "You guys are good?"

His brows knit, but he nods. "She wouldn't even hear me out at first, but after a solid eight of begging and crying like a bitch outside her house that night, she finally took pity on me, let me in and listened to what I had to say."

"But she knew about it already."

"She's known since the day we got home from camp. Dem . . ." He looks away. "She told all the girls."

I scoff, looking off.

"When we argued the other night, it sounded bad. All that shit, anything I've said or done, Nic, it wasn't about protecting Demi. It was about trying to save you from getting hurt in the end."

"I didn't need you to do that, Trent. I don't get in your relationship, why would you get into mine?"

"Because I saw it, the second she agreed, I knew how bad you would want it to be real, and I didn't want you to fall if she . . ."

"If she wasn't?"

He nods.

"Why wouldn't she?" I look to him.

He lifts his hands, holding them up a moment before letting them drop. "You guys weren't friends, you never talked, and she thought you hated her even though I told her several times you didn't."

"You saw how we were together, man," I say, shaking my head. "You're the one that said it seemed too much too fast."

"I know you, Nic, and I saw how much deeper it was getting for you, but I couldn't tell if she was acting. I didn't realize she was into it until I witnessed her jealousy over Miranda."

I look away.

"You need to go over there. I'm sure she's home by now. Explain better. Fix this, Nic."

"No reason, I'm nothin' but a liar to her now." I look his way. "She wanted me for a minute, at least I got that much, right?"

"Wrong, she's fucked up."

My ribs begin to ache. "She'll be good."

"Yeah?" Trent looks up at my mom's bedroom window, dark as always, and back to me. "And what about you, man, will you be good?"

"I am good." Done talking, I push to my feet and hold my hand out.

He eyes me, clapping his into mine as he stands.

"You'll be at the game tomorrow?" he asks as he walks toward the gate.

"Not sure yet."

"You know Coach will let you play, get you excused for the days you missed."

I look away and he walks out.

When he's gone, I drop back in the chair and look up at the sky.

And they say senior year is supposed to be your best year yet.

Yeah fuckin' right.

We're only months in and everything fucking sucks.

Chapter 37
Demi

The knock at my door has my stomach jumping into my throat, but I don't have it in me to ignore the possibility of who might be on the other side or what they'll have to say.

As quietly and gently as possible, I place my palms on the door and lean forward to look into the peephole.

Trent?

I take my hands off the door, sneaking a single step back before his voice floats from the other side.

"I know you're there, Dem. Come on. Please."

A frown takes over, but I give in and pull it open.

One side of his mouth tips up in what's supposed to be a smile, but it's not hard to tell he's got a lot on his mind and happy-go-lucky is the furthest thing from how he's feeling.

"Your mom home?"

"No, she's" —a sad scoff leaves me— "it's just me."

He tilts his head.

"Why are you here?" I ask him.

"Think I could come in?"

I eye him a moment, smashing my lips together as I shake my head. "I don't think that's a good idea." I shift against the frame, putting my hands in the pocket of my hoodie. "Trent, I don't think we should be talking, especially if you haven't worked out everything with Nico yet. I can't and won't get in the middle of your friendship any more than I unknowingly already did. He not only deserves you, but needs you."

314

Trent's eyes grow clear with understanding, only for a heavy sense of guilt to wash over him seconds after, his chin falling to his chest on a long exhale.

He didn't believe in us.

Or more, he didn't believe in me.

He looks up, but only with his eyes. "You love him."

It's not a question.

This isn't why he's here.

He knows everything, other than maybe before Nico and I fell apart again, we had taken the first step to moving past my sleeping with the guy standing in front of me.

"It doesn't really matter how I feel about him, does it?" My eyes sharpen. "I was a forfeitable play piece."

He frowns, taking a half step forward.

"Dem, no," he stresses, eyes grave. "You are so wrong."

I give a lazy shrug, but he knows where to start to keep me from closing the door and leaving him on the other side.

"Nico told me you agreed to fake all this the morning after it happened."

I hesitate a moment, but a frown takes over and I step from the house and onto the porch.

"I'm listening."

He nods, continuing, "I was a little hard on him, told him it wasn't a good idea, and he knew it, too, but once you were in reach, there was no way he'd back out. I knew that as much as he did." He leans against the wall, looking across the lawn.

What he's saying, though, still doesn't make much sense to me.

"At dinner the night after the boardwalk, I gave him more shit, told him it seemed like too much, too quickly and he got mad. It sort of kept on like that, I'd say things that would piss him off. You guys acted like you'd been together for years when it had only been days or weeks. You moved and spoke and looked at each other like you understood the other and like . . ." His eyes come back to mine. "Like you loved each other, but it was fake. Watching you two made me nervous, I was worried."

315

I give a sad smile, guessing, "You didn't want me to get hurt."

A low laugh leaves him and he glances at the sky before releasing a deep exhale.

"That wasn't it, Dem," he says quietly, his words heavy with guilt. "I'd never want you to get hurt, I hope you know that, but if I'm honest right now, and I feel like I have to be, it was him I was looking out for, not you," he admits, shameful.

"It was true what he shouted the other night, he's wanted you for a long ass time, but fear kept him from trying to get close to you. There were a few times when he thought he'd go for it, just before freshman year and then again when he found out you were in his PE class that semester, but both times he backed out, thinking he'd never be enough and decided it wasn't gonna happen for you guys."

"But enough for what?"

"Enough to keep your attention when approaching you would have meant he'd have to fight for it."

I lower myself into one of the patio chairs, so Trent drops into the other.

"I don't understand," I admit.

"What Nico said to you about Alex, how he convinced you to start this in the first place, it's true. Alex does take, he does want what someone else has, but not just anyone. Only Nico, and it started summer of eighth grade."

My head begins to pound. "That's when Nico stopped talking to me."

He nods. "Exactly. Alex pays attention to Nico's every move, and takes everything he can, however he can, always." Trent's eyes bounce between mine. "You, Dem, were the one thing Nico wasn't willing to lose to him."

My ribs constrict and I move my eyes to the grass. "So he stayed away . . ."

"Yes. So, Alex didn't know he wanted you, so he wouldn't sweep in and steal your attention away before Nico had a chance to make you want his more." Trent leans forward, and

I move my gaze back to his. "Nico said he had something to gain, right?"

"He never said what," I whisper weakly.

"Come on, Dem." He gives me a dejected, knowing smile. "It was you. *You* were what he wanted to gain. All this, everything that's happened, was to win you in the end, and not as his prize, as his girl."

My pulse begins to race and I attempt to calm it by taking a deep breath.

"Nic might have stayed away and never told you, I don't know, but all bets were off when Nic realized Alex might want you without knowing Nic did."

And Nico saw I was interested in Alex. He knew I'd have fallen into Alex the second he made a move.

"Oh my god." I close my eyes, covering them with my hands.

He was afraid to lose me, that's why he insisted we play it out longer when Alex approached me only hours after he saw Nico and I together.

This had *nothing* to do with Alex and *everything* to do with me.

I let my arms fall to my lap, looking to Trent. "You should go."

He gives a tight smile, nodding, as he pushes to his feet, and turns to leave.

"Trent," I call once he's halfway down the driveway.

He looks over his shoulder.

My chest tightens. "You think you guys will be okay, you and Nico?"

"Guys are complicated, Dem," he says with a sad laugh. "But yeah, we'll get there."

The corner of my mouth raises.

"See you at school?" he asks.

I nod, opening my mouth to thank him, but as if sensing it, he lifts his palms and gives a small shake of his head, and walks away.

Once he's gone, I pull my legs into the seat, and remain there until late into the night, working through every detail of the last few months in my head.

When I finally manage to bring myself inside and hours later fall asleep, I wake with the same thoughts from the night before.

I take my time getting ready and head for school.

I let the door slam with my intentional late arrival and all eyes fly to the entrance.

Miranda reaches over and presses pause on the music before slowly rising to her feet. Her lips purse.

"Everyone break off with your partner and run one through five," she tells them, not moving her gaze off mine as she takes small steps toward me.

I'm only three feet from her when she tips her head like a petty little bitch.

"Gotta say, didn't expect this."

"I'll bet."

She pops a hip out, crossing her arms. "I'm not letting you back on my team, so if you came here to grovel, don't waste my time."

"Unless you want the school board to know you're sleeping with students, don't waste mine." I step closer to her.

Her eyes widen then sharpen in the same second. "You—"

"Save it. I'm the best you've got, Miranda. I'm taking my spot back."

Her lips thin and she lets her arms fall to her sides. "Nico's gone. Hasn't been back since you made a scene. You dance, you're dancing with Alex."

I laugh lightly. "Funny, you think you're still in control." I set my bag down, pulling my hoodie over my head. "I need this on my college applications, and *you* want to stay out of jail, so you can keep shaking your ass for rappers."

"Watch it, little girl."

I roll my eyes, adjusting the top of my gym pants. "Let's not pretend we like each other but be professional and get the job done well."

I walk past her, slipping right back into the center.

Trent eyes me, both of us aware we can't dance together.

Thompson suddenly slides in behind me, whispering in my ear, "I got you, girl. Let's get it."

I give him a grateful smile, then face forward and wait.

It takes Miranda a second, but slowly she spins around and walks back to the speaker. She gives a tight clap, avoiding my eyes.

"From the top."

I can hardly hold in my smirk.

Chapter 38
Nico

I ditched, figured I'd be cool when game time came, focused enough on playin' hard that my mind wouldn't fuck with me, but the second I pull in, I realize how wrong I was.

It's formal, the night where, every year, the school recognizes the seniors on varsity, and of fucking course this year we're to be escorted by the dance team.

I'm not walking. I don't give a fuck; I'll wait on the sidelines with the few juniors on the team.

Not that it matters, I heard Demi never went back, like she said she wouldn't, which only proves further what a dick I am. I came in and fucked up her little world.

Dance was one of the only things she did for herself and now she can't even look at her coach.

I climb from my truck and grab my bag from the back, slinging it over my shoulder.

At least I won't have to stand there and watch her with anyone else.

The moment I think it, I'm reminded of how nothing in my life ever plays out the way I want it to.

I step between the buildings in time to spot the dance team, all wrapped in their silk coverings to hide their costumes, and the football team gathered together as the guys start handing over their jackets.

My feet lock in place when Trent moves toward Demi, who gives him nothing but a tight smile and nod as she walks off.

Something has Trent's head turning this way, and he spots me.

He tips his chin, so I tip mine back, but decide to cut left, going the long way around to avoid everyone.

I'm dressed out and ready to go before the rest of the guys even filter into the locker room.

I tap on Coach's door, sticking my head in. "I'm feelin' tight, cool if I head out there early, start warming up?"

He eyes me, not believing a word I've said. He might not speak much when it's not football related, but he pays attention. "We're walking with the girls, Sykes."

"Can't, Coach." I don't say anything else, but after a few seconds, he nods his permission, so I avoid eye contact with everyone I pass and head straight to the field.

I don't warm up, but join the JV team on the sideline, watching along as their game comes to an end.

I glance back, finding the stands filling up more and more by the minute, everyone eager to see the show.

Macy catches my eye, Carley and Krista right beside her, already in their cheer gear for when we begin, but I swiftly look away.

Quicker than I'm ready for the game is over, the field cleared, and the announcer comes back on the speaker.

The crowd settles, all to pep back up and louder than before when the guys emerge from the inflatable tunnel and keep forward across the field. In one, solid, straight line, they stand, dressed and ready to play. The only thing they're missing are their helmets.

The crowd dies down, and again grows louder as the girls file out, completely in sync with the speed of each step and the space between them all, the letterman's jackets draped over their left arms, game socks up to their knees and little referee outfits to match.

Demi is in the middle, no jacket across her forearm but her fists on her hips, Thompson right behind her.

I reach up, gripping my gear below my neck, moving from one foot to the next to keep myself calm.

The music starts, but it's a simple hit of a drum, and the girls take one step forward. Another, and they take one step out.

Everyone starts to cheer as our coaching staff slips through the middle and make their way over, the announcer introducing them over the loudspeaker.

Another boom from a drum and the girls turn sideways, each guy strategically removing the jackets and holding them out for the girls to slide into.

But Thompson suddenly drops back, falling into the line of my teammates as Trent steps out and forward.

Toward Demi, his jacket in his own hand.

I clench my jaw, grinding my teeth as he holds it out for her, and her hands slip into the sleeves.

Is he for real?

Is she for fucking real?

I squint when Trent emerges from behind her, quickly jogging this way.

"What the *hell* is he doing?" is hissed, and my head snaps to my left to find Miranda on her knees a few feet away, tripod perched in front of her with a video camera attached.

I look forward right as Trent reaches the sidelines, slipping directly beside me with a smirk in place.

I glare, but my eyes snap toward the field when the music kicks on, and the girls fall in line.

I try to tip my head to the side to see who is behind Demi but can't see.

Trent chuckles and I cut a quick scowl at him before focusing back on the field.

The crowd goes crazy as the girls and their partners begin to go through the shit we'd been practicing, but my eyes stay stuck to D as she makes the same moves, a little more pronounced and all on her own. No partner.

They get to where the girls spin out, holding onto the guy's hand, but Demi doesn't spin. She keeps her legs planted out, her ass facing this way, but she twists her hips looking over her shoulder, right at me.

The team is trained not to move forward until she does.

So, they wait.

For what?

"You even paying attention, man?" Trent whispers. "Look at her."

Pressure falls on my chest as I force my eyes to the last name stitched across the jacket.

My stomach jumps, twisting and turning all at once.

Sykes.

My gaze flies to hers.

Baby . . .

"She's waitin', Nic."

I look to him.

"Go."

My feet carry me to her.

Demi

The second number 24's feet hit the turf; the crowd flips out.

When Carley, Krista, and Macy's screams are heard above them all, I chuckle through the tears that are forming, but I'm too afraid to take my eyes off Nico to glance around.

I keep my position, my head turned, and Nico, being Nico, slides up behind me, his eyes locked on mine and far more intense than ever before.

My body aches to lean into his, but there's no time for anything other than what we're out here for right now, so I slide my hand into his rough one, spinning into him.

His lips press into a firm line, a sudden hopelessness filling his dark eyes, the second my body presses against his, and all I want to do is wash it away.

I will soon.

"Walk me to my spot?" I whisper.

"Where?" he rasps.

"Center."

He steps out and around like he would have in the performance.

We take two strides forward, everyone else sliding with us but staying a space back and the announcer begins to run off the team numbers, giving their starts and ambitions, each one releasing their partner's hand as their name is read and stalking across the field. Nico is the last on the field, and completely reluctant to let me go and walk away, but slowly he does.

The last name mentioned is Trent's, who turns to wave up at the stands then falls back in line with the younger players on the sidelines.

Now it's our turn.

Miranda cues the music.

We run through our routine, and my eyes stay locked on Nico's the entire time, I fight a smirk when the end rolls around and we let the jackets slide from our shoulders, showing the numbers that were positioned inside the jackets to Velcro over the backs of our shirts, each representing our partners. A large 24 now plastered across mine.

Just as quick as it's over, we're hustled off the field as the captains take it for the coin toss. The whistle is blown, and the first quarter begins, Nico and the rest of the starters getting into position.

Miranda wastes no time, charging right up to me before I've even caught my breath. "You little bitch. Who do you think you are?" she growls.

I chuckle, taking the towel and water Carley brings me. I dab at my face, then take a small drink before giving her any of my attention. "What are you worried about? It all looked like part of the plan. Star player gets a little extra, hypes the crowd more. Nobody knows it was a last-minute change."

"You don't get to change my routines."

"I created more than half of that routine while you were off trying to fuck your way into all the guys' good graces."

Miranda's eyes widen and she looks to Carley then back to me.

"I changed my mind," I tell her. "Quit, Miranda. If you don't, well . . . you know what'll follow."

I head for the locker room to shower and wipe the glitter off my face and arms, and change into my formal attire, but I don't go back to the game.

He'll find me.

Chapter 39
Nico

The second the buzzer indicating the end of the fourth quarter sounds, I tear off my helmet, my eyes flying to where I knew the girls to be sitting.

She's still not here.

Macy lifts a shoulder, looking from them to me, and it hits. I drop my helmet and take off.

There're a few teachers in the hall, but I jog right past them, ignoring their shouts of protest.

When I get to that last step though, my feet freeze, my gut twisting.

I take a deep breath, letting my cheeks expand with my controlled exhale and gently push through the door to the rooftop, hanging onto it as it begins to close, erasing any sort of sound I might create.

I don't know why.

I step around the corner and there she is, standing in a long, deep blue gown, my letterman's jacket hanging from her hands.

Her hair is curled and down now, hanging loose over her shoulders, eyes lined in black making the green appear brighter, lips a slick, creamy color.

She's perfection.

My perfection?

"I should have told you," she says instantly.

I shake my head, approaching her slowly. "We talked about this—"

She holds a hand out, cutting me off. "No, I mean, yes, I'm sorry about that too, but that's not what I mean. We can fight more about that later if you want," she says quietly and damn if my chest doesn't ache, my lips twitching.

She gives a sad smile. "I should have told you where my mind was as soon as I figured it out for myself."

I reach her, and she places a hand on my chest, looking up at me. "Why are you standing here apologizing to me when I'm the one who fucked this up?" My hands slide into her silky hair and she closes her eyes a long moment. "You have no idea how much I hate myself for putting doubt in your mind. All I ever wanted was to hold you, baby, and to know you wouldn't force me to let go, but *I* allowed you to believe you were worth less than other things in my life, when that's so fucking false, D. You're worth more than anything I've got."

I slide my palm across her cheek and she leans into my touch. "Tell me I've still got you," I whisper, dropping my forehead to hers.

"You do." She swallows. "Neek . . . you have no idea."

"Say it, baby. Nice and clear for me. Tell me."

She doesn't hesitate. "I love you."

I swallow her words with my lips, and she sighs against my mouth, pulling on my jersey as she tries to get closer. I kiss her, slow and soft for as long as I can until she needs a full breath of air and pulls her lips from mine, all to come back in for another short kiss.

"I want you," she whispers.

I grip her hair. "I'm all sweaty, baby, and you're in your dress already."

"I don't care."

I chuckle and step back, bending to grab my jacket off the floor. I hold her gaze, opening it for her and she spins, slipping her hands in but keeps her eyes on me over her shoulder.

I lean in, kissing her once more, then grab her hand and pull her over to the chairs. She drops into the one beside me.

"Me and Alex used to be friends."

327

"We don't have to do this," she whispers. "Not right now."

"Yeah, I do. I fucked up not being honest with you. Let me break some of this down, and you can ask me anything you want about it later."

She nods.

"So, we were friends and a couple weeks before freshman year we went to this party. Alex wasn't supposed to go, he was grounded or something, but he snuck out anyway. His dad showed up to get him, piss drunk and acting like a fucking dickhead. Alex flew from his seat and was rushing to leave, but his dad decided he was moving too slow, grabbed him by the neck and tossed him out the front door. Alex fell and hit his head on a rock, knocked out cold."

"Oh my god." She frowns.

I nod. "His dad just fuckin' left him there, didn't even notice or care, I'm not sure. He took off. It took a little less than a minute for Alex to open his eyes, and when he did, he was fucked up, dizzy and said he saw spots in his vision. I helped him up and drove him to the ER myself. I didn't even have a license, but he had a car, so we took it." I shrug, a heavy exhale leaving me. "When the nurse asked what happened, I told her. Didn't think too much of it right then."

Her eyes soften. "They put it down as child abuse."

I nod.

"You did what was right."

A low scoff leaves me. "His dad was arrested the next day. He lost his job, lost his pension." I meet her gaze. "Lost his wife next."

Her eyes tighten as she tries to piece it all together.

"Couple weeks went by, and then she came over to thank the father of the son who was brave enough to help hers." I scoff. "My mom wasn't home when she stopped by, she was in the city, where he was supposed to meet her the next morning." Anger forms in the pit of my stomach, but I push it down. "*Dr. Avery Hammons* made herself quite comfortable that night, and when she finally left, Alex already had her convinced to take my dad with her."

"He took from you," she breathes.

"Yep. His mom couldn't get back with his dad after word got out what he did, not if she wanted to keep her practice open and successful. Alex's dad lost everything, he felt *he* lost everything, so he made it his mission to make sure I did, too."

"Your dad walked away, just like that?"

"My dad never appreciated my mom to begin with. The fact that I was never good enough for him made it easier to leave me behind, too. He had an heiress for a wife and gained a doctor. Had a son who started on his team but 'only' held a 3.0, gained one who started *and* was top of the class."

"Second in class," she whispers.

I chuckle lightly, looking to her. "Yeah, second to my Pixie. That was just another reminder he's better for you."

She frowns, stands up and walks over to me.

I spread my legs for her to step between, but she straddles me instead, leaning her elbows on my shoulder pads.

"I don't need another version of me," she says, running her thumb across my bottom lip.

"You deserve someone worth as much as you," I rasp.

"I deserve someone who will love me hard, want me despite my mistakes, and appreciates who I am because of them."

I swallow, and her legs sink farther beside me. "I can do that, D."

"I know," she whispers, kissing me lightly. "Your worth isn't measured in your accomplishments, Nico, even though you have many to be proud of. It's how hard you love that counts."

I pull her mouth to mine, kissing her roughly and she moans against me.

She can feel it, my love for her.

"My silent knight," she breathes across my mouth before sinking into me more.

But I'm a greedy bastard. I want words.

I pull back, looking up at her as she smiles gently at me.

"Mr. Brando said it was about misconception, right?" I start.

She laughs, nodding as I run my hands up her thighs and under the jacket until I'm gripping her hips.

"Tell me, D. What do you see when you look at me now?"

Her palms find my cheeks and she holds my eyes with hers.

"I see a guarded, suffer in silence type who is more than the first glance could ever give. A stubborn, hardheaded guy I want to keep," she whispers, a calm, almost sadness taking over her eyes. "Even more, I see the guy I accidentally fell in love with and wouldn't change if I could. A gorgeous, strong-minded guy I want to love me back."

My pulse is beating out of control, my heartstrings pulled tight as I stare at the girl, I never thought would say half the shit she just did while staring right at me. *Right fuckin' into me.*

My Pixie.

I pull her closer, tilting my head to whisper in her ear. "I do, Pixie. I have, and I will."

She pushes me back, waiting, but not long.

"I love you, Demi," I whisper, and tears fill her eyes. "And not only *can* you keep me, baby, but I'm not against forcing you to, 'cause I'm keeping you, following you wherever you go. Shit, I'll chase you if it comes to that."

She laughs, her head tipping back but only for a second before my palm is spreading across her spine and I'm bringing her face to mine again.

"Thank you."

"For what?"

"Being brave enough to try, even if it was in an ass-backward way."

This time it's me who laughs. "I've never been one to do things right the first time around."

She smirks. "Now *that* I'd have to disagree with."

A loud laugh leaves me.

I bring my hands around to rest them on the curve of her ass, our gazes meeting. "Good to know, Pixie, but just wait." I lean forward, biting on her bottom lip a second. "It only gets better with practice."

330

She lets my jacket slide off her arms, giving me a saucy grin, whispering, "Prove it, Neek."

So, I do.

At her request, we skip the stupid dance knowing there'll be more, and I take her home, showing her over and over until she's putty in my arms, and then falls asleep in them.

As mine.

Epilogue
Nico

"In closing, I want to wish you all the best wherever life takes you, and I hope when you look back on this place, five, ten, even twenty years from now," Demi's slight blush at the time stamp she's giving me in her speech has my chest warming. "It's in remembrance of all the positive ways you changed or grew while you were here, and I hope you never let those memories, or the people who you made them with go." She subconsciously spins the promise ring I gave her as her eyes meet, they hold, then slide past mine as she continues to connect with the rest of our class. "I know I won't," she says gently before the most beautiful smile crosses her face. "Congratulations to us, the Class of 2020!"

Everyone jumps, cheering loudly as they toss their graduation caps in the air, and I dart from my seat, meeting Demi at the edge of the steps.

She holds up her white gown and jumps right into my arms.

I spin her around, both of us laughing as I set her on her feet.

"How's my valedictorian feel?"

"Amazing!"

She kisses me quickly before her friends rush for us screaming, and they hug each other, Trent only feet behind, his gown already off and tossed somewhere.

He steps in for a quick hug, turning to look at the girls. "Can't believe it's over, man."

"I know. If you'd have told me on the first day of senior year it would end like this, I might have punched you for it."

He laughs, looking back to the girls when their laughter hits us. "I can't believe Dem passed on Brown."

I nod.

I was against her decision at first, too, but she deserves to do what she wants, not what others think she should, and one thing she was clear about was not leaving California.

He moves his smile to me. "You ready for UCSD?"

I laugh lightly, my eyes glued to Demi. "Oh, yeah. Thank fuck for coed dorms."

Trent laughs.

"Did I tell you her dad rented her a little spot down there, a little studio to work in?"

"You mentioned it, but I didn't know it all worked out."

I nod. "She's even got a few dozen students signed up and ready to go. She's gonna teach during my practice hours, so we can keep the rest of our time open for just us. She's taking a lighter load than she planned, but she decided she's in no hurry to be done and I like that."

"Thank fuck we're decent ball players, huh, and got to pick what school to go to, or our girls would be headed to colleges far the fuck away from us."

"Like either of us would go anywhere they wouldn't be."

I look to him and we both laugh.

He sighs, clamping a hand on my shoulder. "I'm happy for you, man, really."

"Thanks."

Demi slides back up, and I wrap my hand around her back. "You ask them to come stay next week yet?"

"Not yet."

She laughs, turning to Trent with a smile. "What do you think? You and Krista don't leave until the end of summer, come discover new beaches with us!"

Trent shrugs, nodding. "I don't see why not. Let's talk about it later tonight, I gotta go find my parents, take pictures and shit before we meet you guys at Demi's." Trent holds his hand out, clapping mine again and then walks away, pulling Krista from the group of girls.

"Kids!" I spin around, smiling as my mom, Demi's dad and stepmom walk up together, her mom a few yards behind.

A lot changed in the last half of the school year.

I told Demi about what my dad had done, tricking my mom into giving him everything. Instantly, and against my protests, she went to her dad for help from him and his firm. I got my mom down there and within days, they had everything sorted out.

Like I figured, nothing was as legit as my dad tried to make it seem. Sure, he had friends in low places, but Demi's dad had more in higher ones.

Not that he had to use them, he only had to pretend he did, spew some lawyer bullshit at him and my dad was sweating. Then he threw a single threat out.

He told him he'd expose his wife for writing prescriptions to someone she wasn't treating and Nikoli Sykes walked away with his hands held high.

We haven't seen a sign of him since and an added bonus, Alex hasn't so much as dared lay his eyes on either of us since shit went down.

Mr. Davenport knew what he was doing, he's a smart ass man, and I guarantee every move he made was well thought through and each had a hidden purpose. He had conditions for every step he took in helping us out. Strategic conditions disguised as tasks, the most appreciated being my mom had to check herself into rehab.

It took a little time to get her on board, but after a few conversations with all of us as a group, she agreed.

In the beginning, it was really hard for her. My dad had her hooked on some strong shit he had convinced his wife to prescribe, but my mom's a fighter and she pulled through. She's been clean now for five months, and better than that, she finally let my dad go. She's happy again, and I have Demi and her family to thank for that, her family that I hope will one day become mine.

My mom steps forward, wrapping us both in a large hug, and Demi's parents follow.

We take turns hugging each person, thanking them for their congratulations and take a few rounds of photos.

"Okay, so we've got everything ready and cooked, all we have to do is grab the cake on the way home, but I believe you're stopping for it?" My mom smiles at Demi's dad.

"Yep, we'll grab it on our way over." He nods, wrapping his arm around his wife.

"Perfect." My mom looks over the two of us again, tears in her eyes. "I'm so proud of you two."

Demi laughs lightly, leaning her head on my shoulder. "Thank you, you guys."

"We're proud of you, too, Ma."

I glance at Demi's mom who wears a tight smile on her face as she tries to hide her tears.

When Demi went to her dad for help, it made her mom realize she was losing the only person who loved her, her daughter.

It's been a very slow climb and I doubt they'll ever have the mother-daughter relationship Demi deserves, but there has been some effort to reconnect.

On top of that, and what Demi says is even more surprising, is her mom following mine and learning how to better manage her finances. Really, with Demi leaving, she doesn't exactly have a choice. She hasn't had access to Demi's accounts in months and once we're gone, even if she wanted to ask to borrow when her alimony runs out, Demi won't be here to give it.

My mom and hers have actually become friends because of this — my mom's low maintenance and hers is trying to downscale.

It's also opened up better communication between Demi's mom and dad, since he's the one coaching my mom.

"Okay, sweetheart. We'll see you in a few minutes." Her dad kisses her temple, then pats my shoulder.

"Yep."

They say goodbye to the rest of us and head out.

"We better go, too," Ms. Davenport says. "You'll be there soon?"

"Yeah, we'll be there." Demi smiles and our moms walk away, bickering about what plates to use.

With the help of Demi's dad, my mom decided to sell her house. She says she doesn't need all the space and with only her there, it doesn't make sense to spend so much just to keep the basics running.

We were surprised when Ms. Davenport suggested she stay with her through the process as another way for them both to save, and maybe longer if it worked out between them.

"You think they'll last long as roommates?" I look to Demi.

She laughs. "Actually, I do. They're lonely and they don't even realize it. My mom needs a normal friend in her life." She sighs. "And if not that, they'll at least think they'll have better odds ganging up on us to come home and visit."

I laugh, tugging her in. "They're wrong. Once I have you all to myself, I'm pretty sure I won't be up for sharing again."

She grins, lifting her lips to mine, but I pull her ring finger up, closing my teeth around it and showing her my bite marks.

"See." I run my fingers across the little scar I left on her a decade ago and then do the same with the one I gently added. "I told you I was smart, D. I marked you as mine ten years ago."

"Here's to ten more." She kisses me quickly, whispering, "And to bite marks where the eyes can't see."

I pull her closer, ready to kiss the shit out of her when we're interrupted by a familiar voice.

"Nico Sykes and Demi Davenport."

We spin around, finding Mr. Brando.

He smiles. "The unlikely duo, now attached at the hip, and moving away together. I'm proud to have had a part in that."

Demi reaches out to shake his hand. "Thank you, Mr. Brando, for caring enough to try and break down barriers for people who don't know how."

"Thank *you* for not pestering me to change your partner until I caved," he fires back.

"You wouldn't have." She laughs.

"You're right," he agrees. "I wouldn't have." Mr. Brando looks at me, a knowing smile playing at his lips. "Imagine if I denied you *your* request to be her partner, Mr. Sykes."

Demi's head snaps my way. "Wait, what?"

Mr. Brando lets out a loud laugh, clamping a hand on my shoulder. "Best of luck, you two." With that, he walks away.

I grin from him to her.

Her face slowly softens. "You asked to be my partner. Before everything?"

I smirk, wrapping my arms around her and pulling her in. "It was always my goal to make you mine, that way, if Alex ever tried for you, you'd deny him because you were *mine*." My grip around her tightens. "I wasn't leaving this school without you on my arm, D. One way or the other, I knew we'd find a way. I just had to man up and make it happen."

"So sure of yourself, were you?" she attempts to tease, but nothing but adoration rings through my baby's words.

A light chuckle leaves me, but my features smooth as I pour all my focus into her. "I'd never been more *unsure* of myself in my life, but you, D . . ." I drop my forehead to hers. "Even if we had to fake it to make it, *you,* I was sure of."

She looks to her ring, a small silver band, with a gleam I'll never tire of and a smile I'll forever fight to have on me, she presses her lips to mine.

This.

This is as real as it gets.

Eek!! You guys, these two started speaking to me over a year ago, but I made them wait to tell their story until, finally, they were all I could think about. I knew that meant their story was ready to be written!

I once knew someone who felt alone in a crowded room, who hid their reality from everyone around them while carrying the weight of the world on their shoulders. I think that's where this story came from, though, it is light years different. I felt honored to write it.

Thank you so very much for reading!
I hope you loved Demi and Nico as much as I do!
Xoxo,
Meagan

Stay in touch with Meagan Brandy:

@MeaganBrandyAuthor
@MeaganBrandy
@MeaganBrandyAuthor
@MeaganBrandyBooks
www.meaganbrandy.com

Acknowledgements

First, shout out to my **family!** Thank you so much for putting up with all the crazy long hours this book had me on! I couldn't do this without the support from home!

Ellie (and Rosa!)! You pulled some serious magic and I'm so grateful for it! Thank you for all that you do and for being willing to go above the norm to make things happen! You rock!

Melissa Teo!!! Without you, I'd be a mess! Thank you so much for making my job easier by kicking ass at yours! And for being a true and honest friend.

Danielle, my publicist! Thank you for always knowing what to do when I'm more than clueless. I've learned so much over our time working together and look forward to gaining more knowledge from you!

Serena and Veronica, my #teammeagan girls! Never leave my team! I love having you!

STREET TEAM! YOU GIRLS SLAY! Thank you for taking time from your lives to be on my team!

Stefanie and Kelli! Thank you so much for your honesty! Without it, I wouldn't push myself. Thank you for helping me see what I'm blind to!

Sarah! You're a masterful beta and awesome human! Thank you for being there and talking me through when I couldn't see the light at the end!

To my review team, I'm so grateful to have a team who will follow me across the water when I jump ships! You have no clue what it means to me to be able to go from one genre to another, knowing you will be right there with me! Thank you!

Bloggers and Bookstagrammers, thank you for participating and helping spread the word! I hope you love the conclusion to Nico and Demi as hard as I do!

And to **my readers,** I LOVE YOU! THANK YOU for following me into a brand-new world! If you're new to me, THANK YOU for taking a chance! From the bottom of my heart, I owe you all my biggest thanks and appreciate you more than you'll ever know! Come hang in my Private Facebook Group!